WITH FRIENDS LIKE THESE...

"Whoever gains supremacy in computers will be the great world power for the coming century. Computers will give more power than supremacy in atomic weapons. That's why it is absolutely vital that the United States maintain leadership in computer technology. We simply can't allow anyone, even a 'friendly' country, to take the lead away from us."

The Secretary reached for the wine bottle and carefully refilled the glasses. "You think the Japanese are going to take the lead away from us?" he asked.

"We know they are," Cobb replied soberly. "For the last ten years, our industry has been trying to develop the supercomputer. We're still at least two years away. The Japanese will demonstrate their supercomputer within nine months."

"And we're going to steal it," the Secretary whispered.

"No," Cobb answered. "We're going to destroy it."

THE MASAKADO LESSON

By the same author:
Code Conquistador

THE MASAKADO LESSON

WILLIAM P. KENNEDY

A GOLD EAGLE BOOK FROM
W RLDWIDE

TORONTO · NEW YORK · LONDON · PARIS
AMSTERDAM · STOCKHOLM · HAMBURG
ATHENS · MILAN · TOKYO · SYDNEY

THE MASAKADO LESSON

A Gold Eagle Book/July 1987

First published by St. Martin's Press, Incorporated

Copyright © 1986 by William P. Kennedy

ISBN 0-373-62105-1

This novel is a work of fiction. All of the events, characters, names and places depicted in this novel are entirely fictitious or are used fictitiously. No representation that any statement made in this novel is true or that any incident depicted in this novel actually occurred is intended or should be inferred by the reader.

Printed in Canada

DEDICATION

For Robert Kennedy, S.J.
Priest and Master,
Christian and Buddhist,
American and Japanese

Some spy!

Kaplan was examining the midriff bulge that ballooned out over his belt like an inflated inner tube. He squeezed the roll of flesh in his hands and saw his fingertips disappear into the soft, sagging folds. "Pure lard," he berated himself. "As soon as this assignment is over, you're going to get your ass into the gym and get back into shape." He spent a moment imagining himself stretched out on a bench, pressing an enormous barbell up and down with smooth, confident strokes. Then he reached over to the six-pack of Asahi beer that he had carefully placed on the table beside his chair, detached one of the three remaining cans, and tore off the tab top in disgust.

He wasn't a spy; he was a baby-sitter. He sat before a small computer and a bank of tape drives watching the lights blink on and off and the reels spin back and forth. The damned computer was the spy and the only thing it needed him for was to change the tape reels at the end of the day. Fucking box of junk didn't even know he was out there and sure as hell didn't care. Christ, if he just had some idea of when the transmissions would be coming in and how long they would last, he could leave it to run by itself and go treat himself to a little excitement in Akasaka. But you could never tell. Sometimes it could sit for days, doing nothing more amazing than running its own cooling fan. Then it could turn itself on without warning and run for hours without a break, filling the reels nearly as fast as he could put them on and take them off.

The room was really a loft, built into the storage attic of an abandoned pottery plant on the industrial edge of Tokyo. On the outside, in the pale light of the single lamp that illuminated the fenced-in yard, the building was dilapidated, slowly deteriorating while it waited for an enterprising developer to plow it under. The ground-floor work area was empty, except for the concrete pedestals that had once held production machinery and two stone holding tanks that were obviously impossible to move. It was a relic of a bygone age; the perfect disguise for the electronic wonders that worked tirelessly in the loft.

Over Stanley Kaplan's head, fastened to the inside of the sloping roof, was a huge, wire-mesh antenna. Wave guides, connected to the antenna, curved their graceful paths across the ceiling and then down the wall to two huge amplifier cabinets. Each cabinet had its own fan running constantly to carry off the heat—enough heat to keep the loft comfortable despite the cold outside. From the amplifiers, coaxial cables stretched across the floor to the minicomputer and connected to two tape drives, each a six-foot cabinet in itself. The electronic equipment, with its wiring and cables, took up at least half the space in the loft.

The other half was devoted to Kaplan's living arrangements. There were a refrigerator, stocked with frozen dinners and canned beer, a counter top with a sink and a microwave oven, a square industrial table with two mismatched wooden chairs, and an uncovered box spring and mattress with unmade bedding piled on top. One corner of the living area was framed out to conceal a topless toilet and a washbasin. Both were filled with dark, lifeless water. To Kaplan, the loft represented the nadir of his career.

Some spy! His whole life had been a mockery since the day the recruiter from the Central Intelligence Agency slipped into the chair next to his in the library. He was an accounting major, top man in his class at George Washington and a shoo-in for an offer from one of the Big Seven accounting firms. As soon as he saw the laminated identification card he should have grabbed the bastard and turned him over to the student government. Those were the days of campus riots and student revolutionaries. He would have become a campus legend if he had bagged a CIA agent. Christ, Berkeley would have given him an honorary degree. But, instead, he had been intrigued. When the recruiter told him that he had the stuff the agency was made of, he could feel a Walther PPK snuggled in its quick-release holster under his arm, and a throwing knife strapped to the inside of his leg. His brain flashed images of Istanbul, Geneva, Trieste, and other international cities where he assumed espionage was the major industry. His loins stirred at the scent of the beautiful women he would be forced to seduce in the line of duty.

Audits and trial balances didn't stand a chance.

But his assignments hadn't quite measured up to his expectations. The first was a mail watch at a post office in Chester, Pennsylvania. Each day, Kaplan logged all the correspondence addressed to the residence of one Jonathan Schneider, an electronics wizard with a Philadelphia-based computer giant. Schneider, it was

suspected, was actually in the employ of the Bulgarian
secret police, put in place to expose the identity of CIA
operatives who were working undercover in Bulgaria
as technical representatives of the company. It took a
year for Kaplan to discover that Schneider's mother
lived in Trenton, New Jersey, and wrote him once a
week, and that Schneider had peculiar sexual habits as
indicated by the weekly parcels he received in plain
brown wrappers and the monthly editions of a sado-
masochist magazine called *Whips and Chains*. If he
was a Bulgarian agent, he was a very clever Bulgarian
agent, because he never left any traces.

His next assignment made the mail watch seem exciting. It required neither a pistol nor a throwing knife,
but rather a pair of scissors and an endless supply of
paper clips. Each day, hundreds of magazines and
journals were delivered to his desk: industrial magazines on the Soviet shipbuilding industry, technical
magazines on East German medical developments,
process control magazines from the Rumanian petro-
leum industry, agricultural magazines describing developments in the Ukrainian farm belt. There were
technical papers from Polish mine equipment manufacturers, from Czechoslovakian ceramics experts,
from Russian computer designers, and from Chinese
chemists. Any articles written on any technical subject
in any Iron Curtain country were dropped on his desk
blotter, each with an appended note from the translation department giving the English-language version of
the headline, the sub-headlines, and the first para-
graph of text. Kaplan's job was to cut the article from
the publication, fasten the loose pages together with a
paper clip, and attach a routing slip sending the piece

to whichever of the seventy-one "subject" departments might possibly be interested.

Often, he wondered aloud how anyone could possibly be interested. But, from his superior's replies, he began to understand that the craft of intelligence was undergoing a fundamental change. Quality was giving way to quantity. Instead of using a single agent to steal a single fact, the agency was using thousands of agents to uncover thousands of facts.

"We don't need to steal Soviet secrets," a pipe-smoking director explained to a group of junior spies. "If we're patient and we listen, they'll tell us everything we need to know."

After nearly a decade of magazine articles, Kaplan had witnessed the next revolution in espionage. Just as the quality of information had been replaced by the quantity of information, now the printed word was being replaced by the electronic word. Space satellites were taking over the spy's role.

They circled the earth, listening in on every radio, telephone, and electronic conversation. Millions of conversations and data transmissions traveled every minute from tower to tower in microwave networks, and the satellites recorded every one of them. International transmissions were bounced off any one of a hundred commercial communications satellites, but not before they had been noted and recorded by America's surveillance birds. Communications cables were tapped under the streets where they were buried so that miniature transmitters could send their messages to overflying satellites or to snooping stations a few hundred yards away. Why wait for an article on Polish shipbuilding to appear in an industrial journal when you could listen in as the author dictated his thoughts to a recording machine?

Of course, the satellites had no discretion. They couldn't distinguish the trivial from the important, so they recorded everything: orders for flowers wired from one city to another, conversations between Soviet astronauts and their earthbound controllers, pornographic phone calls from voyeurs to women fond of undressing in front of open windows, homesick children calling home, urgent industrial orders for additional nuts and bolts, currency exchanges between major banks, football scores being flashed to league cities, and diplomatic messages between Arab capitals. They recorded them all, in a babel of all the tongues of the earth, and in all the codes and ciphers invented by all the devious of the earth. The volume was paralyzing.

Each day, giant antennas around the world gathered the messages from the satellites and the listening posts, and flashed them to government antennas in Virginia. Acres of tape recorders spun constantly recording billions of hours of human verbiage. And then these miles of recorded garbage were delivered to the world's largest arsenal of computers, which hummed incessantly as they searched the oysters for pearls.

Each morning, Kaplan waited with a cup of black coffee vibrating in his trembling hands until the clerks pushed the day's work on carts down the aisles. Where he had once received hundreds of pounds of industrial magazines, he now received thousands of pounds of recorded trivia. Slavishly, he forced himself through the material, sorting out the potentially significant, organizing it into bundles fixed with paper clips, and routing it to the appropriate branch.

Another decade passed, and then he met Smith. That wasn't his real name, of course. Smith made it clear that in his line of work one didn't run around leaving calling cards. Whenever he used "Smith," he punctuated it with a quick thin smile and a hint of a wink, as if taking Kaplan into his confidence. But with the exception of his name, the man was all business.

Smith needed an agent. "A professional," he kept insisting. He was engaged in industrial espionage, and was on the verge of breaking into secrets that would take a small computer company and turn it into one of the world's industrial giants. The rewards would be staggering. For Kaplan, $50,000 for a few months of undercover work. And, if they were successful, Kaplan could name his position with the company and share fully in its riches.

Of course, there were dangers. He'd be working alone in a foreign country, with the "other side" using every available means to run him into the ground. The more dangerous it was made to sound, the more excited Kaplan became. Istanbul, the pistol, and the throwing knife seemed possible again. And then, when the job was completed, there would be a top spot as Comptroller with a high-flying computer company. When he learned that the assignment was in Tokyo, he rushed to his branch chief to tender his resignation. What if it wasn't Istanbul? It made sense that if Istanbul was a center of political intrigue, it couldn't be the Mecca for industrial espionage. Tokyo, as the capital of a great industrial nation, made much more sense. He changed his taxi three times just to be certain that he wasn't followed to the airport.

And this was where his journey had ended—alone in the garret of an old pottery plant, watching a computer spin its wheels. Well, not quite alone. Once a day Kado came in his little truck, brought in the bottled water, the frozen dinners, and two six-packs of Asahi beer. He helped Kaplan package the day's tapes into air express envelopes and paste on the labels addressed to the Signet Corporation in Mountain View, California. Signet was probably no more authentic than Smith, and Kaplan realized uneasily that he didn't even know the name of the company that was soon to have him as its chief financial officer.

But even Kado's daily visits didn't qualify as companionship. He spoke no English and, as far as Kaplan knew, no Japanese, but only a symbolic language of monosyllables that he used to communicate with the computer. He would enter through the steel trapdoor that led up from the abandoned work floor below, tapping out a code by knocking the top of his head against the door. Kaplan would pull open the trap and the slight, wiry man, burdened with packages, would rise through the floor like a figure from mythology. Setting the packages on the table, he would walk directly to the computer. He would snap on the video display and begin entering letters from the keyboard. The computer would respond, flashing its own unintelligible words on the screen. Kado would chuckle with delight and then type in his own part of what seemed to be a stimulating conversation.

While the Japanese romanced his computer—apparently running test routines to make sure that it was still working properly—Kaplan would stuff the groceries into the refrigerator and begin packing the day's tape reels into their protective envelopes.

In his loneliest moments, Kaplan imagined that Kado and the computer were talking about him. Suppose, he thought, that besides spying on a distant radio transmitter, the computer was also spying on him? Suppose it was looking out through its display screen and watching his movements about the room?

"Hello," Kado would type into the keyboard. "What's he been up to?"

"Not much," the computer would answer. "He's drinking a bit heavily. Maybe you should bring only one six-pack instead of two."

"Has he had any women up here?"

"You've got to be kidding," the computer would respond.

"Well, what does he do all day?"

"Nothing at all. I can't see him when he's in the bathroom. Maybe he's playing with himself."

"I am not," Kaplan would shout, interrupting the imaginary conversation. And then he would realize that he was probably losing his mind.

HE HAD JUST PULLED the tab from his last can of beer when suddenly the computer sprung to life. Its lamps flickered furiously, indicating that it was loading data into its registers and formatting it for the tape drives. And then the tape reels began to spin, first rocking back and forth to locate the last transmission recorded and then rolling forward as they began writing down the information the computer was copying from the overhead antenna.

Somewhere, out of the darkness, a tap had been placed on a telephone cable. From the direction in which the antenna faced, Kaplan guessed that the tap wasn't located within the city, but rather was in one of the industrial or research complexes that had sprung up along Tokyo's western edge. Connected to the tap was a tiny transmitter, so small that its resistance couldn't be measured by sending a signal down the line. And it was broadcasting at very low power so that its transmissions wouldn't be observed by ordinary radios.

It was the microsignal that was gathered by the wire-mesh antenna and fed into the amplifiers. It was the amplified signal that the computer noted, gathered into internal memory, and then wrote out onto the tapes.

Kaplan's attention was fixed on the spinning reels, and the paths of magnetic tape that arched between them, when he suddenly became aware of the sirens. He should have heard them at a distance, but instead they were very close to the loft when they blasted through to his awareness. He stood frozen for a moment, hoping to hear the shrill sounds peak as they came near and then gradually fade as the sirens moved on toward their destination. But the scream grew louder until he could not only hear it but actually feel it through the walls.

With a quickness he found amazing, he sprang across the room and slid the thick steel bolt on the trapdoor. Rushing back to the computer, he reversed the tape, rewinding it onto its spool. He snatched a large, cylindrical magnet from its metal storage cabinet, connected it to the tape drive, and started the reels spinning again. The tape slid over the magnet erasing all the data that had been recorded.

Then terse commands sounded from below. Whoever had arrived in the cars had entered the building. It would take only seconds for them to locate the iron stairs that led to the loft.

Kaplan next crouched down beside the computer and feeling with his fingers located the switches that had been installed along its base. He closed them in quick sequence, recoiling at the snap of the electrical explosions they caused inside the computer cabinet. Puffs of smoke shot out through the machine's ventilating louvers and, for an instant, Kaplan found himself choking.

He heard the clanging of footsteps on the metal steps that led up from the work floor, but there was no time to guess how many men there were. Instead, he raced to the amplifier cabinets and tripped the self-destructive devices that were connected to its doors. This time the internal explosions were dramatized with electrical flashes that set the room dancing in psychedelic blue light.

He ignored the banging against the underside of the trapdoor. Instead of answering the shouted commands from below, he wrenched the fire extinguisher from the wall clamp and aimed the conical nozzle at the computer. When he squeezed the trigger, the computer disappeared in a white cloud. Next, he tore open the door of the computer cabinet and aimed the foam into the circuit boards. In an instant, the electronic marvel looked like a melting ice-cream cake.

They were pounding against the door, either with clubs or with rifle butts, bouncing it against the bolt. With a quick glance Kaplan could see that the bolt was tearing up from the floor; they would get into the room in seconds. Now he aimed the nozzle at the tape drive and clogged its delicate mechanisms in a wave of foam.

The bolt broke free and flipped into the air as the trapdoor swung open. Japanese, in heavy police uniforms, stumbled up through the opening and suddenly began coughing in the cloud of acrid, electrical smoke. Kaplan glanced back at them, but kept the extinguisher trained on the tape drive. The policemen parted to make way for the officer who now stepped up into the loft and glanced at the banks of destroyed electrical equipment. It was the moment when Kaplan should have wheeled, snapping the Walther from its holster, fired a shot through the officer and then sent himself rolling across the floor to avoid the return fire. Lacking a Walther, he did the next best thing.

"Don't just stand there," he ordered. "Get some water up here before this thing gets out of control." He nodded toward the policemen. "You guys. Get some axes and knock out those walls. We've got to ventilate this place."

The policemen looked at him incredulously, then to their officer for instruction.

"What took you so long?" Kaplan demanded. "I've been fighting this thing for nearly an hour."

The officer smiled and then the smile broadened to a friendly grin. He reached into his jacket, drew out a document, and began reading the warrant for Kaplan's arrest in perfect English. While he was speaking, the fire extinguisher sputtered out its last drops of foam and Kaplan let the nozzle sink to the floor.

"Are you crazy?" he demanded when the officer finished the citaton. "What's industrial espionage? This is a United Nations research project to measure astronomical radiation. Christ, your own government is one of the sponsors."

"That's very good," the officer replied. He turned to his men and translated Kaplan's words into Japanese, which started them all laughing. "Now, as soon as you are finished destroying that equipment, will you please come with us."

Kaplan gave it one more try. "This is a United Nations project," he insisted. "Now, will you get some fire extinguishers up here before this whole place goes up in flames?''

The officer's face registered a moment of impatience, but he instantly got control of himself. He barked some Japanese commands into the hole, and after a few moments two more policemen appeared with Kado supported between them. In his arms were the evening's supply of groceries and yesterday's package of tapes, neatly addressed to Signet.

Kaplan wanted to bite down a cyanide capsule, but he had never seen a cyanide capsule. Instead, he dropped the extinguisher, crossed over to Kado, reached into the grocery bag and pulled a beer from the six-pack. He pulled the tab and offered the can to the officer, who shook his head in refusal but bowed politely to indicate his appreciation.

Kaplan turned to Kado, and noticed the young man's grief-stricken expression. At first he thought Kado was frightened at being arrested. Then he realized that he was shocked at the destruction of his beloved computer. Kaplan looked back at the wreck of the machines. "Fucking thing tried to follow me into the bathroom," he said by way of explanation.

March 1st, 10:00 A.M., Harrisburg

J. P. Toole stopped at the door and smoothed his hair while he waited for the guard to fit the key into the lock. He wished he had a mirror for a final critique of his appearance. First impressions were important to his profession. And he suspected that this was going to be a professional meeting.

He was happy with his grooming. The dark wavy hair was full in the front and combed back neatly to hide the thinning on the crown of his head. He had shaved closely, so there was no hint of the dark beard that sometimes made him look sinister. Instead, his wide blue eyes, framed by dark eyebrows, and his reddened cheeks gave an impression of youthful innocence, belying his forty-two years of toil. But he was disappointed in what a year of idleness had done to his body. His five-foot-ten-inch frame had lost the edge of its athletic trim. He was only a pound or two over his normal 170 pounds, but his weight had begun to rearrange itself so that his form was square rather than tapered. And the poor cut of the short jacket and trousers made him look a bit baggy. He knew he would have to keep his guest's attention focused on his smile.

The guard swung the door open and stood back from the entrance. Toole saw the institutional beige walls, decorated with mass-produced, mechanical oils of the Pennsylvania countryside. There was a scattering of Danish furniture that combined brown vinyl with shiny walnut veneer, and a clever triangular coffee table that stood on three brass-tipped legs. "Tacky," he thought to himself. Hardly an impressive backdrop for the impeccably tailored specimen that rose from one of the chairs.

"Mr. Toole," said the specimen through a lockjawed smile that marked him as a noble of the Eastern establishment. "How good of you to see me."

"My secretary was able to squeeze you in," Toole said sarcastically. He accepted the hand that was offered and shook it vigorously.

"John Cobb," the specimen announced. "I appreciate that you're on a very tight schedule, but I couldn't wait another two years."

"Twenty-two months," Toole corrected. "I know that's two years on the outside, but in here it's only twenty-two months. It's a matter of perspective."

"I thought we might take a walk outside," Cobb said, gesturing to the guard waiting at the doorway. The guard moved more quickly than Toole had ever seen any of the guards move, jumping back from the door and leading the two men back down the hall. Cobb slipped his topcoat over his shoulders like a cape. Toole took the signal and zipped his jacket up to the neck.

"Government," Toole thought. "Governor's office at least. Maybe even federal!"

There were telltale signs. Cobb was tall and thin, with good upper body strength that came through in his handshake. Toole figured him for mid-forties, so his fitness marked him as an exercise freak. That eliminated the possibility of his being police or FBI. They were all out of shape. His thin hair was nicely styled, precisely parted, and blown dry. He had taste, which ruled out any of the lower levels of government. And the guard's reaction showed that he had authority, which meant that he wasn't another one of the endless line of bankers who were constantly visiting, wondering if Toole might examine their computer security systems. "Definitely high government," Toole felt sure.

They followed the guard in silence until he turned to an exit that led out of the prison compound. Toole was impressed. He had thought he was being taken into the exercise yard, which would have been exceptional in itself. But this guy had the run of the countryside. "Federal," Toole decided. "Probably one of the spooks from CIA or the National Security Agency."

"I'm with the Commerce Department," Cobb said by way of small talk as they walked away from the prison wall.

"Bullshit," Toole told himself. "Bean counters don't get to take felons out of federal prison for a stroll."

"Actually, I'm on special assignment from the National Security Agency. On loan to the Commerce Department, you might say."

"Bingo," Toole said to himself. It was encouraging to know that even after years of inactivity he could still size up a mark. This was definitely going to be a professional conversation.

"Playing any poker?" Cobb asked.

"Show-off," Toole thought. "He wants me to know he's done his homework."

"A bit," he lied. "It's hard to get interested in a potful of match sticks. And some of the lads aren't the best of sports when they lose."

"Now, if he's really sharp," Toole thought, "he'll ask about basketball."

"Get to see any of the college games?" Cobb asked.

"Very good," Toole congratulated himself.

Cobb kept up the banter as they walked away from the prison, down a slope toward the trickle of a brook. Toole understood Cobb's need to get outside to make sure the conversation wouldn't be bugged. Now he realized that Cobb wanted to be out of range of long-distance listening devices. This conversation was going to be very professional. And in his comments on poker and basketball, Cobb had indicated that he understood perfectly what J. P. Toole's profession was.

He wasn't really J. P. Toole, which was the first hint that he wasn't to be trusted. He was James Patrick O'Toole, the youngest son of the largest family of that name that inhabited the Irish ghetto on New York's Rockaway Beach. James Patrick O'Toole had set himself apart from nineteen other kids with the same surname by doing amazing things with a basketball. At thirteen, he had made All City with the St. Christopher's team in the Catholic Youth Organization grade school league. He wasn't big and he wasn't fast. But with a twinkle of an eye he could persuade an opponent he was going to shoot, when actually he was going to pass. With the bend of a knee he could convince the lad guarding him that he was about to drive and then take a shot as soon as the boy backed off to block the lane. What made him great was his ability to sell lies— to send the defense rushing off in one direction while he moved leisurely in another.

He had won a scholarship to the Christian Brothers' high school and packed the house for all the freshman games. He was already planning an athletic scholarship to St. John's and probably a career with the New York Knickerbockers. But then he had run into his first black basketball player.

The kid was six foot six, which put him a good seven inches closer to the basket than James Patrick O'Toole. He ran like the wind. And, miracle of miracles, he could stop on a dime, jump straight into the air, and with a flick of the wrist toss the ball twenty feet into the basket. The scoreboard would be registering the points before the black kid came back down to the floor.

"So what," O'Toole had reasoned. "There's nothing shabby about being the second-best player in the city."

But the next time he turned around there were five black players. And then ten and then twenty. All tall. All fast. All immune to his most convincing fakes. He thought of the first slave trader who had found these guys in the jungle and envisioned them in a field picking cotton. The poor sap! With any brains he would have envisioned them as the Boston Celtics and made himself some real money. It was the black kids who convinced O'Toole that he wasn't a great basketball talent and that he wasn't going to make his fortune with the New York Knickerbockers.

But there was money to be made in betting on basketball, a skill that financed O'Toole's college education. All he had done was talk up one team, wait for the word to circulate among the undergraduates, and then bet on the other. He had organized a pool, with runners bringing in money from other campuses, when two linemen from the football team had taken exception to his methods. He still had a scar buried somewhere under his right eyebrow, a reminder that even football players will catch on if you try the same con often enough.

He had drifted into poker, favorably impressed by the amounts of money that even the worst card players like to toss onto the center of the table. Once again, his ability to package deceit had proven invaluable. His expression announced a straight flush when all he held was a pair of threes. By simply flexing a nearly invisible muscle in his cheek, he could look pathetic while he was holding all the aces. People had paid dearly to watch his performance.

Other weapons were added to his arsenal. With a little practice, he learned to pluck from the top of the deck the exact number of cards he wanted—any number from one to fifty-two. Handing him a deck to cut was as suicidal as playing Russian roulette with a bullet in every chamber. He could deal four hands of draw poker and put all four aces in any hand he chose. Then he discovered the added profitability of putting all four kings in another hand to encourage competition.

He could have made a career at the card tables. Nothing tremendous, he reasoned, because you did have to lose a couple of times a week to keep people interested, and you couldn't really make a killing without some of the more dangerous professionals getting very interested. But still, if you weren't greedy, it was a pleasant way to pocket a couple of thousand a week.

But then he had seen the light. He was making a cash deposit at a midtown bank when he noticed that no paper changed hands. He had given the teller cold hard cash. She had punched a few keys on her computer terminal, and then a liquid crystal display had blinked "Thank you."

"That's it?" O'Toole had asked. "I give you fourteen hundred in cash and your machine tells me, 'Thank you'?"

"We're computerized," the teller had answered, obviously proud of the fact. "Your deposit has been credited to your account."

O'Toole pondered what he had just witnessed. Money had been turned into electronic impulses and it was now under the protection of a gum-chewing moron who had obviously gotten her education in response to an ad on the back of a matchbook.

Forgetting that night's poker game, he rushed to the library and began a ten-day reading session on computer technology. Never again would he waste an evening bucking cash back and forth across a card table. Money wasn't cash any longer. It was computer records.

COBB AND TOOLE REACHED THE BROOK, which was frozen over, with chunks of opaque ice tossed to its edges by an earlier thaw. The ice was split down the middle and a thin stream of dark water was splashing in the narrow chasm. Cobb turned up the collar of his topcoat and thrust his hands into the pockets. Then he turned and looked all around the countryside. He didn't want to get into his subject until he was sure they were completely alone.

"How much of Citibank's money did you manage to keep?"

"Oh, Christ," Toole thought. "Not this again." But he realized that the government hadn't sent a National Security agent, on loan to the Commerce Department, to ask questions they knew he wasn't about to answer. Obviously, the guy was just warming up to his real purpose.

"I made full restitution," Toole said, with a twinkle in his eye that told Cobb they both knew he was lying.

"It was damn slick," Cobb said, ignoring the denial. "Citibank figures you kept two hundred thousand. Not that they care. They were delighted to get the million back. Our guys have looked over their records. We figure it was closer to three hundred fifty. Personally, my guess is that you kept at least half a million."

Toole picked up a handful of stones and began tossing them at the thin line of water. He didn't want to talk about Citibank. "Let's walk a little further," Cobb suggested, pointing in the direction away from the prison. He picked up a few stones of his own and tried to match Toole's shots as they walked.

The actual figure had been $350,000. The actual amount Toole had returned to Citibank had been $1.2 million. The bankers appreciated the refund, especially Toole's willingness to give back more than he announced. The bonus, plus the insurance coverage, had gotten them off about even. What did they care if Toole kept a bit for himself? As bankers, they knew that insurance companies had too much money to begin with.

Citibank hadn't been Toole's first adventure with computers. Beginning with his binge in the library, he had made computers his sole interest, raising his reading to increasingly technical levels and taking a night school semester in computer programming. Then he had applied to several banks for computer-related work, finally landing a position next to Manufacturers Hanover's IBM 370. His co-workers had run the machines. But James Patrick O'Toole had done much more. He had spent all his time trying to understand the mind of the machines.

He had seen clearly what few people even considered. Money was no longer bars of precious metal or even carefully minted currency. Money had become information about wealth. A billionaire didn't have a billion dollars or a roomful of gold ingots. Rather, there was information, stored in someone's computer, that said he was a billionaire. Erase the information and he was a pauper. Or put someone else's name on the information and someone else would become a billionaire.

And all this information traveled over telephone lines. Over ordinary, twenty-five-cents-a-call, hanging-on-a-wooden-pole telephone lines. Wealth was being transferred from bank to bank, in and out of brokerage houses, from buyer to seller, from citizen to government, from country to country, over the same lines he used to tap as a kid to beat the friendly Bell Telephone Company out of a dime.

He had quit the bank, paid the price of an Apple II personal computer, and gotten the dealer to throw in a modem so that he could connect his computer to telephone lines. For two months he had done nothing more dangerous than dial into public commercial data bases to look up boring facts and figures about subjects that he didn't understand. What he gathered was firsthand experience in data communications procedures.

He had developed an algorithm to hunt down passwords, starting with a random number generator, and then random letters. It took days, even weeks, but eventually the computer developed the password and gained him access into private data bases. Generally, the access wasn't worth the effort, like the time he broke into the records of the New York City Water Department, only to discover that it was thirty-six years behind on its preventative maintenance program. His procedures had failed to get him even a "hello" from a savings and loan association, much less a first-class bank.

So he had changed his image. He dropped the stiff blue suit and white shirt he had bought for his employment at the bank, and changed to grander stuff: French-cut shirts and Italian ties. He threw away his dark gray topcoat and replaced it with a leather, thigh-length jacket. His appearance changed from "industrious" to "casually well heeled," and in the process his name changed from James Patrick O'Toole to J. P. Toole. The ladies loved it.

Of course, it was only for very special ladies that J. P. Toole gave his full performance. All were secretaries to high-ranking officials in New York's biggest banks. All were liberated women, with a need to demonstrate their own importance to the business world. Most, after dinner at the Palace and stops at clubs frequented by celebrities, discussed their work freely. Some had even gone so far as to talk about the Machiavellian procedures their banks used to safeguard their access codes.

So J. P. Toole found his way into the information files that determined who was rich and who was poor. Then he began to invent his own records—small records representing insignificant amounts. He watched them flow through the bank's auditing procedures, learning which ones were caught immediately, which ones lingered a few days before they were discovered, and which ones the bank missed completely. "No one can think of everything," he reminded himself whenever he seemed to be getting discouraged. Every system had its flaw, and Toole devoted the best part of the year to learning the flaw in each bank's software.

Then he began taking a modest profit on his investment. He moved small amounts of money through the banks' records, accumulated them in fictitious accounts, made a legitimate transfer to another bank, and then closed the accounts in the original banks. His legitimate accounts prospered on transfers from other accounts that vanished as soon as they had served their purpose.

He expanded his holdings, increasing his accounts at one bank, Citibank, until the electronic records declared him a millionaire. He was within hours of transferring his newfound wealth into tax-free municipals when he detected the first hint that his transactions had attracted the attention of the bank's generally unconcerned computers. Every instinct that had been bred into his bones by his years as a con man told him to leave the money and run. But, instead, he made his one fatal mistake. He tried to cash in on an investment that he suspected was compromised.

COBB STOPPED ABRUPTLY and looked back at the bleak walls of the prison. He decided that they had gone far enough.

"Toole," he began, tossing the last of the stones he had gathered back into the brook, "I have a proposition that I think you'll find interesting...assuming, of course, that after a year in that morgue you can still find anything interesting."

Toole glanced back toward the prison. "It's not such a bad place," he said with mock seriousness. Cobb ignored the comment.

"This is an opportunity to do something for yourself and, if you'll pardon the suggestion, for your country. Something very important for your country."

Toole nodded reverently. "Tell me what I can do for myself," he said.

"You can get yourself out of prison and back into the real world. You can go get your things and leave before you have to sit through one more of their gourmet meals."

"That's interesting," Toole answered. "And how long would I be apt to stay out?"

"The assignment begins today and it has to be completed by early December. During that time you'll be under government control. When it's over, assuming that all goes well, we'll just continue you on government assignment for another eighteen months. That would take you right through the end of your term, which means that you'll never have to go back."

"If all goes well . . . ?" Toole wondered aloud.

"If you cooperate and make a good effort," Cobb explained. "This is an extremely complex operation. It could fail despite all of us giving it our best. No one could hold you . . . or me . . . or anyone else directly responsible for its failure. All we ask is your full cooperation. You do the job for us and, no matter how things turn out, I'll see that you don't have to finish your term."

"That's very generous," Toole said, letting his eyes flood with gratitude. "I don't suppose you could be more specific as to what the operation might entail."

Cobb smiled. "Of course I couldn't be more specific. I can't tell you anything about it until you've joined us. And even then, all I would be able to tell you is only what you absolutely have to know. As I said, this is big. A hell of a lot bigger than anything you tried with Citibank."

Toole knew he was hooked. But the idea was not to let Cobb know that Toole was hooked. "You want me to transfer the national debt to someone else's account," he chided.

"That's not exactly what we have in mind," Cobb answered. "But what you'd be doing is just as big."

"Would there be any foreign travel involved?" he asked casually.

"I shouldn't say. But the answer is yes. You'd be out of the country for most of the next nine months."

"Where?"

Cobb shook his head. "I've already told you more than I wanted to."

"You know I don't speak any foreign languages," Toole tried.

"I know," Cobb answered. "And don't try to get any more out of me. Do you want to come with me, or do you want to stay here? There are other people I can talk to."

"Bullshit," Toole thought. "No one else took Citibank apart. It's me you need." He looked up dejectedly. "I'm sorry," he told Cobb, and then with an impish grin, "Particularly since you've appealed to my patriotism. But this place has to have a better Michelin rating than a Russian prison. And I'm not sure the Russians would be as fastidious about letting me out in twenty-two months. I think I'll stay put."

"It's not Russia," Cobb admitted reluctantly.

"Well, then, say Red China, or some other barbaric land...like England. It's all the same," Toole explained. "I've got to choose between another twenty-two months here and nine months of danger in some foreign hellhole. I'm better off staying where I am."

"There's more," Cobb interrupted. "I know you can do the rest of your time here standing on your head, because you know you've got all that money waiting for you. But I can promise you that you'll never get to enjoy a cent of it. You turn me down and

I'll have people waiting at the gate the day you get out.
I'll have them following you every minute for the rest
of your life. The first time you try to spend a penny of
the Citibank money, I'll have you right back in for another three years.''

"Sounds like sour grapes," Toole chided.

"On the other hand, if you help me, we'll forget that
there's money waiting for you. When we're finished,
you're free. Take your money and enjoy it. I'll forget
that it even exists."

"It doesn't exist," Toole lied. "And even if it did, I
couldn't spend a penny of it. You have to understand,
Mr. Cobb, that I am a changed man. Thanks to the
spiritual guidance that I've received here in Harrisburg, I've renounced the kind of life I used to live." He
lowered his voice reverently. "In fact, I'm thinking of
the priesthood."

Cobb began to laugh. "Toole, you're pure horseshit. But you can help us and we need all the help we
can get."

"Here comes the 'sincere and friendly' approach,"
Toole warned himself.

"I'll lay all my cards out on the table," Cobb continued. "The government authorized me to pay for
your services. I figured the money wouldn't mean
anything to you so I decided to offer you your freedom. But I guess we can put them both together. You
help me and you've got your freedom . . . including the
money you kept from the Citibank deal. On top of
that, I'll pay you the hundred thousand that the government authorized. It will be deposited immediately
to any bank you name."

"A hundred thousand," Toole considered. "For a
deal as big as the national debt, the government is

willing to pay a whole hundred thousand. Which has to be nearly as much as they pay to keep the silver polished on the presidential yacht . . .''

"One-fifty," said Cobb.

"Oh, it's not the money," Toole continued. "It's just that I'm trying to get some idea of the importance the government attaches to this particular mission."

"Two hundred," said Cobb. "And if you say one more word, I'm going to leave you here to rot."

"Not to mention the danger to my person," Toole continued. "I mean, I don't suppose there's a group life insurance program for the little team you're assembling?"

"Two-fifty and you can buy your own fucking life insurance," Cobb said.

"I'll get my things," Toole answered.

"Bigger than Citibank," he thought to himself as he checked out the clothes he had worn to prison: a soft camel's hair jacket, charcoal-brown slacks, a beige knitted shirt, and tasseled loafers. Citibank had been big enough. He had moved nearly $50 million around the bank's computer records before he siphoned off $1.5 million to his own account and began transferring it to six other banks. But then he had ignored his primordial instincts and gotten greedy. "This time I'll play it smart," he promised himself as he stepped through the gate and walked toward Cobb's waiting car.

Cobb began to smile as they drove the winding country road that led from the prison to the massive concrete interchange of the Pennsylvania Turnpike. The smile expanded to a broad grin and then to a self-satisfied laugh.

"You must enjoy your work," Toole noticed. "Exactly what is it that you do to provide for the security of our nation? You don't seem the type to crush genitals and tear off fingernails."

Cobb answered through his obvious amusement. "I'm a bit of a con man myself. Not in your league, of course. But I did manage to beat you out of two hundred and fifty thousand dollars."

Toole looked wide-eyed.

"I was authorized to go to half a million."

"My God," Toole allowed himself to gasp.

Cobb nodded. "That's right. Half a million and you settled for two-fifty. You're slipping, Toole."

J. P. Toole pursed his lips. "I must be out of practice," he admitted. "Of course, give credit where it's due. You played me perfectly. More than a 'bit of a con man' I'd say."

He let Cobb go back to his gloating. "You dumb bastard," he thought to himself. "I'd have paid you two hundred and fifty thousand to get out of that tomb."

Toole tried to look humbled.

April 3rd, 11:00 P.M., Tokyo

She was the most beautiful woman Yamagata Fujii had ever seen. Tall for a Japanese woman and straight rather than cherubic, with high, firm breasts that held the open collar of her yukata robe away from her throat. When she bowed her deferential greeting, he couldn't help noticing the enticing cleavage that separated the folds of the thin white cloth.

Her eyes were like dark almonds, cast downward by two thousand years of training, but burning confidently beneath the veil of black eyelashes. And at the corners of her mouth there was the suggestion of a smile that seemed to be welcoming him to a new world of pleasures. He would gladly have foregone the ceremony and carried her directly to the sleeping mat. But that would have been a scandalous breach of bathhouse etiquette.

It was a new world. Fujii had been to many of the bathhouses that his company provided for the discreet pleasure of its executives and their guests. But never one such as this. This was available only to the very highest officers and directors of the company and their guests from the summit of the world's industrial empire. Perhaps no more than a hundred men from the world's business elite had ever seen the inside, which was clearly as it should be. It would be sacrilegious for a god of steel or of banking to share a woman with an executive of lower rank.

Fujii was certainly the youngest man that this glorious woman had ever undressed. And, he was sure, the most desirable. He understood that the bathhouse attendants were trained professionals, emotionally uninvolved with their patrons. But after ministering to the overweight and the balding, the soft and the slow, how could she help but be stirred by the sight of a real man?

She hadn't seen many. In the strict hierarchy of the Japanese industrial community, rank was a function of age. The young labored for the old, paid the required deference, walked a step behind and a little to the left, and patiently waited their turn. "How stupid," he thought, "that the most desirable women were assigned to minister to the aged whose passion for desirable women had long since burned out, while the younger men were admitted to houses of lesser rank and offered women of lesser beauty. And how stupid of the younger men to accept positions of inferior rank in blind obedience to a geriatric code."

Fujii had not waited his turn. With dogged determination and blinding brilliance he had smashed through the traditional barriers. His superiors may have hated his brashness, but they needed his talents. They had swallowed their ancient pride, received him, into their ranks, and opened the doors to their cherished private bathhouse. Worthy or not, he was ready, to share their women.

She moved slowly about him, never looking directly, into his eyes. With weightless fingers, she removed his jacket and his tie, hanging them carefully in a private closet. Then she knelt and removed his shoes, replacing them with slippers so that his stockings never touched the floor. Ceremoniously, she folded each article of clothing as he undressed. She drew a yukata over his shoulders and fastened it with a sash, then opened the door leading to the bath.

It hadn't been easy. Despite his world-acclaimed successes with digital technology, and the vast wealth his computer designs had brought to his company and to his country, his superiors had fully expected him to wait his turn. They would collect the profits of his inventiveness and reward him handsomely with money. But acceptance to their ranks only partially depended on accomplishment. The real test was endurance. And there was no scientific breakthrough he could produce that would hasten the process of maturity. He had despaired of their ever offering. He had decided simply to take.

What could they do about it, besides snarl their useless resentment? He was the world master of the computer. And the computer held the key to their survival. Certainly, they could buy a few more years of prosperity with their marvelous automobiles and their clever little televisions and radios. But the industrial age and its final generation of trash were drawing to a close. The information age was already upon them and they were bright enough to see that whoever led in computer technology would be crowned leader of the new world. They needed him. In the final analysis, they valued him more than their traditions.

Fujii enjoyed the memory of his triumph. The incident had concerned an automobile, one of a fleet of a half-dozen chauffeured limousines kept waiting at the pleasure of the company's highest-ranking officers and directors. He had simply climbed into one and ordered the startled driver to take him on a petty errand. On his return, he had ordered himself deposited at the building's executive entrance.

Moments later the summons had come, brought by a frightened secretary who had scarcely been able to utter the name of the mandarin who demanded Fujii's presence. He had walked confidently into the president's office, passed a row of shocked faces that were obviously aware of his transgression. Then he had taken a chair across the massive desk without waiting for the invitation to be seated, which certainly would not have been given. The president asked for an explanation, hoping that Fujii would produce a story of an emergency need that made the use of the car clearly essential to the company's interests—some excuse that would provide a suitable explanation to his deeply offended associates.

"I needed it for personal business," Fujii said without a moment of hesitation. "I will need it every day from now on. In fact, I will be using it again in just a few moments."

The president's eyes had widened and flashed explosively. A deep growl had sounded in his chest. But before he could speak, Fujii reached into his pocket, produced three letters, each in a white bond envelope, and pushed them carefully across the desk. The older man had shifted his gaze from Fujii to the offensive envelopes, understood that they were the only explanation he was going to receive, and reached into his breast pocket for his reading glasses.

Each letter was on the executive letterhead of one of the world's leading computer giants, two from the United States and one from France. Each was addressed with great deference to Yamagata Fujii. Each offered him the highest position in the company's technical organization at a salary far in excess of his present income. The president turned from page to page reviewing the lists of options and perks that accompanied each salary offering. He understood that, unlike every other employee in Japan, Fujii placed a higher value on himself than he did on his employer. He was a heretic who didn't believe in the national religion, who didn't need his company as much as the company needed him.

The president had grunted his acknowledgment, carefully replaced the letters in their proper envelopes, and pushed them back to Fujii. It was the moment of triumph Fujii had been planning.

He entered the bath, a room forty feet square, with a washing stool and basins, and with a twenty-foot pool to one side. Fujii couldn't control his smile of pleasure. Every appointment in the room was clearly a cut above the bathing rooms he had been entitled to use in the past. The water was perfectly clear, freshly filled for his individual use. "Of course," he thought. "At this level no one could tolerate sharing his bath water." A film of white steam danced across its surface. The tile, which covered the floor and the lower edges of the walls, was an art form. There were delicate floral patterns worked with the intricacy of a mosaic instead of the white blocks that had once been good enough.

Fujii stood beside the stool while she untied the sash, then stepped behind him to catch the yukata as it fell from his shoulders. He couldn't see her face, but he knew that her eyes would be cast downward. Ridiculous, of course. In a few moments, she would be ministering to his body in great detail. But for this part of his entertainment she was functioning as a servant, observing a strict code of deference.

He squatted down on the stool and leaned forward as she began to spread the liquid soap across his back and work it into his skin with her fingers. Her hands seemed hard as they pressed up between his shoulder blades, but softened when they curved around his sides and up under his arms. Then she reached the top of his shoulders, and Fujii thought he heard her breath quicken. Her fingertips seemed to linger as they traced the edges of the muscles in his upper arms.

"Beautiful," she told him. "And strong." She smiled, letting seconds pass before she plunged the cloth into the basin of water and began bathing his chest, her eyes darting up from her work to ask his approval.

"That's not part of the ritual," he assured himself, thinking of her touch. "How could she say 'strong' if her fingers were sinking in fat?" He was special, the first real man she had been given to bathe. She would ask him about his body and his strength, and he would enjoy telling her of his physical triumphs.

They hadn't all been triumphs. There had been humiliating defeats. But he had used the defeats to steel his determination and to feed the fires of his ambition.

In his first year at the university he had hurdled over propriety and presented himself as a candidate for the Olympic gymnastic team. His credentials were impeccable; an unbroken string of victories that had made him a secondary school champion and the best first-year athlete at the university. But his coaches advised him against competing. He was not yet ready to challenge the nation's best.

Defiantly, he submitted his application and went to the Olympic trials, where he appeared without a coach or a sponsor. He would show them who was ready!

So exasperated were the officials at his arrogance that he had to beg a trainer to boost him up to the rings. But once hanging in the air, high above their petty preferences and procedures, he had given them an exercise that had drawn a spontaneous burst of applause. He had spun like a propeller between the ropes with speed and grace that seemed to make his strength unnecessary. There wasn't a flutter of effort in his handstands. And in the excruciating pain of the cross, he had held himself, arms outstretched between the rings, for a full ten seconds, twice as long as any of the other contenders.

His dismount had been a miracle of twists and spins that deposited him precisely on his toes with a quick flex of his knees and without a single gesture of imbalance. The building had rocked, and then exploded again as 9.8s and 9.9s appeared on the white cards above the judges' heads. But when the team selection was announced, his name was never mentioned.

The young woman scoured his skin with the long, thin brush, bringing its sharp edge across his shoulders and down each arm. Her fingers followed the curve of each of his muscles, and she looked up laughing, amazed at his lean strength. She put the brush aside and tried to knead his muscles with her fingers. Then she shook her head in mock despair. "So hard," she told him. "I'm not strong enough."

He laughed, then extended his legs so that she could scrub them. She again took the brush, and began to slide it down his thighs. But she stopped abruptly when she reached the knotted scar at the side of his right leg.

Four years later, he had gone to the Olympic Games as a clear favorite for the gold medal. He had soared through the first qualifying heat, posting the highest score of any of the contenders. In the second heat, his exercise had been even more precise, right up to the final instant of his dismount. He landed too far back on his heels, an imperfection that the judges failed to notice. But the enormous forces created by his spinning body sent a shock wave up the bones of his legs. One had shattered in an excruciating spiral fracture.

He was out of the competition, according to his trainers. His leg needed a cast, and even the lightest cast would throw his balance off. The doctor's hand was on the telephone to deliver the bad news to the team officials when Fujii ripped the instrument from his fingers. There would be no withdrawal. There would be no cast. Fujii would compete with one shattered leg.

His plan had been impossible. He would enter the arena with his arm over the shoulder of a teammate, supporting his leg in a typical gesture of sportsmanship. His coach would carry him to the mat and lift him into the rings, just as all competitors were lifted into the rings. During the exercise, the broken bone would be of no consequence since it would never bear his weight. Only the dismount would present a danger. He would have to land awkwardly, taking the full shock on one leg. Probably he would lose fractions of a point on the imbalanced landing. But the skill of his exercise would overcome that handicap. He would win his gold medal.

The trainer had protested furiously. The pain of the landing would be blinding. How could anyone perform up to potential, knowing the agony that was waiting at the end of the performance? But Fujii was just as furiously determined and the trainer had backed down.

He had grasped the rings, hung suspended for a moment, and then, with the smooth flow of the muscles in his upper body, lifted himself into the exercise. The pain had come with his first spin between the ropes. The tug on his leg caused by the inertial forces the exercise created sent a spear of pain cutting into his body. He felt his mind shutting down in response. His first movements had been labored and heavy; correct in meeting the mandatory requirements, but lacking the grace and style that separated "good" from "outstanding." His medal was slipping away. In an instant, through sheer will, he shut down his sensitivity to pain. His mind locked into the details of the movements and he forced his body to trace the precise patterns of the exercises. In his headstand he held the legs perfectly perpendicular to the floor, his toes delicately pointed, even though the leg seemed about to explode. He welcomed the cross, when the pain in his arms and chest would be so severe that the leg would become only a minor annoyance. The gasp that erupted from the audience as he hung motionless for five seconds, then ten, and finally fifteen seconds, told him that he was still in the running. But now, there was the dismount, and he knew that because of his slow start he needed a perfect dismount to win.

The decision had been instantaneous, made in the fraction of a second between his final swing and the moment he let go of the rings. There would be no awkward one-legged landing. He was going for the gold!

He had flown into the air, tumbling and twisting through space as he first rose, reached the apogee of his arc, and began plunging toward the thin mat. The spin raised the gravity force at the end of his legs as the plunging weight of his body built to a tremendous moving force. Fujii extended both legs, ankles touching, toes pointing toward the floor. Both feet stuck together, the broken leg taking its full share of the enormous impact.

He had landed perfectly, fixed his position, and actually heard the first rumble of applause. Then the agony had broken through the barrier of his will and reached his brain. In a sickening shock of pain, his mind had gone blank. His body dropped like a rag doll into a heap on the spot where he had landed. Fujii never saw the scores that the individual officials awarded. He had been unconscious for nearly a minute, with a small crimson stain expanding on his tights, over the spot where a pointed edge of the broken bone had burst through his skin. The scores had been excellent; good enough to earn him the bronze medal. Later, when the judges realized that they had witnessed the most courageous exercise ever performed on the rings, they regretted that their point awards hadn't been higher. They had, quite properly, deducted points for a poor landing, when in reality, they had never seen one better. "An incredible achievement," the judge from the United Kingdom later told the press. But to Fujii, it had been a moment of failure. The bronze was worthless when compared with the gold.

She carried a heavy pail of clear water to his side, somehow making it appear as if the water had no weight at all. With a large dipper, she drew the water and poured it over his head, repeating the movement as she splashed all the soap from his body. Then she dried him with a large, soft towel and ran the palms of her hands over his skin to be sure that all the soap had been removed. Smiling in satisfaction with her work, she reached out and took his hand. Fujii rose from the washing stool and allowed himself to be led to the edge of the pool.

He walked down the steps into the water, pretending to be oblivious to the heat that boiled his feet and legs. Then he lowered himself to his chin, feeling his skin pucker and flash into crimson. Finally, he stood in the chest-deep kettle and turned to look back at her.

She was staring at his body in admiration, smiling her approval and her gratitude. It was a look intended to flatter; the same breathless anticipation she would have registered for pendant breasts and a stomach that hung down over the genitals. But Fujii knew that in his case it was genuine. In the fifteen years since he had abandoned his gymnastics, he had allowed himself to add just ten pounds, a sacrifice to his taste for martinis, an occasional cigarette at the card tables, and late nights of work that interrupted his scheduled exercises.

Now it was her turn. The time for ceremonial shyness and deference was over and the real delights of the evening were about to begin.

She undid her yukata, slipping it away from a naked body clad only in brief white pants. Her eyes never left his as he admired her long neck, the graceful slope of her shoulders and the firm, erect breasts with pronounced nipples that tipped slightly upward. She stepped to the hooks on the wall where she had hung his robe and placed her yukata beside it. Then she slipped out of her slippers, slipped the pants down over her legs, and hung them carefully on their own hook.

He was transfixed as he watched. Her legs were long and thin; Western rather than Oriental, like the blond women who were the favored dancers at the better Japanese nightclubs. They widened gracefully through her thighs, then blossomed into the curve of her buttocks. She could have been a statue, except she was moving rather than still, with each movement stretching the honey-colored skin right across her contours. She was glorious and Fujii could feel his body responding just to the sight of her.

She turned back toward him, her eyes locking on his own, and walked confidently back to the edge of the pool. He stared at the flat, hard belly that descended to a triangle of thick ebony hair, trimmed to fit easily between the stride of her legs. She paused only long enough to settle her pointed toes on the top step, beneath the water. Then she descended slowly and moved toward him without even rippling the surface.

She stood next to him, the surface of the water caressing her breasts and providing the pretense of a modest covering for her body. She began to push the water up over his shoulders, an innocent excuse that allowed her body to brush gently against his in foreplay. The feel of her skin and the pronounced mounds of her breasts were wildly exciting. Yet his role in the ritual was to be passive. Her task was to torment him with pleasure. His was to maintain his dignity. The fantasy would continue until he led her out of the water and into a bedroom, and then it would be only as a concession to her needs. Men, according to the rules, didn't rush ahead impulsively. The intellect was always in command and, in its excruciating logic, the intellect moved deliberately, one step at a time.

To Fujii, this was the genius of his people as well as their downfall. It explained the plodding determination toward quality that had made their manufactured goods the envy of every factory manager in the world. But it also explained why they continued to lag beind their Western competitors in innovation. Their step-by-step, ritualistic approach produced few flashes of brilliance. Rather, they followed the paths blazed by the scientists of the United States and Europe, and earned their living by building reproductions of Western products more carefully than the Westerners themselves could build them.

They ran second in computers, the spaceships of the information age, because every component of their best machines had been invented in the West. They used semiconductors that had been invented in New Jersey and microcomputers developed in California.

Eventually, they would build them better, with much higher yields than the impatient Americans. But by the time they moved ahead in quality and performance, a flash of American brilliance would produce an even more wondrous design and once again they would fall behind.

Fujii thought he understood how his associates could remain docile under the tormenting movements of a woman's body. Docility had been poured into them with their mothers' milk. They would spend their lives in slow, carefully orchestrated movements, never crashing through the time barriers to be first with a brilliant insight. They would always copy—whether it was the details of a bathing ritual established centuries ago or the blueprint of a circuit invented a year ago.

But not Fujii. To him, anything less than first was failure. In his laboratory he was copying nothing. He was reaching out dangerously, much further than any of his countrymen would ever dare to reach. Even further into the future than his American competitors were able to see. The computers he was inventing were unlike anything running anywhere in the world, based on principles born in his own brain. For the first time since the early days of World War II, the Japanese were ahead of the Americans. Not in clumsy ships or in tons of gunpowder, but in something truly important. His computers were smarter and faster—ten times faster than the best the United States could produce. And computers were the power plants of prosperity in the information age, just as the steam engine had been the power plant of the industrial age. He was ahead because he had dared to violate the time-honored code that rewarded compliance and punished aggressiveness. And he would stay ahead because he would continue to reach out and take what he wanted no matter who was offended by his arrogance.

The girl was standing behind him, smoothing his hair as if it were essential that it not remain disarranged. He could feel her breasts rising and falling against his back and her thigh sliding against his legs. As he turned toward her, she ducked playfully under the water, leaving him smiling as he looked around the misty surface. Moments later, she rose out of the steam directly in front of him, her hair tight against the sides of her face and disappearing behind her shoulders. She moved forward to brush an imagined lock of hair from his eyes, allowing their bodies to touch once again. Then she smiled at the effect that her maddening dance had upon him and tipped her face as if to ask if he were ready to complete the ritual in the privacy of a bedroom.

Instead, he reached out and locked her shoulders in his viselike grip and pushed her back against the edge of the pool. There was no surprise in her face. She understood immediately what he was demanding. With her back pressed against the tile side of the tub, she let her legs float to the surface, on both sides of him. She smiled as his hand released her shoulder, clutched at her hair and pulled her head back. Then her lips parted, awaiting his kiss.

Fujii felt her legs tighten around his back. Instead of resisting his outrageous breach of etiquette, she was helping him take everything he wanted now, when he wanted it.

She understood. He was a man who wasn't bound by rules.

April 7th, 12:30 P.M., Washington, D.C.

Cobb circled the block twice before he pushed open the
iron gate and climbed the three steps to the front door
of the Secretary's townhouse. It was probably a needless caution. Even the most eager of the reporters and
stringers who made their living by haunting the homes
of government officials took Saturdays off. But still,
anyone who called on the Secretary of State was fair
game for the press. The reporters knew the regular
callers, and could pretty well speculate on the reasons
for a visit from an ambassador or foreign dignitary. It
was the people they didn't know that they would ha-
rass, rushing up and demanding identification as if
anyone who called on a public official automatically
sacrificed all rights to privacy.

A butler opened the door and pronounced his name
before he had a chance to identify himself. "Good afternoon, Mr. Cobb. The Secretary has asked me to
make you comfortable in the parlor. He will be joining you in a moment."

As soon as Cobb stepped into the room, he knew
that the house had been found for the Secretary. The
man was a political appointee of no particular distinc-
tion; an industrialist whose campaign contributions
and professional success in gouging resources from
underdeveloped nations had won him his position. He
was strictly chrome and Formica, but the furnishings
of the parlor were breeding and history.

There was a large, floor-mounted globe with sepia outlines of the continents as they had been perceived in the sixteenth century. It was an ideal stage prop for a man who posed as a shaper of the world, even though he had once asked an assistant who presented him with a contract for mineral ore, "Where the fuck is Chad?" The books on the shelves were all original editions of historical works—the annotated *Treaty of Almutz, Minutes of the Washington Naval Conference, Recollections from the Hague*. Cobb doubted whether anyone in Washington had ever read them. Certainly they weren't the bedtime fare of the current Secretary of State. The desk against the wall was an impractical piece with a brass plate on its edge that identified it as being from Woodrow Wilson's home in Princeton and there was a rocking chair that screamed "John Kennedy sat here." Cobb could reconstruct the conversation when the Secretary learned of his appointment and instructed an assistant to get him an apartment in Washington.

"Just make sure it's expensive and in the best part of town. And have the accounting boys look at the contract to make sure it's tax deductible."

"Would you like to interview a few decorators?"

"Hell, no. Just tell them I'm the Secretary of State, and that it damn well better look like it belongs to a Secretary of State."

It looked like it belonged to a decorator who thought he was the Secretary of State.

COBB HATED THE TRAPPINGS of government and the pretensions of its officials, both elected and appointed. They were showmen, performing for a constituency of ignoramuses, whose fancy they were forced to court to secure their positions. By necessity, they were more concerned with appearances than results, happy to fail as long as their failures could be made to look like victories.

Results, Cobb knew, depended on his secret government, which was designed to operate out of earshot of the general public. No one had elected him to his position, so he owed explanations to no one. Operatives of Central Intelligence and National Security earned their positions by succeeding, and paid the penalties for their failures. They were the ones who gave the nation its muscle.

But the satisfaction was solitary. Their success, by design, could never be known. Only their failures were publicized, by the elected officials they served, who delighted in exposing their "excesses," and in appointing watchdog committees to bring them under public scrutiny. The hypocrisy was sickening. In times of difficulty, they turned to the secret government to do their dirty work. If Cobb and his associates succeeded, the accolades were claimed by the politicans who attributed success to their sound policies. But should the venture fail, then the same politicians became publicly outraged at the audacity of their underlings and launched investigations to assure that the public will would never again be violated.

The door opened and the Secretary charged into the room. "Cobb?" he asked as he held out his hand. "I've never heard of you. Neither has my staff." The entrance was designed to rattle a subordinate and leave Cobb groping for an explanation of his existence.

"That's the way it should be," Cobb answered dryly, offering his own hand only after he had seen the Secretary's confidence drain. "I'm on a need-to-know assignment. Until now, you didn't need to know."

The Secretary recovered quickly. "Well, I sure as hell need to know why a simple request to the Justice Department ends up with the Attorney General and why the Attorney General gives me you instead of an answer."

As he spoke, he pushed open the French doors and gestured Cobb into the dining room, which was set for their luncheon. "We can talk over lunch. The whole room is wrapped in a copper mesh to make it bug proof. Damn place is so tight you can't even get a radio to play."

The butler was waiting, already drawing Cobb's chair back from the table. "What will you drink?" the Secretary asked, and Cobb placed his order for a martini. He toyed with the idea of naming a gin that he knew the Secretary wouldn't have stocked, but he decided that there was ample time to put the man in his place.

"Let's get down to business," the Secretary said with a glance at his watch as soon as both men were seated. "Who the hell are you and why do I have to talk to you in order to find out how Justice is doing with an investigation into an industrial espionage case?"

"Signet is a very special case," Cobb answered.

"Signet? Is that the name? The outfit in California that got caught stealing Japanese software?"

"That's the only one you asked about at Justice," Cobb assured him.

The Secretary shook his head, then lifted his fork and plunged into the pâté. Cobb took the invitation and raised his own fork.

"There are so many of them," the Secretary said despairingly. "It's hard to keep track. I bet we've got a thousand complaints from foreign governments about our companies stealing secrets and infringing on patents. And I'll bet we've got a million cases where our companies are prosecuting foreign nationals. Stealing seems to have replaced research as the way to get ahead."

"Excellent pâté," Cobb complimented him.

"It's basically staff work and there's no way that I can follow every case. But Signet has the Japanese in an uproar. They caught one of the spies and they confiscated tapes with their computer secrets written on them. They even have the address in California where the tapes were supposed to be delivered. It's an open-and-shut case, and they want action."

"Understandable," Cobb sympathized.

They were interrupted as the butler entered the room, bearing a martini for Cobb and a double martini for the Secretary. He placed the drinks down, picked up the appetizer plates, and vanished.

"The Japanese are pushing me for action and I have my people pushing their contacts over at Justice. But they were getting stonewalled at Justice, so they kicked it back up to me. Now I get you..." He pointed at Cobb with his knife. "A guy from...Commerce? Who the hell makes a career at Commerce?"

Cobb held his martini up to the light as if it were a chemical experiment. "I'm on temporary assignment at Commerce," he allowed casually, while examining the drink. "It's not really my home."

"Well, where are you really from?" the Secretary demanded, beginning to show his annoyance at being toyed with by a subordinate. Cobb was about to respond when the door swung open and the butler entered with two silver-domed plates balanced on his arm. In frustration, the Secretary turned to his martini.

Both men remained silent while the plates were placed before them and then the domes removed to reveal glazed chicken breasts garnished with fresh broccoli.

"A beautiful presentation," Cobb told the butler, who acknowledged the compliment with a barely perceptible nod.

"I'll take care of the wine," the Secretary insisted by way of ordering his man out of the room. He pulled the chilled Chablis out of the ice bucket and dispensed with the usual amenities of tasting. He filled each glass and slammed the bottle back into the ice.

"So, where are you from?"

Cobb passed the rim of his wineglass near his nose, then raised it slightly to examine the color. "National Security," he said casually.

"National Security Agency...on assignment to Commerce?"

Cobb nodded, his attention still absorbed in the vintage. "Lovely color," he said. "You know, the President is taking a bit of a ribbing for pushing California wines, but I really believe some of the domestics have the French beaten."

"Cobb," the Secretary whispered, his impatience coming to a boil, "if I wanted a review of my kitchen I'd have invited the food critic from the *Post*. What I want to know is what in the name of God the National Security Agency has to do with a bunch of computer thieves called Signet Corporation?"

"We are Signet Corporation," Cobb answered, raising the wine to his lips. He enjoyed the sound of the

Secretary's fork dropping onto his plate. "Well, not really. But we own Signet Corporation. Its stockholders don't exist."

"The government owns Signet Corporation...the company that the Japanese want us to prosecute?"

Cobb shook his head vigorously. "Not the government. You won't find it mentioned in any General Accounting Office records. It's an undercover operation of sorts, set up out of NSA discretionary funds."

The Secretary pushed his plate aside with the back of his hand, indicating that he had lost his appetite. "Jesus Christ," he prayed. "What am I going to tell the Japanese?"

Cobb was already cutting into his chicken. "We'd like you to tell them that we share their sense of outrage and that we will leave no stone unturned to find out who is responsible for stealing their industrial secrets. We want you to promise them our fullest cooperation."

"In exposing the United States government," the Secretary offered sarcastically.

Now it was Cobb's turn to be annoyed. He put down his fork, folded his hands at the edge of his plate, and fixed his eyes directly on the Secretary's. "No, but we will tell you exactly what response we want made to the Japanese and exactly what action you will take in following up on your promise. The capture of the agent in Japan wasn't the end of the Signet Corporation operation. It was just the beginning. And you have a very important role to play in the operation we have planned."

"A role to play in spying on the Japanese? You want the State Department to involve itself in industrial espionage against a friendly nation? Are you crazy?"

The niceties of dining were no longer being used as a pretense. The two men were at each other's throat.

"Exactly. Without the cooperation of the State Department—you and one or two of your top-ranking officials—the plan won't work. And in this case we can't afford to fail."

Slowly, the Secretary folded his napkin and placed it on the table, all the while keeping Cobb fixed in a cold stare. "Mr. Cobb, before I ask you to leave my house, I want to make sure that you understand something. I want you to understand that I have spent all my life in the business world and that I have probably done my share of . . . less than ethical things under the pressure of competition. I'm not a moralist . . . I'm a practical man. I understand the need for some of our undercover activities and while I may not like them, I can appreciate the value of . . . looking the other way. But there is no way in hell that I will look the other way while you spooks run off and try some harebrained scheme that could compromise the good name of my country. Is that clear?"

"I can appreciate your misgivings," Cobb said unemotionally.

"Misgivings, my ass. It's my outrage that you're seeing. And I don't think you appreciate it at all. But you will, I can promise you that. As soon as you've cleared my front door, I'm going to call the President. I'm going to tell him exactly what you've told me, and I'm going to demand that he run you and your associates down, whether you're hiding in Commerce, or NSA, or the Boy Scouts of America."

"If you have a phone handy, I'll call the President for you," Cobb responded.

The Secretary was already on his feet. "You smug little shit . . ." he started to say.

"Please sit down, Mr. Secretary." It had the tone of an order. The Secretary's mouth tried to form a response, but no words came out. Instead, he found himself settling obediently back into his chair.

"As you can understand, the President would prefer to keep as much distance as possible between this operation and his office. But if you need his official confirmation, then you will leave me no choice but to get him on the phone for you."

"The President knows about you?" the Secretary stammered. "He . . . approves?"

"He's not overjoyed at what we're doing. But like you, Mr. Secretary, he's a practical man. What we're doing with Signet Corporation is probably as important—maybe even more important—than the Manhattan Project. It affects a vital national interest. He understands that this is easily the most important competition that the United States has ever entered into."

"Competition with the Japanese? They're our allies. Our friends. It's not as if you were talking about the Russians, or . . ." He tried to think of another nation that could possibly be as dangerous to the United States as the Soviet Union.

"We're not competing with the Russians," Cobb said easily. "The Russians are so far behind us that the only ones they can compete with are the polar bears. Oh, of course, they can blow us up and we can blow them up. But that's not likely. What is very likely is that our good friends, the Japanese, will run us right out of the industrial world with their technology."

The Secretary's serious expression softened and then his tight lips spread into a relaxed grin. "Jesus Christ, is that your Manhattan Project? Your vital national interest? Japanese technology? Televisions and compact cars are more important than Russian rockets? Jesus, Cobb, you belong with the Commerce Department. Everyone over there has nightmares about foreign imports. If we weren't worrying about the Japanese, we'd be worrying about the English and the Germans."

Cobb ignored the Secretary's amusement. "The English," he said dryly, "can't even keep a fender from falling off. And the Germans haven't had a new idea since they invented the volkswagen. It's a two-man fight. Us and the Japanese. And right now, they're about to score a knockout blow."

"With a price cut on their tape recorders," the Secretary howled. He enjoyed his joke so much that he felt a case of hiccups coming on and reached for his water glass.

"Mr. Secretary, how much do you know about computers?" Cobb asked. The water glass paused in midair.

"Computers? Quite a bit. Not how they work or anything like that. But I know how they're used. We have computers to get out our payrolls and keep our books."

"To keep your books," Cobb repeated sarcastically.

"Well, of course, I know that they do a lot more than that. Christ, the damned things talk to you on the telephone. I guess they're all over the place. All over Washington, anyway. But what's your point?"

Cobb rose from the table and walked to a side chest where he lifted the top from an engraved cigar box. "May I?" he asked as he selected his cigar. The Secretary nodded. Cobb performed the traditional licking and biting ritual, then lit the cigar with a table lighter. "Cuban?" he asked suspiciously.

"A gift from the Chinese Ambassador," the Secretary admitted.

Cobb paced the floor as he launched into his monologue. "Computers, Mr. Secretary, run the industrialized world. I don't just mean that they keep our records and pay our bills. I mean run it, just the way a gasoline engine runs your automobile or electricity runs your home. Take the engine away and your car stops. Take the electricity away and your home is plunged into darkness. Take the computers away and the industrialized world grinds to a halt."

"Probably true," the Secretary admitted, unconcerned at conceding such a trivial point.

"Not probably," Cobb corrected. "Absolutely true. Everyone deals with computers every day. They handle our bank deposits, check us out of the supermarket and, as you say, even talk to us over the telephone. So we assume we know all about them. But what we don't stop to realize is how totally dependent we have become on them. Take our industries, for example. Computers do all our engineering studies, design our products, and draw our blueprints. Then they run the machines that make our production equipment, and the production equipment that makes the final products. Whoever has the best computers is obviously going to have the most efficient and most productive industries."

The Secretary nodded his agreement and waited while Cobb drew deeply on the cigar, rolling the smoke around in his mouth and letting a pearl-gray cloud escape into the air.

"They also run our financial institutions. Computers handle all our domestic banking transactions and all our foreign exchange transactions. There's no money anymore! Just computer records that are flashed from country to country over communications links that are managed...by computers. The banks that got heavily into computers are now the major banks in the world. So, it's reasonable to assume that whichever nation has the best computers will inevitably become the world's financial center. Its currency will become the key currency for international exchange.

"It's even more obvious when you look at national defense. All our strategic information is gathered by satellites, which are launched and then constantly repositioned by computers. Our missiles are aimed by computers and fired by computers. Computers fly all our high-performance aircraft, navigate our submarines, direct our artillery fire. Christ, there are even computers built into our tanks."

The Secretary nodded that he understood where Cobb's lecture was headed. "So, whoever has the best computers has complete military supremacy."

Cobb smiled. "Exactly, Mr. Secretary. The industrial age is over. We're entering the information age. And that age will be ruled by whichever nation has the most advanced computers. I appreciate that it sounds like an oversimplification, but it's absolutely true. The British invented the steam engine and with it they ruled the world economy for nearly a century. We invented the production line and that made us the key nation of the world for the last two generations. What is at stake right now is which country will dominate the world economy for the next few generations.''

The Secretary glanced up suspiciously. "I think you're stretching your point, Cobb."

Cobb wasted a few moments picking the loose leaves from the stub of his cigar. "Exaggerating? I don't think so. Let me give you an example. How do you think the next war will be fought?''

The Secretary shrugged his shoulders. "Nuclear weapons?" he ventured.

Cobb shook his head. "Not with nuclear weapons. Not even with conventional explosives. Why would we waste time trying to blow up an enemy's factories when all we'd have to do would be to erase his computers? Put the computers out of commission and you would put the factories out of commission. Erase the computers," Cobb continued, "and you would wipe out all his manufacturing, all his communications, all his financial institutions. Shut down the computers and you shut down the complete economy, plus all the country's defense capabilities. If someone could disable our computers they could turn the United States into a blind, bumbling giant in a matter of hours.''

"And you think the Japanese will destroy our computers?" the Secretary demanded incredulously.

Cobb waved away the suggestion. "Certainly not. I was just illustrating a point. Whoever gains supremacy in computers will be the great world power for the coming century. Computers will give more power than supremacy in atomic weapons. That's why it is absolutely vital that the United States maintain leadership in computer technology. We simply can't allow anyone, even a 'friendly' country, to take the lead away from us."

The Secretary reached for the wine bottle and carefully refilled the glasses. Cobb settled back in his chair.

"That's what Signet is all about?" the Secretary asked. "You think the Japanese are going to take the lead away from us?"

"We know they are," Cobb answered. "For the last ten years, our industry has been trying to develop the supercomputer. We're still at least two years away. The Japanese will demonstrate their supercomputer within nine months."

The Secretary looked bewildered. "Supercomputer?" he wondered aloud.

"A totally new kind of computer," Cobb continued. "Instead of processing its instructions one at a time, it has the intelligence to break the task up into its logical parts and process them simultaneously. Just for starters, it's ten times faster, ten times more efficient, than the best machines we can manufacture today. The supercomputer is to ordinary computers what the jet engine was to the propeller. There's no comparison in its efficiency and its performance."

"And we're going to steal it," the Secretary whispered.

"No, we're going to destroy it," Cobb answered. "We're going to throw it a few years off schedule, to give us the time we need to catch up."

The Secretary's face was ashen. His hand trembled as he lifted his wineglass. "I don't believe this," he tried to convince himself. "It's like Pearl Harbor, only we're the ones planning the sneak attack."

Cobb smiled as he repeated the Secretary's worst fears. "Like Pearl Harbor...in some ways. I suppose there is a parallel of sorts."

"It's the same godawful thing," the Secretary blurted. "What you're talking about is another sneak attack."

Cobb shook his head. "There are differences," he insisted. "Our Pacific fleet was just so many tons of steel, so it could easily be destroyed. But the supercomputer isn't just metal. It's really knowledge. And you can't destroy knowledge. The only way you can sink information is to discredit it. You have to stop people from believing in it by making fools out of those who do believe in it. It's much more difficult than simply dropping a bomb on something."

"But the principle is identical. It's a rotten sneak attack that violates every rule of decency no matter how it's done. I can't consent to this. I can't be a party to it..."

"Before you make up your mind, Mr. Secretary, I'd ask you to consider the consequences of letting the Japanese pull ahead of us. Think of what will happen to the United States if we allow ourselves to become another over-the-hill, has-been industrial nation. God knows, there are enough of them trying to defend what we fondly call civilization. It's the United States that keeps Western Europe free and it's our industrial might that gives us the strength to do it. Take away our economic power and what do you think happens to the Western world? Who do you think will defend Germany and Italy and France and England? The Japanese?"

"But when they know what we've done, when the world realizes what we've stooped to..."

"The Japanese will never know what we've done," Cobb said, leaning confidentially across the table. "Because we're not going to do it."

He relished the Secretary's total confusion. "With Signet and with your help, Mr. Secretary, the Japanese are going to do it themselves. They're going to destroy their own supercomputer."

April 10th, 3:00 P.M., Nagatsuda

Kaplan had expected to be tortured.

It made sense. He was a spy on a secret mission captured behind enemy lines. The barbarians would insist on the valuable information they had every right to suspect that he possessed and they would become understandably impatient when they found him uncooperative.

But how could he cooperate? He knew nothing. He could tell them that he worked for Signet Corporation, but they had already figured that out for themselves. Jesus, it was printed right on the address label of the package of stolen tapes. So, naturally, their next question would be, whom did he work for, and the only answer he could give them was that he was controlled by a Mr. Smith. Smith! Christ, they'd be holding their sides laughing while they tore off his fingernails.

Or they might ask him what information he was gathering. And, of course, he had absolutely no idea. It was just electronic transmissions that were being recorded. No, he really couldn't say what they were or where they originated. He hadn't a clue as to why he was there or what he was up to. He could visualize a sadistic Japanese squinting through a cloud of cigarette smoke and asking in Harvard English, "Do you really expect us to believe that your entire responsibility was to baby-sit for a computer?" And he could hear himself answering, "Exactly. I have no idea what I was up to. You see, what I really want to be is an accountant."

It would take them just seconds to stuff his balls into a vise!

But there had been no physical torture. Instead, he had been fingerprinted by a lovely young lady who said "please," and "thank you," and went to great pains to get all the ink off his fingers without soiling his shirt. A polite, well-spoken police officer had typed his statement, apologizing for the inconvenience caused by his frequent typing errors. A civilian, probably a lawyer, had explained the nature of the charges and the procedures under which Japanese justice would dispose of those charges. Bail could certainly be posted, but that would require his contacting his Mr. Smith who, as he had already explained, was impossible to reach. So, regrettably, he would probably have to await his court date in prison. However, they would do everything possible to make his prison stay comfortable and enjoyable.

Of course, Kaplan said to himself, they don't hang you by your thumbs anymore. It's psychological torture. And in his mind he envisioned his cell. It would be a bamboo cage, probably two-foot by two-foot square. And it would be hung from the end of a rope so that it could be lowered into a sewer each night, allowing the rats to nibble at his flesh. During the days, they would drag him out of the cage and force him to attend educational sessions. They'd tell him that no one cared about him, and that while he remained silent, Smith was living comfortably in Kaplan's home and screwing Kaplan's wife. He could hear the sadistic interrogator mocking him. "Why are you protecting Smith, when at this very moment he has your daughter out on the street, whoring for the goyim? Why won't you tell us about Signet Corporation? After all, they've left you here to die while they've hired another accountant to keep track of their exorbitant profits." Why would they ever believe that he had no wife and no daughter, that he had no idea of Signet Corporation's address, much less its line of business?

But there was no cell. Instead, he had been driven out into the country, through the gates in a stone wall that was topped by an inconspicuous curl of wire into a two-story institutional building with large, bright windows. His room was small, but by no means uncomfortable, with a metal bed covered by a decent mattress, a writing table and chair, and a small washbasin with fresh towels and a new bar of soap. All in all, they were superior accommodations to those he had enjoyed in the attic. The only hint that he wasn't free to come and go as he pleased was the heavy weight of the door with its small, glass window, and the fact that the doorknob and keyhole were on the outside.

Drugs, he told himself knowingly. So that's it! This had to be some sort of medical facility. A loony bin where political prisoners were kept in a state of trouble-free bliss by constant injections of mind-altering chemicals. They would drag him to a tile room with bright chrome flood lamps, strap him to a metal table, and shoot him so full of truth serum that he'd babble everything he knew about the CIA. He'd tell them about all the magazines he had reviewed, and the thousands of yards of fan-folded computer printout that had covered the content of every electronic transmission from every corner of the earth. Maybe then they would understand that they hadn't uncovered one of the world's top agents.

But there were no drugs. Instead, as he learned over the first few weeks of his imprisonment, the penalty they had chosen to inflict was boredom. Their pleasant little routine never varied from day to day, leaving him alone in his room hour after hour, with nothing but old American magazines, or new Japanese magazines, for company. The boredom was interrupted each day by two trips to the dining room for bland meals of rice, fish, and meat, and by a weekly visit from his lawyer who recounted the massive evidence against him, the total lack of a plausible defense, and the difficulties he was having in scheduling a trial. Inevitably, the lawyer pleaded with him to reveal the true identity of Smith and the names of his contacts at Signet Corporation, so that they could at least arrange for bail. Then he smiled knowingly as Kaplan explained that he had no idea who Smith was, or where he could be found, and that not only had he never been to Signet Corporation, but, in fact, he had never been to California.

It was in the third week of his isolation that Kaplan began to figure out what had happened to him. Smith, or whoever he was, had sent him on a suicide mission and now, as far as Smith was concerned, he was dead. Obviously, neither Smith nor Signet—if there was a Signet—had any intention of coming to his rescue. To admit that they knew Kaplan was to admit that they were involved in his crime. And, he guessed, they were probably standing right then in a courtroom, their innocent palms upturned, convincing some magistrate who was in their pay that they had never heard of Kaplan and had no idea what he might have been up to. He began to understand that he might well spend the rest of his life in this room, his declining years cheered only by the visits from his pessimistic attorney. Faced with this bleak future, he began to plan his escape.

He started with physical conditioning: sets of two or three sit-ups, a few push-ups, and thirty seconds of running in place. At first, even this modest effort left him breathless and caused fits of coughing as his lungs tried to expel the effects of a thousand cartons of cigarettes. But within just a few days, his frantic struggling took on a sense of rhythm. He cranked out his sit-ups at fifty to a set and began counting his push-ups by the dozens.

Kaplan begged his jailers for two scrub buckets and a broom, which they gladly delivered for the sake of cleanliness. Instead, he filled the buckets by squirting water from his washbasin, then carefully inserted the broom through the handles of the buckets. The result was a crude barbell that he pressed as he lay on his back and curled up over his chest.

The prison menu made dieting easy, and Kaplan limited himself to just the meat and fish, washed down with pitchers of water. Instantly, the fat began to disappear from his huge, six-foot-five-inch body, replaced by large, if not sculptured muscles.

Each day he exercised for hours, lifting and running, while his captors peered curiously through the small glass window. They were puzzled at first, on guard against the possibility of foul play that any change in a prisoner's routine seemed to threaten. But, gradually, they became involved in Kaplan's quest for physical purity and began to count his push-ups in unison, their voices rising to a frenzy as he neared one hundred. They brought him a set of weights to replace his buckets and rolled in a serviceable exercise mat so that he wouldn't have to stretch out on the floor. Finally, they left his door ajar so that whoever might be passing could stop in his room, watch his routine, and offer him encouragement.

He grew a mustache, which curved down over his mouth in a cruel sneer, and then shaved his head bare. He became a frightening sight, although his keepers assumed he was becoming deranged and enjoyed his antics more than they feared them.

Part of Kaplan's routine was his effort to increase his tolerance for physical pain. He laid the bar from his weights on the bare floor and knelt on it, constantly extending the time during which he withstood the agony in his legs. He unscrewed the bulb in his lamp, allowed it to cool, and then turned it back into the socket, keeping his palms wrapped around the glass. He continued to hold it as the temperature rose to a white heat, grinding his teeth against the excruciating pain. Each day, he forced himself to hold on for a few additional seconds.

He persuaded the Japanese to let him run outdoors on the grounds surrounding the building and, at first, they had consented warily. But later they enjoyed his progress and sat watching him, counting his laps around the building. Kaplan ran barefoot, across the uneven ground and over the gravel drives, ignoring the gashes and punctures in the soles of his feet. Pain, he explained to them, could be mastered. It had to be mastered if he was to succeed at the mission he had in mind.

What drove him was his mission—the most comprehensive and purposeful plan he had ever assembled. He was going to escape, hand over hand, up the sheer face of the stone wall, and over the top, ignoring the sharp barbs that protruded from the coiled wire. He would live off the land, avoiding the cities and the main thoroughfares, working his way to a fishing village or seaport. There, he would stow away on a boat or ship heading back to North America. Then he would find Signet Corporation and through Signet he would pick up Smith's trail. Some night in the not too distant future he would hurl himself through a glass window and land upright on the balls of his feet in Smith's living room. He would stand for a moment, looking Smith in the eyes, which would be yellow with terror. And then, once Smith had a moment to recognize him as one returned from the dead and fully understand exactly why he was there, he would kill Smith with his bare hands.

It wasn't a matter of "if," but rather "when." And now, as Kaplan completed his tenth lap around the grounds and realized that he wasn't even breathing heavily, he knew the time was coming near.

April 15th, 2:00 P.M., Washington, D.C.

She didn't fit.

Cobb glanced from the woman who had just entered the conference room to the records that were on the table before him.

Karen Albert. Age thirty-five. Senior systems analyst for IAC, the world's premier vendor of large, mainframe computers. Previously vice-president, software development, for Pacific Microsciences; associate professor, advanced mathematics, MIT; Ph.D., MIT; M.S., summa cum laude, Harvard; B.S., physics, Georgia Tech. The résumé, to his eye, was a portrait of a figureless matron with bad skin, who would wear ill-fitting clothes.

The woman standing before him was tall, with a straight yet provocative figure, clothed in a tailored, gray chalk-stripe business suit. Soft, sandy hair cascaded around a triangular face with large blue eyes above high, pronounced cheekbones. Her mouth was small, as if unused to smiling, and her nose was perhaps too long for modeling. But still, she looked more like an aspiring actress than the paragon of achievement described in her résumé.

Cobb stumbled to his feet and blurted an introduction, uncertain as to whether he should offer his hand or not. She ended his dilemma with a vigorous handshake and settled easily into the chair next to his own. Her skin, he noticed, was flawless; light as if from

Nordic origin and taut over the collarbones that were visible through the soft, open neckline of her blouse.

"You're not what I was expecting," he said, regretting the chauvinistic implications of his words as soon as they were spoken. He tried to redeem himself by indicating the résumé. "You look . . . younger."

She nodded a thank-you.

"I'm with the federal government," he began. "The Department of Commerce." He caught a trace of disappointment in her expression. Commerce meant trade balances and export licenses; issues that would be of little interest to her. "But I should tell you right away that this isn't a routine Commerce Department inquiry. It concerns the security of computer software. Supercomputer software." Her eyes widened, telling Cobb that he had gotten her attention.

"I've been asked to give you any help you need," Karen told him. She was leaning forward in anticipation of his questions.

"That's the problem," Cobb admitted. "I'm not sure what help I need. Perhaps if I begin with a theoretical situation—a hypothesis—you might begin to understand the area of my . . . the government's . . . concerns."

"All right," she answered, but now the anticipation was replaced with a puzzled narrowing of the eyes.

Cobb rose from his seat and began to pace around the long conference table. He launched into his scenario, addressing his remarks to the walls and ceiling of the room rather than to the woman who was his only audience.

Suppose, his theoretical case ran, some foreign power wanted to detail the development of our supercomputer efforts. Obviously, they couldn't simply destroy our machines because that would cause only temporary inconvenience. And obviously they wouldn't destroy the tapes and disks of the software code we were developing, because there would be numerous duplicate tapes and disks, which could be readily substituted. In fact, there would be no point in destroying anything. The whole system was simply the embodiment of ideas and knowledge, and those ideas would obviously survive damage to the hardware or software.

He glanced at Karen and she responded by nodding her agreement.

It would become, Cobb's monologue continued, a matter of *misdirecting* the whole thought process. Of persuading the designers that their ideas were wrong. Of discrediting their present efforts and pointing them off—at least temporarily—in the wrong direction.

"Making good work look like bad work," Karen interrupted.

"Exactly," Cobb answered, pleased that she had reconstructed the problem so quickly. "Is such a thing feasible?"

"Not really," she answered, "even theoretically. I don't think the government has anything to worry about." Now Cobb looked disappointed.

"In the first place," Karen continued, "there isn't just one U.S. supercomputer program. There are dozens in other companies. Some in universities. I don't see how anyone—any other country—could discredit all of them simultaneously. Second, all the programs are very well protected against information leaks and industrial espionage. We have very few people with access to our supercomputer development and they're all people who have been thoroughly screened."

"So you rule out the programs being sabotaged by people who are working on them?" Cobb questioned.

"Well, not rule out," Karen had to admit. "But I think it's very unlikely. What is impossible is that all of them could be sabotaged at the same time."

Cobb agreed, but asked for Karen's patience while he continued his hypothetical case. "Suppose there were only one program. Further, suppose that all the people working on it were absolutely loyal; incapable of being compromised. Would it be impossible for an outsider to misdirect their work without their even being aware that it had been misdirected?"

Karen seemed suddenly annoyed. "Mr. Cobb, it might really help if I knew what you were driving at. Do you suspect that someone is trying to sabotage IAC's development program? Or that someone at IAC is trying to disrupt one of our competitor's? Because I can assure you..."

Cobb's hand waving stopped her mounting anger. "No. No. Of course not. Nothing of the sort. As I said, this is entirely hypothetical. And I'm asking for nothing more than your expert advice on the supercomputer technology, and for you to consider whether what I have proposed is technically possible."

Karen eyed Cobb suspiciously. "Is my company aware of the nature of your question? Do our managers fully understand what you're asking me to discuss?"

Cobb nodded, then leaned across the table to bring his face close to hers. "Bill Howard knows exactly what I'm asking," he told her, using the name of the company's chairman and chief executive officer as familiarly as if they were regular golf partners. "But he's the only one who knows. If you need verification, you can't talk to your supervisors. You'll have to talk with Howard directly. He has assured me that if I call, they'll put my call through immediately so you can have all the assurances you need."

She watched him walk to a side table and lift the handset from the telephone. Then he turned to her indicating that the next move was hers. Karen shook her head, dismissing Cobb's offer. "It's just that this is something of a touchy subject. It is possible. We've been concerned about it ourselves. But it can't be done by an outsider. At least not easily. The person who did it would have to be intimately familiar with the machine language."

Cobb's pursed lips told her that she was losing him. "Do you know anything about the levels of computer languages?"

"Not a great deal," he admitted.

Karen stood up, slipped off her suit jacket, and hung it over the back of her chair. "Why don't you take off your coat and sit down," she advised Cobb. "This is going to take quite a bit of time."

He watched her as she walked around the table toward the blackboard. She had a purposeful stride, but still the sway of her hips was enticing. As she reached up with the marker to begin writing at the top of the board, the hem of her skirt lifted and unconsciously Cobb leaned out from the table to notice her thin but nicely tapered legs. Again, he thought that she simply didn't fit the credentials in the records that he had read and reread, and he found himself wondering if she had achieved her lofty positions entirely on merit. Physical attractiveness was certainly no disadvantage to a woman's career and Karen was more than passively attractive. Perhaps his researchers hadn't dug deep enough. Perhaps an academic love affair or board-room romance had pushed her past failings that would have disqualified other competitors.

But his doubts vanished as she began to talk. Cobb was well briefed on the black arts of computer software and within a few sentences he knew Karen was genuine. She began with a description of the hardware; basically billions of electronic circuits, which, taken by themselves, could do nothing more than store, forward, or change the direction of electrical current. Then, using the analogy of a freight yard, where cars from hundreds of different tracks can be assembled into a single train, she explained how the individual electronic functions were interrelated.

"It's the machine language that makes the computer a computer," she said, turning back toward him. "At this level, it might take several thousand individual commands to move a single bit of information from one place in the computer to another."

She went to higher-level languages, where a single command could generate hundreds of machine-level commands. And then to the applications languages where one- or two-word commands could cause the machines to perform thousands of individual, electronic functions.

"This is the problem area with supercomputers," she explained. "We want a command to generate not a specific chain of actions, but a whole process of decision making. And that's where the vulnerability arises. The machine is making judgments and it isn't immediately apparent whether the judgments are right or wrong. Errors are a bitch to detect. Everything isn't black or white the way it is in an ordinary computer."

Cobb was nodding, but Karen could tell that he hadn't yet grasped the implications of what she was saying.

"Suppose I could trick the machine into issuing the wrong commands even though it had analyzed the problem correctly. You wouldn't be able to find the error, because it wouldn't be an error that would be obviously different from the instructions you had given the machine."

He still didn't register recognition. Karen groped for a simple analogy.

"If I tell you to go left and you go right, I can spot your error immediately." Cobb nodded that he agreed.

"But if I ask you which way you want to go and you go right, how do I know that you should have gone left? I don't know that you went the wrong way until you end up at the wrong place. I have the wrong answer and I don't know why I have the wrong answer."

"Can you?" Cobb asked.

"Can I what?"

"You asked me to suppose that you could trick the machine into issuing the wrong commands. Can you? Can you screw up someone's supercomputer?"

She pursed her lips and then she nodded. "Yes," she said, almost as an admission of defeat. "I can screw it up so badly it would take us a year to find out where it had gone wrong."

"So the supercomputer programs can be sabotaged," Cobb concluded, rising out of his chair in triumph.

"I can ruin *my* supercomputer," Karen corrected, "not any supercomputer. I understand our project intimately. I've worked at screwing it up precisely to build in safeguards so that no one else can destroy it, intentionally or accidentally. But I couldn't destroy anyone else's supercomputer because I simply wouldn't know enough about it."

"Suppose you did know enough about it?"

The notion was ridiculous, but the answer obvious. "Then I could cause some serious problems."

"How much would you need to know?" Cobb pressed.

Once again, Karen was becoming infuriated by the hypothetical questions. "Mr. Cobb," she snapped, "if you would just tell me what it is you're worried about I could probably give you a direct answer."

"How much information about your program would someone absolutely have to have in hand before he could ruin it?" he demanded.

"You'd need the code for the operating system," she finally said uneasily. "Not all the code, but enough of it to understand the basic command structure. And you'd need one or two of the algorithms that the system uses to analyze problems and select the appropriate instructions from memory."

Cobb seemed startled. "That's all?" he asked incredulously. "You wouldn't need to know all the memory instructions?"

She shook her head. "Why would you?" she asked. "Once the machine picks the wrong course of action and starts working with the wrong mix of instructions, it's going to get lost even if it follows those instructions perfectly."

She saw the confusion in his eyes, so she tried to simplify her explanation. "We're asking the computers to make judgments, so simple errors in the judgment process can lead to ridiculous consequences. Look, suppose I tell you that you're having dinner at the White House. Based on that information, you would make very logical and accurate decisions about what you should wear, and you would probably show up in black tie. But suppose what I really meant was the White House hamburger stand. Then all your correct decisions about what to wear would make you look like a fool. I didn't have to foul up your thought process or change all the clothes in your wardrobe. All I had to do was to help you make one simple little error. It's the same with supercomputers. Just help them make one or two errors and even if they do everything else perfectly, they are ultimately going to crash.''

She watched his eyes light up and then saw a smug smile spread across his face. "It's possible . . . hell, it's easy." He laughed to himself.

"If you know the system," she corrected.

Cobb relaxed back in his chair, closed Karen's file, and folded his hands in a judgmental pose.

"Miss Albert, what I'm going to propose may seem strange to you, but I can assure you that it concerns a matter of the greatest importance to your company . . . and even to your country."

Her eyes narrowed.

"I'm working on a government project that absolutely requires your help. I've discussed it with Bill Howard and he has suggested that I ask you to join our team. The entire project should be completed in about eight or nine months and Mr. Howard has agreed to give you a leave of absence so that you can help us. In fact, I think I can go further and say that he very much wants you to help us . . ."

"But . . . that's impossible. We're up to our necks in our own supercomputer program. Mr. Howard told us

that this was the most important development program in the company's history. I can't leave now. I'm
needed."

"I know you're needed," Cobb sympathized. "And
I appreciate how bewildering all this must seem. I think
you would understand how important this is if I could
just tell you what we're trying to achieve. But I
can't . . . at least not until you're fully committed and
we're much further along."

She had her own image of what would be vitally important to the Department of Commerce. The development of a set of rules and regulations for using
supercomputers in government. Or trade restrictions
on the export of supercomputer technology to foreign
governments. How in God's name could some bu-
reaucrat understand the total revolution that supercomputers would cause? How could this pinstriped
pencil pusher begin to understand what being first with
technology would mean to her company—and her
country?

Mr. Howard understood this. He hadn't been exaggerating when he called the supercomputer the most
important project that IAC had ever undertaken. But
how could he say "no" to a government request for
cooperation on some stupid federal study? The damn
government was his biggest customer. He had to
cooperate.

But why her? There was plenty of dead wood around
IAC that would feel perfectly at home working with the
government.

"Perhaps you should call Bill Howard," Cobb suggested.

"No," she snapped. "I'm sure this is something he
wants me to do. But this isn't his decision. It's mine.

And I already know my answer. I can't help you, Mr. Cobb.''

He seemed startled.

"I'm sorry," Karen continued. "I'm sure this secret project of yours is very important to you. And, obviously, it's important to Mr. Howard. But it's not important to me. What is important to me is winning the supercomputer race. I think I can do it. But just between the two of us, I'm behind right now and I don't have six months to spare. In fact, I don't have another minute to spare, so if you'll excuse me, I'll be getting back to New York.''

She rose abruptly and Cobb found himself jumping to his feet before he had a chance to protest her decision.

"I'm sorry," she repeated, as she put on her suit jacket.

Cobb thrust his fingers into his jacket pocket and pulled out a pen. Quickly, he tore the corner from a sheet of paper in Karen's file and scribbled a telephone number. As she offered her hand to say goodbye, he thrust the paper into her palm and closed her fingers over it.

"I want you to think about this conversation on the way home," he said. "Think about it carefully... word by word. Ask yourself why Bill Howard would take you off his most important project just so you could work on my project. Then call me tonight, at that number.''

"But..." she started to argue.

"If your answer is still no, I'll accept it. But if you really think about it, I believe you'll find good reason to join me.''

She slipped the scrap of paper into her pocket and walked from the room. Cobb watched her hips, then looked skeptically at the folder that rested on the table.

Karen was seated aboard the plane before her boiling rage cooled to a simmer. She knew perfectly well why Mr. Howard would move her off his most important project. She had been there before. Someone on the supercomputer program had become jealous of her success, just as the lettered dons in academia had become jealous of her success. A young woman moving quickly to the top was an intolerable affront to their male egos. As soon as they found they couldn't control her, they found a way to move her out.

It had begun in high school, each time her military family had moved to a new community. Her father was an army warrant officer and electronics technician who disassembled the radar and field computers of the new high-tech army, located the factory-built failures, and reassembled working equipment. Like most itinerant children who never stay in one place long enough to belong, Karen had been close to her father and had nursed his love of science. While still in grade school, she had moved into the high school curriculum of algebra and then calculus. Her brilliance had made her the favorite of the eighth grade faculties.

But in high school, when the family moved again and she entered a new adolescent community, brilliance was not a treasured commodity. Appearance was the key to acceptance, and her tall, straight figure, with squared shoulders and oversized hands, made her an outcast. Parties and proms had come and gone without her phone ever ringing, and the isolation drove her further into the studies that were her only area of accomplishment. Her grades had drawn rave notices from her teachers, but had widened the gulf between Karen and the friends she wanted so badly.

"I have lots of friends," she had lied to her father. But the truth was that boys called her only on the evenings before math and physics examinations, when they needed her best efforts to squeeze through with a "D." And then they ignored her to prove to their friends that they had never needed the help of a stringbean of a girl. She had retaliated by building up a protective wall of indifference.

The scenery had changed by the time she reached college, but the plot was basically the same. She had blossomed into a very attractive young woman, but her only security was still in her work. "My oh my," her freshman counselor had cooed, "a lovely young lady like you enrolling for the toughest physics course in the catalog. That certainly is ambitious. But don't you think you might enjoy a course in home economics? It would be easier and probably much more practical."

They were all admiration until she pulled a straight 4.0 index and finished at the top of her class. Then it became: "That Karen Albert certainly is a strange one. I wonder just what it is that she's trying to prove?"

The chivalrous swains had been certain that they could use her. "Hell, once she gets me between her legs she'll do all my homework just to keep me fresh and fit," she had overheard a fraternity hero boasting to his fellow Greeks. She accepted his invitation for an evening out and had taken her rage straight into his bedroom. Then she had stepped out into the hall, within earshot of the expectant brothers, and shouted back into the room. "Hell, you aren't any better in bed than you are in a classroom. I wouldn't even give you an 'F.' You better settle for an 'incomplete.' "

The pattern had intensified in the competitive atmosphere of graduate school. The ambitious overachievers tried to use her in order to surpass her. But by now she had developed a foolproof radar that gave precise ranges and bearings toward insincerity. Ten words into a conversation and she recognized all the subtle invitations to trade her academic support for temporary acceptance into their social ranks. Once they failed at manipulation, her classmates turned to destruction. "Sure, she gets great grades from Professor Moran. Hell, she's probably sleeping with the old pervert!"

There had been a significant change when she reached the rarefied air of a faculty position. The great minds of the university were too pure to denigrate her, but they still tried to profit by her. Get Karen Albert on your research team and your chances of success improved immeasurably. And the nice thing was that you could keep all the credit. Who would ever suspect that an attractive young woman, stylishly dressed, could be anything more than an ornament?

Now she was sure someone had gotten to Howard. Some frail, threatened ego who was terrified at the thought of the inventor of the supercomputer rocketing past him and into the boardroom. Probably not one of her immediate associates. They, like here, were immersed in the project. It had to be someone higher—a division or group vice-president. A super sales type who had parlayed the rentals from a few choice corporate or government accounts into hundreds of millions in income, and who had successfully maneuvered to get the supercomputer program into his domain.

Someone who had been preparing the speech he would give when he took credit for the success of the supercomputer and who now realized that the technology had a life of its own that he couldn't control.

She had met them all. Each, in one way or another, had suggested an alliance. "I know you're too busy to put together a report, but I would like to keep current on the progress you're making. Perhaps we could meet some evening and discuss it over dinner." Or, "I'll be staying in town this weekend to catch up on things. I wonder if you might be able to drop over for a few hours so we could discuss your program."

She had found polite ways to refuse, sending confidential documents that they wouldn't understand in her place. She needed no sponsors and she certainly had no intention of paying the price of sponsorship.

So now one of them had decided that she was dangerous. Someone had arranged for her to be transferred to a "critical" government program. Not permanently, of course. Just long enough so that the space she left in the supercomputer program would have time to close over.

She was home in her apartment when she found Cobb's scrap of paper in the pocket she was emptying. And she was in a hot tub, trying to make her body accept the calm determination that filled her mind, when she began to review Cobb's conversation. Why in the name of God would the federal government be worrying about someone sabotaging the IAC supercomputer? Or was it the IAC supercomputer? Maybe they thought that someone at IAC was planning a raid on someone else's supercomputer.

The length of the assignment didn't make any sense, unless they wanted her to find a way to make all supercomputers immune to attacks. And then why would IAC volunteer her efforts in order to develop a program that its competitors would use? The company wasn't a philanthropy! Let the competition solve its own problems.

She was pulling on her terry-cloth bathrobe when she remembered that Cobb had never said a word about protecting the supercomputer. That had been entirely her assumption as to the meaning behind his questions. Cobb had been asking how to destroy a supercomputer, not how to protect one. Well then, why in hell would the government be interested in screwing up IAC's program? And why would Howard volunteer her services to help in the effort?

Unless they were going to raid someone else's supercomputer! That certainly would be all right with Howard, but how could the government let itself become involved in helping one American company punch out another American company?

The answer struck her as she was slipping her nightgown over her arms and she dropped down on the edge of her bed with the soft material still bunched up at her shoulders.

"Sweet suffering Jesus," she said to herself, as she reached for the scrap of paper she had left next to the telephone. "Commerce Department, my ass," she said to herself, and she began to dial the number. "Mr. Cobb, you're a spook."

He answered the first ring.

"This is Karen," she said. "I know what you're up to. I'd like to join you."

"Fine," he answered. "Finish up whatever you can in the next few days. I'll be in contact with you."

She felt a chill run down her back as she hung up the phone and it had nothing to do with the fact that she was still wet and half naked.

April 23rd, 7:00 P.M., Tokyo

They were the most perfect specimens of the most perfect economic system that had ever been created.

Fujii looked at the members of his staff who had gathered in front of the open, electronic racks of the supercomputer—men and women in their twenties and thirties, with sparkling eyes that illuminated serious faces.

They were bright, educated in a school system that screened out normal intelligence so that it could devote all its efforts to superior minds. All had earned their places in secondary school by posting impressive achievements from the moment they left their mothers' breasts. All had earned their places in college by triumphing over their friends in a glorious battery of competitive examinations. All had captured a job with the company by rushing to the top of their college classes. And finally, all had made it to Fujii's team by mastering the normal industrial tasks in a matter of weeks. Unlike their American competitors, who were coddled by a tolerant and inclusive society, they had stood the test of an exclusive society that was intolerant of ordinary performance.

They were loyal. In joining the company they had willingly submerged their own identities and proudly taken as their confirmation names the firm's world-famous logotype. Their personal achievement was invisible, seen only in the company's corporate achievement. Their personal joy existed only in the ever-rising curve of their company's worldwide sales. They toiled endlessly to increase the firm's productivity. They formed their own quality committees to criticize one another's work, and in the spirit of the monastic chapter, they joyfully accepted criticism as if it had come directly from God, all in an effort to improve their product. By their selflessness and teamwork they multiplied their efforts. In the process, together with their brothers in other industries, they had created the most efficient, productive economy on earth.

Japanese radios and television sets had humbled the great American names, slamming shut the rusting factories of RCA, Zenith, and Emerson. Japanese steel had cooled furnaces from Pittsburgh to the Ruhr. Japanese automobiles had driven the great European marques off the road. Their calculators tallied the day's take at Monte Carlo, their tires guided racing cars through the turns at Monza and their telephones connected worldwide businessmen who discussed their chances of surviving the Japanese onslaught.

The technicians in Fujii's laboratory had written the convoluted algorithms that enabled their machine to weigh all the parts of a problem, determine the most effective avenue of approach to the solution, and write the computer programs that would lead to the answer. They had developed methods of segregating and then searching enormous banks of electronic memory. They had redesigned the computer's architecture to reduce the connections between circuits to the shortest possible path. Then they had written the billions of words of computer code that gave their Frankenstein life, and even intelligence. They were two years ahead of the Americans and light-years ahead of the Europeans in opening the door of the supercomputer to expose a new age of mankind. They were, beyond doubt, the best and the brightest.

Fujii thought they were insane.

Not that he didn't use them. He gathered them into his laboratory, set impossible tasks before them, encouraged them to work round the clock, and nodded his approval of their achievements. Grandly, he bestowed upon them all the company's tokens of success. He gave them tee times at the company's golf course, memberships in its bathhouses, and parking spaces on its property. For those who delivered revolutionary breakthroughs—achievements that saved months in the development cycle and vaulted them further ahead of their world competitors—he provided better apartments in more prestigious buildings, family vacations at seaside resorts, even the opportunity for foreign travel. He marveled at the added efforts these insignificant gestures of appreciation could inspire. But still, he could not understand their dedication and their loyalty. He was baffled that bright people would work so hard with so little thought of personal gain.

There had been some who did not fit the mold. Occasionally, he had found individualistic rebels who, like himself, demanded rewards proportional to their contributions and insisted on receiving personal credit for their personal accomplishments. But these people were quickly expelled from his team. In Fujii's laboratory there was room for only one individual—Fujii himself. All other members of the team labored joyfully to help him achieve his just measure of fame.

As he gathered them close to the display terminal, Fujii looked upon them with pride. He had assembled them. He had motivated them. He had given them the challenge of creating the computer that would do all the world's thinking. Like him, they were the best. They had proven it over the last three years by outperforming the very best teams that had been assembled by the great American computer companies and the best minds of the world's leading universities. Now, he was going to show them exactly what they had achieved.

He watched one of the technicians slide into a chair behind the display terminal. Quickly, the young woman typed in commands and smiled at the response that appeared on the screen. Within a few minutes the machine language was loaded, converting the mindless racks of electronic components and miniature circuits into an integrated, logical system. Fujii nodded his approval, although he sensed she had no idea of what she had just done. To her, it was an interactive routine of furnishing the proper commands as they were requested. To Fujii, she had breathed life into the machine, just as a biblical God had once breathed life into a handful of dust.

She relinquished her place to a young man who began loading in the high-level language—clusters of electronic commands that would be activated by a single word. Just as the simple request to "set the table" would cause a cloth to be spread, dishes to be placed, silverware to be arranged about the plates, glasses to be positioned, and candles to be lighted, so a single command, "save," would cause thousands of circuits to be actuated, moving a stream of electronic pulses into a specific position of memory. Fujii had often thought that billions of years had evolved before living matter uttered its first word. Within minutes, his electronic being had evolved to a state of linguistic intelligence.

Next the operating system was read into the machine, establishing the patterns and sequences by which it would interact with its peripherals. It now had access to the memories that stored its logical tables and the vast banks of silicon components that stored the information it would use to make decisions. Fujii's supercomputer had instant use of more stored facts than any computer that had ever been assembled.

Of course, it was a trivial file of information; certainly fewer observations than a three-year-old child would gather during a two-minute stroll through the park. Unlike the child, who could gather, store, and interrelate thousands of facts with a single glance, the computer had to learn its information one fact at a time. It would take years, perhaps decades, before even the supercomputer could absorb the range of information that the average person uses each day. In a sense, the human mind with its incredible versatility was the only true supercomputer. But the memory in Fujii's machine was entirely concentrated in a few, clearly defined areas of knowledge. As long as the problems stayed within the confines of these borders, the supercomputer was as well informed as any human being, and a billion times faster in putting its information to work.

The machine was ready and the technicians stepped back, clearing a path to the console for the master. Fujii rose dramatically and walked to the keyboard.

With one finger he typed in his command: RUN WAREHOUSE.

The staff understood. WAREHOUSE was a test program that exercised the company's largest computers. It attempted to fit a thousand boxes, each of different dimensions and different weight, onto the shelves of a mythical warehouse. The precise patterns of the boxes had to be fitted on the shelves with the minimum of waste space. And the heavier boxes had to be allocated to the bottom shelves to avoid exceeding the strength of the shelf structures. Even the most powerful machines took hours to solve the problem.

While the staff crowded around the console, staring anxiously at the blank display screen, Fujii walked away from the computer. He lit a cigarette, casually let a cloud of smoke escape from his lips, and glanced up at the clock with its sweeping second hand. Before the hand had completed one sixty-second sweep, he heard the cheer that exploded behind him.

He turned and looked at the young men and women who were jumping up and down as the figures of the problem's solution rushed across the display screen. They were like children at a sporting event, so carried away by their excitement that, on many of the faces, he saw tears of joy. For an instant, he was puzzled. And then he remembered where he had seen the same frenzied joy before. It was on the flight deck of *Akagi*, the flagship of the fast carrier strike force that had attacked Pearl Harbor.

He had been studying old black-and-white documentary footage; film that had been reprinted and reprinted in the months immediately following the Pearl Harbor attack. The focus was imperfect, and the worn sprocket holes caused the image to jump. But still, the group of planes approaching from the south could be seen clearly.

The deck seemed deserted, except for a distant figure who guided the returning pilots with hand signals and a close-up figure whose head intruded momentarily into the frame. Centered in the image was the first plane to land, a Val dive-bomber with wide wings and two-fendered wheels feeling uncertainly for the landing surface. It touched down, seemed about to bounce back into the air, and then jerked to a stop as its tail hook caught one of the arresting cables. A crewman scampered into the scene, crouched behind the plane's tail, and freed the aircraft, which immediately rolled slowly down the deck toward the camera.

While it was still rolling, a figure rose from the open rear canopy; the bombardier, who only an hour before had held the fleeing *Nevada* in his cross hairs, watched two bombs float down beneath him and disintegrate the battleship's superstructure. In his hand he held a small Japanese flag, which he began to wave furiously.

Suddenly, a human tide rolled across the deck toward the plane, enveloping it in a sea of hysteria. Men sprang up on the wings and lifted the bombardier out of the cockpit. The pilot scarcely had time to turn off his engine before he, too, was lifted out of his seat and passed down to the crowd. And then everyone was dancing; duty-hardened sailors jumping up and down and reaching to touch the hands of the pilot and bombardier. Fujii imagined he could hear their voices above the chatter of the projector as they punched their fists into the air and shouted, "Japan . . . Japan . . . Japan . . . Japan."

They were crazed with their first taste of victory. A victory beyond their wildest dreams. And their joy destroyed all the bounds of behavior. Suddenly it was fitting for common seamen to scream their joy into the faces of their honored officers. Suddenly it was a mark of strength to cry like a child. They had come from nowhere and caught the great self-satisfied American giant before he had become aware of the danger. In one stroke they had destroyed his entire fleet of impregnable warships, raising themselves to supremacy in the Pacific. With their awkward ships and fragile airplanes, they had raised their country to the pinnacle of power.

Fujii's technicians were dancing around their computer, just as the crew had danced around the Val dive-bomber on the deck of *Akagi*. They were swinging their fists in the air, and in unison crying, "Victory... victory... victory."

He congratulated them on their accomplishment, and spent a few minutes reminiscing over the many occasions when their task seemed impossible and when their laboratory was shrouded in gloom. They laughed together at the memory of their own discouragement, which seemed so absurd in light of the demonstration they had just seen. But then he called a halt to their celebration.

"We still have much work to do," he reminded them cheerfully. And then he outlined the agenda for the coming weeks. As he spelled out the details of the work still ahead, the staff joined in a groan. "I know"—Fujii laughed—"it's an impossible workload. But you're used to doing the impossible. And doing it immediately." Once again they were cheering.

"The victory is in sight," he reassured them. "It won't be long before we're ready for a full demonstration." He pushed through the crowd and led his staff to a large calendar that hung on the wall.

He began to assign time periods to each of the functions still before them, crossing out the dates on the calendar. "How many days to check the results of this test?" he asked. Numbers were shouted back and forth among the staff members, until they agreed on five days.

"We'll do it in three," Fujii said, laughing at their protests as he marked three days off on the calendar. Together they built a schedule that stretched through the fall into the first days in December.

"Then this is our target date," he concluded, and he began to draw a circle around the fifth day of December. "We'll be ready on the fifth," he said, "and we'll schedule our demonstration for the following week. That will be the date of our victory, when all of Japan will know exactly what we have achieved." He accepted their bows and then he bowed himself in respect. He watched them break into small, animated groups and leave the laboratory.

"One more thing," he called after them. They stopped and turned, breaking off their conversations to give him their full attention.

"Our computer needs a name. A word descriptive of its capabilities or its purpose." He watched the smiles appear on their faces. "Try to think of something truly fitting. A name that people will recognize instantly and realize exactly what we have achieved."

Words were called back at him immediately; words that described great speed and great strength. He held up his hands defensively. "No, no, not now. Think about it. There's no hurry. But I want the machine to have the perfect name when we announce it to the nation.'' They were already arguing about names before they were out of the room.

Fujii slipped back into his chair and sat alone in the room, staring at the display terminal, which still showed the results of his successful experiment.

History was about to repeat itself, not with a military attack that was significant in the past, but with a commercial attack significant for the future. He was about to fly his unlikely machine over the anchored hulks of America's industrial might and destroy it in a matter of hours.

It was the same scenario. The Americans knew that they were on a collision course with the Japanese, just as they had known it in 1941. Then, they had watched Japan extend its political influence throughout the world by the strength of its military might. Now, they were watching the Japanese extend their economic influence throughout the world by the strength of their technology and industrial might. In 1941 the Americans had been incapable of coming to grips with the technology challenge.

Fujii was a student of history, fanatical about the details of every major military event that had shaped his country's rise and decline. Today he began to see his supercomputer as Japan's superweapon. The American computers were like the lumbering battleships, swinging slowly at anchor beside Ford Island. Their captains assumed they were indestructible, without ever making an effort to test their assumption. Yet their destruction was now being planned.

He realized that he had already decided on the date for his demonstration. It would be December 8th. The

Americans, on their side of the international date line, would receive the news on December 7th. It would be news from which they would never recover.

And he had found the perfect name for his machine. He would call it the Akagi computer. It was the flagship of his attack force, a fitting successor to the fast attack carrier that had humbled the Americans on a December 7th morning of a bygone age when military weapons had been the symbol of a nation's greatness. It was the perfect name for the supercomputer that was the new symbol of Japan's greatness.

May 8th, 9:00 A.M., Cambridge

Toole was on his own, which was the way he preferred it. He needed a training period to reclaim the skills that had atrophied during his stay in prison. Skills that were, he assumed, the reason he had been singled out for the assignment. And he fully appreciated that his sponsors in the federal government had to avoid any association with the activities he was planning.

He spent his days in academia, plodding through the libraries in search of information on Cobb's "Manhattan Project," mastering the subject matter of his task. And he spent his nights practicing the skills of his trade. Each evening, he connected his personal computer to his telephone and searched for the telltale response of computer data banks. They had gotten smarter over the last year and made access much more difficult. But he wrote new programs to run down the access numbers and worked his way into secret files. There were hundreds of them around the Boston campuses, most of them meaningless to an outsider. And there were commercial data files, like the real costs of the articles put on call in Filene's basement. Nothing of value, of course, but then Toole wasn't looking for profit, simply for practice.

Late at night, he made his way into poker games to sensitize his fingers to the feel of the cards. His artistry, he found, had not deserted him, and he was tempted to bring the cash that Cobb had provided to a promising table and add to his pocket money. But, he suspected, notoriety would not be an asset in the more important work that was still before him. He kept his profits modest.

Most of all, he reacclimated himself to freedom, practicing the luxury of coming and going as he pleased. He found that his confinement had elevated his appreciation for the simpler things: walks along the river where tiny mountains of ice drifted aimlessly; for fine meals of fresh seafood or paper-wrapped sandwiches thick with mustard; the stimulation of ideas recorded in dusty documents or spoken over a cool drink; the touch of a woman's breast beneath fresh white sheets. It was a delightful existence that he would gladly have enjoyed forever, except that the deadline was drawing near. He knew from his research that Cobb's assignment couldn't be postponed indefinitely even though Cobb had not mentioned when his real work would begin.

In March Cobb had driven him from Harrisburg to the airport in Philadelphia and handed him an unmarked brown envelope. Inside, he had found a listing of the flights to Boston, the address of a Back Bay apartment with its door key, and $5,000 in cash. There was a short note, indicating that there were study assignments waiting for him in the apartment and that he had to be out of the apartment in one week. Finally, there was a phone number that he was to call each morning at exactly nine o'clock. The phone wouldn't be answered unless there was a message for him.

He had picked the next available flight, purchased a first-class ticket, and ordered two Irish whiskeys, which were served in tiny bottles with two glasses of ice cubes. Then he had settled back in the seat, looked aimlessly at the cloud cover obscuring the wing tips, and considered his many alternatives.

The most obvious was simply to run. With Cobb's obsession for secrecy, he doubted whether there would be anyone waiting in Boston to keep him under surveillance. Hire a spy to spy on a spy and then you needed still another spy to keep track of the second spy. The line grew infinitely long, with each link in the chain a source of potential compromise. The best way to keep a secret was to limit the number of people who even knew that a secret existed, which meant that Cobb's most secure method of operation was to give Toole the assignment and leave him to operate on his own. So, he could simply land in Boston, walk to another ticket counter and purchase a ticket to, say, Cleveland. Then, with a simple name change and perhaps the addition of a beard, he would be a free man, at liberty to choose his own assignments for his own profit.

Another possibility was the classic double cross. Whatever he was about to learn would be of great value to two people: Cobb, of course, but also to whomever Cobb was scheming against. There were usually quick gains to be made in marketing information about plots to their intended victims. Immediate payments, to be sure, but also undying gratitude, which frequently served as a basis for other profitable ventures.

It was while he was waiting for his third drink that he realized it was too early to make a choice. If he were going to run, knowledge of Cobb's plans would provide a valuable measure of security. After all, Cobb would hardly arrest someone whose testimony could sink a plan he had described as "bigger than the Manhattan Project." And you couldn't be too arbitrary in disposing of someone who might have left a written record of what he knew in an envelope addressed to the *New York Times* or the *Washington Post*. On the other hand, if he were going to sell information to the intended victim, he had to have the information to sell.

Either way, the first course of action was to get to the apartment and begin digesting the information Cobb had provided. Only then could he make an informed decision on his best course of action.

It wasn't until he had finished Cobb's material that he realized he had no choice at all. Give credit to the man, Toole admitted. He had picked his accomplice carefully. Cobb had known that Toole would find the information fascinating and that once he was fascinated there was little danger of his running. In the apartment, Toole had found a stack of reports and technical papers on the development of supercomputers. Still wearing his shirt and tie, he had stretched out on the sofa, prepared to labor through the first few pages before setting out in search of the perfect restaurant. Instead, he had read straight through the night, surprised to find sunlight streaming in the window as he turned to the final page of the last document.

It was incredible. Machines that could think for themselves. Boxes of circuitry that could analyze a problem, instantly write their own programs for solving the problem most efficiently, and then execute the programs in a small fraction of the time that an ordinary computer would require. He had found the coffee in the kitchen, watched it perk, and then taken the whole pot back into the living room where he had tried to appreciate what he was reading.

First, the impact. Whoever was first in developing a supercomputer would leap light-years ahead of his competition. Competitors would be left to write off their inventories of conventional computers, take their losses, and look for another line of work. But that was just a minor consideration. The real impact would come from the use of supercomputers. The first factories to use them would increase their efficiency overnight. The first banks to use them would become bankers to the world, processing and posting the most complex transactions instantly, giving their customers use of needed funds before other banks even knew that the funds existed. And in military affairs, the effects would even be more dramatic. The development of these genius machines was certainly not as dramatic an undertaking as the development of the atomic bomb under the pressure of a world war. But Cobb had not been exaggerating. The stakes of the race were every bit as impressive.

Next, Toole considered the contenders. There was a group of American corporations, aided by the major universities and research organizations, in a race with Japan, Incorporated, the combined and highly integrated clout of Japan's technical, financial, and manufacturing resources. Friendly competitors, to be sure, each mouthing its good will toward the other, publicly alluding to the benefits that their developments would bring to "all mankind." But, in fact, they were engaged in a struggle to the death for leadership in an age of information. The winner would claim the new age as its own, while the loser would fall quickly behind and drown in the backwash of progress.

And he considered the weapons that each brought to the battle. Unlike the heavy ships and supersonic missiles that determined the outcome of conventional battles, each side in this contest was armed with its knowledge. The victor would be the side with the best ideas for solving the complex challenges that super-computers presented.

Unaware that he hadn't slept for more than twenty-four hours, Toole began drawing up his plan of attack. And he had followed that plan relentlessly for the last several weeks.

He began at MIT, where several of the articles he had found in the apartment were authored. First, he purchased a small microcomputer, connected it to his telephone, and entered himself as a graduate student in the university's financial and academic records. Then, dressed in a shabby tweed sports coat, which he carefully selected from the racks at the Salvation Army center, he presented himself at the library and secured a library card, which gave him immediate access to the collection of all of Boston's major libraries. He borrowed and read everything in print on the theory of supercomputers.

Armed with a smattering of information and equipped with the requisite vocabulary, he next purchased a gray business suit that he felt would be appropriate to a senior editor of one of the computer industry's myriad trade magazines. Then he secured interviews with those supercomputer experts based at the Cambridge learning factories, and those who worked for the computer companies that ringed Boston. Most of those he asked were too flattered at the prospect of being interviewed to press for his credentials. And, in the course of the interviews, they leaked information which had not yet found its way into print.

Another leg of his strategy was the kind of internal espionage that had once gained him the access codes to the computers of the leading New York banks. He was sure that even after his stint in prison, he would still have his pleasing way with the ladies and would find them an endless source of freely offered inside information. But his initial encounters brought him up short.

At first, he thought that women had changed remarkably while he was out of circulation. But then he realized that Boston was simply a very different city, attractive to a different breed of women. It was one giant university campus, spilling over onto both banks of the Charles and reaching out to its surrounding highways, which were dotted with the homes of high-technology corporations. It attracted thinkers: physicists, chemists, mathematicians, educators, graduate students, and research assistants. Toole was overwhelmed by his first few conversations with young women and embarrassed by his own simplistic attempts at small talk. His surefire lines were returned with a cold stare, or worse, with a response that dismissed him as a boring simpleton.

He spent a week of monastic chastity trying to impress women who weren't easily impressed. Building on the knowledge and vocabulary he was developing through his research, he tried to pass himself off as a computer expert, only to find that the young lady he was leaning against was already sleeping with a computer expert. He tried his role as an editor and was berated for the shallowness of most of the articles appearing in the trade press. Once he tried to bargain with his credentials as a graduate student, only to learn that half the sanitation workers in Boston were also graduate students. In despair, one evening, he blurted out to a thin and thirtyish woman in a Back Bay lounge that he was actually an ex-con who had served time for computer theft. The bored stare behind her heavy glasses suddenly exploded in interest. "You're shitting me," she said, and turned on her bar stool to hear the rest of the story. She added nothing to his knowledge of supercomputers, but in a two-hour session on the floor next to her sofa, she restored him to the ranks of the sexually active.

With his regained confidence his trips to the lounges and his encounters in the bookstores became more productive. He began targeting women whom he knew to be associated with the computer research programs he was learning about. And while they were not well enough placed to deliver definitive information, they at least served to balance the excessive claims of the men they were working with.

Piece by piece, Toole assembled the supercomputer game board. He understood which strategies seemed promising and which had been abandoned, which players were wandering aimlessly and which ones had a definite direction. Most important, he saw who was out ahead, within one or two throws of the dice of claiming victory. And then he understood clearly what his assignment was to be. It was the Japanese group, headed by Yamagata Fujii, that was poised at the edge of the finish line. His job would be to overturn the board and scatter all the pieces.

He searched the libraries, and retrieved every article by Fujii and every report written about his work. Hunched over the reading tables, he followed Fujii's mathematical analyses as far as he could, until he was completely lost in the labyrinth of symbols and equations. He read descriptive articles that commented on Fujii's approach, understanding the general directions the man was taking but unable to grasp how Fujii could solve the dilemmas he was uncovering. He read biographical information that traced Fujii's rapid rise to the top of the Japanese computer hierarchy and his emergence as a world figure in the technology. But while he began to appreciate the man's genius, he learned nothing of his character. For all the information that was available, Fujii might just as well have been one of his own computers... fast, precise, colorless.

It was by accident that he stumbled on Fujii's self-portrait. He asked the librarian at MIT for a paper on random numbers that Fujii had presented to an international group of physicists. When he called back at the desk, there were two papers waiting for him. One was the document he had requested; the other a miscataloged paper on card games. Toole left the first document on the counter as he rushed to copy the second.

He took the paper, along with a delicatessen sandwich, to a bench that overlooked the cold waters of the Charles and settled into some easy reading. Fujii, it seemed, was a poker player. And poker was Toole's

game—the one subject where he could keep abreast of
the adversary he had never met.

Fujii was writing on probability, describing the cal-
culation of odds for various poker hands appearing
during a game. But the man emerged not so much in
his calculations as in his commentary. He wrote with
insufferable arrogance, calmly claiming for himself the
position as the world's most skilled card player, cred-
iting his analytical capabilities and recounting in smug
terms the occasions when he had confounded the
professional gamblers who thought they were running
a string of luck. "There is no string," he wrote, "but
only discrete events that occur with perfectly predict-
able frequency. Because I have made it my business to
know these frequencies and never oppose the obvious
odds, I have repeatedly beaten the world's best at their
own game."

Toole turned from one passage of self-adulation to
another, finding a man who was absolutely certain that
he had mastered the science of his own invincibility. He
flaunted credentials that were supported by his
achievements with computers as well as his winnings in
poker. But in his self-assurance, he revealed a weakness that made him vulnerable to the skills where Toole
admitted no equal. Toole closed the paper, licked the
mustard from his fingertips, and looked happily out
over the moving water. Fujii, he thought, was the key
to his own downfall.

Toole changed back into the role of journalist and
revisited each of the sources he had interviewed who
had commented on Fujii and his work. Each tried to
give him a technical analysis of Fujii's past accomplishments and his approach to supercomputers, but
Toole cut those conversations short. What he was in-

terested in was the man himself. Had any of them worked with Fujii? Did they know him personally? The responses were disappointing. Fujii was very much a loner who kept his work to himself. His papers, Toole learned, generally appeared only after his accomplishments were a matter of record, when they could reveal little of value to the scientific community. "He's not a true scientist," commented a dean at Harvard, "in that he has no interest in advancing the state of the art. He shares nothing. Fujii works for profit. He knows the monetary value of an idea and he reaps all the rewards of his work."

It was at a card game that the portrait was completed. Toole was playing every night with an ever-changing group of researchers and instructors from Boston University in a dorm room at Kenmore Square. It was a friendly game that opened with pocket change and never saw more than fifty dollars in a pot. But the level of play was excellent, affording Toole an opportunity to reacquire his card table skills. He had folded a hand, watched the pot go to a young Japanese instructor who was new to the game, and had idly commented that, according to his countryman Yamagata Fujii, the winner had foolishly bucked the obvious odds.

"That son of a bitch." The Japanese laughed as he gathered in his winnings.

"You know him?" Toole asked in disbelief.

"I worked for him," the Japanese answered. "And don't believe that shit about his being the world's greatest poker player. I've played with him and I've seen him lose his shirt. Most of the time, people let him win because he's such a lousy loser."

Toole was cautious. The odds against his sitting down at a card table with someone who happened to work for Fujii were longer than any of the odds in a poker hand. There was every chance that his inquiries into Fujii's work had attracted too much attention and that someone was now inquiring into his own work. But unlike the Japanese master, Toole did believe in luck and this could be the break he had been hoping for.

"What did you work on?" he asked casually, as he shuffled the cards, and tossed a chip to the center of the table.

"The 64K RAM," the man answered, referring to a semiconductor development that had once been revolutionary, but was now state of the art.

"Oh," Toole acknowledged, as he began dealing. "I read most of Fujii's stuff on the 64K. I must have seen your name in the credits. What is it, again?"

"You wouldn't have seen anyone's name . . . except Fujii's. That's the way the bastard works. It's all one big team until you get close to the results. Then Fujii takes all the papers and puts his own name on them. You can't build a career working for Fujii. He doesn't like to share the glory."

"Are we playing cards?" a cranky voice interrupted.

Toole let the subject drop, but he manipulated three kings into the Japanese's hand and congratulated him on his second straight pot.

Toole picked up the subject during a beer break and again at the end of the evening. He kept his comments casual, well within the limits of social conversation. But the answers were revealing. Fujii, he learned, was idolized by the younger technicians who worked within the restrictive Japanese system. If you were dedicated to the company, then you were dedicated to Fujii, because he was clearly leading his company to supremacy in the industry. But if you had any initiative or personal ambition, there was no place for you in Fujii's laboratory. He provided all the initiative and took credit for all the ideas. "When we were ready to demonstrate the chip, Fujii collected everyone's notes and records," the Japanese explained, shaking his head in disbelief. "The day the chip ran, Fujii was the only one who could explain it or put it into production. All the rest of us got was a bonus."

Toole stopped asking questions. Instead, he read his notes on Fujii and his supercomputer over and over again. And he took to long, leisurely walks along the bank of the river, his topcoat collar turned up, his hands thrust into his pockets, his blank expression concealing the blazing activity in his brain. He invented complete conversations with Fujii, trying to fit phrases into Fujii's mouth and discarding those that didn't seem appropriate. He invented situations in which Fujii was offered a level of risk and tried to guess what his response would be. In his mind, he flattered the man and watched to see if he accepted the praise as genuine, and threatened him to see if he could detect any sign of cowardice.

He spent nearly a week pantomiming his exchanges with the man he hoped to victimize, watching the river out of the corner of his eye as it turned from winter to spring. The shrinking ice slabs had disappeared, replaced by small sailboats that leaned precariously as they shivered into the stiff breeze. And then the boats had relaxed as the water began to regain its blue color.

Then one morning, he made his mandatory stop in a public phone booth, waited until his digital watch showed 0900, deposited a fistful of quarters and dialed the number he now knew by heart. He was startled when the phone was answered on the first ring and he heard a woman's voice.

"This is Mr. Toole calling," he tried. "Are there any messages?"

The pleasant voice at the other end was as uncertain as his own.

"This is Karen Albert. I think you and I are supposed to be meeting."

May 10th, 2:00 P.M., Mountain View

They met like flint and steel.

Karen had assumed that the colleague flying in from Boston would be a world-class computer theoretician, heading a supercomputer program at one of the great universities. Toole had expected to find himself working with the government's top operatives—people who used "big con" to discredit kings and topple governments. Their mutual disappointment was explosive.

As soon as Toole stepped off the plane in San Francisco, he recognized that his seedy New England tweeds had to go. Hollywood had spread like a virus up the California coastline and infected the entire Bay peninsula. Silicon Valley seemed to have been cast on the lot at Universal, with Italian shoes, designer jeans, and bare-chested sports shirts the standard business attire.

He left his Eastern flannels in a men's shop at the airport, and appeared at the car rental counter in dark slacks, a Giorgio Armani blazer, and a white silk shirt. The reflective sunglasses were his own touch.

Toole drove down the peninsula until he reached the valley, and turned west on one of the winding highways that crossed the mountains to the coast. Then he headed south, with the mountains to his left and the Pacific surf crashing against the cliffs to his right. He recognized the driveway that led back into the mountains before he could even read the name on the sign. The giveaway was the freshly washed sedan pulled to the roadside with its hood raised. The two men pretending to examine the engine were wearing dark blue suits, perfectly styled for government agents just flown in from Washington, but as out of place on the Pacific highway as his tweeds would have been. To Toole, they were as conspicuous as the eagle over the door of an American Embassy, and he nearly laughed as he glanced into his rearview mirror and saw one of them raising a radio to announce his arrival.

The driveway wound back and forth as it climbed up the rock face, then turned suddenly back toward the ocean. The house was a modern knock-off of Spanish stucco and tile, casually looking out over the Pacific, but actually an impregnable fortress, invisible from the road below, accessible only by the road that he had just traveled.

He was surprised to find the front door open and the house empty. For a moment he was puzzled, wondering who had been alerted by the radio message sent by the two guards he had passed below. Then he reasoned that there must be another checkpoint at one of the switchback turns he had navigated on his way to the top. The privacy of the meeting was to be protected, but the guards would have no idea of whom or what they were protecting. Toole was pleased by the thoroughness of the arrangements.

He wandered through the rooms; a comfortable living room oriented to a glass wall that framed a panoramic view of the Pacific, a modern kitchen with a tinted skylight, a dining room with two dinner services tastefully set, and a bookcase-lined study with one wall given over to a projection television and a stereo system with enough amplifiers to thrill a rock band. A glass breezeway led to a separate structure that housed the bedrooms, each with its own bath, and a patio with the requisite California hot tub. The government certainly wasn't skimping with the taxpayers' money, he thought.

He hid the one valise he was carrying in the back of the closet of an empty bedroom and began to prowl. To his disappointment, Karen Albert's bedroom announced itself, first by the trace of perfume that filled the doorway and then by the scattering of personal items across the dresser. There was an address book that read like a family tree, linking the woman to every associate she had ever worked with. There was a telephone bill that provided her most recent address, plus a chronology of all the numbers she had contacted in the last two months. And there were letters in which friends and relatives detailed all Karen's concerns. Toole examined the jewelry, which provided a profile of her financial status, and read the jackets of the two books that were stacked on the night table, proclaiming her to be a mathematician with an interest in computer logic. Suddenly, he recognized the taste of bile in the back of his throat and felt the perspiration beginning to bead on the palms of his hands. This was the undercover operative he was going to be working with, the person whose performance would be critical to his own safety and survival. Yet her personal effects were like a billboard, advertising who she was and what she was up to.

He stepped into the closet and began checking through the row of suits and dresses, all Eastern cuts with New York, Boston, and Washington labels. His fear moved toward panic. Whoever Karen Albert was, she would be in a Japanese jail within minutes of her landing in Tokyo. And he was going to be her traveling companion. He thought of the cardinal rule of his profession, which he was about to violate—always work alone. And he took his first step back toward his room to reclaim his bag and start running. But then she burst through the door into the bedroom.

Karen never looked toward the closet where Toole was standing, but crossed straight to the bed, dropping the terry-cloth robe she was wearing. She kicked off her sandals and at the same time slid the straps of her black, one-piece bathing suit off her shoulders. Quickly, she peeled the top of the suit down over her body until it was bunched up around her waist. Then she pushed it down over her hips and bent over, with her back toward Toole, as she slipped the wet fabric over one leg, then over the other. Toole admired her long, slim, naked form. It figured that she would be beautiful. Dumb and beautiful went together, he despaired.

She pranced across the room to the bathroom, giving Toole an unobstructed profile. He wasn't disappointed, even though her breasts were smaller than his ideal. And the front view was actually exciting when she emerged from the bathroom with a towel over her head, her arms raised as she began drying her hair.

"You don't hide anything," he finally announced.

Her body froze as she tried to believe that she had heard a voice. Then she dropped the towel to her chin and peered out over it with wide, startled eyes. Toole leaned casually against the doorjamb, his arms folded, his head shaking slowly in profound disapproval.

She lowered the towel and pressed it over her breasts. But before she could utter a sound, she realized that she was still naked from the waist down, the area where Toole's gaze had found a point of focus. As she pulled one corner of the towel down over her hips, her breasts appeared over the top. When she instantly pulled the hem up to her chin, her pubic hair reappeared at the bottom. Toole watched the juggling act with casual interest. "Jesus Christ," he finally muttered in despair.

He walked toward her and steered her with his fingertips until she backed to the edge of the soft chair. Then he pushed her gently so that she fell backward and dropped into the chair with the towel in her lap.

"Who the hell are you?" she finally demanded, rearranging the towel for the maximum possible coverage. Toole reached into the bathroom and picked a larger towel from the rack. "I'm your partner," he answered as he dropped the towel into her hands.

Her shock turned to anger and she started up out of the chair, frantically wrapping the new covering around herself. "And that gives you the right to break into my bedroom..." she started through clenched teeth.

Toole guided her back into the chair and silenced her with his own look of rage.

"Let's talk about you," he threatened. "Let me tell you everything that I know about you, besides the obvious facts that you're a natural blonde and you're missing your appendix." She pulled the bottom of the towel down to her knees.

"Your name is Karen Jean Albert and your Social Security number is 083-28-8109. You're thirty-five years old, a United States citizen, and you live in New York, on Seventy-third Street. From the address, you're probably just east of Third Avenue. You work for IAC, doing some very high-level programming . . . probably systems development. Your pay voucher says they're paying you better than eighty grand a year, so you have to be doing pretty important stuff. At any rate, you're all business because all you own are business suits and pajamas."

He watched her eyes growing wider.

"Your real home is in Athens, Georgia. At least that's where your mother lives. And she thinks you're something special because she writes you every week."

"How dare you search my room," she shouted, starting again to her feet. He pushed her back into the chair, this time not as gently as before.

"I didn't search anything," he snapped back. "That's just the information you left lying around for anyone to see. If I had searched I probably could have found out about your sex life which, by the way, can't be too hot since you didn't even reach your minimum of local telephone calls. Just how long have you been doing this kind of work for dear Uncle Sam?"

Her fury melted into confusion and he read the bewilderment in her eyes.

"You don't know what the fuck I'm talking about, do you?" he finally realized. "You have no idea what you've gotten yourself into."

She stared back at him blankly.

"Holy shit," he sighed, as he turned his back to her, thrust his hands into his pockets and walked absently toward the window.

She used the moment to jump to the foot of the bed, where she replaced the towel with the terry-cloth robe she had carried in from the pool. In the process, she began to compose herself and then to resent the bullying she had just undergone.

"Okay," she began, turning on her attacker, "now let's talk about you. What the hell do you bring to the party that gives you the right to be such an insufferable bastard?"

"Brains," he answered quickly without moving his gaze from the window. "They're in short supply."

"They're also a well-kept secret," she snapped back. "I've checked every directory of every university and firm in Boston, and the only Toole I've been able to find is a janitor. What project are you working on?"

Now it was his turn to be bewildered. He turned slowly. "What the hell are you talking about?"

"Computer project," she answered. "You're supposed to be an expert in intelligent computer logic. How come I've never heard of you?"

She began rattling off the names of major development projects—names he remembered from his research but which he couldn't link to the technology involved. Then moving to the technical terms involved in research, she saw that she was leaving him behind. They stared at each other for a moment, her eyes becoming angry while the confidence drained out of his.

"Holy shit," she finally said, echoing his earlier sentiments. "You're the genius who's supposed to help me derail a supercomputer and you don't have a clue as to what's involved."

It took her only a moment to make her decision. "Why don't you just leave so I can get packed and get out of here," she told him.

Toole turned back to the window. "That's just what I was going to do," he answered. "But I don't think that's possible."

Her eyes narrowed suspiciously. Toole touched her elbow and moved her to the window.

"See the guy sitting beside the rock?"

She didn't.

"Just follow the road to the first turn and look up about thirty feet."

She swept her eyes in the direction he had indicated and found a hunched figure ridiculously attired in a suit jacket. "Who is he?" she wondered.

"A guard," Toole answered. "I knew he was there somewhere because the guys at the turnoff called someone on their radio. I thought they were there to protect us."

"I don't need any protection," Karen snapped. "All I need is about ten minutes to get packed."

Toole ignored her outburst. "I thought they were here to keep other people out. And maybe they are. But they're also going to keep us in. I'm not sure that they'll just let us leave."

She walked back to the window and stared at the guard. "He can't stop me," she announced. "I'm an American citizen, and I'll come and go as I please."

Toole looked at her with his first expression of sympathy. "You really don't have any idea what you've gotten yourself into, do you?" he said. He started across the hall to his own room and unpacked the few belongings he had brought with him.

They spent the rest of the day ignoring each other. Toole sat at a poolside table, his chin propped on the back of his hand, and stared vacantly into the water. Occasionally, he changed his position and dealt hands from a deck of playing cards that he manipulated absently. Karen sat in her room, reviewing the mountains of fan-folded computer printout that had occupied the two days since she had arrived at the house. But her fascination for the material was changed. Instead of being absorbed by it, the columns of code were only a distraction between her glances through the window at the guard posted above the road.

They passed in the kitchen during the dinner hour as each selected a silvery parcel from the freezer and emptied its rock-hard contents into the microwave. But there was no conversation other than the traffic conventions they were forced to exchange as they maneuvered around the appliances. At dinner, the only sound was the scratch of the silverware on the plates.

But there was only one coffee pot, which forced them to pool their efforts to make coffee. And that moment of cooperation broke the silence.

"Look...I'm sorry," Toole began. "It's just that you're not what I was expecting."

She acknowledged the apology with a nod as she spooned the coffee into the pot Toole was holding.

"And I didn't mean to go through your things," he continued. "But they were so obvious. I mean...I thought you were a pro and I was mad at how sloppy you were. Then it was pretty obvious that you were an amateur and I got upset at the idea of working with an amateur. But it was professional concern. I wasn't snooping for personal reasons."

She assembled the components of the coffee pot, and switched it on.

"Some of your observations seemed very personal," she responded as she turned to leave the kitchen. But she stopped suddenly and when she turned back to Toole her face held a smile that was rapidly becoming a laugh.

"God, I must have looked like a real idiot trying to cover myself with that hand towel."

Toole didn't know how much to tell her as they shared their coffee. He was determined to end their partnership as soon as Cobb arrived, and his passion for secrecy limited the number of topics he could open for discussion. But he did admit to his interest in computers and allowed himself credit for some of the programs he had developed for his microcomputer. Taking a pencil and paper, he began to explain the steps in his procedure for breaking access codes and he was pleased to find her interested. Karen, in turn, spelled out some of the traps her company was using to frustrate the hackers who tried to crack confidential data bases. The conversation quickly became a parlor game with each jotting down the commands that would overcome the other's attack or defenses.

Eventually Karen went back to her room and returned with the printout of the Japanese transmissions she had been studying. She began to explain the difference between dealing with a small microcomputer and the enormous mainframe machine that the code was written for. It was nearly midnight before they realized how much time they had spent in conversation and how many pots of coffee they had absently gone through. As they said their good nights and closed the doors of their separate rooms, their relationship had warmed to one of mutual respect. It was this relationship that Cobb found when he arrived the next morning.

"She's a very bright lady," Toole began after leading Cobb out to the privacy of the patio. "But this just isn't going to work. It's too goddamned dangerous to get into something like this with an amateur. She'll blow any cover you give her the minute she unpacks her suitcase."

"You can't be serious," Karen protested to Cobb when she found herself alone with the government official. "How is he supposed to get me the code I need when he doesn't even know what a supercomputer code looks like? I need someone who understands this stuff."

Cobb patronized each of them with glib assurances that everything would work perfectly. He withheld all discussion of his plan until they were together over sandwiches at the table by the pool.

"I'm delighted that you two are getting along so well," he began. There were startled looks of protest which he dismissed with a gesture. "You have very different talents. But both those talents are absolutely essential if we're to have any chance of success." Karen and Toole looked suspiciously at each other.

"First," he said, turning to Toole, "you should know that Miss Albert is one of the world's leading minds in supercomputer technology. There are perhaps a dozen people on earth who could handle the problem we're giving her. None of them has any experience whatsoever in undercover operations. Which means that you have no choice except to work with what you properly call an amateur."

He turned to Karen. "Mr. Toole, on the other hand, is completely unfamiliar with advanced computer technology. You're absolutely right on that score. But he's a genius when it comes to . . . shall we say . . . deceptive activities. He could relieve any one of your supercomputer colleagues of his bank account, home, probably even wife and children, before the poor soul even knew what had happened. So if you work together, we should have the best of both worlds."

"You mean he's a crook?" Karen demanded, snapping her eyes toward Toole. Toole started up out of his chair in protest, but Cobb's hand held him in place.

"Miss Albert," Cobb asked coldly, "is there any doubt in your mind about what we are attempting to accomplish?"

She thought back to her Washington meeting with Cobb, and the realization that had prompted her to phone him.

"No," she admitted.

"Then, in a sense, we're all crooks," Cobb concluded logically. "The only difference is that he's better at it than you or I." He felt Toole relax back into his chair.

"Now, let's get to work." Cobb focused on Karen. "What have you learned from the reading material I gave you?"

Karen launched into a description of the architecture of the Japanese supercomputer, describing its basic techniques for handling information. As she spoke, she walked back and forth in front of the table, addressing most of her comments to Cobb, but occasionally glancing at Toole. He was shuffling a deck of playing cards, but he was listening intently and obviously grasping most of what he was hearing.

"The basic structure of the language and of the operating system is no surprise," Karen concluded. "It follows the description that Fujii laid out in his technical papers, and it's quite similar to the approach we've been taking at IAC. But the logic matrices are different. Very different from what we're using and, good God, ten times more powerful. He's at least a year ahead of us. Maybe two."

"When will IAC have a machine up and running?" Cobb interrupted.

Karen shrugged. "Hard to say. If we get lucky, maybe in two and a half years."

"Then he's two years ahead of us," Cobb told her. "Fujii is committed to demonstrating by the end of this year."

She looked startled. "That's impossible," she said. "The code I reviewed is nowhere close to being finished."

"It's old code," Cobb admitted. "We lost our source three months ago."

Karen nodded. "Then Fujii has made tremendous progress in the last three months."

"Can you work with what you've got?" Cobb questioned.

Karen thought carefully about her reply. "To a point, yes. Assuming he keeps the same structure and the same vocabulary, I guess I'm confident that I can fix it so it won't work. But I'd have to have more recent code. As close to the finished product as I can get. And I'd have to have access to the machine so that I can make the substitutions."

Cobb nodded. Then he turned to Toole. "Which brings us to your part of the project," he said. "Can you get us the latest code? And can you substitute Karen's altered version for the genuine product?"

Toole finished shuffling his cards. He cut the deck with one hand and stuffed it into his shirt pocket.

"This is crazy," he announced. "Wouldn't it be a lot simpler for the government, or IAC, or someone in the United States to take out a license on Fujii's technology?"

Cobb showed his frustration. It was the same question that dozens of laymen had asked him, including the President of the United States. He was getting sick of explaining to idiots that the reality of a thinking computer wasn't just some piece of hardware that could be licensed and reproduced.

"Of course," he responded to Toole. "The Japanese would be happy to license us their two-year-old technology. But with a supercomputer up and running, they'd be ten years ahead of us by the time we put their technology to work. So in the next round, they'd be licensing us ten-year-old technology. We'd go on forever paying a fancy price to fall further and further behind."

Toole accepted the answer. It was the one he had expected. "You're asking me, 'Can we do it?'" he said. "I'm sure it can be done, given enough time. But if Fujii is going to be ready by the end of the year, I'm not sure there's enough time."

"I can't wait until the last minute to have the code," Karen interjected. "I'll need time to work with it. And, if at all possible, I'll need to be able to run tests on Fujii's computer."

Cobb turned back to Toole, who responded by shrugging his shoulders. "He's obviously a very bright guy," Toole said. "That makes all this very difficult. But he's also a very arrogant guy, and that should make it easier. All we can do is try. And, of course, be ready to cut our losses and run like hell if something goes wrong."

"Nothing will go wrong," Cobb assured him. "But if it should, we're already working on a cover."

Toole walked back into the house, leaving Cobb and Karen to their computer talk. He searched the kitchen cabinets until he found the liquor supply, then made three tall gin and tonics, which he carried back to the pool.

"What's our deadline?" he asked Cobb, as he handed out the drinks.

"December seventh," Cobb answered. "That's the date Fujii has set for his demonstration."

Toole looked up from the rim of his glass. "December seventh?"

Cobb smiled. "He's picked one hell of a day to try to sink the U.S. economy, hasn't he?"

"I wasn't thinking of him," Toole answered. "I was thinking of us. That's one hell of a day for a sneak attack on the Japanese."

They drank in silence.

May 29th, 9:30 P.M., Tokyo

Tokyo was the uneasy love affair between the mysti-- cism of timeless religions and the urgency of modern technology. Glass skyscrapers that housed the world's most progressive financial empires cast their shadows over the Imperial Palace Gardens, where the Emperor's family planted rice as a gift to the rice goddess. Bullet trains fired industrial czars from their electronic offices to their paper homes, where they removed their shoes on the doorsteps, donned embroidered kimonos and rang tiny bells before their personal Shinto altars. High-rise apartment houses, built of concrete and steel, had walls lined with wood to simulate the vulnerable construction of past ages that had made appeasement to the gods of fire and wind a necessity. And in the huge Mitsukoshi department store, a three-story-high image of the goddess of sincerity filled the central atrium, looking down with benevolent approval at the computerized cash registers totaling the day's take.

The love affair was a scandal to all. Monks and priests decried the fact that the temple bells could no longer be heard over the roar of automobiles on the thruways, and that the ceremonial chrysanthemums were choking to death in the noxious engine vapors. Businessmen reluctantly counted the number of work hours lost to the never-ending Matsuri festivals. The old lamented the heritage of peaceful solitude, now shattered by squawking televisions and the incessant ringing of telephones. And the young looked at the reverence of the stone and lacquer gods as an embarrassing reminder of the past centuries when they had locked themselves in isolation from the progress of the West.

Yet the love affair was the source of the city's strength. The intimacy of tradition and technology made work a religious endeavor and gave moral approval to profits. The businessman bowing before the image of the fertility god wasn't concerned with the growth of his progeny, but rather with the growth of his sales. And messages dipped into the curative waters of temple shrines didn't concern withered limbs and broken bones, but were addressed to withered bank accounts and broken businesses. Workers saw the gods not as alternative masters, but rather as stern reminders of the loyalty they owed to their employer masters. Employers, in turn, found only one definition of sin in their meditations—failure to earn the returns that would enable them to meet their sacred obligations to their workers. Since its founding at the dawn of the seventeenth century, Tokyo had prospered by fusing practical administration with ethereal values. Now, that same unlikely coupling was making it the unchallenged capital of the high-technology world.

In the daylight, the two forces could be seen in dynamic competition. Blocks of tiny houses, with streets guarded by ritual gateways that warded off evil spirits, pushed against commercial buildings adorned with corporate insignia. But at night, the cho neighborhoods and the ritualistic shrines were plunged into darkness, and the city surrendered to the brilliance of the gaudy new age. Each building blinked the ideographs of its occupation or flaunted the symbol of its corporate owners. The only visible shrine was the Eiffel-like tower, trimmed in lights rising sixty feet higher than the symbol of Paris, and dedicated to the uninterrupted broadcast of radio and television signals.

It was this Tokyo that Toole watched from the window of the suite in the Imperial Hotel. He had landed at the airport just one week before, presenting a passport that identified him as David Joyce, a sales representative for an electronic components company. Then he had gone directly to an apartment rented in the company's name, located in the Shinagawa district, on the city's southern edge. It was a disappointment.

Shinagawa was a replica of the colorless high-rise communities found in any American city. The angular, concrete structures climbed ten stories above sparse gardens with paved walkways, stacking families on top of one another. The size of the apartment was even more disappointing, hardly more spacious than his accommodations at Harrisburg. The largest room had a Western sofa and chair grouped around a low, lacquered table. Tatami mats were rolled into two small alcoves in one of the walls, so that the room could double as sleeping quarters. The kitchen was modern, but with miniature appliances, suited to its walk-in-closet dimensions. There was a small bath with a washstand and a galvanized metal hot tub that could have doubled for a soup pot. He stepped in to try it for fit and found himself sitting on his heels. As he tried to extend his legs, his knees crashed into the side, setting the whole structure resonating like a snare drum. The final room was the children's quarters, sized for miniature bodies and furnished only with the tatami mats.

The walls throughout the apartment were covered with a light wood veneer, framed out to resemble the flimsy structure of traditional Japanese homes, and there were sliding screens that pulled across the doorways. The intended effect was a visual link with tradition, effective if one could forget that there were identical links to the identical tradition on all sides and that the mandatory garden was fifty feet below.

Toole stopped in there only long enough to change his shirt and connect his computer to the telephone in the main room. Then he left the apartment and packed himself into the commuter train headed to the Marunouchi district in search of his prey.

He started at the major hotels, which shared the city's central district with the glass and steel industrial and financial temples. At each hotel, he tipped the bell captain lavishly as a way to buy into the businessmen's poker games that were part of night-life ritual. At each game, he played well enough to establish himself as a worthy competitor, and manipulated the cards to assure himself a small, polite loss. Inconspicuously, he made chatty inquiries about other games and then moved each night to a more serious contest. By the fourth night, he found Fujii's game. Now, he stood in a suite atop the Imperial Hotel, sharing the view with a Japanese businessman who bowed each time he caught Toole's eye. They were waiting in silence for the rest of the players to arrive.

Six men assembled; two other Americans and three Japanese. One of the Americans was a gray-suited banker who played in a vest and described himself as a venture capitalist looking to put U.S. dollars into high-flying Japanese technology concerns. As Toole watched his poor play, he wondered whether there would be any funds left to invest. The other American was a jovial tourist in a sports shirt who claimed to be selling printing presses. Toole caught him palming the cards the first time he dealt and realized that he would have to fold early whenever the man held the deck. Two cheats in one game could only confuse each other.

Two of the Japanese were older men who sat down in their suit jackets and carefully hooked wire-rimmed spectacles over their ears. They smiled continuously, dipping their chins whenever they received a card, and chatted constantly with each other, retaining their good humor no matter what cards they were dealt. And then there was Fujii, who certainly was not what Toole had expected, based on his writings and the depth of his work.

He was young, under forty according to his biographies, but less than thirty if judged by his physical appearance. His hair was fuller than the approved style of Japanese executives and he wore it in a long shock that cut across his forehead, nearly touching his eyebrows. His face was thin, rising from a small mouth and narrow chin to prominent, high cheekbones. In contrast to his skull, his neck was broad, flaring outward toward his shoulders, which were too broad for his bone structure. From the wide shoulders, his torso tapered to a thin, flat waist.

But it was his eyes that dominated Fujii's appearance. They were black, set like pools of ink in the narrow space above the cheekbones and beneath the tapered eyelids. They panned constantly, like the lenses of television security cameras, swinging across the faces of all the players, taking in every feature and nuance of expression but revealing no reaction to what they saw.

He played in his shirt-sleeves, which he rolled up above powerful forearms that were wired with veins. He positioned his chair back from the table so that he could take in the entire game with each swing of the lenses. While the others held their cards fanned out in their hands, Fujii left his in a miniature deck, stacked face down on the table. There was no need for him to refer to them. Once he had seen them, they were committed to memory, and he would bet any sum without ever pausing to reexamine them.

The waiter asked for drink orders, and nodded to the expected "mizu-wari" that rose like a chant in praise of whiskey and water. Only Fujii differed, requesting a glass of ice and a pitcher of water. He sipped ice water throughout the early evening, changing to black coffee as the evening wore on.

The early play was uneventful, with small pots generally decided before the last card was played. Only the sports-shirted American created any interest by the outlandish combinations he dealt himself from the bottom. Toole noticed that Fujii, like himself, folded early whenever the American held the cards. He wondered whether the Japanese had detected the bogus deals or whether he was simply puzzled by the failure of the distribution to meet any reasonable standard of probability.

In the first hour, one of the Japanese businessmen took the lead, winning a series of boring hands. Then the American cheat parlayed three queens into a substantial pot, putting himself ahead. Fujii seemed to wait, watching the game from afar, minimizing his losses by dropping early, taking occasional winnings when the cards were obviously in his favor.

Toole stayed with the odds, imitating the professional tone of Fujii's game, refusing to stack hands to create competition. He was down less than $100 when the vested American, who had contributed over $3,000 to the evening, looked at his watch and announced that he was leaving after one more round of deals.

Toole let the other American run his scam, and contributed another hundred to the pot by betting two kings against the three tens he watched the incompetent bungler deal himself. When Fujii dealt, Toole feigned a hunch and bucked the obvious odds against drawing a fifth club to a flush. Fujii looked surprised as he raked in a few of Toole's chips. Then the deck came to Toole and he brushed his fingers against the cloth of his trousers before he began to shuffle. He called for seven-card stud, the same game he had chosen all evening, and began dealing the first two cards, face down, to each of the players.

The vested American and the two Japanese businessmen showed their disappointment as they turned up the edges of their cards. Toole had given them a scattering of twos and threes. The cheat's expression was sour, an attempt to disguise the two aces he found on the table before him. Fujii showed no reaction to the king, nine that Toole had dealt him, and Toole made sure to examine the jack and five that he had given himself. Then he dealt the first round of up cards, giving the cheat a ten, himself a second jack, and Fujii a second king. Fujii's king was high, but he didn't want to show early enthusiasm for the pair of kings he now held. He bet modestly and the wager was matched around the table.

Toole dealt the next round of up cards, again leaving the vested American and the Japanese businessmen with nothing. He gave the printing press salesman a second ten, giving him pairs of aces and tens. Fujii remained expressionless as Toole laid a meaningless seven next to the king that was showing. Then he turned over a queen and placed it next to his jack. "Two tens bets," he said, referring to the pair that the cheat was showing.

"Well," said the American, "two tens isn't as good as getting laid, but it's the best around and it is the end of the night. I think I'll back it for two hundred." He pushed a short stack of chips into the pot.

The vested American tossed his cards into the center. "I've already made a big enough contribution," he said pleasantly. "I think I'll get an early start on tomorrow." He rose and walked to the sofa to get his jacket. The two Japanese stacked their cards neatly and pushed them toward the center, still smiling and nodding. One of them spoke to Fujii in Japanese, making a long speech through happy teeth.

"They say 'good night,'" Fujii translated for the benefit of the two Americans. Toole tried to match their smiles, bowing his head to each of them. Then he turned his attention to Fujii. "The bet is two hundred," he continued. Fujii pushed $200 to the center of the table. Toole did the same.

The hands turned with the next face card. Toole dealt the American an ace, adding to the pair of aces that he knew were already in the hole, and leaving the pair of tens showing. The cheat feigned disappointment, which amused Toole since he knew the bumbler was probably about to wet his pants in anticipation. He already held the strongest hand of the evening and he still had two more cards to go. He gave Fujii his second showing king and then gave himself the second showing jack.

"Look at this," he said in controlled amazement. "Three pairs showing: tens, jacks, and kings. Somebody is going to get rich." The comment brought the vested American back to the edge of the table. The two Japanese businessmen saw the surprise in his face and joined him to overlook the play.

"Pair of kings," Toole said to Fujii, and then he held his breath. If Fujii believed what he was seeing, then his mathematical mind would confirm his obviously strong position. There were three players, each with a pair. The odds of that occurring were slim. But he held a third king. To beat him, one of the other players would have to draw either four tens or four jacks. Those odds were out of sight, even though a ten or a jack had not appeared in any of the discarded hands.

"Three hundred," he said, organizing the amount into two stacks and pushing them out to the center.

"Christ," Toole said in relief, disguising the comment as apprehension. Then he added absently, "Well, one of us could get three of a kind." He matched the $300 stack of chips. He looked at the American, letting anxiety wire itself all over his face. Of course the cheat would bet. He already held three aces, backed by a pair of tens. But Toole had to pretend he was absorbed in the tension while he enjoyed the man's efforts to hide his ecstasy.

"Could be me and I'm feeling lucky," the American finally allowed. "So I'm going to raise that bet. Five hundred," he announced, pushing the wager to the center. He turned to Fujii. "Two hundred more, if you think it's going to be you."

Fujii added $200 and, after reexamining his down cards, Toole put up $200 more to stay in the game.

He dealt the final card face down, then looked at his own hand, which contained three jacks. It was better than anything that had been showing, so to maintain credibility with Fujii, he had to open the betting.

"Dealer bets a hundred," he said.

"Dealer should save his money," the American chimed in, "because I like what I'm seeing." He raised Toole's bet by $400 and turned to Fujii. "Five hundred to stay in," he said, scarcely able to suppress the smile that was twitching at the corners of his mouth.

Toole swallowed hard as he saw Fujii's eyes narrow in suspicion. "Oh, Christ," Toole thought to himself. "The bastard smells a rat."

Fujii recognized that the improbable was happening and he had little faith in the improbable. The American's bet made it obvious that he had drawn at least the third ten and the quickness with which he had pushed the bet indicated that he was absolutely certain that he held the winning hand. Fujii would have guessed that he had already held a ten down and was betting four tens. But as he looked at the neat stack on the table before him, four tens was an incredible hand. The last card that Toole dealt to Fujii was the fourth king, and the odds against two players in the same hand holding four of a kind were too high to calculate. Still, what did it matter. Even if the American did have the four tens, Fujii's own hand was still the winner. Unless . . . unless the American had been given two aces as his down cards and then another ace as his final down card. That, plus the single ace showing, would make the printing press salesman in the sports shirt the evening's big winner.

But it was too improbable. The man had been betting the two tens big even before he saw the upturned ace. Even with two aces in the hole, the best he could have was a full house and that wasn't enough to win. And what were the odds of his drawing a fourth king? Impossible, unless the cards weren't falling at random. Unless the dealer knew when and where the cards were falling. His eyes slid upward across Toole's chest until they reached his face. Then the black lenses fixed on Toole's eyes and began to turn with colorless heat.

"He knows," Toole worried as he began to wither under Fujii's stare. "He knows something is wrong and he's guessing I'm working with this guy."

"Five hundred," Fujii said, still blazing at Toole, "and five hundred more." His eyes never left Toole as he pushed the chips out onto the table.

"Mother of God," Toole blurted. He looked back at his down cards and pretended to be reexamining his hand. But what he was actually doing was recalculating his losses. At this point of time, he was down $2,000 to Fujii, which was exactly the kind of round number he had been looking for. He looked up at Fujii and returned the stare. "You're not playing games," he finally told Fujii. Then he pushed his cards to the center. "I'm out," he said softly, and he turned his eyes to the American.

He found fear. The American had recognized that Fujii wasn't a gambler but rather a calculator. And the size of his bet meant that he had calculated his hand to be a winner. But what was he so positive that he was going to win with? Undoubtedly, he had gotten a third king. Was Fujii positive that the best he could have was three tens? Or did Fujii have a hand that could even beat four tens, which would, of course, beat the full house that he had been backing? All of a sudden, his sure thing wasn't all that sure. And the horror of losing was visible in his eyes.

"Five hundred more to stay in," Toole reminded him.

"I'll look," the American said, and he pushed up the additional $500 needed to see Fujii's hand.

Fujii turned over his neat deck and spread it out on the table without even looking at it. If the American produced four aces, then he and Toole had to be working together. But Fujii wasn't anticipating that. If Toole had dealt the American a winning hand, then the American would have known it was a winning hand and he would have raised the bet still higher.

In despair, the American spread out his own cards. "Full house," he mumbled. "Aces and tens. When was the last time you saw someone lose with that kind of hand?"

Toole joined in his disappointment. "Christ, and I thought I had something with three jacks. I should have gotten out sooner."

Fujii smiled as he raked in his winnings, but his joy had nothing to do with the size of the pot. His faith in the laws of probability had been restored. The odds had told him that no one else at the table could possibly have four of a kind and that was exactly what had occurred. Toole had gotten only three jacks, a good hand, which would generally have been a winner. The American had reached a full house, an extraordinary hand, which fully justified his aggressive betting. And he had gotten four kings, which made him an obvious winner. An unlikely hand, but yet the logic of numbers demanded that it should turn up every now and then.

The American counted out his debt in cash and dropped the stack of bills in front of Fujii. "You were lucky," he said, unable to contain his bitterness at losing a sure thing. Fujii folded the cash into his shirt pocket without looking up until after the American had slammed the door behind him.

"I'm sorry," Toole said, as if compelled to apologize for his countryman's poor manners. "I'm afraid he's not a very good loser."

"He's also a cheat," Fujii said impassively.

Toole looked surprised.

"The cards went crazy every time he dealt," said Fujii. "I don't know how he was doing it, but he was obviously controlling the deck. I'd advise you not to play with him again."

"You can tell just by the way the cards fall?" Toole said in amazement bordering on awe.

Fujii responded while he walked to the bar and fixed himself his first drink of the evening. "I can't tell from just one or two hands, because at any moment you can get an extraordinary mix of cards...like the four kings I just held. But when you see several combinations that are highly unlikely and when they occur only when a certain person is dealing, then it's a safe bet that they are not chance occurrences."

"I never noticed," Toole said as he fixed himself a drink.

Fujii raised his glass in a toast. "You play very well," he said by way of congratulations. Toole shrugged his shoulders modestly. "Only once did you try to buck the odds...when you went for that flush. You didn't even have a one in four chance because there were more clubs showing than any other suit."

Toole nodded in agreement. "You're right. But it was getting late and nothing exciting was happening. I just felt that maybe that was my moment."

"Don't bet moments," Fujii advised. "Bet probabilities."

"It's not as much fun," Toole offered weakly.

"It's more profitable," Fujii counseled.

Toole raised his jacket from the sofa and slipped a checkbook out of the inside pocket.

"Can I give you a company check?" he suggested. "I get a break on my taxes if I can make it look as if I've bought something." Fujii nodded, and watched Toole write out a check for $2,000 spelling out the words in a very open hand.

"That's my bank," Fujii said with pleasure. "It will clear right away."

"No problem," Toole assured him. "The company keeps cash over here for small purchases and entertainment of customers. You Japanese require quite a bit of entertainment."

When they reached the lobby, Toole said that he hoped they might play together again. "I'd like to win some of that back before you get a chance to spend it all."

"Can you play tomorrow night?" Fujii offered. "It's a much stronger game. Not as much money, but the quality of play is much higher. They're all computer people, too smart to try for a club flush when all the clubs are already on the table." Toole wrote down the address and the time, thanking Fujii for the invitation, and watched the Japanese walk crisply through the swinging doors and disappear into the crowds moving up and down the street.

"Bingo," he said to himself. He had his prey inside the cage and he was getting ready to set the trap.

June 15th, 12:05 A.M., Tokyo

A few moments after midnight, a light began blinking on the telephone attendant's console at a Ginza branch of the Tokyo National Bank. It was the only sign of activity on the darkened banking floor, which had closed to the public at the end of the business day and been abandoned by the cleaning crew a few hours earlier. A green lamp was illuminated on the keyboard of one of the teller's stations and the blinking telephone lamp switched to a steady glow. Over private lines, the teller's terminal dialed the bank's data center, located in the basement of the headquarters building a few blocks away. The call was answered by a small communications computer, which recognized the caller and signaled back that it was ready to process an information request.

The teller's terminal paused for a moment and then sent the control signal for a question mark, asking the communications computer for help. The machine obliged, sending back a menu of the various files that the teller's terminal was authorized to examine.

In the living room of his scaled-down apartment in the Shinagawa, J. P. Toole watched the exchange on the screen of his Apple computer. An uncontrolled smile broke across his face, grew to a laugh, and exploded into a victory whoop. He was in. He was talking over public telephone lines to the banks' central computers just as surely as if he had tunneled into the building's basement, brushed the plaster from his clothes, and seated himself at the computer's control console. From now on, the machine would tax its billion-dollar logic and its trillion words of memory to deliver exactly the information he was requesting.

He asked for transaction records of the day after he had handed Fujii the first $2,000 check. Within seconds, the computer asked him the type of transaction he was interested in. From the menu of choices, he selected intrabank transfers, looking for just those checks that had been drawn on one of the bank's accounts and made payable to another. The first page of data appeared and he began scrolling through the listing, looking for his check number and the number of his own account. A blur of entries flew by before he spotted it. He stopped the scrolling and examined the information, noting the account number to which the check had been deposited. Then he requested the system's main menu and a statement on that account.

Fujii's bank statement appeared on the screen.

It was too easy and he felt again the wonder he had experienced the first time he had linked up to the records of an American bank. The banks buried their computer records in concrete bunkers and barred entrance with stainless steel gates, opened only by electronic codes in combination with secret keys. Then, for the price of a telephone call, they made the information they were guarding available to anyone who asked.

In his trial, the bank lawyers had explained to an impatient judge why it had to be this way. With great satisfaction they told the court of the lengths they had gone to in order to make their computers "user friendly,'' prompting the judge to laugh that they had certainly made it friendly to burglars.

"It's a matter of customer service," the lawyers pointed out. It was important that every teller be able to answer the customer's question about the status of an account and the tellers weren't necessarily skilled in computer protocol. So, the computers couldn't ask too many questions. Instead, they delivered the information requested. Customers wanted to be able to check their account status simply by inserting a credit card in a slot. The computers had to talk to credit cards. And customers wanted to make bank transactions at night from automatic teller machines that demanded only an account number and a password. So, the passwords couldn't be too complicated.

There was no doubt that the banks could develop procedures that would make their sacred trust of confidential information virtually inaccessible. That's what their security people and financial managers were demanding. But such a step would keep the computers from being user friendly, which was unacceptable to the commercial people. They tried to do both, limiting access to those who knew access codes and passwords, but making the access codes and passwords simple enough to be generated by a cash register or credit card machine. And since they were so simple, they were easily reconstructed by the simplest of computers, which explained why microcomputer hackers all over the world were breaking into commercial files and even the most secure military data bases. College students at Dartmouth were tearing up data files at Columbia in a prank that replaced stealing the other school's mascot before a football game. Cub Scouts in Chicago were rewriting the CIA's confidential files in Washington.

And Toole was examining Fujii's bank account in the financial center of a foreign country.

Language was no barrier. Computers had delivered on the dream of Esperanto, creating a universal language of binary pulses that flowed like enzymes through the brains of all machines. While the displays and printouts appeared in the same cacophony of Cyrillic and roman symbols, the computers that produced those words spoke in a common language of bits and bytes. Fujii's bank statement used English roman letters and arabic numerals instead of the kanji symbols that confused Toole's walks through the Ginza and Akasaka. It was as simple as talking to the computers at Citibank had been. Ironic, thought Toole as he manipulated the tables of data. The discipline of kanji had trained the Japanese to be masters of the electronic age. The skills of eye and hand coordination demanded to create the precise ideographs, where the shape of a line could change the meaning of a word, had made the Japanese masters of the miniature art of electronic assembly. Now the products of that skill—computers and calculators—were eliminating the use of the kanji characters.

He made a simple change to the figures in Fujii's account, changing the value of his check from $2,000 to $200,000. He left the original $2,000 in the account, but added a transaction transferring the balance to a secure account at a bank in Zurich. Then he moved to his own account, changing the balance to cover a $200,000 check, then reducing that balance as the funds were transferred to Fujii's account. Next, he moved to the deposit slip balance, and added a $200,000 deposit to his own account to the detail and summary of the file. He knew the deception would never survive a bank audit. But it would create a balance when the computers matched one record against the other and prevent any premature alarms from sounding in the computer center. By the time the lack of paperwork was discovered and auditors attacked the individual entries to discover the fraud, it would be too late for Fujii and too late for his plans to sink the American information economy.

The process would be repeated when the more recent checks he had written to Fujii reached his bank account. During the last week, he had spent three evenings at the card table with Fujii, making sure to win modestly on one occasion but to lose heavily on the other two. Each would create a record that he would rewrite.

He finished the changes he was making to the bank records, signed off the conversation, and saw his display screen go blank. In the Ginza branch office, the green light on the teller's terminal went off and the light on the telephone console disappeared.

There was no evidence that anyone had ever been there.

June 28th, 9:30 P.M., Tokyo

The crowd exploded as the two kimono-clad giants entered the arena, then broke into competing factions, each chanting the name of its hero. The wrestlers lumbered down the aisles, seemingly oblivious to the applause, and with great effort raised their enormous bodies up to the level of the ring. As if by signal, the cheering stopped, suddenly becoming an uneasy, shuffling silence. Two thousand spectators bowed their heads in a moment of reverence for the contest that was about to begin.

The wrestlers stripped off their kimonos and there was a spontaneous gasp from the audience at the bulk of their bodies. Both men, fed on enormous quantities of carbohydrates since their childhood, weighed more than three hundred pounds each. They stood like mountains of soft flesh, clad only in loin cloths, displaying sloping shoulders, enlarged bellies and thighs with the diameter of tree trunks.

As the audience watched, each man wove his own path around the sand-covered ring, tossing salt into the air to drive away any evil spirits that might attempt to thwart his victory. Then each took a position on the outside edge of the circle, crouched down on his haunches and stared balefully at his opponent.

Cobb smiled at the expressions on their faces. To understand the sumo wrestler, he thought, was to understand the Japanese. They looked at one another, not with hatred, but with something much worse than hatred. It was contempt, which seemed to question whether the opponent was worthy even to enter the contest. They flaunted their girth as if each pound of flesh was proof of the thoroughness of their preparation, as if preparation alone had predetermined the outcome of the contest.

The referee, in a ceremonial kimono, entered the circle and summoned the two contestants to the center. Each rose slowly, stepped carefully over the rope that rested on the floor to mark the limits of the combat area, and turned in a series of poses to the delight of his supporters. Then they walked to the center without wasting a glance on each other and took their positions, setting their feet wide apart and carefully balancing their weight to position their centers of gravity between their feet.

The arena was still with anticipation as the referee raised the fan he held in his hand. He studied the two contestants as they let their weight move forward. Then, at the instant when they would have lost balance and fallen on top of each other, he let the fan fall.

The crowd screamed in a single mad voice as the two giants launched themselves, their bodies meeting with a shock that shook the platform. Thick arms intertwined as shoulders and chests pressed together. There was a brief, twisting struggle as the bodies fought for leverage, but then the motion froze. They stood as still as statues in the center of the circle, pressing all their weight and the enormous energy of coiled muscles against each other as if each were testing his strength against a brick wall.

The struggle was internal. There were no quick moves, no vying for position, no feints to throw an opponent off balance. Instead, there were strength and weight, which had been nurtured over a lifetime, and determination, which was the heritage of centuries. All this preparation was marshaled into a single force aimed squarely at the opponent. And the force was sustained by an iron will which refused to admit the possibility of defeat.

One of the wrestlers began to weaken, the evidence plain in the trembling of his knee. As his weight was forced backward a few fractions of an inch, he slid his foot back to find a new, more favorable grounding. But at the first sign of weakness, his opponent drove forward, shifting his weight to his toes. The weakening fighter took another quick step back, but the constant force pressed against him never allowed him an instant to regain position. There was another step and still another, and suddenly his heels felt the rope that outlined the ring.

He made one last effort, crouching down quickly, and then springing up with all his force against the other man's chest. But the gesture was useless. The opponent was moving forward with a quickening pace that converted his weight to ever-increasing levels of energy. The faltering wrestler sprung up against not just a brick wall but an onrushing locomotive. In an instant he toppled backward, falling like a building onto the floor outside the rope.

The crowd launched itself into a frenzy of adulation for the victor, who gasped for breath, then raised his arms to acknowledge the salute. But Cobb stood silent with a smile traced on his face. The match, like most sumo contests, had lasted only a few seconds. But it had been decided much more quickly, at the instant the loser's knee began to wobble. Like the sumo, the Japanese pressed against you until you showed the first sign of weakness. Then they increased the pressure relentlessly until you were driven from the arena. America's industrial might had become uncertain. Its underpinnings had begun to tremble. And the Japanese, with their years of patient preparation, focused by their national will, had driven it backward until its heels were touching the edge of defeat. The outcome seemed certain.

COBB RECALLED the evening's entertainment as he showered the next morning. The moment had come to reverse the inevitable. Rather than following the sumo tradition of force against force to its ordained conclusion, he preferred the model of judo. Instead of allowing America to be muscled out of the ring, it was time for a sharp kick into the instep, and a pain-inflicting twist of the wrist. He would take the incredible momentum of Japanese girth and energy and use it against them, letting their own lead in the supercomputer race carry them head over heels across the rope and crashing to the floor in defeat.

He walked from his hotel to the headquarters of the Japanese Ministry of International Trade and Industry, where he took the elevator to the sixth-floor conference room. When he entered, his hosts were already waiting.

There were nine men, all middle-aged to elderly, except for the single youthful figure whom he recognized as Fujii. The introductions were elaborate. Each began with a bow that rose into a handshake. As soon as the hands were released, each of the Japanese presented a business card and waited patiently for Cobb to respond with his own business card. He handed over simple white cards that bore no identification other than his name, and watched the momentary confusion of his hosts.

The Japanese gestured him to a seat at the end of the table. Only after he was seated did they take their own places, arranged in order of their rank from the head of the table and down each side. The director of MITI held the place of honor, flanked by a representative of National Security and an officer of Fujii's corporation. Next to the security officer were two assistants, one charged with industrial affairs, the other assigned to relations with the United States. Next to Fujii was his company's chief of security—a man who fought with Fujii constantly over his careless attitudes toward company policy. Finally, there were secretaries on each side of the table, taking notes for the two groups represented.

"My name is John Cobb," he began. He held up one of the cards that had confused the Japanese executives. "Officially, that's all the information I'm able to provide about myself." He gestured toward the two secretaries who were transcribing his every word. "I suppose it's necessary that there be some record of our meeting, but I would respectfully ask that there be only one record kept. And I would ask that as soon as we are finished, it be turned over to your senior security officer and handled as top secret." Cobb noted the moment of embarrassed confusion as questioning looks were exchanged around the table. "I think you will all appreciate this precaution as soon as I have given you the details of my mission and outline the nature of the cooperation I'm requesting."

The MITI executive nodded, to one of the two scribes, who immediately sat up and closed the cap over his pen.

"Thank you," Cobb said to the assembly. He pushed aside the leather briefcase he had placed on the table and folded his hands in front of him.

"Officially, I'm representing the United States Department of State, assigned to service your request for cooperation in a matter of suspected industrial theft by citizens of the United States. Actually, I'm with a United States internal security service, assigned to work with the State Department on this particular matter. My immediate superior has Cabinet rank in the executive branch, which I hope indicates to all of you how seriously we are concerned about this matter.''

Heads bowed to indicate their appreciation.

''Let me briefly review the situation as it was presented to us,'' Cobb continued, ''and bring you up to date on the progress we have made so far.''

There was no objection.

''Several months ago, you apprehended an American citizen who had been using a phone-line tap to copy transmissions of computer code for a new computer that you have under development. Through documents found on his person, you were able to learn that he was an agent for Signet Corporation, an American computer company that, while not known to be a factor in the computer industry, seemed to be engaged in the development of a new line of computer products. You assumed as we did initially that Signet was stealing your technology to use in its own products.

''Naturally, we began what we thought would be a routine investigation into Signet, aimed at bringing to justice the persons responsible for violation of the laws of both of our countries. But we soon learned that Signet Corporation was not the guilty party.''

He paused to give their eyes time to widen in dismay, and then narrow again in suspicion.

''In fact,'' he continued, ''we learned that there was no such thing as Signet Corporation. It's a shell . . . a corporation with no assets, filed by fictitious shareholders. The mailing address is a post office where there was a drawer in the name of Signet Corporation, taken out by a person who used forged identification. There was no indication of who was receiving the copies of your computer data that were sent from Japan or where they were finally being delivered.

"Our only link to the tapes was the man you held prisoner and, as you have informed us, he has refused to give any information on other people who might have been involved and has had absolutely no contact with anyone outside. So, all we knew for certain was that someone was in the process of copying your secrets and transmitting them to a post office drawer in the United States, hardly the kind of information we're used to gathering in cases of this type, and certainly not the kind of results you have every right to expect from a friendly and cooperative government. I hope this gives some explanation of the delays you complained about in your communications with our State Department."

"Certainly not complaints," the MITI director began to apologize. "We were naturally concerned that the time being lost was jeopardizing the recovery of our computer data."

"Naturally," Cobb agreed. "But now I'm happy to be able to report that we have made significant progress. We have identified the man who set up Signet, and who was receiving the tapes. And we believe that, with your cooperation, we may be able to use him to discover where the tapes were to be delivered."

The Japanese leaned forward in anticipation. Cobb searched their eyes eagerly. They were hanging on his every word. So far, everything was going exactly as he had planned.

"First, the man." He opened the flap of his briefcase and slid out a thick file folder. As he spoke, he skimmed through the pages, revealing his information layer by layer.

"His name is Toole. J. P. Toole. An American citizen, forty-two years of age, with a criminal record for theft and embezzlement. Until March of this year, he was in a federal prison in Harrisburg, Pennsylvania, sentenced for stealing over one million dollars from one of our largest banks. He had taken the money by manipulating the bank's computers to create deposits in his own name.''

Of all the serious expressions around the table, only one changed. Fujii's face broke into a smile. He enjoyed the mastery of the computer literate over those who had never troubled to learn the craft.

''Toole usually works by himself,'' Cobb continued. ''But he usually works for cash. In this case, we doubt that your computer secrets would be of any value to him, unless he intended to sell them to someone else. Our conclusion is that Toole is just a small fish in this particular venture. We're betting that if we track him carefully, he'll lead us to someone very big in the computer industry. Someone who could take your ideas and put them into production immediately.''

''One of your major computer companies,'' the Japanese head of government security offered.

''Or one of yours,'' Cobb corrected. ''The use of an American postal box could simply be a diversion. While it's likely that it is an American computer company, we have no way of knowing for certain. It could even be that Toole has broken from his pattern and is stealing this information for his own interest. That's what we have to find out. We gain nothing by arresting Toole. All we would have would be two small-time thieves in your prisons, without knowing who is actually responsible for stealing your technology.''

''Arrest the son of a bitch,'' said Fujii, breaking his silence. ''Let's see who comes to claim him.''

Cobb shook his head. "No one will come to claim him. No one came to claim the other man you arrested. What we have to do is help Toole steal his secrets and then see what he does with them."

He looked at the faces staring at him. No one had registered shock at his suggestion except Fujii. Cobb zeroed in on his most important adversary.

"We have to let him steal something authentic. Remember, this man knows computers. If we give him garbage, he'll smell it immediately. He'll run and once he runs we're out of business. He's the only lead we've got and we have to use him very carefully to lead us to the people responsible for this operation. That's what you want and that's what my government is committed to."

There was silence around the table as the executives looked from one to another. But Cobb's eyes never left Fujii as he searched his face for a reaction. He didn't like what he saw.

"Absolutely not," Fujii said without a trace of emotion. The words were the product of a logical process that was running in his brain. "What we're working on is much too important to use as bait. Just arrest the son of a bitch. That will give us all the time we need to complete the project. And once it's completed and publicized, no one would dare to steal the technology. The fraud would be too obvious."

Cobb felt his plan sinking until the company's security officer took up his argument. The man turned viciously on Fujii.

"What do you know about these matters?" he demanded. "We have asked the American government for assistance and that's exactly what they are offering. They have a plan for catching and punishing the thieves who are stealing our technology. Do you think your project is the only secret that Japan has to protect? Don't you see how important it is to punish the thieves publicly, so that there won't be another attempt on our next project?''

Fujii sneered at the suggestion. ''It's the supercomputer they're after. That's the only thing we have that's worth stealing. That's what we have to protect and we won't protect it by delivering authentic code to an American embezzler.''

The faces at the table reddened in indignation at the arrogance of the statement. All of the Japanese reverted to their native language and pounced on Fujii, castigating him for his indifference to the needs of his country for industrial security.

''Mr. Fujii,'' Cobb interrupted, ''I can appreciate your concern. I've read about the importance of your work in advanced computers and, while I don't really understand the technology, I know that we're discussing extremely sensitive information. I want to assure you that your work will be completely protected.''

Fujii looked cautiously at Cobb, then at the angry faces surrounding him.

''How will he try to steal the code?'' he asked.

Cobb answered by throwing up his hands. ''We won't be sure until he makes his move. I doubt if we'll find him tapping telephone lines. They tried that already and it didn't work. But I do think that he'll make his move very soon. We know he has left the United States and he's now here in Tokyo.''

The remark had its intended effect. An expression of fear swept from face to face.

''We expect him to contact someone in your program, Mr. Fujii. Someone with access to your work who could deliver the information he needs. We would expect him to test that information for its authenticity. Perhaps steal it from two sources and check to see if the information is identical. Once he is convinced he has valid information, we would expect him to run to his employers. That's when we'll move in. We'll get Toole, but we'll also get the people who have directed this outrage."

Fujii's jaw was set in anger. Through clenched teeth he demanded, "Are you suggesting that one of my associates would betray my work?"

"Of course not," Cobb corrected. "That's exactly the problem we are addressing. If approached, you or your associates would immediately turn Toole in. And that is exactly what we can't allow to happen. What we need is for the person approached to pretend to cooperate. To deliver authentic information."

"My people would never do that," Fujii insisted. "They would be dishonored even by the suggestion."

Cobb nodded that he understood. He looked around the table for an expression of support, but found only confusion. The men appreciated Fujii's response and would not urge him to compromise his own staff. They were waiting for Cobb to offer another suggestion. Instead, he slowly began to push his files back into his briefcase.

"I'll deliver your views to the appropriate people in my government," he said. "I know they will be disappointed. We were intrigued by the fact that Toole was released from prison before his sentence was served and we suspected that perhaps some very important people might be involved in this theft."

He paused to give the scent of the bait time to fill the room. "Perhaps even some Democrats," he said with a smile. "But, of course, we certainly won't proceed without your approval and cooperation. Given the circumstances, I think that your best course is simply to arrest our Mr. Toole and end the investigation right there."

They were disappointed in the choice he had given them; exactly the reaction he was hoping for. He rose, smiled at the group, and reached out to shake the closest hand. Then he stopped suddenly, and, as if by afterthought, reopened his briefcase.

"There is one more thing I can do. I have a file on Mr. Toole that will be useful to your police." He removed the file, ran his fingers across the edges of the papers, and slipped out a large black-and-white photo.

"Here's our man," he said, and pushed Toole's image out onto the table.

Cobb kept his head turned on the photo, but from the corner of his eye he kept his attention fixed on Fujii. He saw the thin, hard mouth go suddenly slack and watched the lips part as he swallowed. While everyone else leaned forward to study the face, Fujii fell away against the back of his chair.

"Mr. Cobb," Fujii said in a voice so soft that it demanded attention, "I know this man."

Cobb snapped his face toward Fujii, letting the Japanese take in his expression of shocked surprise. He glanced at the other men, all turned dumb by the announcement. Then he slowly slumped back into his chair.

"There will be no need for me to involve any members of my staff," Fujii said, his face expressionless. "I'm the one that he's after."

"He has approached you?" Cobb asked in a whisper.

"He's using the name David Joyce. An electronics representative. He plays cards with me. He joined my poker game a few weeks ago."

"High stakes?" Cobb asked.

Fujii shook his head. "Very reasonable stakes. It's a friendly game, more to sharpen the skills than to win a great deal of money."

"And you're in debt to him," Cobb suggested.

Fujii sneered. "I don't lose at poker, Mr. Cobb. I play the game very well. In fact, he has lost a bit of money to me."

"You must play extremely well," Cobb complimented him. "Toole used to make his living winning at poker. I'd guess that he's amazed to be losing." He let his head sink thoughtfully into his hands. Then he looked up suddenly. "Is it possible that he is setting you up? Letting you win small hands so that he can turn on you and win one big hand?"

"Not at all possible," Fujii said. "I don't lose big hands. If that's what he is planning, he'll be very disappointed."

Cobb paused again as if weighing the evidence. He gestured his frustration. "I frankly don't understand what he's up to, but the fact that he's sitting at the same table with you confirms our thinking. He's going to make a move soon that will force you to give him information. Probably the code that they were trying to get by their wire tap."

"And I'm to give it to him," Fujii concluded.

Cobb nodded. "It's our best chance." He watched Fujii's eyes narrow.

"Authentic code?" Fujii asked, addressing the question as much to himself as he was to Cobb. Then he shook his head slowly. "Too risky," he concluded.

"If we lost track of the code and it got into the hands of one of the American manufacturers, it could cut our lead in half."

"But if we don't catch the people behind the theft," Cobb countered, "they'll try again. Sooner or later, something that they try will work. In fact, it's very possible that they have two or three plans running simultaneously. The best way to protect your technology is to catch the bastards who are trying to steal it."

Fujii reached for a cigarette and lit it ceremoniously as he thought. "You said this man Toole was a computer expert?" he asked.

"He knows computers," Cobb responded. "But he certainly didn't get a great deal of practice in prison."

"And the people he's working for?" Fujii wondered aloud.

"We'd have to expect them to be expert. Perhaps they're people working on a competitive program."

Fujii sneered. "There are no experts on competitive programs." Then he turned his attention from Cobb and addressed his Japanese colleagues. "I think I can minimize the risks. I can give them sections of code that will be authentic, but incomplete. What they get from me will test out perfectly, but they won't realize that important sections are missing until they assemble all the pieces." He turned back to Cobb. "By that time, perhaps you will have concluded your investigation."

"Nice work, sonny boy," Cobb rejoiced to himself. "You've just slipped the noose over your oversized head."

He smiled appreciatively at Fujii, and then at the relieved faces around the table. "Then we're agreed," he said. The Japanese looked from one to another and then nodded in unison.

They tightened the conversation to make the procedural arrangements that would be necessary. Fujii would be directed by his company's security officer who, in turn, would report to the National Security Officer and the MITI executives.

"I hope you can now appreciate," Cobb concluded, "why I asked that we not keep records of this conversation and that we treat the entire matter with the highest confidentiality. No one, absolutely no one, should know what Mr. Fujii is doing. Nor should anyone outside this room know that Mr. J. P. Toole even exists. Just one break in security, and we could end up with just Toole. It's the bigger fish that we want."

WHEN HE RETURNED TO HIS HOTEL, Cobb dialed room service and gave meticulous instructions for the preparation of his martini. He specified the gin and the exact ratio of dry vermouth. The glass should be chilled, wiped carefully with a lemon peel, and filled with ice. The martini should be served in a separate pitcher. As an afterthought, he inquired as to the heritage of the caviar, and ordered a portion with a few dry crackers. It was a shame that he had to celebrate alone. But that was the very nature of his work.

He slipped off his tie and opened the collar of his shirt. Then he picked up the hotel directory and planned his evening's entertainment.

It wouldn't be the sumo wrestlers. Tonight, the sight of two behemoths pounding tons of beef against one another simply wouldn't fit his mood. He needed to watch something fast and deceptive. He needed to see devious skill overcome self-assured strength. He turned to the listing for the judo matches. Tonight he could truly appreciate the artistry.

Across the city, Fujii typed in the commands that loaded code into his computer and began exercising his own devious skills. "Experts on competitive programs," he mocked to himself. "Let's see how expert they are."

The idea had struck him as he sat at the meeting weighing Cobb's suggestions. It was absurd to give the Americans genuine codes. No matter how little he delivered, he would still be providing insights into the supercomputer and making it easier for them to duplicate his efforts. But what if he embedded traps into the code; hidden commands that would cause the computer to make errors in logic? They had to be subtle so that they would go undetected by the American "experts." But they had to be deadly so that they could take the computer down and make it impossible for it to recover by normal procedures.

Suppose that the code did get into the hands of the "experts" on an American program. Suppose they tried to work with it—maybe even redesigned their machines to fit the software. And then their computers crashed. Even if Cobb couldn't catch the thieves, the trapped code would destroy them.

He began working on the changes, enjoying the thought of the American genius who wouldn't even begin to understand what he had done. Who would invest thousands of hours in duplicating his efforts only to have the entire project fail.

He worked quickly, growing more and more pleased with the elegance of his efforts, unaware that he was setting the board for a chess match with an American woman who had a game plan of her own.

July 15th, 11:00 P.M., Tokyo

Toole had no respect for pickpockets. But now he wished that he had cultivated his hands in the art. It was improbable enough that he would be able to get the wallet out of Shigawa's pocket without the energetic young man detecting him. But what made the job impossible was that he also had to put the wallet back.

He had picked his target randomly from the group of lab assistants leaving Fujii's laboratory and watched him cross the parking field to his car. Then he had rushed back to his apartment, dialed his computer in the Tokyo motor vehicle data base and inquired into the plate number of the automobile. After a brief pause, he had gotten back the registration record, listing all Shigawa's vital statistics, including his home address and telephone number, and the fact that he was employed as a computer programmer. The information made him a promising mark.

Next, Toole dialed into the telephone company record base and asked for billing data on Shigawa's home phone. There were frequent and prolonged late night calls to the exchange that served Fujii's lab. Toole inquired on the number and found that it was a direct line to the laboratory, listed under the company name and assigned to its Special Programs Division. When he dialed the company number, he heard the telltale response of a computer, followed by a request for his password. He had disconnected immediately.

Tonight, he had been parked near Shigawa's home when the car pulled into the driveway. He waited for over an hour until the young man reappeared, clad now in light slacks and a white, short-sleeved sports shirt. Toole followed him, taking off his own jacket and rolling up his sleeves as he drove.

He had to be careful. As a tall Caucasian, he was a poor choice for surveillance work in a population of short Orientals. So he kept a safe distance, waiting outside the bars and clubs that Shigawa window-shopped on his journey down the narrow streets of the Asakusa district. One club, a huge café with topless waitresses, had seemed safe because of the large groups of American businessmen seated at the tables. Toole had taken a place across the circular bar from Shigawa and eyed him casually as the Japanese made small talk with the hostesses.

He had no plan because he had no idea of what Shigawa's next move would be. He could only follow, keeping himself inconspicuous, and wait for an opportunity. But what kind of an opportunity? He would need the wallet, about thirty seconds to examine its contents, and then a chance to slip it back into Shigawa's pocket. And he had to do it all without arousing even a moment of suspicion.

He watched greedily as Shigawa twisted on the bar stool and took the wallet out of his pocket to pay the bill. He set it down casually on the bar as he waited for his change, ignoring it as he stole one last glance at the vibrating breasts of the dancer. In Toole's mind there flashed the image of the long poles with pincers at one end that grocers once used to pluck canned goods from the high shelves of their stores. He saw himself reaching across the bar with the pole and fastening the clamps around the wallet, then slowly swinging it across the bar area and setting it down in front of himself. The idea was ridiculous, but somehow the fantasy eased the frustration of seeing his prize only a few feet away, but being unable to reach out for it. Shigawa broke the spell as he gathered his change and pushed the billfold back into his pocket.

Toole had been so absorbed in his reverie that he had forgotten to signal for his own tab and as he fumbled with his change, Shigawa crossed the room and disappeared through the front door. Toole moved after him quickly, still trying to appear casual and avoid attracting notice. He panicked momentarily when he was unable to locate the young man in the sea of bobbing heads that jammed the street. But then he saw him crossing to the other side, skipping between the automobiles that inched their way through the crowds. Toole moved quickly down his side of the street, keeping Shigawa in sight across the tops of the cars. Then, when he saw his mark turn into one of the brightly lighted doorways, he recognized the opportunity he had been waiting for.

It was called a tea house, but artistry in the tea-making ceremony wasn't the major requirement for employment. With prostitution illegal since the American occupation, all the establishments in the red light district masqueraded as baths or tea houses, lending new meaning to the traditional entertainments of Japanese culture. Each of the small chambers would have its table set with the ceremonial utensils. But few of the patrons would pause for tea before making their way to the tatami, with its unrolled bed quilts.

Toole lingered at the doorway until Shigawa climbed the inside steps and turned at the top. Then he entered, walking softly on the steps until he could hear the male voice surrounded by female giggles. He peeked in carefully and saw Shigawa in the process of being introduced to a hostess. There were smiles and pleasantries, and the young man with his newfound escort disappeared into a hallway.

Toole entered, exchanged a few words of uneasy talk with the hostess to determine his charges, which were outrageous for tea but quite reasonable for the implied services. A moment later, he was headed down the same hallway that Shigawa had taken, on the heels of a small dark Japanese girl who looked to be more child than woman.

There were rooms on each side of the hall, with closed screens across the entrances. Toole listened carefully as he moved slowly past each of the doors. Behind the third screen to the left, he heard chatter rather than the amorous silence behind the other screens. Someone had just entered and was still engaged in the conversational preliminaries. It had to be Shigawa.

The girl stopped at the fifth room on the right, slid the screen open and stepped back to let Toole walk in ahead of her. As soon as he entered he began studying the floor plan. There was a small dressing screen to his right, elaborately carved, with hooks on the wall for hanging clothes. Near the entrance was a low table, set for tea, with cushions on either side. The tatami mat was already unrolled from the back wall, with the quilts stacked on the floor to one side. In his mind, he reversed the room to position it across the hall. He knew where Shigawa would be if he and his girl chose to use the mat and quilts. And he knew where Shigawa's trousers would be hanging with the wallet waiting in the

back pocket. They would be scarcely fifteen feet apart.
The young woman had already begun to undo the sash
of her kimono when Toole turned around. She gave
him the required shy smile and gestured toward the
screen where he could undress in privacy.

"Tea," he suggested, and the smile disappeared
from her face. In confusion, she looked from the table
to the tatami mat and then back to the table.

"Tea," Toole repeated with his most ingratiating
smile, making it more of a request than an order, and
he settled himself comfortably on one of the cushions.

Her confusion turned to resignation. Perhaps the
American simply didn't understand the true business
of the establishment. Or perhaps he had read that the
tea service was part of every Japanese social event. But
he was a cash customer and if he wanted tea then tea
was required by her tradition of sincerity. She patiently knelt down beside the table and began to spoon
the tea from its container into the porcelain pot. Then
she lighted the paper-thin wood that waited beneath the
coals.

"It will take time," she said to Toole in slowly paced
words. He smiled pleasantly, indicating that he had all
the time in the world.

But he was counting the time carefully. He didn't
want to interrupt Shigawa in the process of undressing
or while he was engaged in preliminary rituals. He had
to give him time. Yet he knew nothing of the young
man's style. Perhaps his visit was more medicinal than
recreational and, if Toole waited too long, he might
enter the chamber when Shigawa was no longer dis-
tracted.

He reached for the kettle and handed it to the young
woman. "Fresh water," he said, still smiling to make

his request sound polite. She took the kettle, stood up easily, and bowed as she left the room, drawing the screen door closed behind her.

The instant the door closed, Toole was up and leaning against it. He heard her footsteps disappear down the hallway, and then he slid the door open and crossed the deserted hallway to the room where he had heard the chattering. Now, all was silence.

With his fingertips, he slid the screen open an inch, and pressed his eye to the crack. The chamber was dark except for a single small candle burning on the table, throwing an uneven pool of light that barely reached the sleeping area. Under the quilts, there were two forms, lying quietly together. Behind the screen, visible from the doorway, a shirt and trousers hung from a hook. Shoes and socks were lying on the floor. Toole took a deep breath to flatten out his stomach, pushed the screen quietly until there was a foot of space between its edge and the wall, and slipped into the room. With his eyes fixed on the sleeping mat, he closed the door behind him. Then he eased along the wall until he was hidden behind the screen.

He froze for a moment, his breath silent, as he listened for any sound of suspicion. The lovers were still, hardly stirring in their bed. There was no sound from the hallway that he had just left. Carefully, he ran his hand up the leg of the hanging trousers and slipped his hand into the pocket. With his fingertips, he withdrew the leather wallet.

In the darkness behind the screen, he couldn't see its contents. But he could feel the hard texture of the bills as he flipped through them. There was nothing but cash in the billfold section. Next, he felt into the two sides of the fold. On one side, there was a series of plastic pages, thickened by the photos that they probably held. On the other side, there was a group of small cards. He slipped these out and held them in his hand.

The silence was suddenly broken by a sound from the bed. The girl had spoken a few words in Japanese and then laughed softly. Then there was a quiet laugh from deep within the throat of the man. They tossed as they repositioned themselves within the quilts.

Toole stepped noiselessly to the edge of the screen farthest from the bed. He held the cards out into the flickering light from the candle and began to examine them carefully, one at a time. On top were several business cards with the kanji characters arranged in neat, vertical rows. He examined both sides of each card, finding nothing but the formal printing. Next there were two credit cards, each sealed in clear plastic. He slipped past those without even examining them. Then he found what he had been looking for.

Behind the last credit card was a small piece of paper, folded once. When Toole opened it, he could see the hand-written characters that appeared faintly. There were two arabic letters, "HA," followed by a dash, two roman digits, a dash and then two final digits. He stared at them for a second until he was interrupted by the sound of footsteps in the hall. His girl was returning with the kettle filled with fresh water, probably after pausing to complain about the insane American who had been assigned to her ministries. He had taken too long.

Toole could feel his heart rate accelerating as he slipped back behind the screen and began rearranging the cards in their original order. Carefully, he slipped the packet back into its compartment in the wallet.

Now he heard hurried footsteps in the hall. The girl had discovered the empty chamber and was rushing back to find where her temporary lover had gone. With his eyes fixed on the screen, which he expected to slide open at any second, he moved the wallet back up the leg of the trousers and felt for the pocket. He jumped as his hand hit the shirt, and then watched in sudden terror as the shirt slipped off its hook and dropped to the floor. The rapid beating in his chest seized like a frozen pump.

It was the silent sound of the cloth landing, with just a few ticks as the buttons struck the hard wood. But to Toole, it sounded like an explosion. He felt himself press against the wall as he waited for a panicked reaction from the disturbed lovers, suddenly aware that their privacy had been violated. Instead, he heard a rhythmic thrashing of the quilts, followed by the quickening sound of labored breathing.

At the same time, there was a new noise in the hall outside. Two or three women were arguing, their voices animated but hushed. A screen door slid open somewhere outside the chamber. Then there was a male voice, less hushed and sounding disturbed.

A shout came from the other direction; a muffled scream of unbearable pleasure that the woman breathed professionally at exactly the right moment. From outside the room, the man's voice was becoming louder and more agitated. And a few feet away, Shigawa was now barking in unison with the girl's groans, both orchestrated in time with the rhythmic tossing of the bedding.

Toole pushed the wallet down into the pocket, his mission completed, but totally useless if he were discovered. Yet discovery seemed certain. There was no way that he could slip out of the room without moving into the arms of the crowd that was gathering in the hallway outside. And now that Shigawa and his girl had achieved their moment of ecstasy, they would quickly become aware of the disturbance. Shigawa would come for his pants.

Toole ran his options. He could rush from the room, taking his chances that the suddenness of his appearance would confuse the people outside the door. He could push quickly past them and make for the street, hoping that they would think he was a sick voyeur who got his thrills from watching and had been caught in the act. Shigawa would be outraged at the intrusion, but would have no reason to think that his wallet had been examined. Or he could wait hoping that Shigawa had the endurance for a second encounter and that the people outside would assume he had left the building and would get back to business as usual.

The decision was made for him. Past the edge of the screen, he could see Shigawa standing up from the mat, his naked body shimmering in the uneven light from the candle.

Toole stepped softly for the door and was reaching out for the screen when he noticed a red metal box fixed to the wall at the door's edge. Without an instant's hesitation he pulled down on the metal lever.

The fire alarm bell blasted through the building. Behind him, he heard Shigawa yell at the girl and heard her scream with fright. There was an eruption of shouting from the hallway and the sudden sound of running. As sliding screens began banging, Toole slammed open the screen. He jumped backward into the doorway so that he was facing into the room, looking straight at Shigawa and the girl. She was standing on one leg, facing Toole as she stepped into her pants. Shigawa had his back to the door as he struggled to untangle the underwear he had tossed off so carelessly.

"Hurry, hurry," Toole yelled, as if he had just opened the door from the outside. He slammed it closed behind him.

When he turned into the hallway, the girls were yelling into each of the chambers. Other girls rushed out, holding their kimonos before them, revealing bare backs as they turned down the hallway. Toole joined the rush out into the reception room. Without losing a step, he turned through the doorway and headed down the stairs, right on the heels of an overweight Japanese, who ran naked with his clothes bunched up under his arm.

The noisy alarm had attracted a crowd of people outside the doorway. Their faces were concerned until the naked figure emerged and then they turned to laughter at his embarrassment as he hastily dressed on the sidewalk. Because he was fully dressed, Toole wasn't part of the attraction. He passed unnoticed through the crowd that was cheering each of the undressed women who rushed into the street, then frantically struggled into her clothes. Toole walked casually to the corner and turned toward the street where he had left his car.

He could hear the clanging of fire engines approaching from the distance.

July 23rd, 11:30 A.M., Takanawa

Karen didn't recognize Toole when she entered the garden of the Sengakuji Temple at Takanawa. He was seated on a bench, his face hidden by an oversize straw hat. Two camera cases hung from straps around his neck, resting against a sports shirt of colorful pineapples and palm trees. He was wearing white trousers and canvas-topped crepe-soled shoes.

"Where did you get that outfit?" she chided when he whispered her name and beckoned her to the seat beside him. "You look like a tourist."

"Sorry," he responded in a whisper. "I was trying to look like a spy." He took in her outfit: a white long-sleeved blouse, blue slacks, and a large straw handbag that hung from her shoulder. "I liked you better in that towel you were wearing when we first met. But at least you didn't wear a gray business suit."

"I'm learning, Toole," she answered pleasantly.

"You're doing fine," he said. "I watched you walking around here for fifteen minutes. Nobody else was watching you, so I guess you weren't followed."

"Nobody else even knows I'm in Japan," Karen responded. "I really don't understand why you had me walk in and out of buildings and change cabs twice. And getting on and off the same train? I probably attracted more attention than if I had just taken a taxi straight here."

He ignored the protest, and handed her a slip of paper. "Try these access codes in your computer, I think you'll like the results."

She looked at the numbers and started to fold the paper into her purse. He grabbed her hand.

"Memorize them," he said. "Then we'll burn the paper as an offering at the temple altar."

There was a flash of exasperation in her eyes. Then in resignation she turned to the slip of paper. "Where did you get these?" she asked.

He raised his head and looked around the flower garden as he spoke. "One was taped to the bottom of a desk in a young woman's apartment. I found another after the plumbing struck a leak at a bathhouse. The third one fell into my hands during a whorehouse fire."

"Fell into your hands?" She laughed.

Toole allowed himself a self-satisfied smile. "Everyone is told never to write down access codes, but everyone writes them down. The problem is getting them without anyone knowing you've got them. So you have to create little diversions."

"You know, Toole, when this is over, I'd like you to think about a job at IAC. With you on the team, I think we'd walk away in the supercomputer race."

He shook his head under the great straw hat. "It's bullshit stuff."

"I thought you were a con man," she teased.

A full grin broke across his face. "I am," he told her. "It's a much higher calling than picking pockets. Do you know that this place is the only shrine in the world dedicated to con men. Right over there," he said, pointing to a section of the temple garden where a line of Japanese schoolchildren were standing with their teachers, "the ashes of forty-seven con men are buried and the kids come from all over Japan to pay them honor."

She looked at him skeptically as he led her toward the shrine. When they reached the area, he pulled her down next to him on an iron bench.

"The forty-seven con men were servants . . . really soldiers . . . in the service of a great warlord named Asano," he began. "Asano was from Ako and he was visiting Tokyo, then called Edo, as the guest of the shogun. The shogun's right-hand man, a despicable character named Kira, was jealous of Asano, so he tricked him into drawing his sword within the confines of the shogun's castle. Drawing the sword was a terrible violation of the sanctuary that the shogun provided in his castle, so naturally Asano's personal honor required that he forfeit his own life in retribution."

"Just for drawing his sword," Karen interrupted.

Toole nodded gravely. "Honor counted for a lot in those days," he reminded her. "Asano did the right thing. He went out into the garden and disemboweled himself, pouring out his spirit along with his guts. His castle at Ako was confiscated by the shogun, and his forty-seven warriors were banished from Edo.

"The law of the country prohibited revenge in such matters, so Kira should have felt quite safe. But he was no fool. He knew that the samurai code required the warriors to avenge their master's death. After all, the code said that a man couldn't live under the same sky with his master's killer, so Kira ordered that the forty-seven be watched closely to make sure that they weren't organizing into an army. He doubled the guard at the shogun's castle just to make sure that the warriors didn't come looking for him. And the leader of the forty-seven warriors, a man named Oishi, knew they were being watched. So he worked out a plan with his companions.

"They became con men. They pretended that they were so shattered by the loss of their master they could no longer serve as soldiers. They put away their swords and scattered across the country as idle drifters."

"And Kira fell for it," Karen said, trying to complete his thought.

"Not at first," Toole answered. "He didn't trust Oishi, and he ordered him followed and kept under close watch. Kira's spies followed Oishi to Kyoto, then Japan's major city, and kept him under round-the-clock surveillance. But Oishi knew that he was being watched. So he pretended to be exactly what Kira wanted him to be. He became a bum. The man drank all day and whored all night. Kira's men watched him disintegrate right before their eyes. One night they followed him to a pleasure palace and were absolutely revolted by the things they saw him doing with women. 'How can such an animal ever again take up the sword of a warrior?' they asked themselves."

"What was he doing?" Karen asked, eager for the details of his hedonistic revels.

"Things not fit for your virginal ears," Toole told her. "It was the same with the other warriors. Reports came to Kira from all over the country that Asano's soldiers had become the dishonored inhabitants of the foulest corners of the nation. Kira smiled in satisfaction and ordered his men back to the castle where he relaxed the guard.

"One night, a few months later, Asano's forty-seven warriors came over the wall. Kira awoke in his bedchamber to find Oishi standing over him, his armor

shiny, a glistening sword held high above his head.
'This is a dream,' he screamed. But it wasn't a dream.
It was one of the greatest cons in the history of the
world. The very last thing that Kira knew for certain
was that he had been taken. Oishi gave Kira the chance
to kill himself. But Kira didn't have the courage. So,
Oishi swung his great sword and Kira's head came off.
Oishi picked up the head by its hair and carried it to
Asano's grave. He placed it on top of Asano's body.
And then Oishi was free. He would never have to spend
another night under the same sky with his master's
killer."

Karen turned from Toole's story and looked at the
shrine that the schoolchildren were honoring. They
were lighting candles and placing them on the stone
marker.

"Oishi is buried here?" she asked.

"They all are," Toole answered. "All forty-seven of
them. You see, they were not only con men but also
honorable. By killing Kira in the shogun's palace, they,
too, had violated his sanctuary. So they left in small
groups and killed themselves. All forty-seven of them.
Their bodies were cremated and the ashes are buried
here. The shrine of forty-seven men who conned the
shogun's right-hand man into thinking they were
wastrels."

Karen watched the steady procession of children to
the monument, which was streaked with the wax of a
thousand similar honors. They stood in their school
uniforms, uncharacteristically silent for children, their
heads inclined and their black eyes shining in awe.

"Of course," he told her, "the Japanese tell the story
to their children a little differently. So the kids don't
understand that they're honoring con men. What they

get out of the story is the importance of faithfulness and duty. To them, the moral of the story is that the warriors were so respectful of their master that they sacrificed not just their lives but even their personal reputations. They made themselves nothing in order to assure the success of their master. Which," he added with a smile, "may explain why the Japanese auto worker cares more about the fit of a fender than the American who builds Chevrolets."

Inside the building, there were dozens of midday worshipers, standing in groups before the stone figures. Each had written his petition on a simple strip of white paper and was waiting his turn to drop the paper into the sacred fires. The petitions would rise with the smoke to reach the attention of the gods.

Karen held the paper with the access numbers out over the fire. But then she pulled it back and handed it to Toole.

"I can't do this," she said. "It doesn't seem right."

He took the paper. "It isn't right," he told her. "It's a rotten thing to do." Then he dropped the paper into the flames. "Just say a prayer that they don't change the access numbers."

They left the temple and walked together to the gates of the garden. When they stopped to say good-bye, she reminded Toole, "I still need the sample code. When do you think I'll have it?"

"Within a few days," he answered. "I've invited Fujii to play poker at my hotel suite tonight. He doesn't know it, but he's the only one I've invited. Tonight, I spring the trap."

"Good luck," she said.

"There's no luck to it," Toole answered. "After all, I'm a master con man."

July 23rd, 9:30 P.M., Tokyo

Toole wiped the sweat from his hands with the bar
towel, then stepped back to survey the arrangements:
a tray of glasses, a bucket of ice cubes, a large pitcher
of water, and a new bottle of Chivas Regal. There was
also a bottle of gin, some dry vermouth, olives, and
lemon peel. And there was a pot of hot coffee steaming on an electric burner. The ice water and coffee were
for Fujii, with the scotch standing by in case the young
man found himself in need of a drink. The makings of
a dry martini were an afterthought; the preparation for
a solitary celebration if the evening went the way Toole
hoped it would.

In the center of the room was the card table, with
five chairs pulled up against it. Two sealed decks of
playing cards waited in the center of the green felt table cover and a tray of colored poker chips was pushed
to one side. On a side table there was a huge stack of
small sandwiches with the crusts cut from the bread.
He doubted very much whether Fujii would be able to
work up an appetite for the sandwiches, but he wanted
the room to look as normal as possible when he entered. He intended to open with his strong suit of surprise.

Toole was seated at the table when Fujii pushed open
the door, which had been left ajar. He strode into the
room, already in the process of taking off his suit

jacket, and pulled up short when he found the room empty.

"Am I first?" he asked, sounding surprised. He was nearly fifteen minutes late for the appointed starting time.

Toole nodded, then gestured toward the bar. "Fix yourself a drink."

Fujii, now in shirt-sleeves, carried a glass of ice water back to the table, and took a seat across from Toole.

"Is everybody coming?" he asked.

"Everybody's here," Toole answered. He watched Fujii's eyes narrow.

"Just you and I?" the Japanese wondered. "That won't be much of a poker game."

Toole smiled. "It's going to be the best game you ever played," he said. He reached into his jacket pocket and tossed several sheets of paper, fastened with a clip, across the table to his adversary. "Here's my openers."

Fujii picked up the pages and saw that they were Xerox copies of checks—the checks he had received from Toole to cover the poker losses. On the copies of the backs of the checks there were deposit notations and Fujii's scrawled endorsements. He was about to toss them back to Toole when he noticed the amounts. Each thousand had been raised a hundred times, so that a $2,000 check was now a $200,000 check. Even the written statements of the amounts had been altered.

"How did you do this?" he asked curiously. So far, not a single nerve in his body had been disturbed.

"It's easy to add the zeros and the hundreds when the checks come back," Toole said, leaning over to

admire his work. "The hard part is to lose in exact
thousands so that I have the right numbers to change.
It sort of looks as if I've paid you one hell of a lot of
money, doesn't it?"

"You were able to lose an exactly predetermined
amount," Fujii said, unable to conceal his admiration. "That's incredible. I'm usually too busy counting cards to worry about the money."

"You have to watch both," Toole agreed.

Fujii nodded. "I compliment you. I could see that
you played well, but obviously you didn't want me to
see exactly how well. But I'm puzzled. What's the
purpose of all this? If you're trying to increase your tax
deductions, I would have been happy to give you a receipt for any amount you wanted."

"No," Toole contradicted. "Nothing like that. I
really wanted you to have the money."

Fujii raised his hands in bewilderment. "But what
difference do the forged checks make? My bank records will show the actual amounts."

Toole lifted some chips from the rack and pushed
them to the center of the table. "Want to bet?" he
asked. While Fujii watched, he reached back into his
pocket and withdrew a copy of a bank statement.

"You'll have to fill in the Japanese characters at the
head of the columns," Toole said. "I can't reproduce
them on my printer. But I think you'll recognize all the
entries."

"You've changed it," the Japanese said when he
looked up from the document.

"No," Toole corrected. "It's accurate. It matches all
the checks you deposited, including the ones I just
showed you. You're a very rich man, Mr. Fujii. You'll
find the total is a million dollars."

Fujii looked at the copy of the bank statement, studied it for nearly a minute, and then looked back at Toole. "Let me see if I understand this. You wrote checks to me for ten thousand dollars, but you changed them to represent one million dollars. Then you changed my bank records to indicate that I actually had deposited a million dollars."

Toole nodded.

"So, I now have one million dollars in my account."

Now Toole shook his head. "Not anymore. You did as of the close of business yesterday. But this morning you wired all that money to a numbered account in Zurich."

"A fake account," Fujii commented absently.

"Fake nothing," Toole insisted. "It's a real account, and it just received a real million dollars. I won't tell you the number, but if anyone inquires about that number, they'll find that it holds a million dollars and it's in your name. Obviously, you've been selling me something very valuable."

Fujii smiled. "I'm sure all this is leading someplace, but I honestly haven't any idea where. Exactly what is it that I've been selling you?"

"To tell you the honest truth, I really don't know," Toole answered. "But apparently it's computer secrets that are very valuable to the people I work for. I have some copies. Would you like to see them?"

"Please," Fujii said, the smile on his face growing.

Toole got up from the table and crossed to a dresser. He opened the top drawer and took out several folded stacks of computer printout. "I hope you're impressed," he said to Fujii as he dropped the printout in front of him.

For a long moment, Fujii kept his eyes fixed on Toole. Then he glanced casually down at the printout and began to flip through the pages with the fingertips of one hand.

"Where did you get this?" he finally asked.

"From my employers," Toole responded. "I have no idea where they got it. But obviously it's genuine. You seem to be impressed by it."

"It is genuine," Fujii said. "But it's also old. It won't do them much good."

"That's exactly what they said," Toole agreed. "They were hoping you might provide them with some of your more recent work. Something that would be valuable. Of course, they're willing to pay a very substantial sum."

Now Fujii took a stack of chips from the rack and began restacking them on the table as he talked. "How substantial?" he asked.

"A million in cash up front," Toole said. "And then the number of the Swiss bank account when they have everything they need. That way you can withdraw the million that's already deposited before anyone else finds out about it. All in all, two million dollars. I'm embarrassed to tell you that it's a great deal more than they're paying me."

The black lenses held Toole fixed for a long time. "You're right," he finally said. "It was an exciting game. And you just lost. I'm not interested. In fact, I'm disappointed in you—you and your employers, whoever they are. I'm going straight to our security officer just to make sure he appreciates what an honorable person I am."

He started to rise, but Toole stopped him by raising his hand. "The game's not over yet. I haven't told you how much you just lost."

Fujii looked at him cautiously, then relaxed in his chair. He took another sip of his ice water. "How much have I lost?" he asked.

"Everything," Toole said. "Because you've got all the problems of a man who just took a million-dollar payoff. But you don't have the million dollars. That sounds like a loser to me."

Fujii repeated the word "problems" as a question.

"Tomorrow morning," Toole continued, "The president of your company is going to receive a package from an honestly outraged, but unfortunately anonymous American, who is going to accuse his own people of stealing Japanese secrets. It will, of course, mention that the secrets were bought from you, at a price of one million dollars. Think of the confusion. You will have just reported that you turned down a million and here will be a letter saying that you have already accepted a million. My guess is that the president will do a little investigating. Especially when the package also contains samples of top secret code that could have come only from you or someone very close to you. And when he investigates, he's going to find the one million that was processed through your bank account into a Swiss account. Your claims are going to look like a panicked attempt to save your own ass, don't you think?"

The lenses clouded over and shifted uneasily away.

"Unless, of course, the president loves you like a son and trusts you like a wife. Does he love you like a son, Mr. Fujii? Or does he hate you? I've heard conflicting reports."

Fujii got up from the table, the confidence missing from his stride. He walked to the bar and opened the bottle of Chivas Regal.

"They can audit the bank," Fujii offered. Toole nodded. "Of course," he agreed. "The system is exact. The auditors will find the fraud after they've hand-sorted a few billion computer records. That should take them six months to a year, wouldn't you say? But they'll never find it in their computer runs. I can guarantee that fact. The records are unanimous in calling you a millionaire."

Fujii carried the scotch back to the table. "You know, I could just pick up your sleazy ass and throw it right out the window."

"You could also draw to an inside straight," Toole added. "But you're too smart for long shots. It would just look as if you'd resorted to murder to cover your tracks." He waited for a response from Fujii, but none came.

"As I see it, there are just two ways to play this hand," Toole continued. "You can go to your security officer and then to the police. Without a doubt, in the long run, you'll be exonerated. But let's say it takes a year. Hell, let's say it takes only six months. What happens to your program while your security officer keeps you locked out of the lab for six months? I understand he's not too fond of you either."

Still, there was no interruption from Fujii. "I'd guess that the program falls behind. All your wonderful work counts for nothing. And financially, I'm not even sure they'd keep you on salary during the investigation. It seems to me you end up the loser."

"And the other way to play the hand?" Fujii questioned.

"Take the money," Toole advised. "Whatever you give to my employers, it will take them months to put to use. You won't lose a step, so you'll still be first, and if you keep your nose to the grindstone, you'll always be ahead of them. You lose nothing. Christ, your company will license the technology to my employers anyway. The only difference is that instead of being under suspicion as a traitor, you'll be a wealthy man. It's the winning play!"

"But not the honorable play," Fujii added.

Toole shrugged his shoulders. "I respect your sense of honor. Truthfully, I'm not proud of myself for asking you to compromise it. But you don't have much of a choice. What happens to your honor when half the people in the country think that you're a traitor and a thief?"

Fujii downed the drink and went back to the bar for another. "How will the money be paid?" he asked while he was adding the ice cubes.

"In one-hundred-dollar bills," Toole said, still seated at the table. "The money is already here in the city. You bring me some new code and as soon as my people agree that it's genuine, you get the money. When you've delivered all the current programs, you get the account number. All in all, you can have the money and be rid of me in probably no more than two weeks."

Fujii shook his head. "It will take longer. The code has to be assembled. I could deliver it in four...maybe five installments over the next eight weeks."

"That should be acceptable," Toole answered and watched Fujii toss off the second drink.

"Where can I reach you?" Fujii asked, reaching for his jacket.

"You can't. I'll reach you."

"You're a good poker player," Fujii commented as he opened the door. "You played your cards perfectly."

Toole tipped his head to acknowledge the compliment, then watched Fujii close the door behind him.

He sat for several long minutes stacking and restacking the handful of chips without raising his eyes from the green felt table cover. He had played his hand perfectly, just as Fujii had said. He had turned his cards over one at a time, showing his opponent every possible option and then showing him how the option was blocked. There was no safe escape from the trap he had set and, with a $2 million prize, there was little reason to take risks. Fujii had played the odds, exactly as Toole had expected. And now it was time to celebrate.

He walked listlessly to the bar, selected a glass and filled it with ice cubes. Then he drained the water from the pitcher, poured in a healthy measure of gin and added a pinch of the dry vermouth. With one hand, he swirled the mixture while with the other he tossed a few olives at the glass. He carried his drink to the window where he had a commanding view of the Tokyo skyline.

The drink tasted sweet, so he returned to the bar to doctor it with an added touch of gin. He tasted it again when he returned to the window, but it still wasn't the stuff that celebrations were made of. He had won, so why wasn't he enjoying his victory? As he watched the traffic below, the drink cradled in his hands, he played back every word of the conversation and reviewed Fujii's expression as the man's composure had eroded. The evening had run perfectly according to script. Yet something was bothering him. For some reason, the sweetness of victory had gone sour and he wasn't sure why.

FUJII LEANED AGAINST THE WALL of the elevator car as he rode down to the street. Then he walked through the lobby without turning to notice the glamorous women who were flocking into the hotel in their evening attire. In the parking garage, he paid his charge and drove away from the gate without even waiting for his change. On the way home, he drove cautiously, never venturing out of his lane, never snapping the powerful car into a lower gear to rocket through the traffic as he generally did.

It wasn't until he was safely in his house, with his jacket off that he allowed himself a smile. The smile grew to laughter as he fixed himself a drink and carried it into his bedroom. There, he removed his shirt and undershirt, and began unpeeling the tape that covered the left side of his chest. From beneath the tape, he removed a small recorder, along with the wire that led to a button-sized microphone that had been taped under his necktie.

He turned on the recorder and heard his own voice ask, "Am I first?" Then he heard Toole's voice, subdued in the distance, telling him to "fix yourself a drink."

There was a shuffling sound and then his own voice asked, "Is everybody coming?" Toole's response was close and clear. "Everybody's here."

Fujii snapped off the recorder and left it on the bed as he carried his drink toward the shower. "You're right, J. P. Toole, you stupid ass," he yelled in ecstasy. "The whole Japanese government was there."

August 25th, 8:00 A.M., Nagatsuda

Kaplan was about to become a national hero, although there was some doubt as to which nation.

"He's an American," the Minister of Prisons argued, stating the obvious. "How are we honored if an American convict wins the Tokyo marathon? It would make us look ridiculous." He grunted his displeasure with the whole idea.

"But he has been reformed in a Japanese prison," the warden pointed out. "Wouldn't it be a tribute to our rehabilitation program if an American discard were to find purpose and determination in one of our correctional institutions? We were given a dissipated wreck, destroyed by selfish American values, and in just months we are able to turn him into a world-class athlete."

The minister looked suspiciously at the warden. "You're sure he can make a good showing?"

The warden almost laughed. "He's only two minutes off last year's winning time, and he's been running with a knapsack filled with rocks."

The minister still wasn't totally comfortable with the idea, but the only time his department ever received publicity was after prison breaks or in response to allegations of brutality by prison guards. He commanded an area of the government that was difficult to glamorize. He reached out and signed Kaplan's entry form.

There was no doubt that Kaplan was ready. He had been training since the first day when the guards allowed him to run on the prison grounds. What was the point of running, he had reasoned, unless he set some standard by which to measure his progress? Methodically, he had paced off the perimeter of the grounds along the inside of the wall, and calculated that exactly fifty-one laps was equal to the distance of an official marathon. Then he had begun his program.

His first attempts had been disastrous, leaving him propped against the wall, gasping for air, less than five miles from his starting point. The guards were puzzled by his seemingly pointless effort. But each day he had run; a two-mile attempt one day at his best speed, followed the next day by a more slowly paced attempt to reach his maximum distance. Then one day, several weeks after his initial failure, the guards suddenly became aware that he wasn't stopping. First one of the uniformed Japanese who walked along the top of the wall realized that he had been running for nearly two hours. His telephone call brought several off-duty guards out into the yard where they had stood together, their heads slowly turning as they watched him wind his way around them. By the end of the third hour, they sent up a cheer each time he pounded past them. Well into the fourth hour, the guards on the wall were shouting encouragement to him, and the prisoners were cheering from the windows of their cells. The prison lights were already turned on by the time he broke stride, staggered a few steps, and then dropped onto the grass. The guards rushed across the yard and supported him as he limped back toward the main building.

An hour later, his sentences still broken by gasps, he explained that he had just run the marathon distance—26 miles, 385 yards. From his pocket he produced a newspaper clipping that called for entries in the Tokyo marathon, pointed to the article and then to himself.

"You think you can finish the Tokyo marathon?" the warden asked in disbelief. Kaplan shook his head, forced his lungs to take in air, and blurted, "I think I can win the Tokyo marathon."

They had spent the night laughing at his insanity, but the next afternoon he was running again; a short distance at full speed. And, as if to drive home his determination, he was running with a knapsack on his back that he had carefully filled with twenty pounds of rocks.

Day after day they watched his efforts in awe. One day he would race madly for half an hour. The next day he would run more easily for better than three hours. Finally, he declared his intention of going the distance. He wanted to run on the roads and streets outside the prison, accompanied, of course, by guards who would ride in a car both to watch him and call out the miles. He would run the first fifteen miles wearing the extra weight of the stones. Then he would discard the knapsack and cruise the rest of the way unencumbered.

The warden, quite naturally, refused. Kaplan, he explained to his enthusiastic guards, was a criminal, and criminals were not allowed to run freely through the countryside. But the next day he stood in the yard with his guards while Kaplan dashed along the base of the wall. The agonized pounding had vanished. Kaplan ran with long, effortless strides, almost floating above the ground. And when he glanced down at his digital watch, the warden realized he was turning in five-minute miles, certainly not a pace that he could maintain throughout the entire marathon, but a time that put him well ahead of the casual running freak. He agreed to the test outside the walls.

The entire prison, inmates and guards, stood at the open gate as Kaplan placed his hands on his knees and then sprinted out into the open. "Banzai, Kaplan-san," they screamed until he disappeared over the first hill, followed closely by a pace car with a speaker mounted on the roof and gun muzzles pressed against the windows. They returned to their day's work, but only halfheartedly. Their eyes repeatedly darted to the nearest clock and then turned toward the gate for a sign of his return.

The first hour passed slowly. During the second hour, rumors began to circulate. "He's still running and he's only a few minutes behind last year's pace," started in the dining room and became, "He's running rings around last year's pace," by the time it reached the workshop. The pessimists had their competing rumors, which ranged from "he broke his ankle" to "he tried to escape and the guards shot him in the ankle." But by the end of the second hour, they were using any excuse to leave the building and wander across the yard toward the main gate. At 2 hours, 28 minutes, the previous year's winning time, they were standing five deep at the iron fence looking up at a guard who stood on top of the wall watching the road with binoculars.

"He's coming," the guard screamed, and the watchful silence had immediately exploded in frenzy. Then, over their voices, they heard the wail of a police siren. The pace car was celebrating his return with the siren turned on and all its lights flashing. They tore open the gates and saw Kaplan running toward them. He was picking up his pace, smiling easily and waving in acknowledgment of their cheers.

The warden clicked his stopwatch and read 2 hours, 33 minutes, and 14 seconds. He went to his office and picked up the application form for the marathon. Then he climbed into his car and drove straight to the office of the Ministry of Prisons.

THE DAY OF THE MARATHON ARRIVED. At 7:00 A.M. Kaplan passed by a formation of all the prison guards, wearing a warm-up suit, a gift from the warden's wife, over running shorts and shirt that the guards had bought out of their own pockets. His knapsack was slung casually over his shoulder. He bowed his respect to each guard, then reached out and shook the man's hand emotionally. "Banzai, Kaplan-san," they whispered in turn. The same ceremony was completed with the formation of inmates, some of whom were moved to tears. He was their man; a representative of all the world's losers. And he was going out to win. Then he climbed into the prison car, sitting in the front seat next to the driver. The warden was in the back, crouched uncomfortably between his wife and a uniformed guard who tried to hide a short-barreled shotgun under the flap of his jacket.

There were prison officials posted all along the marathon route, each armed with a pistol and equipped with a radio. The Minister of Prisons was waiting at the finish line, surrounded by government officials and business leaders whom he had invited for the occasion. By his side was the warden, whose radio kept them all in constant communication with the check-points along the route.

"He's off," the warden informed the group nearly a minute after the race officials had announced that the race had begun. The minister grunted, causing the warden to explain that there were over two thousand runners and that Kaplan's starting position had been well back in the pack.

"He's moving up," the warden shouted, echoing the report from the first checkpoint. "He plans to start with a fast pace to move up close to the serious contenders."

The news from the five-mile post was even more encouraging. Kaplan had blazed by only thirty seconds behind the leader. He had made up half his starting handicap in the first five miles, carrying his twenty pounds of rocks as if they were a handful of feathers.

Their spirits sank with the ten-mile report. He had given back nearly fifteen seconds to the leader. The serious contenders were bunched up at the front, eight or ten runners only a few seconds apart. There was a long gap between them and the second group, running about thirty-five seconds back. Kaplan was in the middle of a third pack and he seemed unable to break out.

"Just finishing a marathon is an extraordinary achievement," the warden offered. The minister's grunt had a decidedly bass tone.

Kaplan was a full minute behind when the lead runners entered the city at the fifteen-mile point. "He seems to be tiring," the guard reported over the radio.

"Is he still wearing the knapsack?" the warden questioned and he nodded as he listened to the affirmative answer. "You have to jettison the rocks," he said anxiously as if Kaplan could hear him. "Drop the weight and go for it."

The runners were weaving through the suburban streets at the city's southwestern edge. The leaders had broken into two groups with three running shoulder to shoulder about ten seconds ahead of a second group of three who were less than a second apart. Thirty seconds behind them came a giant of a man running with a knapsack. And to the spectators, it seemed that he was closing the gap.

The guard at the twenty-mile point was so excited that the warden could scarcely understand him. "He's only fifteen seconds behind . . . running up the heels of the second group. He's in seventh place. He's still carrying the weights."

The warden leaped into the air. "He's right behind the leader. When he drops the rocks, he'll fire into the lead." A smile shattered the ice of the minister's expression. "Good . . . good," he let himself say. Then he turned to his entourage. "He has fired into the lead. He is winning."

The leaders were running through crowded business streets only four miles from the finish when they saw him over their shoulders. Two men were running side by side, and now a huge American with a fierce mustache had joined their elite company. He seemed fresh despite the fact that he was wearing a knapsack.

"He's side by side with the leader," came a shouted voice over the radio from a checkpoint one mile later. "It's anybody's race."

"Drop the knapsack," the warden shouted. "Tell him to drop the knapsack."

"He has already turned the corner, but I think he was in the lead," came the response.

Furiously, the warden summoned the next checkpoint. "Can you see him?" he demanded.

"I can see runners approaching," came the reply.

"Tell him to get rid of the rocks. Tell him he has less than three miles to go," the warden commanded.

The minister snatched the radio from the warden's hand and yelled into it, "I command him to drop the knapsack. That's an order, do you understand!"

"He's not wearing a knapsack," came the immediate reply. "None of the leading runners is wearing a knapsack."

The minister smiled. The warden laughed out loud. There was a crackle of static. "I don't see him at all," came an incredulous voice. "He's not among the leaders. He must have fallen."

Now the warden grabbed the radio from the minister. "Of course you see him. He's in the lead," he shouted.

There was a pause. "The leaders have all gone by me. Two runners together, then three or four in a line. There's another group approaching. Kaplan isn't with them. He must have dropped out."

When the prison officials interviewed the winner, a young Japanese student who had been about two minutes behind the previous year's time, he remembered Kaplan very well.

"He was running right beside me. Then we passed a subway kiosk, and when I looked over, he was gone. I thought he must have collided with the kiosk, but I guess he didn't see it and fell down the stairs. Was he hurt?"

The officials found a Japanese woman who had been coming up the steps. "He ran right past me," she said, recalling the moment with great excitement. "A huge man. He ran down the steps and rushed straight into the men's room. I've never seen anyone in such a hurry!"

"Do you think he was planning to escape from the first moment he began training?" the warden timidly asked the Minister of Prisons, who was holding the newspaper article on one of the humorous sidebars to the marathon. The minister growled instead of answering.

"Amazing," the warden ventured, hoping to distract the minister from the grim implications of the article that the entire Ministry of Prisons was going to be investigated. "He was leading after twenty-three miles and he was carrying a sackful of rocks."

"The only rocks are the ones in your head," the minister screamed, leaping to his feet and crumpling the newspaper. "Did you check his knapsack before you and your wife drove him out of the prison gates?"

"But he always filled it with stones," the warden reasoned.

"This time he filled it with civilian clothing," the minister explained through lips that never moved, "and probably with his razor and a change of underwear."

"We'll find him," the warden promised.

"Where?" the minster asked. "Do you think he plans to enter next year's marathon?"

August 27th, 4:00 P.M., Tokyo

Smith was in Tokyo.

Kado didn't know exactly where, but through his cousin who spoke passable English, he recounted the story to Kaplan. After his arrest in the loft, he had been taken to the police station and held for questioning. His information had been even more meager than that which Kaplan had provided. He was only a messenger, hired to bring food to the abandoned pottery plant and to carry air express packages to the airport. He had no idea what Kaplan did with the food, nor did he know what happened to the packages when they reached their destination. No, there was nothing unusual about the equipment. He had been paid handsomely by an American named Smith—how should he know that it was a very common name frequently used as an alias?—and he had performed his assignments with laudable Japanese devotion. The magistrate set the date for his hearing and released him without bond.

Kado had returned to court for hearings that were repeatedly postponed. And he had been summoned over and over by National Security officials to repeat his story and look at photos that he was never able to recognize. Then one day—June 29th, he remembered—he had been climbing the steps of the Justice building on his way to still another repetition of the same questions, when he had seen him. It was Smith, coming down the steps, arm in arm with the director of

National Security, a man who made frequent appearances on Japanese television, and who had personally sat in on one of Kado's interrogations.

"He said he was working with an American corporation," Kaplan insisted to Kado's cousin, who turned and repeated the words to Kado in the baffling language. Kado's eyes widened as he listened. Then he snapped his head toward Kaplan and shook it furiously. "No. No," he managed in English and then he aimed a stream of Japanese into Kaplan's face.

"He says, 'No, that's impossible,'" the cousin translated with far less emotion. "He is sure that Smith was with Japanese security officials. He must be working for the Japanese."

Kaplan rose from the cushion and nearly tripped over the hem of the kimono that Kado's aunt had provided. He paced back and forth in the small room, ducking his head under the center support beam each time he passed it. If Smith was working for the Japanese, why had he been hired to steal Japanese secrets? And why were the computers and recorders that he had tended in the attic of the pottery factory made in America? It couldn't be. Smith, or whoever he was, was clearly an American, working for someone in the United States. But what was he doing in the company of Japanese security officials? If they knew who Smith was, then why had he been held in jail for failing to reveal Smith's identity?

As he marched back and forth, his own plans changed. Instead of bursting into the room, wherever the room might be, and killing Smith with his bare hands, he would have to take the lying bastard prisoner. Then he would beat the truth out of him; get a full confession of exactly what Smith was up to. That information would indict Smith and might even buy Kaplan his freedom.

He clasped his hands together and pulled them one against the other until he could feel the huge muscles that had grown in his arms straining against his skin. He would grab Smith by the head and lift him in the air until his toes were barely touching the floor. He would hold him, letting him hang from his neck until he realized that he was dying. Smith would beg to tell the truth and, just in the hope of escaping death, he would repeat his story to the Japanese authorities.

Kaplan was so excited by the prospect that he forgot to duck his head as he rushed back toward the table. He smashed his forehead on the supporting beam for the third time since he had arrived at Kado's house.

He had planned to escape during the marathon, although he had no idea when the opportunity might present itself. All he had known was that he had to stay with the pack until the race reached the dense inner city where even an American of his size could get lost in the crowd. He had gotten caught up in the euphoria of the race, and when he found himself challenging the leaders he had momentarily entertained visions of himself standing on the winner's platform, a laurel wreath placed on his brow. Then, as he had been about to shed the bag of rocks, he had remembered that he wasn't carrying rocks. He had realized that, moments after being in the winner's circle, he would be on his way back to prison.

The subway kiosk had appeared before him. In an instant, he had veered to his right and, without breaking stride, continued running down the steps and into the men's room. Changing to civilian clothes, he shaved his mustache and boarded a train away from the central city. Then he had switched trains, taking a route to the Shinjuku district, where he had found the small neighborhood cho that Kado had once given as his address.

But the name of the neighborhood had been of no use to him. There was no uniform pattern of street identification and the small signs of the buildings were written in kanji characters. He had been forced to walk through the cho searching for Kado or his battered truck, always aware that as an oversized American he was an easy target for the police who were bound to be searching for him.

He had finally spotted the truck nosed onto the sidewalk in front of a fish store. Then he stood in a doorway, out of sight, waiting for someone to return to the truck. Kado had come out of the store carrying a wooden box filled with fish. As the tiny Japanese had slipped the box into the cargo area, Kaplan dashed across the street, slipped into the passenger side of the cab, and crouched low. The door across from him had opened, and Kado was halfway on the seat before he noticed his companion. His first reaction had been confusion. The muscled, menacing Kaplan bore no resemblance to the soft, dissipated spy in the attic. He had turned quickly and tried to jump out of the truck. He had found himself looking into a frantic face, and suddenly recognized Kaplan.

They couldn't communicate, but Kado had quickly sized up the situation. Kaplan's exhausted appearance and anxious expression made it clear that he hadn't been set free. He was a fugitive, in full flight from the police. Kado had known that his home was well known to the authorities and that they were certainly aware he was the only friend Kaplan had in the country. Instantly, he gestured Kaplan down on the floor where he would be out of sight. Then he had backed the truck into the street and headed across the city to his cousin's home.

But even after just one day in hiding, Kaplan was explosively impatient. He was ready for action. If Smith were working for the Japanese, then sooner or later he would return to the Ministry of National Security. The building had to be watched. Every American who entered had to be followed as he left on the chance that he might be working for Smith and in the hope that he would lead them to Smith. The building was the one link he had to the American whose confession—and Kaplan would enjoy helping him to confess—could win both Kado and Kaplan their full freedom.

They formulated their plan. Kado and his cousin would spend each day near the steps to security headquarters. Since Kado could recognize Smith, his job would be to wait for the man himself to show up. His cousin would handle the task of shadowing other likely-looking Americans. Kaplan, no matter how much it pained him, would stay in hiding. It was too dangerous for him to be out in the streets, especially in the vicinity of the security building. He would emerge only when Smith had been identified and his house located.

"Then," Kaplan told his confederates, "I'll take over. And I promise you this. Once I get these hands on the son of a bitch, he'll be begging to go to the police and tell them the whole story."

He was in his element. An undercover agent stalking his prey through one of the world's great cities. He didn't need the pistol in the shoulder holster or the throwing knife strapped to his leg. He was a weapon in himself.

He jumped to his feet in his excitement and waved his fist in the faces of the two Japanese, who immediately thrust their own fists into the air and gave a cheer. Kaplan whirled around in ecstasy, cracking his head against the timber.

"Jesus Christ," he screamed in pain.

"Jesus Christ," the Japanese joined in, proud that they had learned a new battle cry.

September 29th, 10:00 A.M., Tokyo

Toole was already feeling depressed, and his first look at Karen's house only added to his gloom. It was an estate: a large stone structure with a heavy planked roof, surrounded by a concrete wall. As he drove past the iron entrance gate, he could see into the manicured gardens with a railed wooden bridge over a still pond. He thought of the small, prefabricated apartment that he lived in, bumping his knees as he squeezed between the appliances. The contrast in accommodations was further proof that he had been relegated to the outskirts of Cobb's plot.

He continued past the house and began circling the streets of the neighborhood. Many of the homes of the Meguro district were palatial, miniature villas surrounded by immaculate gardens. The walls and the dense plantings of shrubbery and trees made his task all the more difficult. There were thousands of places that would provide perfect concealment for anyone who was keeping a watch on Karen's house.

As he drove around the block, he looked for the more clumsy signs of surveillance; people waiting in parked cars, repair crews working on streets or utility lines, delivery trucks that seemed never to complete their deliveries. There were none.

Karen's greeting was all business. "You have it," she said factually as he slipped the folded computer print-out from beneath his coat. She was already absorbed in the columns of numbers as she led him through the magnificently appointed living room, decorated with Chinese art, and pushed open the screens to a large room at the back of the house. Toole stopped suddenly in the doorway. He thought he was entering the data center at Manufacturers Hanover.

"Holy shit," he said, by way of opening the conversation.

She looked up from the printout and followed his glance around the racks of computer equipment that were bolted against the delicately papered walls. "It's not all that impressive," she apologized. "It could have been built into a couple of cabinets. But they brought it into the country one piece at a time and assembled it here.

"This is the computer," she said, beginning the tour at two large frames that were packed with circuit cards. "It's a very fast, scientific mini with distributed logic. Same kind of architecture as Fujii's machine. When you buy it commercially it all comes in one box about the size of a refrigerator. Cobb actually had it disassembled in the States and shipped in card by card."

Toole nodded, even though he had no idea what he was looking at.

"I'm programming it to emulate one small section of the supercomputer—the part of the processor that looks at the instructions and decides what memory files the machine has to access to solve the problem."

He remembered reading about this function in most supercomputer designs, but he'd never appreciated the amount of processing power that the function required. "All this for just one part of the operation," he mumbled toward Karen.

"That's what I thought," she agreed, "until I began working with the first batch of code you brought me. Then I realized that I don't have nearly enough processing. I've been defining this machine as a smaller and smaller sector of the Fujii machine."

"A problem?" Toole asked.

"Not really," Karen reasoned. "Even a small screwup in this area can send the supercomputer running off in exactly the wrong direction." He nodded again.

She walked past a screened window to another pair of frames, these holding subassemblies that were wired together with thick connector straps. "This is all communications equipment," she continued. "I use the passwords you gave me to get into Fujii's lab. I can actually watch them working and copy what I need." She turned and gestured around the room. "And, of course, printers, disk drives...the whole bag of tools."

He smiled. "Imagine what I could have done to Citibank with this stuff," he allowed. "Jail, hell. They'd have given me a seat on the board."

They walked back through the living room, passed by a dining area that was set with Western style table and chairs and entered a fully appointed kitchen. Karen took two coffee mugs out of the cabinet and reached for the coffee pot.

"Have you got something stronger?" Toole asked. She brought a bottle of scotch to the table and handed him a flat, thick drinking glass. He poured a casual measure and sat staring into the amber liquid as if he were watching a fish in a bowl.

"I'm making progress," Karen continued as she sipped her coffee, "but there's still such a long way to go. I'm not just copying what Fujii is giving us. What I'm trying to do is understand the whole structure of the program. It's like learning a foreign language well enough so that you don't just translate it, but you actually think in it. If I'm going to write traps into his code, I really have to understand what I'm working with. But just when I think I know what I'm doing, I find commands that don't seem to make any sense. It's really a bitch."

Toole was still staring absently into his glass.

"The one thing I've learned is that he really is two years ahead of us," Karen said, trying another topic. "We've been working on one problem for about six months—all the addressing and subaddressing needed to identify the various memory files. There are thousands of them even in our development machine and there will be hundreds of thousands of them in a commercial system. Fujii has invented a whole new addressing system that solves the problem. It really has nothing to do with the hardware. It's a whole new theory. But it lets you do things much more simply. And it makes the whole machine look as if it's running much more quickly."

Toole had taken his first sip of the scotch, but he still wasn't making eye contact with Karen.

"If only we were working together," she mused. "Not just Fujii and me, but his company and IAC. If we were cooperating instead of competing, I think we'd have a supercomputer running right now."

"How many people could do what you're doing?" Toole interrupted.

Her eyes, looking back over the rim of her coffee cup, were suddenly puzzled. "Do what?" she asked.

"You're looking at a new computer language, and analyzing it from scraps and pieces. From the language, you're deciding what the machine must look like and then you're setting up a different machine to run just like the one that the language was written for. It's like archeology. You find a broken stone with a few characters cut into it, and from that you piece together a whole civilization. How many people understand computer languages well enough to do it?"

"Lots of people," she said, realizing that she was reddening in embarrassment over Toole's compliment.

"How many?" he persisted.

She shook her head. "How would I know? When you read the literature on some of the other supercomputer programs you realize how many truly bright people there are."

"Would anyone believe that I could do it?" Toole demanded.

She spent a moment looking thoughtful. "Well, you've done some spectacular things with microcomputers. Probably the people at that bank you violated would figure that you could do damn near anything."

"Would Fujii believe that I could do it?" Toole demanded. "Or, for that matter, would you believe that I could do it?"

"Toole," she reminded him, "this isn't really your field. Why would you expect that you should be able to..."

He cut her off. "After Fujii's computer crashes and he figures out what's happened to him, he's also going to figure out that someone besides me was fucking up his work. He's going to be absolutely positive that someone else was involved."

"I guess so," she admitted.

"And he's going to know that the 'someone' isn't just some systems analyst with a computer company or some engineer who solders wires for a living. In fact, he's going to be damn sure that it's one of a dozen or so people who are working on supercomputer programs in the United States."

She nodded. "It would have to be someone in a well-defined position. Or maybe a theorist from one of the universities."

"And how many of those are there?" he asked, returning to his original question.

"A few hundred," she finally answered, shrugging her shoulders to make the number seem unimportant. She saw his eyes narrow sternly. "Okay, maybe a few dozen. We probably are a very specialized fraternity."

He drained the glass. "That's what I was afraid of," he told her. He got up from the table and took the bottle and the glass into the living room. Then he sat staring at a pale colored fresco of a past emperor and empress of China that had been cut from its original structure and reset into the living room wall.

Hours passed and daylight vanished before he walked back into the computer room where she was working. Karen heard him behind her and, without turning her head, called him over to the display terminal that she was using.

"Do you believe that bastard?" she demanded. Toole looked over her shoulder and tried to focus on the list of computer commands that was scrolling up the display screen.

"Do I believe what?" he finally confessed.

She talked without looking up from her work. "I'm connected into Fujii's lab. One of the people whose password you borrowed is writing some corrections to the program. It's the same part of the program that you brought me last week."

"Great," he muttered sarcastically.

"It's fantastic," she corrected. "Whoever it is, he's solving the problem I was having."

There was no comment behind her.

"Remember, I told you that there were commands that didn't seem to make any sense. Well, they don't make any sense. They're not in the original code. I'm running a comparison between the code that Fujii gave you and the same code that he's running in the lab. He added those commands to the version that he gave you."

Toole tried to understand the significance of her discovery. "So?" was the most intelligent comment he could manage.

"So, the bastard put traps into the code. They're commands that look authentic. But they direct a sequence of steps in the wrong direction. I didn't understand what they were. But when you compare the version he mined with the original version, they're obvious. Fujii was thinking the same way we were. But now that I know what he's up to, it's easy to take his traps out and replace them with a few land mines of my own."

"Easy as pie," she heard him say. When she turned, he was standing over her left shoulder. He still held the glass in one hand and the bottle in the other. But now the bottle, which had been half full, was empty.

"Too easy," he continued, slurring the word "easy."

"Are you all right?" Karen asked.

"I'm great," he answered, holding up the empty bottle and examining it with disbelief. "It's all so fucking easy that I'm celebrating."

She checked the equipment to make sure that the transaction she had been watching was being copied on the disk drive. Then she turned away from the terminal to face Toole. "What's wrong?" she asked.

He shook his head slowly, then set the bottle and glass on top of the disk cabinet. He dropped into one of the straight backed chairs, thrust his hands into his pockets, and stared vacantly at the ceiling.

"It's too easy," he answered. "Everything is running too perfectly. Everyone is cooperating. It's just too goddamned wonderful."

"I think you need some coffee," Karen suggested.

He agreed. He got up from the chair and shuffled behind her into the kitchen. He stood leaning against the sink while she spooned coffee into the pot.

"I'm good at what I do," he began. "You're good at what you do and I'm good at what I do."

She suppressed a smile as she nodded her agreement. He was obviously dulled by his bout with the bottle and there wasn't any point in taking anything he said very seriously.

"In my field, you have to know how people are going to react. I mean, I'm not a highwayman, hitting people over the head and stealing their coins. What I do is create situations. Situations where people are very happy to give me their coins.''

"And I'm sure you're very good at it," she said as she brushed against him to fill the coffee pot with water.

"Very good," Toole stated as a matter of fact. "Maybe the best. So I know how people should react when they know that they're cornered. They should squirm a little. Maybe even try to fight back. Fujii's a very bright man. Not as bright as you, but still smart. Maybe one of the dozen smartest bastards in the world. He should have tried to fight back. But he didn't.''

"What could he do?" she asked, leaning against the computer beside him. "You had him trapped." Toole dismissed the suggestion with a huge sweep of his arm that nearly cost him his precarious balance.

"Threatened me with a slow death. Or maybe warned me that he was going straight to the authorities. Or maybe even tried to pass a few hundred pages of bullshit off as authentic code. It wouldn't matter what he did. It's just that he should have put some kind of pressure on me to see if I would back off. After all, he's handing me his life's work. Does it make any sense that he would just hand it over without even trying to scare me off?''

"Well," Karen reasoned, after a few moments of thought, "you were offering him a great deal of money."

"Forget the money," he said, his voice taking on an angry tone. "Would you have packaged up all IAC's secrets and delivered them to my doorstep for money? Any amount of money?"

She pursed her lips, indicating the logic of his point. "No," she admitted, "money isn't that important to me. Certainly not as important as my work."

He smiled at her. "See what I mean. And it isn't that important to Fujii. Christ, I play poker with the guy. He doesn't care about the size of the pot. All he cares about is winning. So why would he sell me his big triumph for a suitcase full of money? Why wouldn't he at least try to scare me off?"

She had no answer to the riddle he was posing.

"It was almost as if he had been expecting me to drop a bomb on him. As if he knew what I was after and was only too happy to give it to me."

"Maybe you've misjudged him," she tried.

"And why hasn't he changed the access codes?" Toole persisted.

"Because he doesn't even suspect that you've compromised them," Karen answered assuredly. "And why would he think you would be dialing into his computer when he is already giving you the code you need?"

"Do you know how many times the banks change their access codes?" Toole asked by way of an answer. "And all they're protecting is money that doesn't even belong to them. This guy is protecting his brainchild. He knows I'm in the process of stealing it, yet he hasn't taken even the simplest of precautions."

Karen watched him worry as she poured a mug of coffee and handed it to him.

"Christ, he's helping us steal it," Toole added. He looked at the coffee and then handed the mug back to her. "I really don't want this," he said. He bolted from the counter and began pacing in circles around the kitchen table.

"I'm not being watched. I keep looking over my shoulder and no one is following me. My apartment hasn't been searched. Jesus, they're not even tapping my telephone. Fujii knows who I am and exactly where to find me, and he doesn't have anybody watching me. It's as if he knows exactly what I'm up to. As if he's conning me instead of me conning him. It's all just too easy. Too fucking easy."

"It's a good plan. Why shouldn't it be going well?" she offered as consolation.

He stopped his pacing and stood unsteadily in the center of the kitchen. "Am I the con man or am I being set up?" he asked no one in particular.

"Set up by whom?" Karen demanded.

Toole looked at her helplessly, his infuriating self-confidence suddenly drained. "I don't know," he admitted. He seemed to be shrinking as he stood before her.

"Why don't you stay here tonight?" she finally said. He shook his head in response and turned absently toward the doorway. But even this simple movement upset his balance and he reached out and grasped the back of a chair.

"Stay here," she repeated, "You're too tired to drive across the city and the last thing we need is to have the police checking into your driver's license after you've taken down a traffic light."

He stared at her for a moment through unfocused eyes. Then his confused face broke into a broad grin. "I'm not too tired," he corrected, "but I am too drunk. Do you have an extra nighty?"

Karen led him to a large bedroom, unrolled a mat and began spreading the quilts. When she turned around, he had already removed his shirt and tie, and dropped them in a heap on the center of the floor. "Be careful," she teased. "I don't iron shirts."

He kicked off his shoes, then let his trousers drop in a separate pile. Clad in oversized white boxer shorts and a T-shirt, Toole slipped into the quilts. Karen watched him patiently, then picked up his clothes and began folding them. She turned off the light and started out through the doorway.

"Karen," she heard him call. She turned and saw him lying in the bed, his face turned away from her. "When are you going to be finished with the code?"

She was amazed that he was still thinking about the problems she had explained to him earlier.

"On time, I hope," she answered. "It's a very tight schedule."

Toole rolled over quickly so that he was facing her. In the dim light from the doorway she could see that his eyes were no longer confused.

"When you have the code finished, I want you to show me how to substitute it for Fujii's programs. Then I want you to get out of here."

"Why?" Karen demanded. He suddenly sounded as if he were issuing an order and her response had been immediate.

"Because there's no reason for you to stick around once you've sabotaged the code," he told her. "And because things could get dangerous right at the end."

"Out of the question," she told him abruptly. "I signed on for the full tour. Besides, if it's dangerous for me, it would be just as dangerous for you. I couldn't just walk off and leave you."

"This isn't a game, Karen," he answered softly. "I don't have the answers yet, but this thing could get very rough. I'm beginning to think that our little scheme is part of someone else's big scheme, and that somewhere along the way the plan calls for us to get crumpled up and thrown aside. I want you out of here."

"I can take care of myself," she assured him.

Toole raised up on his elbow and stared at her shadowy form, backlighted by the doorway. "No, you can't," he said factually. "Not if you don't know where the danger is coming from. And I'm not sure I'll be able to take care of you."

She took a step back into the room. "You're afraid I'm going to screw up, aren't you?" she demanded.

"No," Toole said. "I think you'll do just fine. But I'm afraid that I'm going to screw up. And I don't want to take you down with me. When this crazy scheme started, I thought that you were in over your head and you'd be a danger to everyone. Now I'm beginning to realize that I'm the one who's in over his head. I'm the danger because I think I'm in control when the truth is that someone is pulling my strings. I'm being set up for something. I can feel it in my gut and I've learned to trust my gut."

She felt a sudden chill that she recognized as fear. Slowly, Karen backed out of the room and closed the screen carefully so as not to make a sound. He was right. Of course it wasn't a game. She had become so absorbed in the mechanics of her task that she had forgotten what the task was. They were stealing secrets. Important secrets with a commercial value of billions of dollars. But even at that level, the money was of secondary importance. The real prize was national leadership in the technology that would dominate world economies. It was a prize that people would kill for.

October 14th, 8:00 P.M., Over the Pacific

Toole turned in his seat to watch the sunlit cone of Fujiyama sweep past the wing tip, looking exactly like the color photograph in his grade school geography book. The mountain was every child's symbol of Japan, sparse yet beautiful, a timeless vent for incredible energy. It was the last sight he would see for nearly thirteen hours as the plane curved a great circle across the top of the world, dropped through Canada and down into New York.

He had reserved his ticket in his fictitious name, dialing the reservation directly into the airline's computer. He had left his apartment without luggage, carrying only a light windbreaker to disguise his travel plans. All the habitual caution of stepping on and off trains, leaving taxis at the front of office buildings and claiming new cabs at the rear had been observed. When he boarded the plane, he was positive that neither Fujii nor Cobb would have any reason to suspect he had left the country.

Toole needed answers to questions he couldn't completely formulate; answers that would calm the paranoia he had begun to feel the moment Fujii turned over the first sample of supercomputer code. If they existed anywhere, he reasoned, it would be in the United States, written as electronic pulses in America's all-knowing computers.

The Americans had reduced all current knowledge to colorless binary numbers. The lives of individuals were carefully recorded in every license application, credit transaction, medical claim, and tax return that began with a space for a Social Security number. The lives of businesses were chronicled in corporate registration forms, proxy statements, quarterly reports, and financial disclosures. Every transaction etched its own precise trail of purchase orders, work orders, shipping documents, and invoices, all dutifully recorded in the computers of the company that bought and the company that sold, as well as in the digital records of all the companies that handled the shipments.

Need to know where a person was living? His credit card accounts contained his current address and phone number. Want to know where he was traveling? His driver's license number was a flawless index into the records of rental car companies. Tax records told how he was making his money. And bank and brokerage records told how he was spending it.

Corporations bared their souls in the records of the Securities and Exchange Commission. Lawyers told their secrets to the computers of the State Bar Associations. Even children admitted their academic shortcomings in the records of the college entrance services and their parents' economic shortcomings in the records of the college scholarship services. There was no fact too insignificant to escape the endless process of electronic recording.

Of course, all the information was strictly confidential, protected by privacy laws but, more significantly, protected by its own enormous volume. The facts about themselves that individuals penned in "legible block letters" onto the hundreds of forms they dutifully completed each year, were swallowed up into bubble memories and reels of magnetic tape, and rendered invisible with electronic speed. Or so the individuals assumed when they made their confessions. But, in fact, they were all carefully labeled and precisely cross-referenced, with each computer pointing directly to other computers that held still more information.

Tax records gave the numbers of bank accounts to which interest had been paid. And bank records gave the numbers of brokerage accounts in which securities were held. Auto registrations gave the numbers of insurance policies, and the applications for those policies contained a file of all other policies held with the company. Medical insurance forms pointed to hospital records and hospital records listed treatments for diseases that had never been admitted. Beginning with one simple record, a hacker with a cheap home computer could construct an ever-expanding pyramid that would compromise every financial and social fact about the life and times of an insignificant individual or a world-class corporation. Nothing was hidden. Everything was revealed.

It was time for Toole to begin constructing the pyramids to learn whom he was dealing with and what they were really up to. He was working for John Cobb, a top agent of the secret government, involved in a plot of national survival. But who was John Cobb? Was he really part of the U.S. government, or had Toole committed a cardinal error—believing what he had been told? Cobb had demonstrated his divine authority by opening the gates of a federal prison. But Mafia chieftains had walked in and out of federal prisons. And, as Watergate had demonstrated all too clearly, not everyone employed by the government had the country's interests at heart.

Who was Yamagata Fujii? A top computer theorist, of course. But whose side was he on? He was turning over Japan's most closely guarded industrial secrets with no more urging than a transparent threat and no more reward than a suitcase of money. And he could scarcely contain his joy in the process. Was he the victim? Or was he part of the plot?

Then there was the Signet Corporation, described by Cobb as simply a shell that served as a mailing address for stolen information. But who owned Signet? What was its connection to Cobb or to Fujii? And what was it going to do with computer code that only a dozen or so people in the world could even begin to understand?

He needed answers. He needed to know who was scheming, and who was being victimized. And he needed to know how. Otherwise, he was simply one cog in the machine, and cogs tended to heat up and break when the machine was running at top speed.

His gut told him he was being used. But how? As a washing machine to launder money that Signet was paying to Fujii? As a watchman, to keep Karen from inadvertently compromising a schreme she didn't understand? Or as a victim to take the fall if Cobb's house of cards should suddenly become top-heavy and unstable?

But why did he care? Why not simply fall back on one of the alternatives he had considered on his first flight to Boston? He could run. He could dial up the computers at his banks and transfer the funds he had kept from the Citibank settlement into other accounts at other banks. He could move the money to where

Cobb would never find it, write himself a new identity, and simply disappear. Let them work their complex schemes, and let the losers pay the price of failure. He could get out of it if he moved quickly, before anyone was even aware that he had left Japan.

Or, he could use the second alternative. No matter who was scheming or who was being victimized, the ultimate loser was going to be Fujii's company. He could take what he knew directly to the company and sell it for a handsome price. Then he would emerge the hero—the one honest man in a network of thieves—who had brought down a plot of international piracy. And he'd probably have a generous reward to go with the acclamation.

His problem was Karen. Toole had violated the first rule of his profession. He had become involved. Instead of using Karen, he found himself caring about her safety. His concern hung from him like an anchor, taking away his freedom to move with the currents. Run and he would leave her behind, an obvious victim, since she was one of the few people in the world who could make use of the code that Fujii was providing. Expose the plot to the Japanese and she would be one of the people he was exposing. That was why he had urged her to finish her work quickly and leave the country before Cobb's scheme reached its moment of climax. If the intricate fabric of intrigue should suddenly become unraveled, Toole thought that he might be able to take care of himself. But not if he had someone else to worry about.

But why should he worry about her? Why was Karen important to him? He had worked with dozens of women before, pretending to be involved while carefully keeping a cold separation. They had all been decent people, all honest, all talented. Most had been beautiful. Some even affectionate. It had made no difference to him. He had used them shamelessly to get information he needed about a mark. To get access codes to hidden computers. To make introductions that were essential to his schemes. They were simply pieces on the game board, significant only so long as they helped him to advance to the winner's circle. Why shouldn't he discard Karen as thoughtlessly as he had discarded all the others?

He wasn't captivated by her looks. Granted, she was a very attractive woman, but there had been others who were stunning beauties. Besides, physical appearance held no great interest for him. He had learned in his boyhood that sexual attraction had less to do with physical dimensions or the color of eyes than it did with an openness of emotions or a pattern of thoughts.

Nor was he returning any obvious expressions of concern and affection on her part. She had made it clear from the first moment he had seen her from the protection of her closet that their relationship was all business. In fact, she was a purposefully distant person, almost afraid to open herself up to another person. She seemed comfortable only when sharing herself with her infernal machines.

He wasn't even enthralled by her brilliance. True, she was one of the leading thinkers in civilization's most cerebral technology. But her mind lived in kingdoms that held no interest for him. They had nothing in common, no areas of mutual involvement that could generate even the most feeble magnetic field between them. Yet, Toole was concerned for her welfare. So concerned, that he was putting his own person at risk to protect her. And he didn't know why. His every in-

stinct told him that it was time to cut his losses and run.
Yet he knew that regardless of what he might learn in
the United States, he would return to Japan. He was
powerless to avoid the same stupid mistake that he had
made two years earlier, the one that had sent him to a
federal prison.

Then, the signs had been unmistakable. Someone at
the bank—or perhaps even the computer system itself—had noticed the withdrawals that had reduced the
balance in his phantom account by more than a million dollars. The account had been posted to a list that
required direct officer authorization for any further
transactions. His conclusion should have been obvious: simply sign off the line, forget the half-million
that was still credited to his account number, take his
profits and run. He had been perfectly aware that no
con operation could stand such scrutiny. They succeeded only because they were made to seem insignificant. They were doomed the instant the mark became
aware of their existence. His gut had warned him that
he was in trouble. But he hadn't listened. Instead, he
had walked into one of the bank's branches and presented a withdrawal slip for an officer's signature.

It was audacious, which was probably why Toole
had found it so appealing. He hadn't expected to reclaim the whole amount. But why shouldn't the bank
let him take half of it? Its records would show that the
withdrawal was amply covered, and the account had a
history of large deposits and large withdrawals. He
couldn't deposit the check in any of the banks that now
carried his accounts because that would leave a paper
trail to the rest of the money. But he could launder it
through a foreign bank that respected the confidence
of its depositors.

He had walked up to one of the teller windows and announced that he would like to make a withdrawal. Without bothering to look up, the teller had directed him to one of the banking machines in the lobby.

"I don't think it has enough money," Toole had protested meekly.

Hardly able to contain his amusement, the teller glanced at the slip. "Two hundred and twenty thousand!" he had gasped.

"I don't want to take more than I can carry," Toole explained.

It had taken the teller two tries to pick up the telephone and three attempts to dial the number of the platform officer. The platform officer's hand had reached out from behind his copy of the *Wall Street Journal* and then disappeared behind the paper with the handset of his telephone. A second later, the paper had simply fallen to the desk revealing a scrubbed young face with slicked-down hair that fixed two wide eyes directly on Toole. Then the platform officer had rushed to one of the closed doors at the back of the platform, and emerged with a middle-aged titan who had been interrupted while having his shoes shined. His trousers were still rolled up above his garters. He had looked up at Toole, who returned his confused expression with his most ingratiating smile, and then fired back into his office without closing the door. He had kicked away at the shoe-shine boy while he dialed his phone and then had done a little dance to shake down his trousers while he waited for his call to be answered.

"If you don't have the money on hand," Toole had said casually to the teller, who was still waiting for his message to reach one of the gods on the fiftieth floor, "I'll take a bank check."

The man in the office had hung up the phone, straightened his jacket, and then walked quickly across the platform toward Toole.

"Mr. Toole, how good to see you again," he had bubbled, offering a handshake that included his left arm extended to grasp Toole's elbow. "Perhaps you'll join me in my office while we're preparing your check."

Toole had sat through fifteen minutes of idle conversation, perfectly aware that he was being stalled while officials at the bank argued with their computers. Then a clerk had knocked and entered, handing a check to the officer who, in turn passed it over the desk to Toole with his best customer relations smile. Toole had nodded toward the amount and the official signature. "If all goes well," he assured the officer, "I'll be bringing twice this amount back to you in a few weeks."

"We'll look forward to it," the officer had answered him, rising and offering his hand.

Toole had crossed the lobby, conscious of the admiring gaze of the platform officer and the open-mouthed awe of the teller. "Nothing to it," he had congratulated himself. "What was there to be afraid of?"

Half-way through the revolving door he had seen the two police cruisers careen up to the curb. And as he had continued around the circle and back into the bank, he noticed the two frantic executives emerging from the elevator and running on stiff legs in his direction. He had continued again around the circle, deciding that he would be more comfortable in the custody of the policemen.

Through all his negotiations with the bank, in which money was exchanged for reductions in his sentence, he had insisted that he be allowed to keep the check. It had been taped to his wall in Harrisburg as a constant reminder of the perils of greed and as the tablet of the covenant of his faith—when in doubt, run!

Toole stepped into the darkened aisle and made his way between the twisted bodies that were struggling to find rest in the tortuous airline seats. The stewardess rushed to meet him at the service area, and swallowed a yawn as she poured liquor into a plastic replica of a brandy snifter.

"Trouble sleeping?" she asked in perfectly accented English. "May I get you a blanket or an extra pillow?"

"It's a troubled conscience," he answered in declining the courtesy. "I'm worried about my drinking."

He walked to the back of the plane and stared out through the emergency door window. There was light outside, the sun peeking over the curve of the Arctic ice cap. It was crazy; passengers pretending to pass the night forty thousand feet over a land where there was no night. All the comfortable conventions were being destroyed.

Why was he doing it? Why was he breaking the covenant and putting himself at risk for the sake of a woman who meant nothing to him? He was a con artist—maybe the very best con artist in the world. His craft demanded cold, icy detachment. Why was he so determined to become attached to another person? That was the other question that he had to answer.

Perhaps a more important question than the ones about Cobb, and Fujii, and Signet Corporation.

October 27th, 1:30 A.M., Tokyo

Fujii tapped the introductory commands into the terminal keyboard, and began the process of breathing life into the Akagi computer.

He had entered the laboratory in the early morning hours, when he was sure he would have no competition from any of his staff for control of the machine. He had shut the machine down, depriving it of the instructions and memory resources that organized its billions of circuits into a functioning computer. It was time to interrupt the long, laborious development process and put his work to the test.

Until now, he had been working with pieces. First, with the codes for simple one-step functions, then by integrating functions, with the instructions for logical routines. Each of his technicians had labored over a single sector of the system and later had helped to assemble the sectors into larger components of the computer's operation. At times, the various routines had been strapped together to test the operation of the entire computer on simple test problems. But no one in the laboratory had ever integrated all the individual efforts into the single massive system that would give the Akagi computer its breathtaking performance. Until now.

From his vantage point at the head of the program, Fujii had seen all the pieces of the puzzle as they were shaped. He alone had observed the interlocking fit of the parts into a complete panorama. He alone had actually put the puzzle together, giving his staff one simple demonstration on the warehouse problem. That was the only demonstration they would witness until after he achieved his moment of glory.

While his team members were polishing the details, he had been assembling the complete system code, gathering it on his own disks and tapes, running it through the machine and honing the edges for a precise fit. He now had assembled all the instructions the computer needed to function to its barrier-shattering potential on a real problem.

Starting with a cold system, he loaded in the machine language, which gave the component-level instructions that made electrical connections, set up electronic paths, and moved and stored pulses of information. Then he read in the higher-level language that converted simple commands into machine instructions. The Akagi computer remained mute. It now had the potential intelligence to solve any properly defined problem. But it still had no way of communicating with the outside world.

Fujii punched a series of keys and heard the disk drives begin to whirl. The operating system was loading, building bridges between the computer's brain and the peripheral devices that would enable it to see, to hear, and to speak. Finally, he entered the memory matrices, the complex algorithms that allowed the machine to decide what information it needed to solve a problem and to locate that information in its enormous storage cells with the same speed that the human brain uses to remember the name of a familiar face.

He looked up from the terminal at the computer, which had not changed its appearance throughout the entire process. It stood like a giant erector-set project; a whole city of metal frames, crossed with the light metal shelves that held the dark and silent circuit cards. In its finished form, the shelves would be tightly packaged into the familiar sheet-metal cabinets. But now the racks were stretched across the entire laboratory, tied together by thick straps of wire that linked one function to another. The processors, each of which would occupy a single circuit board in the commercial product, took up a complete seven-foot frame each. The memory matrices, actually several powerful computers dedicated to a single "look-up" function, would ultimately be fitted into one cabinet. But for the present they occupied several banks of shelves. There were a dozen storage frames holding the Akagi computer's memory files. And these, in turn, were connected to a row of disk drives that served as a library, storing information which the computer might have to retrieve to add to its on-line data banks. All this equipment waited at the ready. There were no blinking lights; no spinning reels. The only sound was the hum of the fans that pushed cooling air through the equipment frames.

Fujii paused long enough to take a deep breath. It was a moment worth savoring. In his mind he could see the deck of *Akagi* when the flight operations flag was hoisted into the pale glow of the predawn sky. He could hear the first feeble cough of a Mitsubishi Kinsei engine and smell its sulfurous exhaust. He imagined the cheer from *Akagi*'s crew as the first plane lurched forward, gathering speed into the wind and rocking itself into the air. While it was still struggling for height, the second and then the third bomber began to roll forward.

They were headed toward an uncertain battlefield, fully expecting fierce opposition and heavy losses. But they were borne aloft on two confident wings. First was their devotion to country. Second was their confidence in the meticulous thoroughness of their planning. They had tested their strategy against every eventuality and rehearsed their tactics over and over. They had even invented special torpedoes for the shallow waters in which their targets rested comfortably. There was no room for hesitation. No possibility of turning back.

Fujii forced his mind back to the present and leaned over the keyboard, entering the designation of the first problem he had prepared. The Akagi computer swallowed the facts. Then Fujii gave it the command to run the problem and watched the machine indicate that it had taken over.

At a speed approaching the theoretical limits of light, coded pulses passed back and forth from one section of the system to another, rendezvousing in temporary storage buffers as parts of the answer were assembled. Finally, all the information was gathered into one register, then written out on the screen that Fujii watched so intently.

He loaded the data for his second problem, then once again typed the run command. Again he glanced at the silent racks of circuit cards and tried to imagine the incredibly complex operations that were taking place beneath their silicon cranium. As the answers began flashing across the screen, he could feel his heartbeat rising toward the incessant beat of the com-

puter's electronic clock. His mind raced to keep up
with the process and his excitement became physical.
He realized that he was no longer seated. He was
standing up, bending over the keyboard in his anxiety
to fire more and more problems into the machine. And
he was laughing, nearly hysterically, at the instant responses that the Akagi computer was firing back.

It became a battle, his own quick mind against the
superbrain he had created. And he was nearly dizzy
with delight that the computer was winning. Problems
that he had selected for their complexity seemed to be
analyzed before they had even been read from his
problem file. Before he could even remember what answers he had expected, they were being written across
the screen.

He worked without pause for nearly an hour until he
had put all his test problems through the system. As the
final answers appeared before him, he dropped in ex-
haustion back into the chair. He was out of breath, as
if he had just finished a strenuous routine on the parallel bars. Yet he was delirious with joy. He had looked
into the world of the future and he couldn't yet begin
to describe it. Not even to himself.

He sat quietly until he could feel his heartbeat slow
down. Calmly, he walked to the disk drives and removed the disk packs containing the completed code
that he had earlier loaded into the machine. These were
his—the keys to the miraculous performance he had
just witnessed; the mind of his supercomptuer. From
this point on, he was the sole possessor of the Akagi
computer secrets. When the power of the machine was
demonstrated, he would be its only master.

There was still work for his staff. The task of loading the computer's memory with more files of facts that

it could use to solve problems would be never-ending. His company would make a fortune creating files of information to be used by its customers with the supercomputers they bought. And it would make another fortune licensing the technology so that customers could create their own memory banks for their specific applications. His associates would be well employed for the rest of their lives simply serving the endless needs of the monster they had created. But the Akagi computer would be his and his alone. He locked the disk packs in the safe in his office.

Fujii returned to the terminal and called up the programs that recognized the access codes he had assigned to his workers. Carefully, he changed the commands. It was like changing the combination to a vault or the locks to the office doors. Now no one could gain access to the system from any of the terminals in the laboratory. No one except himself could call into the system on any of the outside telephone lines.

He wrote a new series of commands that changed the structure of access codes, so any new passwords that were developed would have to conform to a different format. And there would be only one authorized password. His own.

He rose from the chair and began pacing through his laboratory, lighting a cigarette and carelessly discarding the match. His password should have some significance. The pairs of digits would represent an hour, a day, a month and a year. He wanted to fill them with a memorable moment that would serve as his access code.

Normally, it would be a trivial date, chosen because it was easy to remember. Generally, people working with computers used their birth dates, wedding dates, or some other event that was impossible to forget. But such numbers were easily compromised because they were so obvious.

He needed a date that was important to him. Something of historic significance in keeping with the historic moment he was about to create for his countrymen. Yet something obscure so that it could not be easily guessed by someone who knew his love of Japanese history.

In his mind, he turned the pages of the hundreds of volumes he had read, detailing the lives of the great shoguns who had shaped the nation. He flipped through every moment of glory in Japan's past. Twice, he started back toward the keyboard, momentarily excited by an event of conquest or victory. But each time he stopped. He was grasping for a significance even more dramatic.

Fujii was about to settle on a temporary access code; a number he could use while he reviewed his shelves of heroic texts to find the perfect numbers. Suddenly, he stopped his pacing. He turned toward his machine and stared at it, communicating his thoughts to the endless maze of wires and circuits, and then listened as if waiting for the Akagi computer to respond. He smiled slowly at the approval he was sure he heard.

Deliberately, he stepped up to the terminal and typed in the numbers he had chosen, an event no Japanese should ever forget. He shut down the system and left the laboratory.

He was surprised that it was still night. It had been late when he entered the laboratory and the experience inside had seemed to occupy a lifetime. How could he have hurtled so far into the future and returned in just a few hours?

There was still time before dawn, but he was much too excited to think of sleep. He stood at the street corner and turned from side to side, sniffing for a direction. Then he thought of the magnificent young woman who ministered to him at the exclusive bathhouse he now visited regularly. Of course! It was a special night, one that had lifted him to the top of the world. And she was the perfect creature to stand with him at the top of the world.

He leaned into the street and waved at a taxi.

November 9th, 1:00 P.M., Tokyo

Karen hardly recognized Cobb when he opened the hotel door the length of the lock chain and peered out. His precisely parted, short-cut hair was now a few shades lighter and hung in waves that reached the tops of his ears. A short beard covered his chin and his mouth. In place of the dark, English-tailored suit that he generally wore as his uniform, he was wearing a brightly colored sports shirt. The door closed and she heard the chain rattle as it was disconnected. Then it opened quickly and Cobb's arm nearly pulled her into the room.

She found herself laughing at his appearance. "Who are you supposed to be?" she said, gesturing toward his attire.

He didn't join in her amusement. Instead, he snatched the wig from the top of his head and set it, like some giant bug, on top of the coffee table. "Did you follow my instructions?" he demanded. When Karen called the drop number to ask for a meeting, Cobb had suggested a remote hotel away from the center of the city. Then he had given her precise instructions for getting there.

"To the letter," she answered in a tone that indicated she thought his instructions were ridiculous. "I changed cabs twice, walked through two hotels, and ducked in and out of two stores. In the hotels, they thought I was a street walker and I'm sure the store-keepers thought I was a shop lifter. All your damn precautions make me feel more obvious than if I had just taken a taxi straight here."

"No one could have followed you?" Cobb demanded.

"Hell, no! It was all so confusing I almost got myself lost. Do we really need all this cloak-and-dagger nonsense just to have a conversation?"

"I can't risk anyone tying us together," he said, and Karen knew it was the only explanation she was going to get. "Now, what's the crisis that made it so important for you to see me?" he asked. Cobb was talking into the blinds that he had tipped so that he could peek out into the street.

"I wasn't followed," Karen repeated. He turned and looked at her, took a moment to satisfy himself that she knew what she was talking about, then let the raised slat slip from his fingers.

"Sit down," he offered, indicating the sofa. "Can I get you a drink?" She asked for a soft drink and he returned from the kitchen with a Coke, and a tall gin and tonic for himself.

"Is that thing real?" she asked, again fighting to control her laughter as she pointed toward his beard.

He stroked the beard and shook his head. "Stage makeup," he explained. His smile showed that he finally believed she hadn't been followed. "They could have been watching either of us. I took the same precautions that you did. Now, what's our problem?"

"The access codes," Karen told him between sips of her drink. "They've all been changed. I've been working on it for over a week and I can't get into Fujii's computer. He's changed the code number structure. I generated numbers to fit the old structure and they didn't work. Now I'm inventing new password formats, but I'm not getting anywhere."

He looked puzzled. "Why would he do that? Do you think he knows that we've been talking to the computer?"

Karen had no answer, even though she had been asking herself the same question. "It's hard to say. If his staff had been checking the computer time logged against their access numbers, they would have discovered us the first time we dialed in. Someone could have noticed that his password had been used when he hadn't been talking to the machine. They could have found out. Or, it might be just a routine precaution. Maybe they change the whole access system every few months. I really don't know."

"There's another possibility," Cobb offered as he settled into a chair across from her. "According to Toole, Fujii's pattern has been to take complete control of all his programs as they neared completion. Do you think he's close enough so that he could finish his work without any help?''

"I hadn't thought of that," she admitted. "You mean he may be the only one who has a password."

"A possibility," Cobb said. "But only if he has everything he needs to complete the project. Do you think he does?''

She thought out loud. "The machine language and the compiler are ready. They've been ready for months. And I think the memory access matrices are ready. Hell, he could go on making improvements in the programs forever. But I'd guess he's in good enough shape right now to stage one hell of a dramatic demonstration. Just the pieces I've been seeing them work on are absolutely amazing."

"So then he is ready," Cobb persisted.

"For a very limited demonstration to people who don't really understand the full potential of the machine...yes. But the more memory he uses, the more dramatic his demonstration will be."

"He'll want to knock their socks off," Cobb advised. "My guess is that he'll stick to his date. He'll take a little longer to do something with the computer that will get world notice. If he's not there yet, then I wouldn't think that he would cut his assistants off the machine."

Karen shook her head as soon as she saw where Cobb's thoughts were leading. "There's no connection," she pointed out. "The memory addressing is a routine chore. He could take complete control of the computer and polish up his code all by himself. The staff could be loading memory without having access to the supercomputer. All they would need would be an ordinary minicomputer."

Cobb looked thoughtful, then drained his glass and walked back into the kitchen for a refill. When he emerged, he had another line of questions.

"How much more time do you need on the supercomputer to finish the substitute code?"

"I've got all I need," she answered. "I can finish my job right in my own house. But I should get on it once more to test what I've done. I have to be sure that when it's loaded onto Fujii's machine, it looks exactly like the original code. And then, of course, I need to be sure that I can get to his computer in the final minutes before his demonstration."

"What are your chances of developing the password?"

She threw up her hands in response. "No specific odds. My computer is generating random letters and numbers, and trying them one at a time. Eventually, we'll hit it. There's a finite limit on the number of possible letter and number combinations. But I don't know how many figures there are in the new password. I don't know how many spaces there are between figures. And I don't know how many are letters and how many are digits. If we're lucky, I could hit it tomorrow. Or it might take six months. I just don't know. I was hoping you might have a shortcut."

Cobb walked back to the window and once again tipped one of the slats in the blind. While he looked into the street he said, "We should probably have Toole steal a look at one of the staff's access numbers. If it's different, then we'll know that they've issued new passwords to everyone and we'll have to steal a new set for you. If it isn't changed, we'll know that Fujii has changed them without telling the staff. In that case, we'll have to steal it from Fujii."

She nodded her agreement. "How long will it take?"

"Probably a few days, if we can get it from a staff member. I'm not sure exactly how we could get it from Fujii. Toole can't just follow him into a bathhouse, because Fujii knows Toole."

"Can't Toole just demand it?" she asked. "Fujii gave him the code he needed."

Now it was Cobb who was shaking his head. "It wouldn't make sense to Fujii. He's already given Toole the code and gotten his money. If Toole now demands the access code then Fujii will know that we need access to his computer. It wouldn't take him very long to figure out what we were planning to do. No...if we have to get it from Fujii, we have to do it without his suspecting."

"So then I just keep trying numbers and wait to hear from Toole," she concluded.

"That's all you can do for now," Cobb agreed.

Karen shrugged her shoulders in a gesture of hopelessness. "It isn't much of a plan," she finally said.

Cobb returned to the chair opposite her, reached out and took her hands in his own. "Don't worry. We're a lot closer than I really thought we could be. One way or another, we'll get the password. You just be sure that we're ready to use it when we do."

"Okay," she agreed. She tried to stand, but Cobb was still holding her hands and wasn't yet ready to let go.

"Karen," he continued, now in a much softer and less authoritative voice, "I don't want you to worry. What I want is for you to trust me. I came into this thing with my eyes open. I knew the problems and figured our plan was a long shot at best. I think you should know that this isn't our only plan. There are other things in the works that you don't even know about. One way or the other, we're going to slow down Fujii's computer. He's not going to own the world on December seventh.''

''Another plan?'' she asked slowly, suddenly remembering Toole's warning the night he had stayed at her house. ''You mean everything I've been working on is only a part of something much bigger?''

''Much bigger,'' he agreed with a confident, even condescending smile. ''And much more important to you.'' He enjoyed the puzzled expression in her eyes. ''I want you to think about the future. When this is over, you're going to know quite a bit about Fujii's computer. Maybe as much as he knows about it himself. You'll have knowledge of nearly inestimable value. With the right support, the right backing, there's every chance you could vault into the lead in the supercomputer race. Fujii's bound to lose time trying to figure out what went wrong. Trying to put the pieces back together. You'll know exactly what went wrong. You'll know where all the pieces fit.''

''You mean we don't just derail Fujii's program,'' Karen summarized. ''The government wants me to take what I've learned back to IAC so that we can build Fujii's computer ourselves.''

''Karen,'' he said, leaning his face closer to hers, ''the government doesn't even know what we're doing here. One or two people in the government do, but officially you and I don't even exist. When we get back to the States, no one will even acknowledge that we've ever been here. That's the way it has to be. You can understand that. The United States government can't have any awareness of a plan to sabotage an important technical development in a friendly country. What we do here will never have happened. And what we learn here will belong to no one but us. We're taking the risks. Why should we take what we've learned and simply hand it over to IAC or any other company?''

She pulled her hands away and looked at him cautiously. "I'm not sure I like where I think you're heading," she finally said.

"Just think about it. Keep an open mind, at least for the present. Things are going to get quite confusing before we get to the end of this effort. You probably won't understand everything that's happening. But just trust me. I know where all this is heading and I've got every angle covered. I'm going to come out way ahead. And if you stick with me, you'll come out ahead, too. I can promise you that."

She stood up, but Cobb stood with her so that she couldn't escape between the chair and the coffee table. "After we're out of here," he continued, "there will be plenty of time to decide what to do with what we've learned about the supercomputer. But if you think about it, I'm certain you'll agree that we could be a very good team. You have unique knowledge about the biggest technological breakthrough since the computer was invented. And I have the connections to put that knowledge to work. We could be very good for one another."

He stepped back to let her pass. Then he followed her to the door. "I can't look that far ahead," she said in parting. "Right now my only concern is getting the password."

"Of course," he agreed. "We'll get the password. But remember what I've told you. And trust me. If we stick together, everything is going to be all right. In fact, much better than just all right."

She stepped out into the hall and heard the door close quickly behind her.

November 9th, 11:20 P.M., Tokyo

"Trust me."

She had heard it so many times, always from people who shouldn't be trusted. Always they talked about being a "great team" or mentioned that they could be "very good for each other." They had always been very good for themselves.

Cobb's words stayed with Karen after she left their rendezvous in the hotel. She thought of nothing else during the cab ride to her house. And she had been replaying the words as she absently programmed new patterns for random numbers into the computer and connected it to the telephone lines. Let the machine solve the puzzle of Fujii's new passwords. She was working on a puzzle of her own.

Toole's suspicions had been correct. They had thought they were masters of the plot. But Cobb had confirmed that they were part of a larger scheme; a scheme Cobb was unwilling to discuss. Were they being dangled on a string? Were they being used? Was it time to get out, as Toole had feared?

Then there was Cobb's hand-holding advice that they could both profit by combining their resources; what she would know about Fujii's supercomputer, together with his contacts who could put her knowledge to work. Clearly he was talking about walking off with the information they were stealing and putting it to private use. Selling it to someone? Or perhaps starting their own company to exploit it? She had thought she was engaged in a vital mission for the United States. Now Cobb was telling her that as far as the government was concerned she didn't exist. Who was Cobb working for? Himself, obviously. But there had to be a sponsor. Was he connected with the government? Or was that as much a part of his disguise as the ridiculous wig and the theatrical beard? She had seen fear in Toole. Now she was feeling it in herself. But what was she afraid of? Was it Cobb? Was it the uncertainty of their whole scheme? Or was it the fear that she was about to be used again?

As she tossed in her bed, she couldn't escape the memories of George Ettlinger and Pacific Microsciences.

Ettlinger had come to her at MIT, much the way Cobb had. He needed help and wondered if her contract with the university allowed time for consulting. She had been working with the new concept of microcomputers—complete processors grown into a silicon chip. The concept of using these devices to build distributed processing computers was still in the laboratory stage, a prospect that absorbed her completely. But Ettlinger had another idea. There were several companies beginning to build small personal computers, using the microcomputer processors. He needed help in developing simple software that could change these hobbyist toys into commercial products to be sold over the counter.

Karen wasn't interested, but she politely gave him the names of other academic types who, she suspected, would jump at the opportunity. "These two," she said, pointing to two of the names on the list, "do a good deal of outside work." Ettlinger had nodded, then smiled sheepishly. He recited a list of the recent consulting work for each, pointing out their abilities to confuse simple issues and collect hefty fees in the process. "You're the one I want. You're worth twice what any of these people would demand and I'm ready to pay the difference." He had mentioned the fee he had in mind—nearly a year's salary at the university for perhaps a month's work.

She was tempted and had agreed to dinner to discuss the project. But even as she arrived at the restaurant—a fish house on the Boston piers—she had been formulating the phrases of a polite refusal. It was over dinner that she had met a new and more persuasive George Ettlinger. He had come into her office in the standard salesman's attire: a dark blue suit, white shirt with obscure tie, and glistening black shoes. His hair, as she remembered it, was straight and neatly in place, arranged with the same care as the handkerchief in his jacket pocket. He had been a businessman, stating a business proposition and playing his key card when he had mentioned the size of the consulting fee. Now he wore a blazer over an open-collared knit shirt. His slacks carried a faint blue pinstripe and touched the tops of casual, tassled loafers. His hair seemed much softer and disarranged around the aviator sunglasses that were pushed up from his face. She had the impression he had just stepped off his yacht.

Karen knew it was her imagination, but he appeared taller and stronger than the man who had squeezed into the small space across the desk in her office. He was certainly better-looking. And as he led her to their table—a choice corner location that looked out on the harbor in two directions—he was certainly less the boy on an errand and much more the man in charge.

She had expected him to reemphasize the amount of the stipend and then raise it when she refused. But the new George Ettlinger never mentioned money. Instead, he sold excitement.

"You won't believe what they're doing in California," he had begun as soon as the cocktails were ordered. "Kids. I mean high school kids. They're building computers in garages. Then they're writing programs to make the damn things run. I'm thirty years old, and I go to these computer clubs they've formed and I'm the oldest guy in the building."

She had looked skeptical. She had seen the work some of the hot-shot companies in Silicon Valley were doing with microprocessors, but she had no idea of the turmoil that the small machines were causing.

"It's true," Ettlinger had insisted. "I was visiting the top research guy at a scientific minicomputer outfit, trying to get some help with a problem. He wasn't sure, but he told me he knew someone who could help. He made a phone call, talked to someone named Billy, and then wrote out an address for me on a piece of paper. I thought he was sending me to a laboratory, but when I got there it was a private house. A woman answered the door and before I could say anything, she told me 'Billy is out back.' So I walked down the driveway and coming out of the garage is Billy. He must have been all of fourteen years old. We sat down on two broken chairs, in a garage filled with circuit boards and wires, and Billy talked me through my problem in about twenty minutes. This kid builds computers. The companies give him all the parts he needs just to see what he's going to invent next!''

She found herself laughing at his contagious enthusiasm, but uncertain as to where he was leading. "If you have all this talent in California," she asked, "why are you in Massachusetts looking for help?"

"Because I'm not interested in playing games," Ettlinger answered. "There's business in these damn little computers. I want to put together an operating system that will take the micros out of the hands of the Billys and make them useful to anyone. Then I want to start writing programs to run on the operating system."

He had talked all through dinner about the economics of his scheme. All the work was up front and the investment was heavy. It might take a year to develop the operating system and then two more years to build a library of programs. But once you had them, you could duplicate them onto floppy disks for a few cents a copy. And then the copies could sell for hundreds of dollars each. "It's like building a toll bridge." He laughed. "It takes a few years to build it, but then for the next century you get to collect a dollar from everyone who goes across." After dinner, he had gone back to his toll-bridge analogy. "The problem is to build it right. That takes time and dedication. I need someone who understands theory and can translate it into product. Someone who can teach a staff of technicians to do things that have never been done before. I've asked around and I've been told that the best theoretical work was being done here. I came here and I found out that you're the rising star. That's why I need you."

"I thought you said a one-month consulting assignment," Karen had asked suspiciously.

"That's what I'm offering," Ettlinger had answered without a moment's hesitation. "I'm betting that if you get involved for one month, you'll want to stick with it."

He had led her to a maroon Porsche with California plates and driven her home. During the ride, he had switched his sale from the excitement of the new small computers to the excitement of California. "It's a totally new way of living," he had insisted. At her door, he had put together his package. "Give it a month. Just come out to California for one month. I'll show you everything that's happening in the technology and you can try the life style for yourself."

Karen laughed at the suggestion. "I can't just drop my work, give up my contacts, and move to California. I have no idea of what I'm getting into."

"Trust me," Ettlinger replied with a sincerity that was irresistible.

He hadn't exaggerated. In California, he had taken her to the walled-off section of a warehouse where five or six test benches filled with electronic equipment had been pulled into a row under the area's only string of fluorescent lights. "Running a laboratory in here violates every zoning law in California," Ettlinger warned her. "But I think the town fathers are looking the other way. Some of these garage operations could turn this area into the silicon center of the world."

She watched a single circuit card, about the size of a cutting board, running a simulated storage and retrieval problem. "What is it . . . a register?" she asked. The bearded young man in sandals who had given the demonstration laughed. "No way, babe. That's the whole system."

They had gone to another small building and watched other small computers outperform their size. Then he had taken her to a computer fair where people were giving demonstrations, examining each other's circuit layouts and trading programs by copying them onto paper disks. It had been a bewildering day.

"I know this looks crazy," Ettlinger had told her over dinner. "A year ago, all these people were working with other companies. They built computers and wrote programs as a hobby... like collecting stamps. The hit of one of the computer fairs was a kid who used a homemade computer to run his electric trains. But now it's turning into serious business. Those guys in the warehouse yesterday! Three of them are about to become millionaires. One of the New York investment banking firms has given them three million dollars. They're taking them public in a few months and they're going to raise ten."

Karen had nodded through the meal while Ettlinger described the explosion that was about to take place. Over dessert, she had raised the question that had been bothering her since the demonstration in the warehouse. "What I don't understand, George, is why you want me to get involved. All these people are way ahead of anything I've done."

"That's the problem," he had snapped back. "They're also way ahead of me. And I've got to catch up. Look, Karen, these people are tinkerers. Everything is trial and error. I don't have time for trial and error. I need someone who can look at the new chips the semiconductor guys are making and visualize the operating system that will make them as easy to use as a telephone. Then I need to start writing a library of applications in that operating system. Believe me, the programs will sell the machines . . . not the other way around. Don't you see? Once an operating system gets accepted, the hardware types will have to build machines that work with the operating system. If we get there first, we'll own this place."

She had stayed with him, traveling around the valley and talking to researchers at every level. They talked freely, with little fear of safeguarding their work. They all knew that they were on to something, but no one was quite sure what it was. "Here's what I can do, but what can anyone use it for?" seemed to be the prevailing attitude. Karen used up most of her month just finding out what it was they could do. By then, she was hooked on the assignment.

But the challenge of the work wasn't her only inducement. George Ettlinger had become part of the bargain. It shouldn't have surprised her because with all their traveling from company to company and garage to garage, and with their daily conversations that ran late into the evenings, Karen had spent more time with him than with any man she had ever known. In the beginning their relationship had been entirely professional . . . friendly and exciting, but focused on the problem she was being paid to solve. Gradually, they found themselves talking about other things; personal things that revealed themselves and showed a willingness to reveal even more of their inner feelings. He had invited her to social gatherings of friends he had made since coming to California: cocktail parties on patios that overlooked the Pacific and pool parties where the champagne was served from floating bars. He had even asked her to take on the role of hostess at one of his own parties, an invitation which she thought demonstrated that he wasn't seriously involved with anyone else. She had been dazzled by the house, built on a peninsula that extended into a pool refreshed by its own waterfall.

"Just what the hell do you do to make money while you're waiting to build your fortune?" she demanded impishly.

"Nothing right now," he answered. He explained that he had done very well with an investment banking firm in New York and had come to California to study several investment opportunities.

"I was here about a week when I called back to the firm and told them to purchase my shares. I knew I was never going back."

The following weekend, he offered a vacation, and took her on a drive through the wine country. Karen had begun the trip with a description of her ideas for an operating system, talking her technology in an un-interrupted stream. She reviewed the machines she had seen, challenged him to list the pros and cons of each, and then as he finished, she dismissed them all as irrel-evant. "It's the chips," she told him. "In six months there's going to be a new family of processors... much more powerful. And new memories with more storage. They're going to be cheaper, and they're going to be available in quantity. That's what we should work with, because once they're out, that's what all the microcomputers will use."

"So we can catch up," he said casually, as if it were of no import.

"Right," Karen nearly shouted. "While everyone else is playing around with the present generation, we'll be writing for the new generation. When the computers are there, we'll be there. Then everyone else can try to catch up.''

Ettlinger laughed. ''I was worried about this trip. I was going to use it as a three-day sales pitch to get you to stay. Sounds like you're already sold.''

''I guess I am,'' she said to herself out loud.

He had reserved two rooms at the lodge they were to stay at, but by the end of the day they both knew that one room would be enough. After a day spent tasting wines poured from wooden casks, walking through vineyards where the grapes were about to explode, and a seafood dinner on an open patio, they arrived at Karen's door.

''Got a couple of glasses?'' Ettlinger asked. He held up a bottle from the last vineyard they had visited. ''There's one more to taste.''

The next morning, lying in bed with Ettlinger still sleeping beside her, Karen had felt completely happy for the first time in her life. She had found a man who wasn't intimidated. Someone with enough self-assurance not to be threatened by her own. A man who didn't need to bring her down in order to make himself seem more important. They stayed together through the weekend, and when they returned to the valley, they stopped at her apartment just long enough for her to pick up the rest of her things.

She had gone to work, first in one of the rooms of Ettlinger's house where she could break each day for an hour of sunbathing and swimming. But within a few months, her equipment needs had outgrown the space and she needed assistants to work on pieces of the system she was creating. Ettlinger took a floor in a one-story suburban office building. As Karen entered, she saw on the door the name of the company she was now working for, Pacific Microsciences. Within four months, her staff filled the entire floor; fifteen young men and women working all day and into the night at data terminals that were connected to a bank of mini-computers.

Ettlinger remained completely attentive whenever he was in California. But his absences became more frequent as he traveled to New York to "line up the backers." Frequently, he returned with New York investment bankers in tow and Karen's work was interrupted as she spent long hours trying to explain the unexplainable to money men whose eyes glazed over the minute she began to talk.

"Why would they ever invest in something they don't even understand?" she asked Ettlinger on several occasions.

"It's all eyewash," he told her, laughing. "At least when you talk to them, they're listening to a Ph.D. from MIT. They expect to be confused. It's when they're confused by some Jesus freak in shower clogs who's carrying a box of circuits under his arm that they tighten up their wallets."

Whatever Ettlinger was telling them, it was working. The money flowed in and the work progressed beautifully. Ettlinger even got contracts from some of the microcomputer manufacturers for software that had not yet been written, to run on machines that had not yet been invented.

Then Pacific Microsciences had gone public, with Ettlinger owning the largest share and Karen holding a considerable interest. "What did these shares cost me?" she asked. Ettlinger answered with a smile. "I bought them for you," he told her. "We make a great team."

Long before they announced their system and their first line of applications programs, their work was being reviewed in the trade press. They were a hot property. New machines were being introduced with the name of Pacific Microsciences's operating system as their most important claim. Ettlinger was on the road constantly, returning to the house only for an occasional weekend. Even then, he was poor company, totally oblivious to Karen as he phoned all over the world arranging new meetings.

Karen had suggested that they redo their vacation into the wine country. "No time now," Ettlinger had responded. "We're hot and we've got to stay that way." He had spent the evening reciting the features of the new software packages that they needed "right away."

After looking at his list, Karen protested, "This is damn near a year's work. Aren't we going to be together for the next year?"

"That's four months' work," he had snapped back with no hint of humor or irony. "I've promised those programs to the dealers in four months."

She realized that she was no longer a part of his life, except as a factory to turn out the product that he needed. It didn't make sense to her. Judging by the success of the company, they had more money than they could even count. If he wanted to be with her, there was no reason for them to be spending so much time apart.

Her eyes were opened one weekday afternoon when she returned early from a conference. Ettlinger had sent her to a three-day meeting in Texas where a manufacturer wanted to discuss the technical details of a proprietary system they were developing. The meeting had broken up within hours when the company, in a flight of corporate whimsy, announced that it was abandoning the project.

Karen had been amazed to find Ettlinger's car in the driveway and had rushed into the house shouting a greeting. George emerged from the pool naked, grasping for a towel. At his heels was a startlingly developed teenage girl, also naked, who didn't have enough sense to look for a towel. Ettlinger had led Karen back into the house, demanding to know what she was doing back so early and refusing to answer her questions about the wide-eyed child who had simply jumped back into the water. He had become furious when she told him why the meeting had been canceled, yelling that the Texas company couldn't just back out of a project. He had dressed quickly, howling about lawsuits he was going to bring and then had driven off with the girl, who was nearly naked even when fully dressed. A week later, he asked Karen to move out.

Pacific Microsciences, he explained, was doing fine. She should continue to run it. He was putting his time and his money into a new venture. Their relationship? It had been basically business, he told her, admitting that they had enjoyed some good times in the sack. What had she expected? He had given her a company to run, which would pay her a healthy salary. Hell, she had to be making ten times what she was getting when he found her. Had he ever promised her that it was going to be permanent?

"You said we were a great team," Karen had protested.

"We were," George Ettlinger had answered innocently. But there were other teams that he was anxious to join. He was getting into movie production and that demanded a whole new string of contacts.

Karen had thought that the conversation had been the low point of her life until Ettlinger's lawyers had met with her and enlightened her as to the true corporate structure of Pacific Microsciences. She owned a piece of the company. But the company was just a shell that marketed the operating systems and the programs she had invented. Those were copyrighted. And George Ettlinger owned the copyrights. Money coming into Pacific Microsciences was being turned over to Ettlinger in royalty payments. Her personal assets didn't amount to much.

She had driven up to the house for one last meeting with Ettlinger, interrupting a party that mixed people in dinner jackets with people in bathing suits. George's skinny-dipping partner had been replaced by a striking young woman whom Karen had seen playing an airhead secretary in reruns of a discontinued situation comedy. She was still playing the part.

"You used me, you bastard," she screamed when he had finally separated from his admirers.

"We used each other," he answered factually. "Everybody uses everybody. I'm just better at it than most people."

He offered her a drink and turned back to his guests, leaving her standing alone almost as an object of ridicule. On her way out of the driveway, she had swung her car wide, tearing the front fender off his Porsche.

"Trust me," Cobb had said. As she punched her pillow trying desperately to find sleep, she knew that she wasn't about to trust anyone. Particularly someone who promised that they would "make a great team." That "they would be good for each other." She trusted only herself. And she would find her own answers. If things got messy at the end, she would find her own way out. It was time to get ready to fight back. Only she had no idea what it was that she would be fighting.

November 10th, 8:00 A.M., Tokyo

Toole was sitting Buddha-like at the foot of her bed when Karen awoke. She tried to blink away his presence. Then her surprise gave way to outrage at his audacity.

"How the hell did you get in here?" she demanded, sitting straight up with no regard for the revealing disarray of her nightgown.

He held up the nail file he had been using on his fingers. "I have a key," he answered simply.

Karen bounded up from the bed and threw on the robe she had draped over a chair. "Jesus, is there anything illegal you're not good at? Picking pockets...dealing from the bottom...breaking into computers, And now breaking into bedrooms. You're just a goddamned wonder!"

He knew from the tone of her voice that she wasn't paying him a compliment. "I guess you could call me a generalist," he allowed as he rolled off the bed. "Get dressed. I'll put the coffee on. We have to talk."

Karen wanted a bath, but she knew that Toole would walk in and sit on the edge of the tub. She settled for a wet cloth to wipe the sleep from her face and a quick pass with a toothbrush. When she looked up, she was shocked at her own pale color and the redness of her eyes. Then she remembered the hours she had spent tossing over Cobb's comments and the memories of George Ettlinger they had invoked. She fumbled through the bathroom cabinet for a bottle of liquid makeup, then found a lipstick that was lighter than the shade she wanted. She wasted another minute running a brush through her hair. When she reached the kitchen, Toole was in the process of pouring the cof- fee.

"I'm sorry for biting your head off," she began. "I had a rough night." She let Toole assume that she was talking about problems with the access codes.

"It won't get any easier," he responded. He reached into his pocket and unfolded a piece of paper. "I lifted this last night. It's from one of Fujii's people and I think it's the same number I got from him last month. They haven't changed to new codes. Fujii has just canceled the old ones. I think he's cut his own people off the machine."

"Then he's ready," she said, glancing at the paper and confirming with a nod of her head that it was in- deed one of the earlier numbers she had been using.

Toole concentrated on stirring his coffee. "He's ready and we can't get into the computer to stop him. I think it's time for us to head for home."

"Not yet," she shot back. "There's still a chance that I can generate the number. My computer is turn- ing out alphanumeric combinations faster than you can blink. The problem is the time it takes to transmit the numbers and wait for a response. I'm only getting to try about five numbers a minute. At that rate, I'll be at it all year."

"It's a long shot at best," he told her. "Back in the States there are hundreds of hackers who sell phone numbers and passwords. I can get into anything. But I don't know anyone here."

"I've still got to try," Karen concluded, "as long as there's a chance."

"Let me try," Toole said. "Show me how you're doing it, and show me what to do if I'm able to get into Fujii's machine. Then you get yourself out of here. There's no reason for you to stick around."

"Why?" she asked suspiciously, her eyes narrowing.

He shrugged. "Why not? You've done all that you can."

"Why do you want me out of here?" Karen demanded. Toole was startled at the vehemence of her attack. Then he felt his own anger rising.

"Don't ask. Just take my word for it. Pack your things and get out of here. Today, if you can make it."

"Just trust you," she snapped, her voice rising. "Don't ask for explanations. Don't weigh the facts and make up my own mind. Just trust you. Is that it?"

"Look, I'm only trying to protect you."

The comment didn't satisfy her. It seemed only to raise the fire under what was rapidly becoming rage.

"Who asked you to protect me? Do you think I'm some kind of simpleton who needs a keeper? First Cobb says 'trust me.' Now you want to watch over me. Well, I'll tell you what I want. I want some answers. I want to know what in God's name is going on around here. I was the one who decided I wanted to be in on this raid. And I'll be the one who decides when I should get out. I don't have to trust anyone. Not Cobb. Not you. So if you have some information for me, let's have it. If you don't, then finish your coffee and get out of here, because I have work to do."

She jumped up from the table, hitting the leg with her knee. Coffee splashed out of the cups, some landing in a handprint pattern on the front of Toole's shirt. He looked down at the spreading stain, then back up at Karen.

"Could I have a second cup?" he asked impishly.

"Get it yourself," she told him.

Toole followed her into the computer room where she had slammed herself into a chair in front of the terminal. She was staring at the blank screen, trying to decide what to do first.

"I was back in the States," he began again, settling into a chair next to hers and joining her in focusing his attention on the lifeless tube. "I had a lot of questions about what was happening to our little scheme. I wanted to know why everything seemed to be so easy."

"So," she said, as a way of telling him to continue without admitting her interest.

"I got the answers," he said. She turned her face toward his. The redness of her eyes was even more pronounced.

"First, I looked up our associate, John Cobb. Officially he's with the Justice Department, assigned to the investigation of industrial espionage involving foreign countries. Officially, he's not stealing from anyone. His job...and he gets paid modestly for it every two weeks...is to catch people who do steal secrets from foreign countries. Pretty nice cover, don't you think?"

"He's a spy! A secret agent!" Karen reminded Toole. "What did you expect? To find that he was fully vested under a pension plan for secret agents?"

Toole nodded. "Right. There's no surprise in the fact that our friend has a convincing disguise. If he gets caught with his hand in the cookie jar, all he has to do is say he was looking for someone else's hand in the cookie jar. I'd like to have that kind of cover myself. But you know what. You and I aren't listed as working with the Justice Department. We earn our bread elsewhere."

He recognized a sparkle of interest.

"We're working for Signet Corporation. You know the shell that was 'only a mail drop'? Well, it has employees. A lot of people who, as far as I could learn, don't even exist. But there are two employees who do exist. Who draw regular salaries. Whose paychecks are docked for withholding taxes and Social Security." With his thumb, Toole indicated himself. Then he pointed his index finger at Karen. "Officially, we work for a company that's under investigation for industrial espionage. Cobb doesn't. Just you and me."

Karen shook her head. "That won't hold up. I work for IAC and I can prove it."

"That's what I thought. So I looked up your records at IAC."

She leaned toward him expectantly.

"You left them back in April. There's a record of your exit interview. You told them you were going to join an outfit called Signet Corporation. You even cashed in your IAC stock." Her expression went to shock.

"I thought you might be surprised." Toole continued. "You'll also be surprised at the size of your bank account. You deposited the money from the stock sale. And Signet has been depositing your salary. You make a hell of a lot more than Cobb's modest stipend as a civil servant.

"Next, I looked up my own records. Obviously, I wasn't expecting to see that I was out on special assignment to the U.S. Government. But then I really wasn't expecting to learn that my sentence had been reduced for good behavior. Christ, there was even a record of the hearing. My comments about the effectiveness of the federal prison system are very touching. I sound like Patrick Henry and Thomas Paine rolled into one!''

"And when you were released . . .?'' she asked.

"Guess where I went to work?'' he answered.

"Signet Corporation,'' she said with no question in her tone.

"Bingo,'' Toole said without smiling.

Karen walked back into the kitchen, took a fresh cup and filled it with coffee. Toole followed her.

"Why?'' she asked in a whisper.

Toole went to the refrigerator and took out some eggs. He talked while he was setting a skillet on top of the stove.

"I'm not sure,'' he answered. "There are a couple of possibilities and neither of them is very good.''

She watched him crack the eggs into the pan with a quick snap of his wrist. "I like mine over light,'' she said as she took dishes from the shelf and began setting the table.

"Suppose this whole thing falls apart,'' Toole continued. "Suppose the Japanese catch us. All Cobb has to do is say that he was hot on our trail. He congratulates the Japanese for beating him to us. Obviously we're crooks. Our records show we're working for a crooked company. And his records shows he was trying to catch us. He gets a citation from the Japanese government and we get to go to prison. Japanese-American friendship is reaffirmed.''

She stood with the knives and forks in her hand reviewing what she had just heard. "Wouldn't the Japanese be upset that an American government agent had been snooping around in their country without their knowing about it?"

He nodded. "Which means that he would have to be working with the Japanese. Not bad, huh? He pretends he's on their side so that they help him steal their secrets. And at the same time, he's building his own cover in case we get caught. That would certainly explain why Fujii is being so damned cooperative. He thinks he's in on the scheme to catch us."

She shook her head as she continued setting the silverware. "It's too devious. I just don't believe that the U.S. government would set out to screw two of its own citizens."

"Three," he answered, flipping her egg into the air and catching it in the skillet as it turned. "The Japanese have already caught one American who was associated with Signet. The guy who stole that original code we saw back in California. Some lunatic named Kaplan. According to his records he was dismissed from the CIA for activities detrimental to the integrity of the service. He's in a Japanese jail and no one has lifted a finger to spring him."

"What else could it be?" Karen asked. Toole's first scenario made sense but its implications were too frightening.

"Maybe Cobb is exactly what he's supposed to be," Toole offered. He crossed to the table and slipped the eggs onto the plates. Then he went back to the stove to refill his coffee cup. "It's possible that someone else is stealing Japanese computer secrets...someone that this guy Kaplan was working with. Cobb could be working legitimately with the Japanese. In that case, all we're doing is helping him get inside Fujii's operation so that they can find out if anyone in Fujii's company is selling secret information. That would also explain why Fujii is cooperating so readily.''

"But why would they need us?" she wondered.

"Simply as a cover. Someone Cobb could pretend to be investigating while he was digging for the real crooks. All we'd be is a diversion.''

Karen pointed with her fork at the plate. "These are good," she said with obvious surprise.

"You learn when you spend a lot of time by yourself," Toole said. Then he continued his monologue. "The point is that no matter what's going on, you and I are being lied to. We don't know why we're here or how we fit in. And that's dangerous. That's why I think you should pack up and get out. Right now.''

"And go where?" she asked. "Back to Signet . . . if there is a Signet?"

"Go back to IAC," he advised her. "Once they get over the shock of seeing you walk through the door, they'll change all your records. They'll make it look as if you had never left. No one knows you've been here. No one except Cobb and William Howard, and I don't think either of them is in a position to make an issue out of it. Then if this scheme . . . whatever it is . . . runs into problems, you're not involved. You're safe.''

Karen picked up the dishes and carried them to the sink. Toole's eyes followed her as he waited for an answer. It became obvious that she hadn't yet made up her mind.

"Please," he finally begged. "Get out now."

She abandoned the distraction of her domestic chores, turned full face to Toole and looked him in the eye until he began to feel uneasy under her glance.

"There's one more piece of information I need and I want a straight answer. Why did you come back?"

He looked puzzled at the question.

"You were in the United States. You found out that we were being lied to and you guessed that we might be the victims of this scheme. You knew that the best thing we could do was get out. For God's sake, you were already out! All you had to do was disappear. You're smart. You could have had a new identity in an hour. They never would have found you even if they decided to look."

He nodded. Everything she was saying was true.

"So why did you come back and put yourself in danger?"

"I don't know," he tried. There was no conviction in his voice or manner.

"What else did you find out in the United States?" Karen demanded. "You learned something else. Something you're not telling me. Something that brought you back. What was it?"

Toole looked down at the bare tablecloth. "That I cared what happened to you," he admitted. When he looked up, she was still staring at him. "Christ," he said, jumping out of the chair, the confident bravado returning to his voice, "I can't just leave you here. You don't know what you're involved in."

"No, Toole," Karen said confidently, "you're the one who doesn't know what he's involved in. You're breaking your cardinal rule. You're getting involved with one of your marks. I'm not going to let you do this."

"What are you talking about?" he protested. "What was I supposed to do? Just walk away and let these bastards fuck up your life?"

"Remember when we first met," Karen continued. "In my bedroom at the California house. You said you didn't want to be tied to an amateur." His expression showed that he remembered. "Well, that's what you're doing now. You're getting tied up with an amateur. It could get you hurt. Maybe even killed. I'm not going to let you do it."

"Will you get out?" he said with a hint of desperation in his voice.

"Will you?" she answered.

He stared at her. She knew him better than he knew himself. "No," he told her softly. "I'm not going into hiding for the rest of my life. I'm going to see this through."

Karen turned back to the dishes that waited in the sink. "If you'll take that shirt off," she said, "I'll try to get the coffee stain out. It makes you look ridiculous."

He knew that she was right. As he sat in his undershirt watching the computer try one password after another he admitted to himself that he was involved with an amateur. Over the next few weeks, Cobb's scheme would play itself out. It would get dangerous. And, as she had said, he could get himself hurt. Maybe even killed. His safety was in his ability to maneuver—to work with his wits as he had always done in the past. But now he wasn't just watching out for himself. He cared what happened to Karen. And in his caring, he lost his maneuverability. He was putting himself in jeopardy and he felt powerless to avoid it.

He heard Karen come into the room behind him. When he turned she handed him his shirt. "This is never going to make it," Toole said, indicating the laborious process by which the computer was attempting to develop the password. "You probably don't even have the right format."

"I know," Karen answered. "We need help. And the only person who can help us is Fujii. You've got to introduce me to him."

Toole was too shocked to respond.

"It's the only way," Karen continued, filling the unexpected silence. "If I just knew the guy...if I could just spend some time with him...I'd have a much better chance of figuring out what kind of a password he'd be apt to use. Or maybe I could even find it. If he's like the rest of us, it's a number that's very important to him...something he knows he could never forget. Or if it's a truly random number, then he has a record of it somewhere. Probably right in his house taped to the bottom of his desk."

"No way," Toole answered forcefully. "That's the craziest thing I've ever heard."

"It's better than just sitting here watching the computer grind out numbers," Karen countered. "We can let the machine take that approach on its own. Meanwhile I can get to know Fujii...learn how he thinks. It might work."

"Out of the question," he said. "Jesus Christ, the only protection you have is that none of the Japanese knows you're here. I'm not going to let you stick your neck out. Look, I'll break into Fujii's house. I'll find the damn password."

"Maybe," Karen argued. "But if you get caught, he'll know exactly what we're up to. We have to get the password without his knowing that we're even interested in the password. He won't talk to you because as far as he's concerned, you're just a thief...a con man. But he will talk to me. I'm in his fraternity of supercomputer experts. I'm someone who can appreciate all his wonderful achievements. He'll want me to understand enough of his work so that I can be in awe. I think I can win his confidence. In fact, I think I've got a better chance of learning his damn password than you or Cobb or anyone else.''

"What you've got is one hell of a good chance of getting yourself trapped,'' Toole interrupted. "If I introduce you to Fujii, he'll know right away that you're the one who's been analyzing his code. If he's legitimate, he'll never let you leave Japan with what you know. Damn it, Karen, be serious.''

She didn't budge an inch. "If we can get into that computer,'' she argued, "what Fujii wants won't make a damn bit of difference. He'll be a public fool. Look, there are only two choices. We can play it safe and just hope the computer generates the password. But that's a long shot. Impossibly long. Fuji will demonstrate his machine and we'll go home safely...maybe we'll go home safely. But we'll have failed. The Japanese will be the world technology leaders. Or we can take a chance. Of course I'm at risk once you introduce me to Fujii. And if we fail, I'm in big trouble. But if we succeed, Fujii is finished. He loses all credibility. Who would steal a supercomputer that doesn't work? We'll still get out in the end. But we'll have succeeded. We'll have knocked the Japanese supercomptuer off its tracks.''

"Succeeded for whom?'' Toole fired back. "For people we don't even know. For people who have been

lying to us and may be setting us up to take the fall if
the damn scheme fails. There's no one involved in this
thing worth your spending one day in prison, much less
getting your head blown off."

"I'm involved," Karen answered, "and I'm worth
the risk."

Toole was bewildered. "What the fuck are you talking about?" he demanded.

Karen broke the heated pace of the argument. "You
said before that you wouldn't go back because you
aren't going to spend your life in hiding. That's true for
me, too. If I quit now and leave, all I'll be going back
to is more of what I left. More people using me to get
what they want. More people telling me to trust them
to point me in the right direction. For as long as I can
remember, men have been screwing me and I've been
paying for the hotel room. But not this time. This time,
I'm taking charge. Right now, I've got the best chance
of crashing that computer. And I'm not going to sit
back like a good little girl while you screw it up, or
Cobb screws it up. I'm not going to trust anyone except me. Can you understand that?"

"You're going to sleep with the son of a bitch to get
his goddamned password," Toole said, his horror at
the thought obvious to her.

"If I have to," she answered without an instant's
consideration. "How many guys do you think have
tried to sleep with me to get something from me?"

"That's different," he said without thinking of what
he was saying.

"You're so right, Toole." She smiled. "It's going to
be very different. This time I'm going to get what I
want. And Fujii is going to pay the hotel bill. Now, are

you going to introduce me to him, or do I have to go pick him up in a bar?''

"You think I came back to Japan to watch you jump into Fujii's bed?'' Toole protested angrily.

"Don't watch,'' Karen told him.

"I won't have any part of this,'' he threatened.

"Toole,'' Karen said wearily, "I don't need your permission. What I need is an introduction.''

"What the hell have we done to you?'' Toole asked in bewilderment.

"Maybe the biggest favor of my life,'' Karen told him.

He pulled on the shirt and buttoned it to the collar, never taking his eyes off her.

"You know I care about you,'' he admitted.

"Please don't,'' she answered. "You said it's dangerous for someone in your profession to get involved.''

November 20th, 3:00 P.M., Tokyo

Fujii poured a small measure of sake into the porcelain cup that Karen held between the palms of her hands. He laughed as she turned uncertainly toward the stone figure of Taira Masakado.

"Now,'' she asked, glancing back over her shoulder.

He nodded vigorously. "Of course,'' he told her. "Masakado is waiting.''

She poured the sake out over the stone feet. When the cup was empty, she stepped back and spun around in joy. "I did it," she danced, almost as if she had caused a miracle.

"And very well," Fujii said. "You shall have a full year of prosperity."

He was the perfect host, taking the time to acquaint Karen with all the city's mysteries and legends. And she was the perfect guest, lending her full enthusiasm to each venture. It was hard for either of them to believe that they were looking forward to the destruction of the other.

They had met over a luncheon arranged by Toole and Karen opened the conversation with an expression of the awe she held for Fujii's work. He had listened to the compliments with a bored expression and had responded with a few questions designed to put Karen in her place. When her answers showed understanding of his more advanced theories, Fujii turned his full attention to her. They had spent the lunch in animated conversation, drawing circuits and mathematical symbols on the tablecloth while Toole chased the vegetables around his plate with chopsticks that had a mind of their own.

"This is completely insane," Toole roared as soon as he had returned Karen to the hotel room she had taken. "The son of a bitch sees right through us. I've stolen his damned computer secrets and you're the one who's analyzing them. Yet he sits there for two hours chatting with us as if we were old family friends. He's playing with us. We think we've conned him and he's laughing at us because he knows better."

"He thinks he knows better," Karen corrected. "We've still got one more surprise in store for him."

Toole had already been to the bar to fill a glass with ice and whiskey. "I'm not so sure about that," he argued. "I think he might be planning the last surprise."

"He's brilliant," Karen said, trying to change the subject.

Toole would have none of it. "Look, if you were selling me your company's...maybe even your country's...top industrial secret, who's the last person you'd want to be seen having lunch with? Shouldn't he be keeping as much distance as possible between me and himself? In case I get caught, wouldn't he want to be able to say that he had no idea who I was...that he'd never seen me before? Why do you think he feels so safe letting me buy him lunch in a public restaurant?"

Karen had kicked her shoes off and was pinching the blood back into her toes. She dismissed the question with a shrug.

"Because I'm no danger to him," Toole snapped. "And neither are you. That means the authorities—his company and probably the police—already know about us. He must have told them we were trying to bribe him, and they must know that he's stringing us along. Don't you see? If the bastard had anything to hide, he couldn't have lunch with us. But he's got nothing to hide."

"Which means...?" Karen asked.

"Which means that you and I are getting out of Japan. Right now," Toole told her.

"Could you get me a glass of wine?"

Toole found her indifference to his logic infuriating. But he bolted over to the bar and spilled some wine from the decanter over her glass.

"You're right," Karen reasoned as he handed her the wine. "It's obvious that he's cooperating with the police, or with the government, or someone. And I can understand why he wouldn't give a damn about the code he sold you. The stuff was mined. He would probably love to see us try to run it in a computer. It would drive us crazy. But he doesn't know what we're going to do with the code. That's the surprise he isn't counting on."

Toole struggled to see where she was leading.

"If he thinks we're just stealing his software, then it's no wonder he's so damn smug. The software is no good to anyone so he's risking nothing. He knows you and now he has identified me. Christ, he thinks he's rounding up a whole ring of industrial spies. Not only is he going to humiliate the Americans with his technology, but he's even going to turn the key on our jail cells. But we're not going to steal his software. We've got other plans for it. So, if he doesn't understand that, then let him have his laughs. We still have him conned."

"It's too risky," Toole answered. "Even if you're right, we don't have the fucking password. So why are we hanging around waiting for the jailers to pick us up?"

Karen hadn't disagreed.

"Karen," Toole continued, trying a fatherly approach, "do you know what my best moments as a con man were? The moments when I recognized that a mark was catching on. That's the genius of this business; knowing when the scam is coming apart and the time has come to disappear. This is the time. I can feel it in my gut. The last time I had this feeling, I ignored it. I stuck around trying to get just a litle more out of the mark. Instead I got three years in a federal prison."

"We still have a chance," she countered. "And the more sure Fujii feels of himself, the more likely he is to make the mistake that will give me the password. I'm staying."

FUJII MET KAREN FOR LUNCH the next day, and they picked up their conversation at the last syllable of their previous meeting. She described the structure of his address codes, then posed situations where his new technique didn't appear to work. He smiled confidently as he jumped to the question, then backed off when he understood the implications of the puzzle she was presenting. For the next hour they wrote all over the menu and the napkins as their lunch wilted on the plates they pushed aside.

It was the conspiracy of shared secrets that was drawing them together. Both were theoreticians whose minds leaped easily beyond the constraints of technology. He had posed a solution to her which she had dismissed. "We can't do that," she said, chewing absently on a bread stick. "We can't get in and out of memory fast enough." Fujii looked up from his fingers, and smiled deviously. "*We* can," he answered, and with the "we" she knew he meant the Japanese, and that he had pushed her back to her side of the competition.

"There's someone I want you to meet," Fujii offered, breaking the sudden silence that his reference to Japanese technology had caused. "Someone who will help you to understand us. I think it's important." Karen followed him as he dashed across streets through the dense traffic, leading her to the heart of the business district. There, she had met Taira Masakado.

It was an image of a samurai warrior squeezed into a shrine amid the skyscrapers; a character from the past who didn't seem to realize that it was time to retire. Fujii told her nothing of his story. "It's customary to make an offering. Some sake, or fruit, or perhaps flowers." He had gone to a sidewalk vendor, an old man who sold suitable offerings from a small cart, and purchased the sake. Then he had poured it for Karen, telling her that it should be poured out over the warrior's feet. "I think he likes the sake better than fruit or flowers. I always offer sake and he's been very good to me."

"You don't really make religious offerings?" Karen asked while they stood back respectfully before the figure.

Fujii answered without taking his eyes from the impassive stone face. "Taira Masakado isn't religion. He's a fact." And then he smiled and took her hand.

They walked together to the moat that surrounded the Imperial Palace Gardens, and settled on a bench near the Nijubashi Bridge.

"Taira Masakado was a shogun in the tenth century," Fujii began. "He was a great man in his time; probably had half the country under his control. But, eventually he was beaten by a greater warrior and, in time, was pretty much forgotten. He's not an important figure in our history. In fact, I doubt if anyone in Japan would have ever heard of him if it were not for that ridiculous statue."

"It does seem out of place," Karen agreed.

"Very much out of place," said Fujii. "But, unfortunately, that's the place where Masakado wants his statue to be. He insists on it."

She narrowed her eyes suspiciously as a way of asking him to continue.

"No one is quite sure how the statue got there, or even who decided that we needed a statue of Taira Masakado. But as Tokyo grew into the twentieth century, there was the statue right in the middle of the most crowded part of the city. The question is not how it got there, but rather, why didn't anyone move it? Land is very valuable, particularly in this part of Tokyo. But still, the builders worked around the shrine. No one had the courage to simply knock it down.

"Then there was the great earthquake of 1923. The whole city was in shambles, and it was decided that it would be rebuilt not with wood, but rather with steel and concrete. Obviously, there was no room for a shrine to a tenth-century warrior in the middle of what would be the world's most modern city. Tairo Masakado simply had to go. So the city fathers took the statue and moved it away to the edge of the city.

Karen interrupted with a laugh. "You're not going to tell me he came back by himself," she teased.

Fujii nodded. "You're not far from the truth. They built their new city and went on with business as usual. But they found very unusual things. First, businesses began to fail. Fine businesses that had been in operation for a century suddenly lost all their customers. Then a major bank went under and it took down other businesses. There were fires and explosions. A whole rash of traffic accidents. Everyone knew that something was wrong, but no one knew what it could be.

"Then, at a meeting to discuss the problem, a revered old businessman stood up and told them it was Taira Masakado. 'He doesn't like his new home,' the man said seriously. 'He wants to come back into the city.' Everyone bowed to him, because they certainly wouldn't dishonor an old man even if he was obviously crazy. But they did ease him out the door.

"A few nights later, one of the new buildings collapsed. Without warning, in the middle of the night, the whole structure just dropped, one floor falling through the next, and then those through the next until the whole building was a pile of rubble. In the morning, people couldn't believe their eyes. They spent two days picking up the pieces before someone realized what building it was. It was the one that had been built on the land where Masakado's statue had stood for as long as anyone could remember.

"Needless to say, they didn't rebuild the structure. Instead, they moved Masakado back to the spot where he had always stood. And miraculously, all their troubles went away."

"Because of Taira Masakado," Karen said jokingly.

"Of course," Fujii answered. "What he was telling us was that it is dangerous to tamper with tradition. Even if you don't understand it, respect it. If you do, it will be very good to you. But if you don't, you proceed at your own risk."

"But no one would believe in Masakado today. Not here in the Mecca of high technology," Karen reasoned.

"In 1945, we had to rebuild Tokyo again," Fujii reminded her. "After the fire bombings, there was nothing left of the city. Just ashes blowing in the wind. But when we rebuilt it, no one even suggested that Masakado was out of place or that we were too modern to have an old shogun standing in the center of the city. They put his statue back where it had always been, right where you saw it. We're not sure that there would be any problem in moving it. But with everything going so well, why should we take a chance? Some things are hard to explain. They don't make sense. But if they work, don't analyze them. Just follow them where they lead you.''

They ordered tea in a small restaurant, where the blinds were drawn down over the top half of the windows to protect their privacy from the glances of pedestrians passing outside. But the precaution was unnecessary. Before their tea was served they were back into their discussion of supercomputer theory, completely oblivious to everything that was going on around them.

"Beautiful," Karen commented as he described the concept of one of the suboperations.

"Beautiful in theory," Fujii agreed, leaning back in his chair. "Spectacular in operation. You have to see Akagi in operation to grasp the potential. It's a new dimension. A machine that rivals the human brain. Slow to learn, still. But once he learns, the most marvelously efficient thinker that has ever existed."

"Akagi," Karen asked, sounding out the word a syllable at a time.

Fujii smiled. "That's the name I've given it. In English it would translate as 'red castle.' But it has a much more personal meaning to me. Perhaps, someday, I will have the opportunity to explain."

"Perhaps, someday, you'll let me see it in operation. Let me create a problem and try to confound it."

He nodded. "Of course. I'd like that very much. But not until after my demonstration. After all, we are competitors.''

"True," Karen conceded. "But from what I've seen of your code, I think you've already won the first round."

"Just the first round?" he asked suggestively.

Karen held her answer until the waitress had placed the cups and the teapot, and backed away from the table. Then she said, "It's going to be a long race. You've already given us a great deal of help and we have a lot of fine people working on it."

Fujii shook his head. Then, with a smile he said, "I don't think you listened to Taira Masakado."

"He talks?" Karen asked playfully.

"To those who listen," Fujii answered. "Perhaps you have to be Japanese to hear him. I hear him very clearly. He tells me why you will never catch up with us.

"Masakado lives right in the heart of the business district. He represents our tradition . . . our national pride. And, as you can see, he insists on being part of our industry. He and our business are inseparable. So, for us, hard work and industry aren't just what we do. They're what we are. In the West, you keep them separate. Work is what you do so that you can live. For us, work is why we live. The sake that our highest-ranking businessmen pour out at his feet represents their souls. They don't work just for their bank accounts. They work for the honor of their country. Can you compete with that?"

"I think your bank account is very important to you," Karen corrected. "When you sold us the code, you must have given some thought to the money."

"Very little," he said simply. "I was much more concerned with avoiding the disgrace that Mr. Toole could have brought to my name. And giving you the code was a small enough price to pay. Because actually I gave you nothing. By the time you digest that material, I will be on the next level. I'll be that much further up along the learning curve. If I keep working, you'll never catch up. And I can assure you, I will keep on working."

"You may be right," she admitted.

"There's another lesson to be learned from Masakado," he continued. "We all know our place. In Japan, my laboratory assistants want nothing more than to be my assistants. They bend every effort just to help me succeed, because in my success they find fulfillment. Do all the people you work with want you to succeed? Or would they like to see you fail so that they can step over you?"

"There's a great deal of rivalry," Karen admitted after only the shortest pause.

"Here we work together for a common purpose. And we work very hard. You couldn't afford to pay us for the efforts we expend. But fortunately, we don't do it for the pay. To me, the supercomputer will be a national triumph. My reward is in bringing this triumph to my country. I couldn't care less about the money. Power comes from creating, not from a bank account.

"In the past, our sense of deference held us back. No one wanted to stand out in front, so we copied. We willingly accepted a secondary position to Western innovation. But those days are past. Now there are many young Japanese who are willing to innovate. And when they do, their workers gather behind them to help them succeed. The Akagi computer copies nothing. It's a bold, innovative stroke. But it is possible because of the loyalty and devotion of my staff."

"We're not dead yet," Karen challenged.

"No, not dead. But if you listen to Masakado, you'll understand why you can never catch up. Masakado tells me that I must have faith. You Americans don't believe in anything that you can't control. You have no faith."

"That's ridiculous," she said.

He smiled. "What do you believe in?" he challenged.

As he was leaving her in the lobby of her hotel, Karen asked, "Will we have the chance to talk again? I'd like to hear more of your ideas if you don't mind sharing them."

"Of course," Fujii answered. "I'll tell you anything you want to know. It will help make our competition a little more interesting."

He started to leave, but he stopped and turned back to her. "Perhaps dinner tomorrow night," he suggested. "It would be my pleasure to cook for you in my home."

"I'd like that," Karen answered. They agreed on a time.

When Karen opened the door to her room, she saw Toole sitting in a straight-backed chair. He was staring at the door, his hands folded in his lap, obviously annoyed that he had been kept waiting.

"That was a long lunch," he said as his greeting, glancing down at his watch to make his point.

"Toole," she said, returning the disapproving gaze, "you look like my father waiting for me to come home from a date. But you're not old enough to be my father."

"Where the hell have you been?" he demanded. "I figured that they had already carted you off to jail."

"Talking to a statue," she said.

Toole seemed pleased with the answer. "I didn't think you'd find him terribly exciting."

Karen kicked off her shoes and walked toward the bar to get herself a glass of wine. "I didn't mean Fujii. I meant a real statue. He took me to see a statue so that I could learn something about Japanese dedication. He's a smug son of a bitch. Came right out and told me that even if he gave us all his work, he'd still beat the Americans in the supercomputer race. He says we're not dedicated enough!"

She handed Toole a whiskey over ice, and then took her wine to the sofa across from him. "But arrogant or not, the man is an authentic genius. I don't think there is anyone in our industry who could hold his own against Fujii. He's more than just a technician. He has imagination. He's almost poetic. Do you know what he calls his supercomputer?"

Toole's expression indicated that he didn't give a damn, but Karen told him anyway.

"The red castle. What do you suppose red castle means?"

Toole shrugged his indifference.

Karen continued. "He said it had a special meaning to him, and that he would tell me later."

Toole drank morosely, plainly disgusted by her fascination with Fujii.

"Akagi," Karen continued. "That's the Japanese word. The Akagi computer."

Toole choked on his drink. "What did you say?" he demanded jumping up out of his chair. She was startled by his sudden animation.

"Akagi," Karen answered defensively. "That's the Japanese word for red castle. The name of his computer."

Toole's demanding scowl softened and his face broke out into a broad grin. "The hell it is," he told her, and he grabbed her hand and pulled her up out of the chair. "Let's go," he ordered.

She found herself being dragged toward the door and had to free her hand so that she could pause long enough to step back into her shoes. "Go where?" she demanded.

"To your house," he told her. "Karen, you angel, you've just come up with the password."

She was already in the hallway, headed toward the elevator, before she could ask, "What are you talking about? What did I say?"

"Akagi," he answered while he was pumping the elevator button. "Red castle, my ass. *Akagi* was the name of a Japanese aircraft carrier. The carrier that led the attack on Pearl Harbor. Don't you see? To Fujii, his supercomputer is Pearl Harbor revisited. That's the weapon he's going to use to blow us out of the water."

She was still bewildered in the taxi. "Even if he named his computer after an aircraft carrier, how does that tell us the password?"

"Because he's a nut," Toole explained. "The crazy son of a bitch thinks he's about to recreate Japan's great triumph over the United States. He sets his demonstration for the anniversary of the Pearl Harbor attack. And he names his computer after the carrier that launched the dive-bombers. How much do you want to bet that the date of the attack gets us into his computer?"

Karen felt an icy chill at the base of her spine. Then she found herself leaning forward in the seat as if to urge the taxi to go faster. "God, I think you're right," she whispered to Toole.

He looked back at her and shook his head in admiration. "You did it, kiddo! When you said you wanted to meet Fujii, I thought it was the most idiotic idea I have ever heard. I thought your chances of getting anything out of him were absolutely zero. But you were right."

"It hasn't worked yet," she reminded him. But in her mind she was as positive as he was. It had to be the answer.

Toole nearly broke the door down while waiting for her to find her key. They ran through the living room directly to the computer, which was humming softly as it tried one alphanumeric combination after another, always receiving "incorrect password" as a response. Karen typed a command into the terminal, taking control away from the computer. "Twelve... oh seven... forty-one," she said aloud as she typed her offering to Fujii's machine.

"Incorrect password," printed out across the display.

"Eight," Toole yelled at her. "In Japan, it was December eighth."

She nodded quickly and then mouthed, "Twelve... oh eight... forty-one," as she typed the digits.

"Incorrect password," the machine responded.

"Damn it," she hissed.

Toole nearly pushed her out of the way. "It has to be. Let me try it." He repeated the procedure and was rejected both times by the computer. "Damn it," he echoed. "It has to be the password. It's so fucking right."

They were staring in despair at the words on the screen when Karen suddenly shouted, "Wait a minute. That's not how they write dates in Japan. They put the day ahead of the month."

Now she pushed Toole aside and reclaimed the keyboard. "Oh eight…twelve…forty-one," she mouthed.

"Incorrect password," the computer answered.

"Damn," she screamed in frustraton.

"Try the seventh," Toole ordered.

"Oh seven … twelve … forty-one."

"Incorrect password," the machine mocked.

"It has to be," Toole said, suddenly lapsing into despair. "Something to do with the Pearl Harbor attack." Then he told Karen, "Try the name. Try *Akagi*." She did, and once again the computer rejected the signal.

They stood around the terminal for nearly an hour, trying all the words and numbers they could relate to Pearl Harbor. Finally Karen turned the effort back over to the computer. "It was a good idea," she consoled Toole.

"I would have bet my life on it," he answered through pursed lips. "I thought he'd given us the clue you were looking for."

"He will," Karen assured him. "I'm having dinner with him tomorrow night."

The comment did nothing to lift Toole's spirits.

November 22nd, 4:00 P.M., Tokyo

Kado was going broke.

Each morning, instead of going to work, he and his cousin pushed their bicycles down the narrow alley that separated the house from the crowded neighborhood. Then they pedaled through the dense traffic into the federal district and took up their posts on opposite street corners, commanding a view of the steps that led up to the National Security offices. For Kado, it was a boring vigil. He wasted his days searching in vain for the sight of Smith, who seemed to have vanished from the face of the earth. For his cousin, it was an exhausting routine, spent chasing taxi cabs, buses, and private automobiles in pursuit of likely-looking Americans who were spotted leaving the building. The stakeout had been going on for over two months and was getting them nowhere except deeper and deeper into financial difficulty. There were no weekly paychecks to reward their efforts.

Another part of their problem was that their expenses were rising. Their permanent houseguest had an inexhaustible appetite that could be kept under control only with great quantities of fresh fish and lean meat. Kaplan avoided the low-cost rice staples, convinced that they would add to his weight without increasing his strength. Instead, he consumed a week's worth of the expensive delicacies at every sitting.

Each evening, as they pushed back the screen to enter their dining area, they would find Kaplan already waiting, his legs crossed and his massive hands resting anxiously on the edge of the low table. Kado's aunt would bring in the food: large steaming bowls of rice and small flat plates with thin cuts of fish and meat. Then the Japanese would slowly lift the rice into their mouths, staring wide-eyed over the edges of their bowls while Kaplan tipped the plates of fish and meat toward his chin and erased them with his chopsticks. He was graciously polite, complimenting Kado's aunt elaborately in English and then smiling at her while she listened to the translation. Her tradition of Japanese hospitality prevented her from telling him that he had just consumed six days' worth of the typical Japanese diet.

The tea was served in small handleless cups, which Kaplan tossed down like shot glasses. On their first evening together, the woman had inclined her head toward him and delivered a speech in Japanese. "My mother says you honor her humble efforts to please you and begs you to have another cup of tea," Kado's cousin had translated.

"Great idea," Kaplan had answered. The exchange of compliments had been repeated each evening. But now, after weeks of experience, the woman simply held the pot at Kaplan's elbow and splashed tea into his cup with assembly-line indifference.

As Kado stood on the corner, a white mask drawn across his mouth and nose to protect him from the traffic fumes, the answer to his problem was clearly visible. All he had to do was cross the street, enter the offices of National Security and announce that an escaped prisoner had taken refuge in his house. The police would pick up Kaplan along with his appetite. As a reward for his cooperation, there was even a chance that the charges pending against him would be dropped. He could already taste the fresh fish that would be left for him at the dinner table.

Kaplan would never have to know who had turned him in. And there would be no reason for him to suspect Kado. After all, it could be any one of their neighbors. In the dense Japanese community, any American would be as conspicuous as a fireworks display. This American was more conspicuous than most.

Despite the small size of the house and the postage stamp of fenced-in property behind it, Kaplan was determined to maintain his regimen of physical conditioning. Each day he appeared in the yard with the first light, stripped off his kimono to reveal his massive torso, and warmed up with a few hundred jumping jacks.

"One...two, one...two, one...two," he counted aloud with military precision as he bounced up and down and threw his hands together over his head. Screens slid open on the surrounding houses and sleepy faces peered out through the cracks.

Then it was a half-hour of running in place. For this exercise, the methodical count was replaced with shouted commands. "Keep those knees up! That's it. Stay on your toes." The weary faces at the neighbors' windows scanned the small yard to see if there might be two insane Americans, unable to believe that Kaplan was shouting at himself.

By the time he got to the weight lifting, whole families were gathered at the open screens of the neighboring houses, their faces stacked one above the other. Kaplan had taken four concrete blocks and stood them in a column that was nearly five feet high. Then he had woven a length of chain through the holes in the blocks so they were fastened together as a unit. His ritual was to approach the tower of concrete cautiously. Then he would crouch down, bending his knees and extending his arms, and circle the structure as if he were stalking it. He would talk to it, mumbling words under his breath and then pause as if listening to its answer. Suddenly, with a scream that came from the caverns of hell, he would lunge at the monolith, slap his hands together on the sides of the highest block and snatch his voiceless opponent into the air. He would hold it out at arm's length and then begin shaking it like a rag doll. For a whole minute he would hold the blocks suspended, the muscles across his back quivering against the enormous strain. Finally, with a contemptuous shout, he would toss it aside.

In the silence, his laborious breathing blew like a wind through the neighborhood. Then there was a sequence of clicks, as the surrounding screens snapped shut.

"Anyone could turn him in," Kado told himself as he searched the faces on the steps of the government building. "Why would he suspect me?" He had to hold on to the traffic pole to keep himself from bolting across the street and up the steps.

November 23rd, 10:00 A.M., Tokyo

Cobb was shocked at the sound of Karen's voice.

He had heard Toole mumble the introduction and mention an unfamiliar woman's name. Then the faint sound of a soft but unintelligible voice exchanging the pleasantries of a greeting. There had been a few table sounds and background noise that indicated they were in a public place. And, of course, Toole and Fujii opening up the conversation with a momentary exchange of small talk. Then there was the woman's voice, addressed clearly to Fujii, with technical comments about a computer-switching matrix. It was Karen. There could be no doubt.

Fujii's tape recorder sat on the conference table, recreating his first meeting with Karen in the restaurant. He sat behind the miniature machine, inhaling a cigarette, his glance following the smoke as it rose toward the ceiling. On one side of him sat his company's security officer; the government security man sat on the other. Cobb was across the table, leaning forward to catch every word.

"This is Mr. Toole's associate," Fujii narrated over the recorded voices. "As you'll see from the conversation, she is extremely knowledgeable in supercomputer theory. And she has obviously studied very carefully the code I provided."

The two security officers nodded simultaneously.

The tape wound through the lunch, then switched quickly to some comments about offerings of sake to Masakado.

"This is later," Fujii explained to the puzzled faces. "I took her on a brief tour of the city. Most of the conversation is personal and irrelevant. But there are a few comments where she comes right out and states that she is competing with me. I think it's a very clear admission that she plans to use the stolen code in her own development program."

The government security official placed a pad of paper on the table and began noting passages from the conversation.

They listened in silence for nearly an hour, hearing a word-by-word replay of the conversation between Fujii and Karen at the bridge and their later discussion over tea. The company security man lavished a smile on Fujii as he listened to his lecture on why the Americans could never again catch up with the Japanese.

Cobb was only half paying attention to the words of the conversation. Instead, he was thinking through their implications. For some reason and without his authority, Toole had decided to put Fujii and Karen together. His plan was taking a dangerous turn. Slipping out of his control. The puppets he had so carefully put in place were cutting their strings and taking on a life of their own.

Why? What did Karen and Toole hope to achieve? They already had the code. Karen had sabotaged it and was ready to put it to work. All they needed was the password. Could they possibly think that Karen would be able to seduce the secret from Fujii?

He recalled his meeting with Karen in the hotel room. Nothing she had said hinted that she was about to embark on such a bold venture. She had been confused. Perhaps even frightened. What could possibly account for her suddenly trying to play Mata Hari? It had to be Toole. Karen would never have moved so dramatically on her own. Toole was obviously introducing his own sick genius into the scheme. And that could be very dangerous to the entire plan.

The tape stopped, and Fujii reached forward and touched the rewind button.

"Excellent," the government security officer commented. Then he looked up at Cobb and awaited his views.

"You have done beautifully," Cobb told Fujii. "Gentlemen, our plan seems to be working perfectly. We obviously have all the evidence we need to take good care of our Mr. Toole. And now he seems to be implicating other members of the conspiracy. With a bit more patience, I wouldn't be surprised if Toole and his lady led us to the higher-ups."

They were words he had to say. But even as he was congratulating Fujii on his coup, he was thinking of how he could protect Karen. There were things he wanted from her in the future. He had no intention of having her swept up in a conspiracy and thrown into a Japanese jail.

"This next tape," Fujii said, producing a new cassette and snapping it into the recorder, "was made the next night at dinner. I took the liberty of inviting the young lady to my home and she graciously consented." He smiled at those around the table to be sure they appreciated that her consent had been a foregone conclusion. Women never refused an invitation to spend an evening with Yamagata Fujii. "Most of the evening," he continued, "was spent discussing

Japanese history. She was very impressed by my col-
lections of our history and had great interest in the
subject. But I did try to lead her into more incriminat-
ing topics. I think there is a passage here that you will
enjoy."

He advanced the tape as he watched the digital
counter spin off the discussions of history. Then he
stopped the machine and turned it to "play." It was
Karen's voice that Cobb first heard.

"It's the memory addressing system that's pure genius. I think that's the single most significant advance
of the entire design."

Then Fujii's voice, soft and casual. "True, that certainly is critical. But look at the generation of the
commands. Is anyone in the United States letting the
machine write so much of its own code for an individual problem?"

Karen's voice answered, "I think you would be surprised. We've made tremendous strides in that area.
We're using more firmware than you are, so probably
our early machines would be more dedicated than
yours to specific applications. But we were losing too
much time recalling specific instructions from memory. That's the part of the process that was killing us.
You seem to have solved it."

"Who is the 'we'?" Fujii's voice asked. "With all
the information I've given you, I hope you're going to
tell me which American company I can expect to be
first to market my work."

"Oh, Jesus, no," Cobb thought to himself, half
expecting Karen to name the U.S. government, or IAC,
or another valid organization that would suddenly become publicly involved in industrial espionage.

"Signet," she said, sounding surprised that Fujii didn't already know the name.

"Signet Corporation, in California," he repeated like an attorney who wanted to be positive that a witness's words were captured for the record.

"Yes," Karen's voice confirmed.

"I expected a larger company to be at the bottom of this," Fujii's voice challenged.

The men leaning toward the recorder heard Karen laugh quietly. "It will be a larger company once it gets some of these ideas into production," she answered.

Fujii shut off the recorder and smiled triumphantly.

"Fantastic," said the company security agent. The government official agreed enthusiastically. Then he turned his attention to Cobb. "Perhaps there is nothing more required from our side. Fujii has given you a tight chain of evidence. From Toole, to the young woman. And from her, directly to an American corporation. Is there anything more you need before you move against Signet?"

Cobb shook his head. "It wouldn't seem so," he said, trying to appear enthusiastic. "But there are one or two points that I would like to see us tie together."

All three men waited for him to continue.

"First, the woman. I think I've heard her voice before. I'm not sure where, but I'd like to get a positive identification on her before we make any move. It could just be that she is on our side."

Shock rolled like a wave across the three faces he was addressing.

"It's a long shot," Cobb continued, "but the U.S. government isn't always the most efficient of organizations. It's possible that the people watching Signet Corporation had infiltrated the organization and in the interest of security haven't told me about it. I want to be damn sure that this young woman isn't a plant who's keeping an eye on Toole and anyone he contacts."

The Japanese agreed reluctantly.

"The second point is that the stolen code hasn't yet reached the United States. We've got a watch on Signet and it still hasn't been delivered. I think when we hit Signet, it's important that we find your code in their hands."

"Goddamn you, Toole," Cobb thought as he was speaking. He was well aware that his comments sounded ridiculous to the Japanese. He was asking for more time when no more time was needed. Toole and Karen had given the Japanese a wrapped-up case. They were ready to make arrests now, before he made his move against the supercomputer. How could he have involved himself with an irresponsible con man and a bumbling amateur?

"Mr. Cobb." It was the government security officer who interrupted his morbid thoughts. "Do you think your watch on Signet is sufficient? Couldn't the code have been hand-delivered by Toole?" The officer saw Cobb's expression go blank. "You are aware that Mr. Toole made a visit to the United States?"

Cobb felt his stomach turn sour. "Toole? In the United States? When?" he heard himself say foolishly.

"We don't know when he left," the security official answered. "But he returned two weeks ago. Our people picked him up at passport control. He was traveling under his pseudonym."

Cobb recovered from his shock quickly. "He never made contact with Signet," he answered. "We have Signet and all its people under surveillance."

"Mr. Cobb," the Japanese said with vicious courtesy, "you have just told us that you are not even sure who might be working on your side. Isn't it possible that there might be someone working for Signet that you don't know about? Someone who could have met with Toole in the United States?"

He had to agree. In his efforts to protect Karen, he had fabricated the possibility that she might be working with the U.S. government without his knowing about it. Now, with Toole having gone back to the States, he had no choice but to admit that the code might already have left Japan without his detecting the transfer.

"You make an excellent point," he said humbly to his Japanese counterpart. "Just give me a few days to check up on this woman. If she's not with us, then we'll make our move."

"Let's not be too hasty," Fujii said lightheartedly. "I have another meeting planned with the woman. I wouldn't want you to spoil it by arresting her."

Cobb eagerly agreed. He was grasping at straws.

"I wasn't planning on recording our future meetings," Fujii said. And then, with a self-satisfied smile, "I was hoping our conversations might take a more personal turn. And, of course, if the occasion should arise for me to take off my shirt, I wouldn't want her to find a tape recorder strapped to my chest. It could spoil the mood of the evening."

The Japanese security officers laughed hysterically. Cobb forced himself to join in the merriment even though he felt as if he were about to be sick.

They adjourned the meeting with bows and hand-shakes. Cobb started down the corridor toward the front door of the building. He had been shocked and then humiliated by the events that had just occurred. But now he was beginning to think clearly again and to formulate a new plan of action.

He had to move quickly. The date for Fujii's dem-onstration was close at hand and he had no chance of causing the machine to crash unless Karen were able to take control of the supercomputer during the demon-stration. Now that possibility seemed extremely re-mote. Karen didn't have the access code and it was unlikely that she could generate it in the few days left. She had admitted as much herself. Even more fright-ening, there was a strong chance that Karen would be in police custody at the time of the demonstration. The Japanese certainly had all the evidence they needed to justify arresting both her and Toole. He could only delay them for a few more days . . . a few weeks at the very most.

It was time to move to his backup plan, neither as elegant nor as effective as the original scheme but now apparently the very best that he could hope to salvage. All the pieces were in place, just waiting for his signal. Toole was well known to the Japanese as a thief who was determined to upset their supercomputer pro-gram. There would be little difficulty in getting them to accept Toole as the source of the disaster that Cobb was about to create.

Toole, Cobb reasoned, had already played his part in the scheme. Now he was becoming a problem. It was his meddling that had compromised Karen and caused the present difficulty. Originally, he had planned nothing worse for Toole than a return to prison, which was where the bastard belonged anyway. Toole would be exposed and handed over to the Japanese as justification of the American's involvement with Fujii's computer code. But now, the sleazy con man had brought a worse fate upon himself. It was too bad, Cobb admitted. But there was nothing he could do about it. His job was to keep the Japanese from achieving their technical breakthrough. He couldn't allow anything to stand in his way.

It was cold when he stepped outside on the steps of the building, and he turned up his collar against the drizzle that was being driven by an icy wind. He would walk quickly to the lobby of one of the public buildings and use a pay phone to make the calls that were necessary.

Across the street, Kado was doing a repetitive dance to keep his wet feet from freezing. The diminutive Japanese had already made his decision. This was the last day he would waste on Kaplan's mindless stakeout. Clearly, Smith was not about to return to the security headquarters. Just as clearly, the dozens of Americans who entered and left each day had nothing to do with Smith. There was nothing more he could do for the crazy American.

He had formulated his plan. He would return home that evening and tell Kaplan that the security police had spotted him on the street corner. They had even attempted to follow him when he left. For Kaplan's own safety, it was essential that he leave the house immediately and flee the country as quickly as possible. There was no chance of their discovering the whereabouts of Smith in time to do Kaplan any good.

He raised his eyes from his soaked shoes just in time to see a tall American across the street push open the

door and walk down the steps. He blinked the rain-
drops from his eyelids and stared in disbelief. In the
moment when the man turned his face as he searched
the surrounding buildings, Kado recognized him clearly
as Smith.

November 24th, 2:00 P.M., Tokyo

It had to be an event from history. A date, or a name
clearly associated with Japan's rise as a powerful nation. But there were so many events to choose from.

Karen returned from her dinner with Fujii positive
that his password had historical significance. "You
can't believe his home," she told Toole. "It could be a
library. Or maybe it's more like a museum. There are
hundreds of books, most of them first sources...diaries
of admirals and generals...ships' logs...drafts of
diplomatic treaties. If he wasn't such a brilliant computer theorist, you'd swear he was living in the past."

"You spent the whole evening talking about
Japanese history?" Toole asked suspiciously.

"Will you stop acting like a jealous husband?"
Karen snapped, annoyed that he was ignoring her enthusiasm. "We're on to something. I want to set the
computer so that it tries dates. We'll start with the date
he changed the access codes and let it run backward,
generating dates back into history as far as we can go.
Somewhere in there is a date that's important to Fujii.
When we hit it, I think we'll have our password."

"What if it's a name?" Toole demanded. She answered by throwing up her hands.

"Do you have a better idea? All we've been doing is generating random numbers. This is the same thing, only it's a lot less random. It's the kind of number that I think Fujii would be apt to use. Some great triumph, just like the triumph he's planning for his supercomputer."

"Okay." Toole surrendered. "It's a long shot, but it's as good as anything else we've got. You run the numbers. I'll get to the library and see if I can come up with a list of likely names. If a date doesn't do it, we'll start plugging in names of people who could be his heroes."

Her eyes widened in excitement. "I can help with that. I'll try to get him talking about his heroes. Maybe he'll volunteer some names. Or at least a period in history that you can concentrate on..."

"You're going to see him again?" Toole interrupted.

Her enthusiasm drained. "Yes, Toole, I'm going to see him again. As often as I have to to get into his computer."

"You know what he's trying to get into, don't you?" he warned, as he snatched up his jacket and started for the door.

THEY HAD BEEN WORKING around the clock for nearly two days, Toole rushing back and forth from the library with listings from English language catalogs and translations of Japanese historical works, Karen interrupting the computer's automatic generation of dates to try lists of the most promising names as fast as Toole prepared them. The computer had mocked their feeble efforts, flashing "incorrect password" until the rebuke seemed to have etched itself onto the display screen.

He was sitting at the kitchen table, running through volumes of World War II histories when Karen suddenly left the computer terminal. "This isn't going to work, is it?" she said to him.

He pushed aside the books, and answered with a gesture that took in the pages of notes and the still unopened volumes. "It's here someplace. But I wouldn't bet on the odds of our finding it."

"Then we've failed," Karen concluded, hoping that Toole would disagree with her and bolster her sagging spirits.

"It was an impossible scheme from the start," Toole answered. "So many things could have gone wrong. But I wouldn't have guessed that we would finally be stopped by a lousy password. I've been beating passwords all my life."

"What do we do now?" she asked.

"What we should have done weeks ago," Toole answered. "We get our asses out of here before this whole thing comes down on our heads."

"And just turn the next century over to the Japanese?" she challenged.

"We're not turning it over to them," Toole corrected. "They've earned it. And besides, you're not going to be able to do anything about winning it back if you're sewing mail bags in a Japanese prison. The only alternative you've got left is to get out of here and get back to work at IAC."

He watched her hopefully as she seemed to be about to collapse at his suggestion. But then he saw the determination return to her eyes.

"No," she said with quiet intensity. "Not yet. I'm not beaten yet. Not while I still have a chance."

He let his eyes search the piles of paper and books. "Some chance," he reminded her. But she was already back at the terminal typing in new names from one of his lists. Morosely, he turned back to the volumes of history.

It was an hour later when Toole realized that Karen had fallen asleep. Her arms were folded across the table next to the terminal, her face buried in her arms. He lifted her out of the chair and carried her to her bed, ignoring the protests that she mouthed without waking.

He rested her weight against his knees while he pulled back the heavy quilts and placed her carefully on her bed. He slipped off her shoes and started to pull the quilts up over her, then stopped when he realized that she was fully dressed. His eyes darted from the skirt and blouse that were twisted around her body to the nightgown that was folded on the chair. "You should get undressed," he said apologetically, but instead of answering, she rolled away from him, wrinkling the skirt under her legs.

Carefully, he unzipped the skirt and raised her legs as he slipped it down over her ankles, awkwardly holding her slip up as he pulled her skirt down. Then he walked around the bed and tried to undo the buttons on the front of her blouse, lifting her arm carefully. He had succeeded in pushing the blouse off her shoulder, when she tossed away from him, rolling the other arm under her body.

"Christ," he muttered in his frustration. He grabbed the quilt, threw it over her, and started out of the room.

"Some con man," he heard her say behind him.

He turned back to her quickly, then made an uncertain gesture toward her blouse and the nightgown on the chair. "I was just . . . your clothes were getting ruined . . ." Karen sat up and smiled at his babbled explanation, and then laughed as she watched his face begin to redden.

"You can't even con a defenseless woman out of her clothes," she continued. "Are you sure you got all those passwords by seducing secretaries?"

"I wasn't trying to seduce you," he insisted indignantly. "You fell asleep . . . and I put you to bed . . . I wasn't going to try to get you into your nightgown. I just thought you'd be more comfortable . . . oh, shit." He wheeled and started out through the door.

He stopped abruptly when she called his name. "I'm sorry," Karen explained at his back. "I didn't mean to laugh at you. I guess I just didn't want you to leave."

"I figured I should get back to the computer," he said without looking toward her. He knew his explanation had nothing to do with what he had just heard her say.

"The computer doesn't need you right now," Karen's voice responded.

Toole answered with his eyes still looking out through the bedroom door. "Look, you're tired. You're probably half asleep." Even as he spoke, he knew that wasn't the reason, and he guessed that she knew it as well. He stuffed his hands into his pockets as he turned and walked back toward the bed without looking directly into her eyes. "Even if you weren't tired, I couldn't try to con you. I mean . . . there's nothing I want from you. Except maybe to take care of you." He raised his gaze until he was looking directly at her. "But you don't need anyone to take care of you." He shrugged his shoulders as an expression of his confusion.

"I don't?" Karen asked.

Toole started a few unconnected words as he tried to put together a response. Then he threw his hands in the air in despair. "Jesus," he said, "I'm no good at this. I'm so used to lying that I don't know how to say what I really mean. When you're conning someone, all your feelings are fake so they're easy to talk about. These are real and I feel like an idiot because I can't fit them into the right words. I mean, what the hell am I supposed to say to you? You don't bat an eye over the thought of jumping into bed with Fujii just to get his lousy password and I can't even bring myself to take your blouse off. So what the hell can I give you...besides the names of a lot of dead shoguns for you to run on a computer. Damn it, if you were just a mark I could get you out of your clothes without your even knowing I was in the room. And I could be in and out of your bed without even remembering your name. But...you're not just a mark..."

"I haven't jumped into bed with Fujii," Karen interrupted in a soft voice. "I'm frightened stiff whenever I'm with him because I know that's where he thinks we're headed. I'm playing with fire and I'm scared."

"Then get away from here," he pleaded with her.

She shook her head slowly. "I can't," she said, as if that explained everything.

Toole knelt on the bed and Karen came into his arms without an instant's hesitation, her face buried in his shoulder. He stroked her hair and when she looked up at him he kissed her, gently at first and then forcefully. He felt her fingers opening the buttons of his shirt.

He pulled away from her embrace and stood up next to the bed. "You know I can't use you," he told her. "I can con anyone else...but not you."

She answered by completing the work he had started, slipping her blouse off her shoulders and undressing in front of him.

Toole took off his own clothes, leaving them in an untidy heap, and slipped under the quilts beside her.

"I love you," he said as he pulled her against him, finally finding the words that he had been unable to speak. But then she was kissing him and their closeness expressed more than anything either of them could have said.

November 29th, 8:20 P.M., Tokyo

Fujii could scarcely conceal his excitement as he pulled the soft cotton sports shirt over his head and tucked it into the top of his slacks. He smiled as he smoothed the cloth against his body, feeling only his muscular form and not the recorder, which had been taped to his side for all his previous meetings with Karen. Tonight, he would be completely unencumbered when he was with her and the seduction he planned would add one more indignity to her final downfall. Not only would she understand his total victory, but as she was being carted away to prison with her con artist companion, she would realize that Fujii had triumphed over her person as well as her plan.

"I thought we might relax for an hour or so before we have dinner," he suggested after he greeted her at his door. She smiled at the offer.

"I've decided to give you even further help in our competition," he said, leading her through his library' with its historical documents and ship models, and out into the garden that formed the center of his home. "I, haven't really answered your questions about the Akagi's logic matrices. But I see no real harm to my program in helping you along. After all, I'll be demonstrating them in a week and you would need several months just to duplicate them. So feel free to ask anything that you would like me to clarify."

He was surprised at her response. "Let's not spend the whole evening on shop talk," Karen said. "I'm really fascinated by some of the things you've been telling me about Japan's history. You mentioned that your country had only been invaded once and that you were saved by storms that scattered the Mongol fleet."

He looked at her suspiciously. "By the kamikaze...the divine wind," he answered. "That's why we used that word for the planes that dove into the American ships. They were trying to save us from your invasion."

He slid open a door that led from the garden and stepped back so that Karen could enter before him. "We'll talk while we bathe," he said. She stopped just inside the entrance to the steamy room and saw the high wooden tub through the mist. "In the long run," Fujii continued casually, "I think America will value the hot tub more than any of our exports. It's the most perfect form of relaxation."

He brushed past her and began to pull off his shirt. "There's a closet behind that door," he told her, indicating the door with a nod of his head. "You can hang your things in there."

She understood his purpose immediately. He would tell her anything she wanted to know, but now there was a price for the information. He was adding fuel to the fire that she had been playing with.

"Could we have a drink first?" Karen tried.

Fujii poked his head up through the neck of his shirt and looked amused. "Of course," he answered. Then he glanced at the tub. "I hope I haven't offended you. I frequently bathe with friends."

"No, not at all," Karen lied. "But I don't...at least I haven't...bathed with friends."

"We'll have a drink first," he agreed.

They returned to the main room, where he poured the drinks and sat across the table from her while he continued the story of the Mongol invasion. Her eyes followed his tale, but her mind was racing off in another direction. She didn't care about the computer information he had offered. There was nothing more she needed to know in order to crash his supercomputer. It was the historical information she needed; anything that could lead her to the password that still eluded her. She wanted to stay with him and keep him talking, just as he was doing now. And she had considered right from the beginning that holding his attention might force her into his bed, an idea that had never held any appeal for her but which she had been able to subordinate to the purpose of her mission. But now the vagaries were gone. The question was explicit: Would she prostitute herself, or would she give up any hope of derailing his technical wonder? It was her decision to make, but she realized that she would not be making it alone.

There was Toole. He had taken her through the rites of commitment and she had traveled with him joyfully. There had been no spoken pledges, nothing specifically binding. Yet she felt bound. Before Toole, intimacy with Fujii would have been dishonest, but her whole purpose was dishonest. She might have been able to go through with it as part of the price for succeeding in what she knew was a critical cause. Now it seemed to her that it would be much worse than dishonest. It would be destructive; an abortion of the new life that she and Toole had offered each other. Now the cost of success was, in a sense, her own life. That was a price she might be able to pay. But the cost would also include the life that Toole had just found and she had no right to make him the victim of a cause that wasn't at all important to him. Right from the beginning, Toole had been less concerned with the Japanese technical triumph than either she or Cobb. Did she have the right to sacrifice him to her cause?

She focused on Fujii's voice. He was telling her about the hopeless situation the Japanese faced before the enormous Mongol fleet that lay at anchor in the harbor and the prayers being offered throughout the nation for deliverance. She knew she should be making mental notes of the major characters he was describing. That was why she was there. She had to get his password, or stand by idly while his supercomputer demonstration tipped the balance of the economic world. Yet all she could think of was what she was about to do to Toole. She could see herself explaining to him that she had submitted to Fujii, trying to make her confession less painful by avoiding the details of their frolic in his bathtub. She cold anticipate his re-action—a sarcastic comment indicating he had expected as much. Toole, she knew, would go to any length to hide his pain.

Fujii was standing, draining his glass and reaching for the glass that she had nervously emptied. "And now you must join me in my bath," he was saying. "I'll finish the story while we soak." She could tell from his expression that the story would carry long past the soaking and further into the evening. It was time to take Toole's advice. Time to cut her losses and run. But she wasn't beaten yet. There was still time. Maybe, while they were together in the water, he would say something that would help her focus on a name or a point in time that would unlock the door to the Akagi computer. And maybe there would be a path of escape between Fujii's tub and his bed.

She forced a smile as she rose and allowed herself to be led out through the garden.

December 7th, 9:00 A.M., Tokyo

Toole didn't want to continue the fight that had started the previous evening when Karen told him that she was going to spend one more evening with Fujii. "He's having some sort of ceremony. I guess it's a celebration on the eve of his great victory," she explained.

"I thought you weren't conceding his victory," he protested. "Instead of helping him celebrate, we could be taking one last shot at getting into his fucking computer."

"He still might give me a lead," Karen offered, but Toole stormed out of the room. "Like he did the other night," he yelled sarcastically. "You spent half the night with him and all you got was the word for 'divine wind.' He's making a damned fool out of you, and you keep going back for more."

She had followed him through the house, trying to explain what had happened the evening she had been with Fujii, but he buried his head in his books and made a point of ignoring her as he added to his list of historical names. He was still working when she went to bed alone.

Now she was trying to start the conversation again, but Toole was resisting. He didn't want to argue with her, but even more he was afraid of what it was that she might be about to tell him. She had been upset when she had returned from Fujii's home a week earlier and had given him a half-dozen words to try on the computer while she hurried into her room to change. He had noticed that the bow on her blouse was poorly tied and the cuffs open as if she had dressed in a hurry.

"How did it go?" he had asked through the door of the bedroom.

"Those were all the words that I got," she had answered, avoiding what they both knew was the intent of his question. "Try them, for God's sake."

They had moved cautiously around the subject, angered that they were still failing in their attempts to crack the computer password and frustrated as the few days left to them escaped through their fingers. Then, last night, she had told him that she was going back to Fujii for one more try.

"We have to talk about the other night," Karen said when she brought Toole a cup of coffee.

"Which night?" he answered sarcastically. "Mine . . . or Fujii's?"

"Both, I guess," she tried.

He jumped up quickly and started for the door. "I've got some more leads to run down in the library."

"But we have to talk," Karen insisted, following him as he crossed through the house.

"Let's wait until you get back from Fujii's," he shouted from outside the door. "We can cover all three evenings at one time."

He chased through what had become a blur of Japanese history, hardly remembering whether he had covered the names in a previous visit, or whether they were new and potentially useful. He tried to concentrate, but his mind kept going back to Karen. He had been so sure that they were finding something together the night he had slept with her. And yet, she seemed to have discarded it so easily in exchange for another chance to crack Fujii's password. He knew that her purpose was important to her; she had to keep Fujii from winning the supercomputer race before she even left the starting line. But still, he thought they had found an even more important purpose during the moments they had spent in unreserved intimacy. He realized it had been idiotic for him to run out on her when she was trying to answer the very questions that were torturing him. He suddenly jumped up from the long reading table, gathered the references he had been using and rushed out of the library.

Toole had scarcely started driving back toward the house when he noticed a car make a radical movement to take up position behind him. For a moment, he studied it in the rearview mirror, then dismissed its significance. But several streets later, when he casually glanced in the mirror, it was still stuck to his tail.

With growing alarm, he began a pattern of senseless turns, winding down side streets and then circling back to his original route. The car stayed with him. He pulled through the tollbooths and onto the major expressway, picking a direction that led away from Karen's house. The car followed. Finally, he left the highway, turned through several streets and reentered the highway heading in the opposite direction. Anxiously, he looked back. He could see the car emerge from the crowded traffic and take up a position a few car lengths behind.

He had been expecting it. Since his first contact with Fujii he had wondered why he wasn't under surveillance. But still, it came as a shock. After ignoring him for months, someone in Japan had finally determined that it was time to keep watch over his movements. The enemy's strategy—whoever the enemy was—had suddenly changed. The moment he feared, when all the preparation and planning would turn into a few moments of furious activity, was close at hand. And Toole knew that he and Karen weren't yet ready.

Once again, he exited from the expressway. Leisurely, he joined a dense flow of traffic on a major street, letting his pursuer fall in behind him. He waited for the right moment and then, with a sudden turn that caused a screeching of brakes and the blaring of horns, he cut across the traffic headed in the opposite direction and accelerated into a side street. At the end of the first block, he made a skidding right turn, followed at the next intersection by a skidding left turn. Then he

brought the car to a sudden stop, jumped out and
rushed to the cover of a doorway across the street.
Toole waited there for fifteen minutes, watching for the
car to appear. It never came.

Toole had few choices. The moment for his escape
had already passed. If he was being watched, there was
little chance of his being allowed to leave the country
and vanish back into the United States. He couldn't
return to Karen's house without endangering her. He
couldn't even phone her to warn her. If she was being
watched, there was every chance that they would be
listening in on her incoming lines. He couldn't even
return to his apartment. Certainly, that would be one
of the places they would be watching.

They—whoever they were—had him cornered. He
was helpless to do anything to stop Fujii's demonstration which was only hours away. And no matter where
he hid, it was just a matter of time before they would
find him. He crossed the street back to the car, opened
the door, and took out the books and notes he had
carried from the library. They would do him no good.
But when his pursuers found the car, he didn't want
them to find evidence that he and Karen were searching the nation's history in their hunt for a password.
Then he abandoned the car and set off on foot. The
best he could do was find a hotel where he could hide
while he gathered his thoughts and made new plans.
The zero hour had come.

December 7th, 8:00 P.M., Tokyo

It should be obvious. But it wasn't. They were being used. But he didn't know how and he wasn't sure by whom.

Toole sat in the darkened hotel room oblivious to the noise in the street outside. He had selected a small hotel frequented by Japanese even though he knew his appearance would be unusual. It seemed safer than using one of the major tourist hotels because those would be the obvious choices for the police to watch.

The room reinforced his sense of being trapped. It was a tiny cubicle, hardly big enough for the mat and bedding, which were unrolled, and the uncomfortable chair in which he now sat. The toilet was at the end of the hallway, to be shared with the other guests. The common bath was in the basement. Despite the floral arrangement atop a small table and the copies of prints on the walls carefully placed to make guests feel at home, Toole felt as if he were back in prison. He couldn't escape the notion that much of his future would be spent in just such a room. And he knew that unless he could figure out exactly what was happening to him, he could do little more than simply sit and wait for his jailers to come and claim him.

Some things seemed clear. From what he had learned on his trip to the United States, it was apparent that Cobb had set him up to be the obvious culprit if the scheme were discovered. The perpetrator of record was not the United States government, but rather Signet Corporation, which had already been caught with its hand in the cookie jar. Cobb had claimed that Signet was nothing more than a mail drop. But the records indicated that it was a legitimate corporation with assets, activities, and employees. Both Toole and Karen were listed among the employees. So if the Japanese were to discover that someone was stealing their computer secrets, they would have to look no further than Toole and Karen. There would be no reason to search out Cobb and his secret government associates.

"Fair enough," Toole thought to himself. If the U.S. government were planning an operation against a friendly country it would be essential that it take steps to cover its tracks. What better cover than to create a much more obvious group of plotters who could shoulder all the blame? Who could fault Cobb for not letting him and Karen in on the real reason they had been sent to Japan? Toole had never bothered to brief his marks on the full nature of the schemes in which he was involving them.

Then there was Fujii. Had he known what Toole was up to the first time they had sat down together at a card table? If he did, then why had he been such a willing victim? Why had he turned over authentic code? Clearly, the Japanese computer expert had no intention of handing over his great invention for money. From Karen's meetings with him, Fujii still thought his supercomputer was going to sink the American fleet of technology. That meant he was certain Karen and Toole were going to be stopped before they could put his secrets to use. But who did he think was going to stop them? It seemed certain that he had inside information on their activities, but where was he getting it?

How was he managing to spy on them while they thought they were spying on him?

In fact, he realized painfully, he couldn't even be sure of Karen. She was a legitimate computer expert, a fact that was apparent in their conversations and which he had verified in his trip back to the United States. And she had certainly been recruited by Cobb from an important position with a major American computer company. But for what mission? The one that Cobb had presented to him of scuttling Japan's new technical wonder? Or perhaps simply to learn as much as she could about Fujii's work? Was the whole plot simply a device to use Toole as a cover for Karen? If it was, did Karen know about it? Had he simply played into a trap by refusing to escape and leave her behind?

Toole kicked the mat and bedding aside to give himself room to pace the floor. Suppose none of them were what they appeared to be. Suppose Cobb had nothing to do with the government. Suppose Cobb and Karen and possibly even Fujii were working together to move Japanese technology out of the country for their own private use. Could Toole simply be a cover to protect Fujii? That would explain why handing over his secrets hadn't caused him a moment of anxiety. He would have known that he was simply handing them over to himself. But they had the code months ago. Why would Fujii have waited so long to put the police on Toole's tail? And if they had been watching him, why would they have let him leave the country when they had no reason to think that he planned to return?

Everywhere he looked he found a new maze with convolutions just as puzzling as the heaps of historical data he had left at Karen's house. And yet he was sure there was an obvious answer, just as he was sure that

Fujii's password was buried somewhere in his long list of names and dates.

He thought back to the very beginning, to the briefing that Cobb had given to Karen and him by the side of the swimming pool in California. Had Cobb really needed his skills to get the code away from Fujii? Or had Cobb simply needed his reputation as a convicted computer thief to serve as a cover for other activities? Or, had the plan been exactly as represented? And if it had been, what had changed suddenly to cast him from the role of a schemer to the role of a victim? Perhaps it was the password. Maybe when they lost the password the original plan had become inoperative. Maybe Cobb—and perhaps Karen—were simply closing the door on a failed venture. Or, perhaps Fujii had thrown in with them, and now they were disposing of useless baggage. In any event, he had no choice. His only chance was to run. But, suppose Karen was as much a victim as he was? Could he simply leave her behind? It was unprofessional to care about anyone else, but he knew that he cared. He knew from the rage he felt every time she was alone with Fujii and the fear he felt when she was late returning.

He reached the window just in time to see an uncharacteristically large sedan appear at the corner and stop at the doorway below. Toole didn't wait to see who got out. What difference would it make? It was clear they had come for him. In all likelihood, he was the first American who had registered at this hotel. And this was probably the first sedan that had ever pulled up to its front door. The coincidence didn't require a great deal of explanation.

He bolted out of the room and started toward the bathroom at the end of the hallway. But he stopped himself quickly. Once they found the empty room, the toilet would be the logical place to look, and it offered no alternate path of escape. He looked toward the stairs that led to the next floor. They were his only hope, he thought as he rushed toward them. Just as he reached them he heard footsteps starting up from the lobby below. Resisting the urge to run, he walked as quietly and carefully as he could up to the next level. Before he got to the top floor, he could hear footsteps starting down the hallway he had just left, moving toward his room.

There were no apparent escapes from the top floor. All the room doors were shut and the toilet at the end of the corridor was just as much of a trap as the one that he had rejected on the floor below. He moved to the nearest door, took the nail file from his pocket and, with trembling hands, went to work on the lock. It shouldn't have been much of a challenge. The locks in the hotel were simply a courtesy to lodgers. The rooms seldom held anything worth stealing. But he was working under pressure. He had already heard the knocking on the door of his room. Now there were rushing footsteps in the hallway below.

It sounded like two men running together when the feet began pounding on the stairs he had just climbed. He fought back the panic, making his fingers feel the simple mechanism at the end of the probe. The lock clicked noiselessly, and Toole turned the knob and stepped inside the room. He closed the door behind him before he turned around and found to his relief that the room was empty. The mat and the bedding were still rolled against the wall. Behind him, he could hear voices speaking in Japanese. He thought that the two men were moving down the corridor toward the door to the toilet. For a moment, he thought of dashing out into the hallway behind them and racing down the stairs. But the car was still waiting at the front door to close off his escape. But then he heard one voice call from the distance. The answering voice came from the other direction. One of the men had checked the toilet while the other had moved to the top of the stairs. His room was between them.

As he pressed against the door he could hear the steps of the man who had checked the washroom returning back toward the stairs. Then he heard the two men talking. In a moment, there was the sound of descending footsteps.

Toole allowed himself to breathe again. If they thought he had left the building, it would make sense for them to post a guard near the hotel and to move the conspicuous automobile away from the front door. They could come back for him when he returned. But if they knew he was in the hotel, they would probably begin a room-by-room search. He moved to the window to see if he had any hope of escape.

There was no fire escape or safety ladder. The window looked out at an empty, unplanted patch of ground that was at least thirty feet below. And the area was surrounded by the blank façades of other buildings. Even if there were any way of reaching the ground, there seemed to be no exit other than through the lobby.

Toole returned to the door and listened carefully. There were no sounds. He eased the door open and stepped out into the empty corridor. Across the hall, near the stairs, there was a small window that looked out on the front of the building. He crossed to it, forced it open a crack and pressed his face to the opening to see into the street below.

The car was still there. Two men, probably the Japanese who had been outside his door moments before, were leaning into the window, talking with someone inside the car. Toole watched carefully as they debated their course of action. His only chance would come if they decided to move away. If they began a search it would just be a matter of time. There weren't even any beds for him to hide under. But if they posted a guard, then he would find himself dashing from the building with a single man in pursuit. There was a chance he could lose the man in the crowded streets.

He watched the two men stand up away from the car. One took a thoughtful glance back toward the hotel entrance. Then they reached their decision. One started across the street to take up his position opposite the hotel. The other walked around the car, opened the door, and started to slide in behind the wheel. They were leaving. Toole allowed himself a smile. He still had a chance to make a getaway.

He strained against the small opening in the window to watch the man who was crossing the street. It was important to be certain exactly where he took up his post so that Toole would know which way to turn when he dashed out the front door from the lobby. He followed him carefully as he reached the sidewalk, then moved against the flow of the crowd into the doorway of a shop. Toole glanced down. The car was just beginning to edge away from the curb.

He heard a crack and at the same instant realized that his face was no longer pressing against the window frame. The frame had broken free from its old, unmaintained sash and was falling toward the street.

As Toole watched in horror, the small square structure tumbled through the air, sliding outward away from the face of the building as if it were struggling to fly. It almost seemed to hang motionless, held up by the air beneath it. He followed its trajectory carefully as it merged with the automobile making its way into the street. Then it exploded across the hood of the car.

He saw the car jerk to a stop. The driver's door flew open. Toole raised his eyes and saw the man across the street wheel abruptly, and snap his head toward the car. Next he realized that he was staring into two upturned faces. The man across the street had retraced the flight of the falling window and had fixed upon Toole's face, which was evenly framed in the open window sash. The driver jumped from the car and pointed up toward him.

It was all too ridiculous. At the instant of his salvation he had been trapped by careless construction from a previous age. The two men were now running into the lobby and there was no reason not to sit there by the broken window frame and await their arrival. All he could do by dashing back into the bedroom was prolong the agony of his capture.

It was over and the answer had been surprisingly simple. Fujii had turned them in and then simply picked his time for their inevitable arrest. The moment of his glorious demonstration was at hand. He had become bored at toying with them. He had had his laughs with Karen. Now he wanted them out of the way. The police, whose footsteps he could already hear on the stairs, would make certain that Fujii had no distractions at the moment when his aircraft carrier launched its lethal strike against the arrogant Americans.

His arrest was unceremonious. Japanese police, he figured, didn't have to read the prisoner his rights. The two men, both smaller than himself, simply gripped his arms and guided him down the steps.

He thought of his possibilites as they reached the second floor and circled the stairwell for the final descent. He could fire an elbow into one of his captors and pull away from the other. Then it would become a foot race through the crowded streets. There was a chance that he might be able to lose them. Or perhaps he should wait until they reached the car. He could slam the door into one of the men and perhaps kick his way past the other. Toole found himself laughing at the thought. Weren't these the people who smashed heavy timbers with the edges of their hands? Didn't they spin through the air like pinwheels to build up momentum for vicious kicks that could take an opponent's head off? His last act of violence had been a sneaky elbow under the boards in a high school basketball game.

"Admit it," he told himself. "You're nothing but a con man who has finally met his match." Cobb had conned him and then Fujii had conned him. He had been beaten by amateurs, and he deserved whatever fate awaited him. He hadn't been totally gullible. He had suspected that Cobb might be setting him up and he had taken steps to build his defense while he was in the United States—some creative changes in the computer records in case Cobb tried to turn him in as the sole plotter in the scheme to steal the Japanese supercomputer secret. But he had been totally wrong. Cobb hadn't been his enemy. It had been Fujii. And Fujii had taken the simplest course open to anyone who suspected they were the victims of a sham. He had called the cops.

At last, he had the whole thing figured out. But as the two Japanese pushed him through the door and into the back seat of the car, all his doubts came crashing down on top of him like the falling window that had given him away.

The man seated beside him wasn't a Japanese policeman. It was John Cobb.

December 7th, 8:30 P.M., Tokyo

Fujii had retreated into the past.

When Karen reached his home and rang the bell that hung next to the doorway, she had expected to be greeted by the modern, urbane computer genius. Instead, she was met by tradition.

Fujii was wearing an elaborately embroidered kimono that made him seem shorter and heavier. A white band, decorated with kanji characters, was tied across his forehead. He stepped back from the entrance to his home, bowed deeply, and spoke his greeting in Japanese.

Karen was confused. She began to return the bow and then was uncertain as to whether this was the proper response. She had no idea of the meaning of the greeting. She wasn't even sure if it was appropriate for her to enter or whether some further invitation was about to be offered.

"Hello," was the best she could muster and as she said it she felt that it was ridiculously inadequate in the face of the ceremonial introduction.

"Welcome," he answered, with a smile that put her at ease. Then he began the initiation. "It's customary for you to leave your shoes outside the door. Would you mind?"

Karen looked down and noticed Fujii's shoes neatly placed to one side. She balanced from one foot to the other as she removed her heels and carefully put them next to the doorway. When she looked up, Fujii was setting a pair of slippers on the floor just inside the door.

It had been nothing like this on her previous visits. Then Fujii had been buoyant and confident, anxious to begin the joust of intellects and to assert his total control of the situation. Now he seemed subdued; concerned about putting her at ease.

He stopped her at the door to his living room, the library and museum where he had entertained her before. "Would you do me the honor of wearing this during the ceremony?" he said, and he held up a kimono with a floral print that was even more elaborate than the one he was wearing.

"It's beautiful," Karen responded with genuine enthusiasm, turning so he could help her slip it over her dress. As he tied the sash, she asked, "What kind of ceremony are we having?"

Fujii looked thoughtful. "I'm not sure that you have a word for it. Perhaps the Christian concept of 'penance' might be the right word. But I'll explain as we go along, and then you can tell me what you would call it in English."

"Just the two of us?" she asked as he led her through the empty house.

"Just me," he said. "This is a very personal ceremony. But I wanted you to see it. I think it will help you to understand me...us, really. The Japanese." He gestured to one of the cushions beside the table. She sat, even though she was puzzled that the table was bare. Fujii sat opposite her.

"You know, of course, that tomorrow is a very important day for me," he began.

"The supercomputer test," Karen answered.

He nodded, but then he corrected himself. "Not really a test. I've tested it a dozen times and I know exactly how it will perform. It's more of a demonstration. Something to open the eyes of the critics and cynics. My audience will be divided. There will be those who want me to succeed because they recognize the enormous victory that the supercomputer will bring to Japan. It will be a great leap ahead of our rivals in your country and in Europe. But there will also be those who would be delighted to see me fail. Some because I have had to force my ideas through their concepts of rank and privilege. They're afraid that my success will inspire other young people to ignore their authority. I'm more a danger to their status than I am to their Western competitors. And there are others who are simply afraid of success itself. They are quite comfortable living in the backwaters of Western technical leadership. They are used to adapting the ideas of others instead of having ideas of their own."

"So you need to prove your point," Karen offered.

He shook his head. "I need to prove nothing. When they see the machine operate, the scope of the victory will be obvious. What I need is for them to taste victory. That, in itself, will drive them to further exploits no matter what it does to their notions of propriety."

She didn't understand. "But you've already tasted victory," she argued. "Japan has been the technical and economic miracle of the world."

"We have had the full measure of success that you have allowed us," he countered. "And you have been very generous. We have prospered because you have allowed us to sell you our goods. But make no mistake. You in the West have always been in charge. You have been able to cut us off any time our success seemed to threaten your own prosperity. In a sense, we are still a defeated nation. That's what this ceremony is all about. It wipes away the sting of defeat."

"All that was years ago," Karen answered. "You and I weren't even born."

"In Japan," he corrected, "dishonor is never 'long ago.' It is always with you until it is righted. And it doesn't die with one generation. It is passed on from father to son. Throughout our history, men have struggled to avenge an insult suffered by their grandfathers. Why do you think that your life began only when you were born? How can you possibly have a tradition when your responsibility begins with an individual birth and ends with an individual death? How can one short life ever hope to be important?"

"I don't understand where you're leading," she admitted.

He smiled. "That's why I wanted you to be here. Tomorrow I will achieve a great triumph. But before that triumph, I need to erase all memory of defeat. I would like to know that you understand."

"What defeat?" she persisted. "Your work has been one success after another."

"I told you the name I have given to the supercomputer. Akagi. You asked what it meant and I told you 'red castle.' Actually, it means a great deal more."

She tried to look curious, disguising the fact that Toole had already told her what the word signified.

"Akagi is the name of a ship." He stood up and walked to one of the models that waited in its glass case. "This ship. It's an aircraft carrier. *Akagi* was the ship that launched the successful attack on Pearl Harbor. In the months that followed, it roamed the Pacific and the Indian oceans, spreading our victories all over Asia.

"Then disaster struck. *Akagi* was sunk. American planes hit her with all her aircraft on deck in the process of being refueled. They were minor hits with small bombs. But with all the gasoline lines stretched across the decks and all the explosives in the process of being loaded, the ship was completely destroyed. It may be a coincidence, but from that moment on, Japan was on the defensive. It was as if our fate were sealed when *Akagi* went under."

"So your supercomputer is the rebirth of a ship."

"Not the old ship," he corrected. "The weapons of that day are no longer relevant. It's an Akagi for our times. A supercomputer. It will launch us on a new era of victories."

"Why do you see it as a weapon?" Karen asked. "Shouldn't we be putting wars behind us? Can't you see it as a tool that will work for everyone... not just one country or one people?"

He walked to the table and held out his hand, inviting her to stand and come with him. "It would be nice, of course. But the fact is that there is a war. A battle for economic and technological supremacy. You must know that. Otherwise, why would you and your associates be working so hard to steal the Akagi computer's secrets?''

He led her around a central garden, toward rooms in the back of the house that he had not shown her on her previous visit. He slid open a screen and stepped back so that she could enter a space that was no larger than a walk-in closet. The room was entirely empty, except for a small shrine placed in an alcove on the far wall. The shrine consisted of a small image of the Miroku Bosatsu, the Buddha Who Is to Come. Flowers were arranged on each side of the figure. Before it, there was a small brazier holding cherry-red coals.

"You're religious," Karen announced as an expression of her surprise.

"Not at all," Fujii answered. "But remember what I told you about Masakado's statue? No one knows why they are afraid to move it. But if things are going well, why take any chances?''

"But...you pray," she said, gesturing to the statue. "You have your own shrine."

"It's called tokonoma. There's one in nearly every Japanese home. I suppose some people think that when they kneel before it they are talking to a god. I don't believe there is any god who is listening. But I listen. I hear myself say things that are important to me. I guess you would call it giving yourself a pep talk. Is that right?''

"I do it all the time." She laughed, thankful for such a simple explanation of what she thought was going to be a ridiculous ceremony.

Fujii stepped in front of the tokonoma, dropped slowly to his knees and sat back on his heels. He gestured to the place beside him. "Will you join me?" he asked.

Karen started forward, but then stopped. "Is it right?" she asked sincerely. "I'm not sure that I want you to be all that successful tomorrow."

"You said we weren't at war," Fujii answered.

"Maybe we are," Karen admitted. Then she stepped forward and knelt next to Fujii. "You and I aren't at war," she concluded. "At least not now. Not until tomorrow."

He reached into the folds of the kimono and took out a small strip of paper, rolled neatly and secured with a thin ribbon. "This is the moment of our defeat. I've written it on this paper. I am offering up that agonizing moment."

He extend his arms with the paper resting in his fingertips, until it was suspended over the glowing coals. Then he began to speak softly in his native tongue. Karen watched him from the corner of her eye. She could see that his eyes were closed.

When he opened them he continued his explanation. "Now, I will put the paper into the fire. It will disappear and as it vanishes, the disgrace of defeat will disappear with it."

The instant the paper touched the coals it burst into flames. Karen watched it twist as if it were in agony. It began to flake into ashes and pieces of ash rose with the smoke before the face of the Buddha. She noticed that the image was smiling.

Fujii remained on his knees until the paper was entirely consumed. Then he rose and extended his hand to help Karen. "If we don't go back to war until tomorrow, we should be able to have a very pleasant dinner tonight."

She sat silently by the edge of the table while he brought in the food and prepared it. Although the thin strips of meat and fish were delicious, she ate without any particular enthusiasm. Fujii noticed her distraction and set down his rice bowl. "Did my little ceremony upset you?" he asked.

"No," she answered too quickly. And then, after a moment's thought, "Yes, I guess it did."

"Why?" he questioned.

"Because we are enemies," Karen said. "For God's sake, the only reason we're together is that I came here to steal your...your aircraft carrier. You know that and I know that. You want your demonstration to be a smashing success. I'd like to see your supercomputer crash so badly that you could never put the pieces back together again. That would give me the time to catch up with you. So what are we doing eating together?"

Fujii smiled. "It's easy for me," he answered. "The Akagi computer isn't going to crash, I assure you. I'm going to win and no matter what you do, you're never going to catch up. Why should I have any problem dining with you? Think about it. If you won, you would have no problem dining with me. The problem you have is dining with someone who has won a prize you wanted for yourself. We Japanese solved that problem many years ago. Now, I'm afraid, you Americans will have to solve it. Because, from now on, we will be the winners."

"You expect us to just give up?" she asked.

"No, no, certainly not," Fujii said. "At least, not you. You're very much like me. I never gave up, so why should you? I expect you to keep fighting. I expect you to do everything you can to overtake me."

"And you don't mind entertaining a person who will get up from your table, take your ideas, and try to use them against you?" she demanded.

"Of course not," Fujii assured her. "I hope you will be able to keep it interesting."

She nodded. "Okay," she said with finality. "It's a deal. And I can promise you, it's going to get very interesting."

She lifted her bowl and ate with enjoyment. But throughout the meal, she was anxious to get to her house and get back to her computer. Because now she knew exactly how she would be able to sink Fujii's new Akagi before it was even launched from its skids.

In his ceremony of expiation, Fujii had given her his password.

December 7th, 11:00 P.M., Tokyo

"They're on to you. We've got to get you out."

That was all the explanation that Cobb offered. Then he raised his hand, silencing all further conversation. Toole settled back into the seat and watched himself being driven away from the hotel and into Tokyo traffic.

It wasn't the Japanese police. It was Cobb. Cobb was canceling his role in the operation. Or perhaps canceling the complete operation. Without the password they couldn't get into Fujii's computer. If they couldn't get into it, there was no way they could cause it to crash.

And they were out of time. Cobb was simply facing the facts; that was the most obvious conclusion.

Except it was too simple. If he was so willing to call off the plan at the first sign of trouble, why had he gone to such lengths to change all the records on Karen and Toole? And what had he meant when he had told Karen that they were simply part of a larger scheme and that he had a fall-back position? Most likely his attempt to stop Fujii's demonstration hadn't been canceled. Instead, it was just entering a new phase. The larger plan was beginning to unfold.

Toole knew he should have felt safe. If the new tack didn't involve him, it would make perfect sense for Cobb to get him out of the way. The last thing he needed would be an unpredictable con man on the scene who knew him and knew exactly what he was up to. But the bilious taste in the back of his throat told him that he didn't feel safe at all.

They left the center of the city, but instead of heading toward the airport, they headed west, in the general direction of the research center where Fujii had his laboratory. Toole watched the lighted office buildings disappear over his shoulder. "Where are we going?" he finally asked. Cobb simply raised his hand to ward off the question.

They left the highway and entered an industrial district with acres of low buildings devoted to warehousing and light assembly work. The car bumped over railroad tracks and entered an area that was crisscrossed with wire fences. Then it turned through an open gate, circled a darkened building, and stopped at a loading dock in the back. Cobb got out without waiting for the driver to open his door, and Toole followed him into the building.

"We're switching cars," Cobb said without elaboration. Then he led Toole down a narrow hallway and pushed open a door into a large open area. In the center of the room there were several racks of electronic equipment, standing by themselves and apparently connected to nothing. There was a large worktable, covered with wires, circuit boards, and small electronic instruments. Standing by the table were two men, both Americans. They didn't seem at all involved with the equipment spread before them. Instead, they seemed to have been simply waiting for Cobb's arrival.

"There's no reason for introductions," Cobb said before he was halfway across the room. "Let's just get started." Then he turned to Toole. "I want you to see exactly what we're trying to do. I'll need your help with this before I send you home."

The two men left the table and stepped over to the frames of electronic equipment. They were wearing jumpsuits; dark blue one-piece coveralls with baggy pockets on the legs and across the chest. Both were trim with broad shoulders and powerful forearms protruding beneath the sleeves of their outfits.

"Who are these guys?" Toole asked Cobb, wary at the introduction of new players this late in the game.

"They're specialists," Cobb answered. "You'll see." He led Toole over to the two metal frames.

"This is the communications frame that we'll find in the laboratory," one of the men began. He was addressing Cobb and treating Toole as a bystander. "The phone lines from the outside cable are separated into wire pairs and lead into the back of the frame. They're connected here." He pointed to rows of connector clips that protruded from plastic blocks on the back of the equipment.

"From here, there are jumper wires that connect to these fuse panels." As he spoke, he ran his finger along the connecting wires and indicated the plastic blocks, crowded with small fuses, at the front of the frame. Then he pulled out one of the fuses. "There's a fuse for every telephone line. The idea is to protect the equipment in case the phone lines take a lightning strike. It's a pretty standard arrangement."

Cobb nodded. Toole's face remained expressionless.

"We're going to pull one of these fuses and connect our charge here. There are no wires. We're making our connections to equipment that is already installed. Then we leave the building and simply call in on the right line. The ringer current sets off the charge."

"And there's absolutely no evidence," Cobb commented with approval.

The lecturer shrugged his shoulders. "There's always evidence. But nothing obvious. It's not as if we were spilling gasoline all over the floor. The charge, of course, self-destructs along with everything else. The heat sets the wire insulation on fire and the whole place burns. Since it's an electrical fire, the firemen will have to use chemical extinguishers which will hide any chemical residue from the charge. When it's all over, it should look as if they've simply had one hell of an accident."

Toole was looking at the man, whose unemotional cadence might just as well have been used to describe his recipe for a cocktail. Then he looked back at Cobb. "You're going to destroy the supercomputer," he whispered in disbelief. Cobb didn't answer. He was already following the two men back to the table.

"There's just one other component," the lecturer said. He lifted a small glass capsule from the table. "This is really to protect us in case someone energizes the phone line while we are connecting the charge. It's a simple switch called an E cell." He used the point of a pencil to call out the details of the wonder he was describing. "A simple connector . . . wire in and wire out. There's a bit of tinfoil dividing the capsule into two chambers. We put this on the line in front of the charge. It blocks the electrical current. Just before we leave, we put a few drops of acid into one side of the capsule. Then we turn it so that the acid is in contact with the foil. It takes about twenty minutes for the acid to eat through. Once it does, then the charge is connected and everything is ready to go."

"Clever," Cobb commented.

"Pure genius," Toole added sarcastically.

"Anything else?" Cobb asked.

"That's it," the newcomer answered. "We should be in and out of the place in ten minutes. The charge will arm itself while we're driving to the airport. We'll make the call and set it off just before we board our plane."

"And no one gets hurt," Cobb said with a show of concern.

"The only one in the building is the watchman," the man answered. "And if he sticks to his schedule, he'll be nowhere near the computer room."

Cobb turned slowly and took in the two communications racks, which had apparently been used for rehearsal. Then he took one last look at the equipment on the table.

"Okay," he concluded. "Take what you need and get the car loaded. These frames will be disassembled tomorrow and shipped out piece by piece. I need a moment with my assistant here. He'll be joining you in just a few minutes."

"You're crazy," Toole said as soon as the two men left the room. "All you're going to blow up are cards and circuits. They'll be able to rebuild the whole thing in a couple of weeks."

"Not quite," Cobb said. "There's a hell of a lot of semiconductor memory and firmware. We think we can set them back about six months."

"Great," Toole said in exasperation. "But all you're delaying is the demonstration. Fujii already knows the concept works. During the six months that they lose reassembling hardware, he'll just keep adding to the memory banks and improving the software. When he does get to demonstrate the machine, it will be twice as powerful."

Cobb was nodding in agreement. "I know," he conceded. "This isn't the best solution. But it's all we've got left. We simply can't permit the demonstration to succeed."

Toole was walking around the table as he listened to Cobb's answer. He examined the electronic equipment that had been used to develop the method of exploding the bomb. "Well," he said in resignation, "it's your show. But I don't think the Japanese are ever going to buy it. Christ, an explosion and fire the night before the demonstration. If you were they, would you believe it was just a coincidence? For God's sake, Cobb, computers don't explode!"

"Toole," Cobb snapped, his impatience flaring, "there's no other way. Sure, they'll have their suspicions. But as far as they know, you're the only one who's interested in their supercomputer. And you're going to be on an airplane somewhere over the Pacific."

"What about Karen?" Toole demanded.

"She'll be on the plane with you. Don't you see? There will be no one here for them to blame."

Toole nodded, but he was still unconvinced. "Okay, what do you need from me?" he asked.

"I want you to go with those guys. Make damn sure that they do it just the way they said. And study the layout. Make sure the charge is close to the memory banks. I don't want to blow up just some telephone lines. I want to be sure that it blows the brains out of that computer."

Toole was staggered. "I don't know anything about explosives," he protested, "and I wouldn't know a supercomputer from a dishwasher."

"But you're quick on your feet," Cobb answered. "Things are never the way the technical boys tell you they're going to be. If the layout is different or the phone circuits are not what they expect, some quick decisions are going to have to be made. I don't want a pair of bomb-throwers making them."

"They seem to know what they're doing," Toole argued, turning his head toward the door where the two men had left.

"They're experts," Cobb agreed. "They can blow up anything...buildings, airplanes, trucks...they don't care. But I do care. I need the guts of this machine utterly destroyed. I trust you before I trust them."

Toole's only answer was an inquisitive stare directed straight into Cobb's eyes. He was far from convinced that Cobb was telling him the whole truth.

"Before you go, I've got a few things for you," Cobb said. He walked to the table and tossed an envelope in front of Toole. Toole opened it and took out a bank statement. It was in his name and there were two entries. Each was a deposit of $125,000.

"I told you at the prison," Cobb said, "that there were no guarantees we would succeed. I said if you gave me a good effort, you would get the money. As far as I'm concerned, you did everything I asked of you. The money is yours."

Toole nodded his appreciation. Next he took out an airline ticket. It was for the flight that Cobb had promised him he would be on. "You land in San Francisco. Then you're on your own. I'd like to work with you again sometime, but I don't suppose you'll be as easy to find as you were in Harrisburg."

"Probably not," Toole agreed.

The last item in the envelope was a packet of American currency. Toole flipped through one edge and counted a thousand dollars. "For incidentals," Cobb said. "It may make it easier for you to disappear."

"I'm good at disappearing," Toole answered.

The door opened and one of the men in the jumpsuits reappeared. "We should be going," he told Cobb.

"Good luck," Cobb said to Toole as he shook his hand emotionally.

They drove in a small station wagon, Toole in the front seat next to the man who had given the demonstration. His partner, who had yet to say his first word, sat in back, directly behind Toole. The little equipment they needed was packed neatly into a toolbox on the other back seat.

"You guys know the way?" Toole asked, hoping to start a conversation. The driver nodded, never taking his eyes from the road. Toole turned in the seat toward the other figure in the jumpsuit. He pointed toward a package that was folded into a corner of the equipment box. "What's that? Plastic?" he asked. Again, his only answer was a nod. "You're going to be great company on a ten-hour flight," he concluded, curling up into his own pocket of silence.

They kept to the side streets passing through blocks of low industrial buildings that were illuminated by yellow lights mounted on high poles. After a short distance, the car turned into a parking area near an abandoned building. "We're walking from here," the demonstrator said. Then he took an envelope from his pocket. "Here, keep this," he told Toole. "It's the registration. If we get separated, you take the car."

They walked in single file, the mute one at the end of the line behind Toole. The procession hugged the back of the empty building until the street opened out on a large, wire-fenced compound. The low building in the center was well lit and there were security cameras mounted on the fence posts. Toole recognized it as the building where he had spotted Fujii's lab assistants and followed them in search of their passwords.

The quiet one rushed past Toole and across the open area while the camera was swinging in the other direction. From one of the pockets on his jumpsuit, he produced an instrument that he connected to the lock on one of the gates in the fence. In just a few seconds, he pushed the gate open and signaled to his companion.

"Wait," the man commanded Toole, thrusting his hand across Toole's chest. They stood fixed while the security camera panned in their direction. As soon as it turned away, the man commanded, "Now!"

They ran across the open space and through the gate. Without breaking stride they continued up to a side door in the wall of the building. Toole saw that the first man had already attached an electronic box to the door lock and was in the process of fitting a key into the slot. The door swung open immediately.

"I guess you didn't need me to pick the locks," Toole whispered. As he had come to expect, there was no response.

Once inside the door, the procession re-formed, again with Toole in the middle. They started down a hallway with a glass windowed wall to one side that overlooked small programmers' cubicles, each equipped with a keyboard, a display, and printer. As they moved quickly through the building Toole began to feel the pounding of his own heart. It was time to test a sick theory that he had developed during the car ride.

"Wait," he whispered. "I think we're going the wrong way."

"No," the demonstrator fired back. "Keep going. It's straight ahead."

Toole could taste his fear. Cobb had said that the equipment might not be arranged as they expected. But these men had been here before. They should know exactly how the equipment was arranged. They didn't need him to find the building, or to open the locks, or locate the computer equipment. They certainly didn't need him to set the charge. What did they need him for? Obviously, not for what he could do. What was his role in Cobb's final plan to stop the Japanese supercomputer?

They applied the electronic alarm silencer to still another door, which they opened with another key.

When they passed through the doorway they were inside Fujii's laboratory, standing in the midst of towers of electronics, interconnected by cable bundles. The two men walked directly to a group of communications frames, identical to the ones they had just left behind in the warehouse.

Without a moment's hesitation, the silent partner found the fuse banks in the illumination of a penlight. He connected a meter to one of the hundreds of fuse sockets that formed the façade to the front of the equipment. The needle on the meter peaked, and the man turned in satisfaction to his partner, raising his thumb in triumph.

"Call from the airport, my ass," Toole thought. The man had just identified the proper line connection by measuring a signal that was being transmitted on one of the phone lines. That meant that there was a third partner—perhaps Cobb himself—at the other end of the line who was transmitting the signal. If the switch were to be blown, it wouldn't be from a public telephone at the airport. Nothing Cobb had told him was true! As the two men began making their connections to the fuse socket, Toole began planning his escape.

They had no intention of taking him with them when they left the building. His role was to stay behind. Cobb hadn't needed him for what he could do. It was what he was. He was the answer to the question that the Japanese would certainly ask as soon as they had doused the last embers of their supercomputer: "Who did this?" He was the reason they would never look any further to satisfy their suspicions that the fire hadn't been an accident. Toole, as Cobb had so accurately pointed out, was "someone they knew who was interested in their supercomputer." He was a convicted criminal, with links to the Signet Corporation. He had $250,000 and a ticket out of the country in his pocket. He was even carrying the registration of a car abandoned nearby—a car he never reclaimed because ironically he had been killed by his own bomb.

It was all so simple. Cobb could never be satisfied with handing Toole over to the Japanese authorities as the person who had tried to sabotage their program. He couldn't risk the Japanese listening to Toole, and beginning to believe that he had been working with the United States government. But he could turn over Toole's silent body. A body decorated with bank deposits and airline tickets and other items that would confirm what the Japanese already suspected.

Toole saw the silent man looking directly at him. In his panic, he thought that the man might be reading his mind, watching Toole assemble the pieces of the puzzle in his brain and understand exactly what role he was to play in the destruction of the machine. He tried to look interested in the connections that the men were making.

They had connected two short leads from the fuse sockets to a ball of creamy white plastic explosive. The jumper line from the back of the frame had been cut and the small glass E cell had been connected into the line. Now they were in the process of packing the plastic into the space between the frame and the fuse panels. All that remained was for them to put the few drops of acid into the E cell. They would soon be finished.

"Wait a second," Toole said. "There are a couple of disks over here that we have to get." He tried to look purposeful as he walked away from the communications equipment toward the banks of disk drives that were at the other end of the laboratory. There were two doors leading out of the room; the one they had entered at the side and a main door near the disk drives. If he could get to the drives, he could dash to the main door and perhaps get through it before the two men could dash across the room to cut him off.

"We don't need them," the demonstrator called after him.

"We shouldn't take any chances," Toole answered.

He reached the drives without hearing any footsteps following. He paused for an instant, just to demonstrate his interest in the equipment. Then, with a lunge, he started for the door.

He twisted the doorknob with one hand while he turned the lock handle with the other. He heard the lock spring open at the same instant he heard the footsteps rushing up behind him. He pulled the door in and dashed around its edge, into the corridor outside. There was a light at one end and he cut toward it, driving his legs as hard as he could. For an instant, he seemed to be free, running in the open passage toward the light. Then the light went out.

Toole felt sick—waves of nausea rolling from his gut and into his brain. There was a throbbing across the back of his head. He knew his eyes were open and he could see shapes of darkness towering above him. But he couldn't make out what they were. He could hear voices, but they seemed to be coming from very far away. He tried to sleep.

The pain was still there when he awoke. And he was still afraid that he was about to vomit. But his vision was clearer. He was lying on his back looking up at the communications frames which seemed to be as tall as buildings.

"Turn him over," he heard a voice say. "We want the cut on his head to be toward the frame." His arm was lifted straight up and then pulled across his chest. His body followed it, rolling over until he could feel the cold tile floor against his cheek. Toole tried to lift his head, but it felt too heavy. From the corner of his eye, he could still see the frame rising above him.

"That's good," he heard a voice say. "Let's drop this thing on top of him."

"What thing?" Toole wondered, almost with scientific detachment. He blinked his eyes, trying to clear his vision. He remembered turning into the corridor. He realized that one of the men had caught up with him and hit him from behind. Then they had brought him back to the communications equipment they had wired with the bomb. What were they going to drop on him?

The building next to him began to move. The two men had circled around behind it and they were pushing it toward him. The top of the frame began to tip, leaning outward away from its base. It seemed to be rising up over him, hanging unsteadily in space. Then it started down, almost as if photographed in slow motion. It gathered speed, plunging down toward him. It began to disassemble; cards and components falling out of its face. It was collapsing and he was trapped underneath it. Toole heard his voice whimper and he tried to scream. Then he heard the enormous crash and felt the building hit his body.

The pain silenced the sounds. It rushed like an electric shock, starting in his back and running out through his limbs. His arms and legs jumped convulsively. The air in his lungs exploded out through his throat. His vision shut down and his mind went blank.

When he awoke, he was conscious of the sound of the components striking the floor. The blackness had lasted for only a fraction of a second. The heavy frame was still settling across his back. And the sharp pain, which seemed to have been erased by the blackness, was returning. He tried to cry out, but there was no air in his body to power his voice.

Toole looked up. The frame wired with the explosive was still standing right next to his face. The second frame held him pinned to the floor. Above him, one of the men had lifted the E cell from its position connected to the jumper wires that ran across from the back of the frame to the front. With a hypodermic needle, he was in the process of injecting the acid into the capsule. When he finished, he carefully twisted the wires so that they held the cell in a vertical position.

As Toole watched, the two men repacked their equipment into the pockets of their jumpsuits. Then they turned and stepped out of his field of vision without even looking back. As far as they were concerned, he was simply part of the hardware that was to be destroyed. There was no reason for any further involvement with him. Like the supercomputer, he was wired.

Toole heard their receding footsteps. Then the sound of the door closing. Then silence.

As he looked up, he could see the plastic explosive packed into the frame above his head. He could see the glass capsule held in its lethal position by the jumped wire. They were several feet away from him. His right arm, which was stretched out from under the broken frame that pinned him to the floor, could reach upward only a few inches.

He knew it was his imagination, but he thought he could hear the acid burning its way through the tinfoil. Then the sound of the pain that was spreading through his body became deafening. His vision darkened and the sick nausea returned. He knew he was losing consciousness as his body tried to ease his agony.

December 7th, 11:55 P.M., Tokyo

Kado looked up from his newspaper as Cobb entered the lobby. He had been sitting in a soft chair, hiding behind the daily newspaper, which he had read three times, ignoring the glances of the concierge and his army of hovering bellboys. Now he had a new entry for his report.

There were three previous entries:

3:00 P.M. Smith left hotel with two Americans who had arrived half an hour earlier. Followed sugjects to front door where they boarded private car. Unable to follow since taxi was not available.

5:00 P.M. Smith returned to hotel alone. Took elevator to his room on eighth floor. Entered room. I returned to lobby and continued watch.

7:00 P.M. Smith left hotel with two Japanese who had arrived fifteen minutes earlier. Followed subjects to front door where they boarded private car. Attempted to follow in taxi, but lost car at first intersection.

He made the day's final notation. Smith had returned almost at the stroke of midnight, unaccompanied by either the Americans or Japanese. It wasn't much information for a full day's surveillance. Kado knew that Kaplan would be displeased.

He had followed Smith from the steps of the Security building, through two public buildings and then to the hotel. During the journey, Smith had boarded the subway, which had required Kado to part with his bicycle. As far as he knew, it was still leaning against the kiosk at the subway entrance. He had watched carefully as the desk clerk reached behind him and took Smith's key from one of the pigeonholes. Kado had walked directly to the desk and read the room number from the slot. Then he had walked to the elevator and watched the digital display count off the floors. The key slot had said 814. The elevator stopped at the eighth floor. He had rushed back to the house to report his great discovery.

Kado had thought his mission was complete. He could give Kaplan Smith's hotel and room number. Kaplan could go to the hotel and visit the same destruction on Smith that he had been rehearsing on the concrete blocks. Then Kaplan would either be arrested—this time on a probable charge of cold-blooded murder—or he would flee the country. Either way he would be moving out of the house and taking his appetite and exercise regimen with him. Things, Kado had dreamed, were about to return to normal.

Kaplan had been thrilled with the news. But instead of rushing immediately to the hotel, he had summoned Kado and his cousin to a meeting around the family table. It was essential, he explained, that they now keep Smith under constant scrutiny. "We want to know where he goes and when he goes there," Kaplan had explained. "We want to know when he's alone and when he's with other people. Once we know his daily routine better than he knows it himself, we can begin to plan our attack.''

Kado had been appalled. It sounded as if Kaplan's visit was just beginning instead of ending. ''Couldn't you strike tonight while he's sleeping?'' he had suggested through his cousin. He hadn't listened to his cousin's interpretation of Kaplan's answer. From the expression on the giant man's face, he had known that his suggestion was ridiculous. Kaplan would be staying for dinner.

He and his cousin had taken up their vigil, splitting shifts in the lobby of the hotel to keep Smith under close watch. They had kept daily logs, responsive to the format that Kaplan had determined. Each night they assembled at Kado's aunt's house to report the results of their intelligence operations. On the first night, Kaplan had greeted them with a wall-sized map of Tokyo. At its center was Smith's hotel, circled in red. Eagerly, he had listened to the reports, which chronicled Smith's arrivals and departures. He had stood poised with his felt-tip marker ready to enter the various itineraries and locations visited. But the reports had been less than he was hoping for. Smith seemed always to leave by private car. And neither Kado nor his cousin had been able to follow the car for more than a few blocks. Night after night they had returned with their notebooks. But the circle around the hotel remained the only mark on the map.

When Kado reached the house, Kaplan was pacing furiously in his anxiety, his movements resembling a dance step. He crossed the small room in just three strides, so there was more turning than there was walking. And he ducked down automatically as he passed the beam in the center of the room, a habit he had developed for his own survival. His pattern was step, duck, step, turn, repeated over and over again like a baroque ritual. He rushed to Kado and snatched the report from his hands, then ducked back under the beam as he crossed to his map. With his felt-tip pen poised at the hotel, he read the first entry, ready to move his hand in a line that would indicate Smith's route. The line stopped at the hotel's front door. He read quickly through the second notation covering Smith's return from places unknown. Again, he raised the pen as he began the third entry detailing Smith's departure with the two Japanese. Once more, the boundary of the circle around the hotel remained unviolated. The hand with the pen fell feebly to his side as he mouthed the final comment.

He squared his shoulders and took a deep breath. "We've got to change our tactics," he concluded. Kado and his cousin smiled in relief.

"Starting tomorrow, all three of us will keep a watch on the hotel," Kaplan began. He paused after each sentence to give the cousin time to translate. "The only things we've learned are that he always leaves by the front door and he always leaves in a private car. So we'll cover the street. One of us will be posted at each end of the block. And one of you will take up a position inside the lobby. When Smith leaves, the one in the hotel will step into the street and signal the other two. Then he'll try to follow Smith. The two of us at the ends of the street will each be in a taxi. No matter which way he goes, there will be someone waiting to fall in right behind him."

He ripped the map off the wall and turned it around so that the blank side was showing. With bold strokes, he began to diagram the hotel and the streets around it. Then he marked the two stakeout locations at the corners of the street in front of the main entrance. "I'll be here . . . in the direction he has usually gone in. One of you will be here, waiting in a taxi." He looked at the two unenthused faces staring up at him. Kado raised his hand slowly, thinking of the meter that would be ticking off the minutes of his vigil. "No," said Kaplan, then looking at Kado's cousin, "you'll be in the taxi. It has to be someone who speaks English." He drew another "X" inside the box he had used to designate the hotel. "This is Kado's post. Now, if he goes in your direction," he said to the cousin, "I'll leave my taxi and go into the hotel lobby. As soon as you know where he is going, you call me at the hotel. We'll have to get the number of one of the pay phones. I'll go to wherever he leads you. Or, if he goes in my direction, I'll follow him and call you at the hotel." As he spoke, he drew lines showing the paths that each of them would take from the street corners to the lobby. "Kado will follow him no matter which direction he takes. That way, we'll have at least two people on the scene, ready to attack him."

Kado said something to his cousin, who turned to Kaplan and translated. "Suppose he doesn't leave the hotel. We could be waiting in the taxi forever!"

Kaplan smiled as he put the cover back on his felt-tip marker. "We won't be waiting long. Smith's activity is starting to peak. Two Americans in the afternoon and two Japanese in the evening. Something is about to break. He's up to something and whatever it is it will happen soon. My guess is that he'll be leaving his hotel in a day or so. This time we're going to stick with him. And the first instant he lets his guard down, we're going to get him." He watched Kado's expression as he listened to the translation. When the Japanese looked back up at him, Kaplan fired his fist into the air and shouted, "Banzai!"

His knuckles crashed painfully against the overhead beam.

December 8th, 12:20 A.M., Tokyo

Toole had no idea how long he had been lost in the blackness. Was it a few seconds since the frame had been pushed over on top of him? Or minutes, like the gap between the moment his pursuer caught up with him in the hallway, and the flickering realization that he had been brought back into the computer room? Had the acid in the E cell just begun to corrode its way through the foil? Or had it already armed the telephone circuit?

He tried to move. His right hand, stretching out under the deadly frame, was free. But his left arm was pinned beneath the fallen shelves and his legs were spread out behind him. He had no leverage to lift himself and raise the frame that had been pushed over on top of him. He clutched one of the standing shelves with his right hand and tried to drag himself out from under the trap. Nothing moved, either because the weight on top of him was heavier than it looked, or because he was too weakened from his ordeal. He turned his head as far as he could. He could see the plastic explosive connected by its short leads to the fuse sockets. Behind the fuse panel he could see the small glass capsule, connected to the bend in the jumper wire. It was all out of reach. The bomb had been set near the top of the frame, six feet above the floor. His free hand could barely reach the first shelf, which was less than two feet above the floor.

He tried to draw a breath in order to scream. A charge of pain fired in his back and spread like a belt around to his chest. He screamed for help, then almost laughed at the feeble sound that came from his mouth. Even if the security guard had been in the next room, he wouldn't have been disturbed. His only chance was if the guard walked in on his regular rounds. And that wasn't much of a chance. The two men had cased the building thoroughly, examining the locks and the alarm signals so that they had been able to let themselves in undetected. Certainly, they had noted the guard's routine and made sure that he wouldn't be arriving before their bomb was detonated.

He could visualize them, picking up a telephone at some distant location and setting the receiver against a tape player. Then they would simply press a button. The tape would begin to spin, emitting a sound at a precise frequency. The signal would travel down the phone line, past the E cell, which would by this time have broken through the foil and closed the circuit. The detonators, buried inside the plastic, would respond to the frequency, and send a small electric charge through the center of the plastic. And the plastic would explode. Toole would never even hear the sound of the blast.

The men would then simply hang up the phone and pack up their tape recorder with all the detachment of someone who had accidentally dialed the wrong number. There would be no need to call back. The technology was corrected and they had absolute faith in technology. They were, as Cobb had said, "specialists."

In the deathly silence, Toole was suddenly aware of a methodical clicking. From somewhere behind him, he was aware of the sound of a clock and the nearly inaudible "tick" it made each time the sweep hand advanced a second. The seconds, he knew, were building into minutes. Before too many more of them passed, a phone signal would travel into the building along the wires in the cable and climb up the back of the frame to the jumper. Then it would travel across the frame to the fuse socket. And from there to the plastic.

He strained to get a better look at the E cell. The jumper wire came from the fuse panel to the cell and then from the cell it disappeared into a maze of wires at the back of the structure. From the maze, wire bundles ran down to the cable, which emerged from the floor. He stretched out his arm and found that his fingers touched the wires coming down the back of the frame

One at a time, he pinched the wires and pulled down on them. As he did, he watched the rows of jumpers that crossed far above his head. For each wire he pulled down, one of the jumpers tightened as it tried to pull itself away from the fuse panel. If he could find the right wire, he would know it, because it would pull on the jumper that connected through the glass capsule.

Toole began working furiously, selecting a wire, tugging it, and then turning his head upward to see if it caused the jumper to strain against the cell. He found each wire with his fingertips, separated it from the bundle, and then rolled it back into his hands so that he could pull down on it. As he worked, he heard the clicking of the sweep hand behind him. It was taking him five or six seconds to isolate an individual wire, another two seconds to get a grip on it and jerk it down, and still another two seconds to find the responsive movement in the jumper. Nine or ten seconds per wire and there were hundreds leading up from the cable. There wasn't enough time!

He tried to rush his pace, but in his haste the wires slipped through his fingers. He was losing time rather than gaining any. Toole forced himself to slow down. He made his fingers work carefully. He tried to ignore the motion of the clock that moved on steadily behind him with no concern for his plight.

He wondered what it would be like. Would he hear the sound of the phone call being connected? Would he see the cell move as it passed the signal? Would he hear the fuse fire inside the plastic? Did you see the light of an explosion before its intensity seared the sensory nerves at the back of the eyeballs? Did you feel the shock wave before the heat tore into your skin?

The capsule moved. As he pulled down on one of the wires, the E cell bobbed like a cork in water, then quickly righted itself under the tension of the twisted jumper. Toole looked at the hand on the end of his extended arm. He held one of the thin, insulated phone wires.

Carefully, he wrapped the wire around two of his fingers and bent it under his thumb. Then, with all the strength he could muster, he began dragging it downward through the frame. Above his head, he could see the jumper wire begin to straighten. As it did, the E cell began to twist away from its vertical position, pulled from both ends by the wire as if it were caught in a tug-of-war.

He unwrapped the wire from his finger and slid his hand along it, reaching higher up into the frame. Again, he gripped the wire and pulled down steadily. The jumper stretched out tighter, the cell becoming perfectly horizontal. In his mind, he could see the acid flowing away from the foil.

He reached still higher, taking another grip. This time he snapped down rather than pulled. The wire in his hand snapped and fell free from the back of the frame. He had pulled it out of its connection.

He saw the bare copper end land on the floor next to his hand. This was the wire that would carry the explosive signal. Now that it was torn free, it had no way to deliver its deadly message.

Toole smiled as he thought of the specialists who were picking up a telephone at the far end of the line. "Fuck you, fellas," he said to the ripped copper stub. He'd have to stay awake to warn the watchman not to touch the plastic. There was no sense in letting an amateur do the work of professionals.

December 8th, 9:00 A.M., Tokyo

The gods of Japanese industry and finance began filing into the room, a procession of dark blue suits and starched white shirts.

First came the delegation from MITI, the worldwide trading organization, its aged director in the lead
with a trail of progressively younger but equally serious executives strung out behind him like ducklings.
Then there were groups from each of the leading international banks, each an executive whose gaze was
self-contained, followed by subordinates who stared
reverently at the back of his head. The chairman of
Fujii's company followed with a delegation of his
technical and financial advisers. By his side was the
Commercial Secretary of the Japanese government.
Finally the heads of smaller companies that supplied
materials and services to Fujii's company were allowed to enter. They were ranked according to the level
of sales they made to Fujii's firm.

The groups converged in the open area at the front
of the room, between the stage and the first row of
theater seats. As they met, the head of each organization stepped in front of his entourage to greet the heads
of the other organizations. While their junior executives looked on in awe, the directors bowed to one another and exchanged brief words of respect. Then the
younger men stepped forward and exchanged greet-
ings with those of appropriate rank in the other dele-
gations.

The brief ceremony was an exchange of trust. For
although these men represented many different organizations, they regarded themselves as associates rather
than competitors. Their companies were bound together in a holy alliance that had as its sacred duty the
economic domination of the industrial world. The men
assembled knew that they weren't far from delivering
on their pledge.

Their achievements were a tribute to the religious dedication of the Japanese people to their work. But even more, they were the result of the many-tiered organization of the individual companies into a unified, global strike force. Like a finely tuned military organization, each company had a specific role to play in the battle. Each depended for its life on the effective functioning of the other. Everyone knew his place.

The attack could begin anywhere in the world and could involve any product. Electronic components in the United States. Automobiles in Brazil. Chemicals in Eastern Europe. Fabrics in Latin America. It didn't matter what or where. All the leaders of Japanese industry needed to know was that there was a market of sufficient size to justify their efforts and that they could make quality products that would meet the needs of the market.

Time was no obstacle. They were infuriatingly patient. What difference did it make if they lost money for ten years in developing the market? Once they owned it, it would return handsome profits for the next century. One or two of their companies would be assigned to gear up for production. Vendors would be organized to supply the company with the materials and services it needed. The banks would be marshaled to provide the necessary funding at low interest. If a critical supplier were shaky, the lead company would be allowed to buy it. If money became scarce, other companies in already established industries would agree to borrow less and pay higher interest, all for the purpose of funneling the scarce resource to the companies charged with bringing the new produce to the new markets. Toys and fabrics had subsidized consumer electronics. Once consumer electronics became a vast money-maker, it subsidized automobiles. And as soon as the automobile industry was firmly in the black, it gave up financing and vendor services to support the development of electronic components. Then components did its duty in support of telecommunications equipment and computers. As each new company opened a new market, it had only foreigners to compete with. All the other Japanese companies were firmly in its camp.

"Unfair," cried the American companies. "We're competing against an entire nation." But while they were complaining about Japanese ethics they kept right on battling against one another. Their best managers continued to jump from company to company with no interest in long-term plans or long-term results. As they lost market after market, they tried to blame the fiction of low Japanese wages. In fact, they were losing to smarter, more dedicated managers who were simply better organized. They were competing against people who had a national purpose that commanded more dedication than simply the next round of stock options. The American workers weren't the culprits. They were the victims.

Now the Japanese were about to open a new frontier. They had triumphed by doing a better job with borrowed technology. Finally they were about to launch a better technology.

The business leaders took their seats, filling the first five rows of the ampitheater. On the stage before them was a small computer with a keyboard and a display screen. There was a television camera with large monitors on both sides of the stage. By looking at the monitors, they could see the keyboard clearly without leaving their seats. A second camera was trained on the display, reproducing its image on a large motion picture screen that hung at the back of the stage.

When they had settled to complete attention, Fujii appeared from behind the edge of the open curtain and walked to the lighted podium at stage right. There was no applause. His reputation had preceded him. The ranking executives were well aware of the humiliation he had brought upon the chairman of his own company and knew he mocked their traditional privileges of rank. In their tightly structured organizations, mavericks were dangerous. Only Fujii's awesome talent permitted him to survive his own transgressions and there were many in the audience who were anxious for a hint of tarnish on that talent so that he could be properly banished from their presence.

"First," Fujii began, "I want to put a few things in perspective so that you will fully appreciate exactly what it is that you are about to see.

"Today's computers, marvelous machines though they are, are basically quite stupid. They require an instruction for every step of the process and they proceed one step at a time. With better components and circuits, we have been able to make them take each of those steps much more quickly. And with some machines, we have been able to get them to take two or three steps simultaneously. As a result, they take less time to do the same tasks. Because they are faster, we like to refer to them as being smarter. But they are no smarter than an abacus."

The industrialists and bankers were familiar with this scenario. But they tolerated it as a preamble to what they were about to see.

"The leader in this conventional technology is the United States. American computers dominate the world. And their advantage in this technology gives them advantages in many other areas. They build better airplanes, for example, because their computers make their design engineers much more productive. They have leadership wherever advanced technology is involved because their computers are the generators that produce power for technology. Simply put, as long as they hold the lead in computers, we are condemned to second place as an economic power.

"My new computer will put us into first place. It will enable us to leap ahead of the Americans. This is because I have abandoned the traditional step-by-step design for computers and moved ahead to a new concept. And in this new concept, this morning's demonstraton puts us two years ahead of the best American efforts. So far ahead that it is highly unlikely they will ever catch up."

Carried away in his enthusiasm, one of the younger executives began to applaud vigorously. His hands withered under the critical glance of his superior.

"Thank you," Fujii said, with a nod toward his intemperate supporter. Then he continued.

"The new computer doesn't need step-by-step instructions for each operation. It generates most of its own instructions. It sees what work needs to be done, figures out the most efficient way of doing it, gathers the appropriate information and instructions from its own memory, and goes to work. Physically, it is no faster than a conventional computer because both use basically the same components and circuits. But in solving a problem, it is ten times faster. It can be doing many things at the same time, and it doesn't have to keep stopping and waiting for the next instruction. Comparing this machine to the best American computer is like comparing a modern jet liner to a gas-filled balloon.''

He stepped to the keyboard and display terminal, talking through his lapel microphone as he moved. ''I've chosen an engineering problem for this demonstration because I think it will make clear the implications of this computer for all our industries. And I have selected a graphic presentation of the problem because it will be much easier for you to follow. I have taken the design of an automobile . . . a model you see every day on the streets of Tokyo.'' He touched a key and an engineering drawing of the car appeared in dimension on the large movie screen. ''Now I am going to change the size and the horsepower of the engine.'' He made an entry from the keyboard. The image on the screen vibrated and the outlines of the engine immediately expanded. ''As you can see, the engine no longer fits. Changing that one component means that we have to make changes throughout the entire car. We need more space, stronger engine supports, and with the increased weight, stronger structures throughout the entire automobile. So what we are going to do is ask a conventional computer to help us redesign the car. The computer will handle the task one step at a time. It will ask me endless questions and will do nothing while awaiting my response. The whole process, even with the aid of this highly sophisticated conventional computer, would take several days. Certainly, we could never finish it this morning. But I will begin the changes just so that you can see the laborious process that is involved.''

He sat down at the keyboard and began to work. His audience edged toward the fronts of their seats. He typed in references to the engine supports. The computer responded with a range of parameters that affected their design and Fujii, in turn, responded by putting numerical values on one of the parameters. The supports on the drawing of the car expanded, but now they clearly overshot the edges of the frame.

"Solve one problem and you create another," Fujii said, and with swift keystrokes he began changing the dimensions of the frame. He worked for nearly an hour, constantly interacting with the requests and commands of the computer. For each step, he offered an explanation. The audience marveled at the speed with which his keystrokes were converted to changes in the engineering drawing. But they were soon painfully aware of exactly what Fujii meant when he said that conventional computers weren't very smart. At each step, the machine demanded new decisions and new instructions from its operator.

Fujii finally stood up and returned to the podium. "You now see what's involved in catering to the inadequacies of an ordinary computer. What I will do next is to disconnect from the conventional machine and connect to my new computer. Then I will give the supercomputer exactly the same problem. I will change the size and horsepower of the engine. Then I will simply tell it to make the necessary changes in the overall design of the car. I think the difference will explain why the era of American domination is about to end."

He walked back toward the terminal. As he did, he heard a noise behind him and turned to investigate. His audience had risen from their chairs and they were crowding closer to the stage to get a better look at the operation. They were like the crew members, crowding along the edges of the deck of *Akagi*, to cheer the bombers as they took off.

KAREN WATCHED the Akagi computer come to life. Someone had turned the supercomputer on and was beginning to load the preliminary machine instructions. It was a sequence that she had watched many times before and understood perfectly. In just a few moments she would see the operating system being loaded and the special instructions for accessing Akagi's enormous banks of memory. She was only seconds away from the moment that had occupied all her attention for the last half-year. Her fingers were unsteady as she spread them out over the keyboard.

She had rushed back from Fujii's home with the events of the evening burned into her brain. He had taken the moment of the aircraft carrier's destruction, held it before the idol, and then dropped it into the flames. In that one act, the disgrace had been erased. When *Akagi* had sunk, the seas above it had churned violently; rocked with explosions as the trapped air tore through the hull and burst up to the surface. In Fujii's mind, the chasm in the ocean had remained as a constant shrine to his country's defeat. But his ceremony of propitiation had, at long last, calmed the sea. It had created a placid setting onto which the new Akagi could be launched.

In the traditional ceremony, Karen had understood why they had been unable to discover the password. She and Toole had been recreating the dates of Japan's thousand victories. But the victories were not important to Fujii. He chose to live rather with the memory of defeat. He had named his machine not to honor *Akagi*'s triumphs, but rather to avenge its one fatal error; the moment when it chose to fire at the circling American torpedo bombers and ignore the four dive-bombers that were dropping down above it. Sec-

onds later, the standard-bearer of the Japanese fleet
was a raging inferno. In that instant, Japan's last great
military venture had turned to ashes.

She had rushed into the house and gone straight to
the volumes of history that Toole had left strewn across
the table. In the indexes, she had searched out the references to *Akagi* and turned to the descriptions of its
last battle.

It was in early June 1942 that *Akagi*, in company
with a large task force and three other carriers, had
launched an air strike against two tiny islands, surrounded by a coral reef, called Midway. In the following hours, the task force had been attacked by the
pitiful American air forces; outdated planes with
poorly trained pilots. The few Americans who had
managed to get through the Japanese fighter screen,
and then the metal curtain of antiaircraft fire, had
dropped their bombs harmlessly into the sea. *Akagi*,
along with the other carriers, had recovered its planes
and was in the process of refueling and rearming them
for the next strike.

The torpedo planes had lumbered into sight, ancient airframes powered by antique engines that
popped like outboard motors. Only two had made it
through the screen, dropping two torpedoes that had
passed down either side of one of the aircraft carriers.
But while the attention of the Japanese commanders
was fixed on the torpedo planes, a group of dive-
bombers had appeared overhead. It seemed to be a co-
ordinated attack, but in fact the two groups of American planes were from two different ships, each
unaware of the other. The crew of *Akagi* had watched
in fascination as a pair of American bombers dove
down over their heads. They had watched the black

shapes of the thousand-pound bombs separate from the aircraft and float down on top of them. Two had exploded in the water close to *Akagi*. Two more had landed squarely on the flight deck.

The damage would have been insignificant, except that there were Japanese bombs lying about the decks, in the process of being affixed to the wings of the planes. And there were gasoline lines stretched from the storage tanks to the aircraft. Everything exploded at once and, within seconds, the entire ship was salted with fire.

It burned throughout the rest of the day. When night came, it shone like a torch, lighting up the sky over hundreds of square miles of the Pacific. By morning, it was a smoking hulk, hardly recognizable as an aircraft carrier; certainly bearing no resemblance to the proud standard-bearer of the Imperial Japanese Navy.

The Japanese decided to put her out of her agony. At 5:00 A.M., June 5th, 1942, they had torpedoed *Akagi* to keep her from falling into the hands of the Americans. Then they had retreated from their first Pacific defeat, never again to return that far across the ocean.

It was this moment that Karen had found in the histories. At first she had entered 06-05-42 and been stunned when the password was rejected. Then she remembered the Japanese custom of putting the day before the month: 05-06-42. Once again, she had failed. Then she had added the exact hour of the sinking; 0500-05-06-42. The computer had answered "incorrect password."

There had been tears of frustration in her eyes when she remembered the difference between American time, used by the victors to record the events at Midway, and Japanese time. Events happening at 5:00 A.M., June

5th, at Midway, occurred at 2:00 A.M., June 6th in Tokyo. She returned to the computer and entered 0200-06-06-42.

The computer flashed its greeting.

Karen tied into the machine and began testing the code she had created from Fujii's samples. She made the changes that were indicated, loaded her substitute operating system and memory adresses into her own storage system and readied them for transmission. All she had to do then was to wait for Fujii to fire up his Akagi and begin his long-awaited demonstration.

Now the computer had come to life. Fujii was about to launch his planes on their deadly strike. Only this time, the American defenders were ready.

FUJII MADE THE CONNECTION between his demonstration terminal and the supercomputer in his research laboratory several miles away. He began typing in his instructions, telling his audience as he worked the significance of each step in the operation. "The operating system," he said, "is the most complex software package ever conceived. There are only a handful of people on earth who could even begin to appreciate its elegance." With the next commands he explained that the machine was now loading its memory addressing system. "This program doesn't even exist in other computers." He laughed, and then he added, "One of my American colleagues thinks it is the single most important advance in modern computer theory. Perhaps she is right."

Then he turned to his audience. "We're ready," he said. "I'm going to begin in exactly the same way by bringing up the engineering drawing of our everyday automobile." He reached casually across his chest and punched in a command. Immediately the same outline of the car filled the theater-size screen. "Now I will change the size and power of the engine just as I did with the conventional computer." He turned in his chair, typed an instruction, responded to a question, and then entered the data. In the giant image that hung above the Japanese business leaders, the engine enlarged, overriding its mounts and extending past the lines that represented the car's frame.

"So now, we have exactly the same problem that we had earlier," Fujii reminded his listeners. "The change in engine size and power means that the entire car has to be redesigned. Only this time, it will be done by Japan's new supercomputer. Once I start the machine, I am going to step back and join you. As you will see, the supercomputer doesn't need me to solve the problem. It doesn't have to ask me questions because it has the answers it needs stored in its memory. I would only get in the way, because the supercomputer can answer its own questions in a few billionths of a second . . . much more quickly than I could tap a single key. The whole process will take fifteen, perhaps twenty minutes."

He stood up, leaned over the keyboard and gave the machine its run command. Then he walked back to the edge of the stage and turned to watch the action on the screen.

At first, nothing happened. The engineering drawing remained fixed in space. The business leaders glanced at one another and then up at Fujii. His confident, unconcerned smile reassured them that everything was proceeding smoothly. Then the new, larger engine mounts appeared, attaching themselves perfectly to the oversized engine. As before, they now extended beyond the limits of the frame. Then, the frame erased itself, redrawing the appropriate sections so that they captured the mountings. Other sections of the design began to erase, replaced by alternate designs that seemed to be in harmony with one another. A gasp went up from the older men, and was echoed by adoring sighs from their subordinates. Unaided, a computer was engineering a new automobile.

Suddenly, the four wheels disappeared. In an instant they were replaced by enormous wheels, each higher than the entire car had been moments before. The engine dropped down, and sprouted a drive shaft that passed well below the passenger floor, but much too low to connect to the rear axle. The supercomputer solved the problem by bending the back half of the car downward, creating a vehicle that looked as if it were about to be launched into space. The ranking banker began to laugh, with his staff quickly joining in to provide the harmony. And then the laughter became contagious, spreading even as far as the ranking vendors.

The car began disposing of its own parts. The roof vanished to create headroom for rear-seat passengers who had been crushed in the redesign of the back half of the auto. The steering wheel was repositioned to the back seat. With the fancy of a cartoonist who can put eyeglasses on dogs and tuxedos on mice, the computer began creating a strange new machine, replacing headlamps with streetlamps and oilcaps with oilwells.

The laughter grew into total hilarity, the leaders thoroughly entertained by the mindless design exercise that was taking place before them.

Fujii rushed back to the terminal and suddenly the screen went blank. He turned to explain the possible reasons for the malfunction to his audience, but they were laughing too loudly for him to make himself heard.

With abuse ringing in his ears, Fujii turned back to the terminal and took a quick glance at the commands the machine was issuing. It was his code. The proper instructions had been loaded and were operating. It had to be working, unless there was something wrong with the mechanics of the equipment.

He switched from the disk drives that contained his program to the backup disk which held the only other copy of his work. Now, in a near-panic, he issued the commands to load the backup programs. He waited anxiously while the new code flooded into the machine. Then he looked up and saw the original drawing of the auto appear on the screen. The audience hushed, and watched carefully as he once again changed the size and power of the engine.

He turned the problem over to the machine.

This time there was no delay. Ignoring its oversized engine, the car began to reassemble itself with random parts. Its windshield vanished, replaced by a casement window with sliding panels. The wheels were replaced by the retractable landing gear from an airplane. Drafting lines began to stretch and bend into ridiculous shapes. And then body panels flew off in different directions as if the car had been destroyed by a bomb.

The room was in an uproar. Sour-faced business tycoons were staggering under the impact of their own laughter, throwing their arms around one another and pointing to the details of the comedy on the screen. "A computer that thinks for itself," a voice screamed, "but it thinks like an idiot."

Fujii was back at the terminal, attempting to stop the mindless destruction that his supercomputer was engineering. While he worked, pieces of the auto flew randomly about the screen over his head, mixed indiscriminately with parts from houses, airplanes and ships. The images lingered for a few moments even after the computer had been disconnected.

He turned and looked at the jeering faces, then fell back to his console to begin analyzing the error. His computer was selecting instructions at random with no regard to their logical fit into the problem. And it was using any information it happened to come across in its memory. The precise instructions for addressing the memory were being ignored.

He heard a voice behind him and recognized the speaker as the chairman of his company. The man's appearance at the podium quieted his colleagues and now he was mumbling the beginnings of an apology. "Obviously, we were not fully prepared to demonstrate this new system, and I very much regret raising your expectations and wasting your time. I had assumed that we were much closer to an operating system than we seem to be."

There were grunts of agreement from the mandarins.

"I will direct a complete review of all the work that has been done on this project." He glanced over his shoulder to the terminal where Fujii was still punching the keys in an effort to discover the cause of the disaster. "I will also broaden the management of the program so as to be certain that we get an objective evaluation of where we stand."

Over his head, Fujii could hear the screaming engines of the dive-bombers. He knew that if he looked up he would see the dark winged shapes plunging out of the sky. And then he would see the bombs falling freely toward him, floating down on *Akagi* as it writhed and twisted in its effort to escape. The explosions were inevitable. And then the flashing fires that would melt rivets and boil the paint off the steel plate.

Akagi was sinking again. It was about to disappear in the sea of corporate bureaucracy, beneath the surface, without leaving a trace.

December 9th, 2:30 P.M., Tokyo

"It was a complete fiasco. A total disaster. It was beautiful."

Cobb couldn't contain his joy. There were three bottles of champagne chilling in an oversized ice bucket. He pulled one out by the neck. Karen, who had just arrived at his hotel room, wasn't yet caught up in the spirit of the occasion.

"I don't know how you did it," Cobb continued as he twisted the wire from the cork, "but you couldn't have done it any better. From what I hear, Fujii's supercomputer crashed in glorious living color. The damn thing tried to design an automobile using parts from an airplane."

"I'm glad it worked," Karen said without a great deal of enthusiasm in her voice.

The cork popped and Cobb rushed to the cocktail table to catch the cascading wine in the glass. "How did you do it?" he asked as he poured.

"With his own code," she answered, "plus a few basic design changes in his memory instructions. He'll probably find the traps that he put into the software he gave us. But it will take him quite a while to run down the ones we made."

"Beautiful," Cobb said. "Now tell me. Were you able to get it onto his disk files?"

She nodded as she accepted the glass of champagne. "I think so. He put in the original disk and loaded it into the computer. I transferred his code back onto the disk and then sent my code to the computer. As soon as he stopped operating, I wrote my code back onto the disk over his code. That meant his original was ruined. He loaded again, probably from his backup file. I did the same thing. So my guess is that we destroyed both the original and the backup."

"Fantastic!" Cobb said. He raised his glass in a toast to Karen. "Congratulations. You're the one who made it all work."

"Fantastic," she answered sarcastically. "Except what have we done to Fujii?"

Cobb didn't catch the sincerity of her question. "We've ruined the son of a bitch, that's what we've done. We've made him a laughingstock and, believe me, there were a lot of people standing in line for a chance to laugh. I hear that his chairman was so pissed that he'll probably make Fujii a computer salesman in Tibet."

"He's a genius," Karen said. She was still holding the champagne glass, but she hadn't yet tasted the wine.

"He's a smug little bastard," Cobb bounced back. He was already refilling his glass. "He got exactly what he deserved."

"You don't know him," Karen corrected. "Sure, he thinks he's great. But the fact is that he is great. I don't think we've got anyone in our country who can touch him. And what we did to him was rotten."

"Nothing that he wouldn't have done to us if we gave him the chance," Cobb said.

Karen put the glass back on the table. She walked to the window and stared vacantly into the street as she continued. "That's not true. Fujii wouldn't have cheated. He would have competed fairly. He's a very sincere and highly motivated person. I can't help thinking that this is one case where the best man didn't win."

"Sincere?" Cobb asked in disbelief. "Did you know that while he was being so sincere with you he was wearing a tape recorder? And do you know what he did with all those sincere conversations? He took them in and played them for the police. Your 'highly motivated' friend was trying to get you sent to a Japanese prison. The only thing that was delaying him was that he was looking for a chance to sleep with you first!"

Karen turned to him wide-eyed, but she was too stunned to answer. She shook her head slowly and buried her face in her hands. Then she fell back against the wall. Cobb retrieved Karen's glass and brought it across the room to her. She took it, but she still couldn't drink.

Cobb filled his glass again. "You shouldn't have met with him," he concluded. "That was a mistake. The one thing you should have learned from Toole was that you never want to get involved with your victims. Once you start seeing them as people, you lose your touch."

"I had to get close to him," she countered. "I needed his password. If he hadn't invited me to his ceremony, I never would have gotten into the computer."

Cobb nodded. "Drink up," he advised her. "We've earned our little celebration, but we're not home free yet. There are a few things that we have to discuss."

She drank the champagne and held her glass out as he poured the rest of the bottle. "Where's Toole?" she suddenly asked. "Does he know that the computer crashed?"

"I don't think so," Cobb said. "That's one of the things that we have to talk about."

He gestured toward the chair and she sat uneasily. "Did anything happen to him?" she demanded.

Cobb tried to look grief-stricken as he answered. "The Japanese have arrested him." He saw the sudden fright in her expression. "Now don't get upset. He won't try to involve us. It's not part of his code of conduct. And even if he did, no one would believe him."

"Us?" she fired back, her fear turning to anger. "I wasn't thinking about us. I was thinking about him. What happened to him?"

"A real bonehead play," Cobb said. He shook his head to indicate his despair. "Our friend Toole decided to take matters into his own hands. He broke into Fujii's laboratory and tried to blow up the supercomputer."

"Is he all right?"

"He seems to be. My contacts tell me that he knocked a frame over on top of himself. The guard found him pinned to the floor and called the police."

"That can't be true," Karen protested. "He was working with me to try to break the password. He had gone to the library to get more information."

"It is true. Apparently he didn't go to the library. Instead, he went somewhere where they make plastic explosives and fuses. And he got himself caught."

"Can we help him?" Karen demanded.

Cobb threw his hands up in a helpless gesture. "How the hell can we help him? What are we supposed to do...go to the Japanese and say, 'Let him go, he works for us'? Christ, we're the United States government. A guy carrying a bomb into a Japanese computer facility can't work for the government." He let the obvious implications sink in. "Besides," he continued, "it's all going to work out pretty well."

She was on the verge of rage. "Pretty well," she shot back. "Fujii is ruined and we're the ones who did it. Now Toole is in prison and you don't think we can help him. Two people are being destroyed by your damned computer plot and you think it's all going to work out pretty well."

"Okay," he agreed, but now there was an edge of anger building in his own voice. "You're right. Two people didn't survive. But you knew we were going to discredit Fujii when you first took the assignment. So let's not get all choked up over him. And Toole knew he was in a high-risk situation. He was in jail when I found him and now he's back in jail. The only difference is that he's a quarter of a million dollars richer. But let's not talk about the losers. Let's talk about the winners. You and me."

She started to interrupt, but he cut her off. "Remember when I met you in the hotel? I told you we had problems, but I promised you that if you would just trust me everything would come out all right. Well, this is the moment of truth. If you play it out exactly the way I tell you, then you and I will be out of here with the supercomputer secrets under our arm. But I have to warn you. If you get creative, or start feeling sorry for Fujii and Toole, I'm the only one who will be getting out of here. You'll end up in prison with Toole.''

Karen looked bewildered. ''Prison . . . ?''

''Haven't you been listening?'' Cobb demanded, abandoning all sense of sympathy for her feelings. ''Fujii was wearing a tape recorder. The police have a long-playing record of you admitting that you were stealing his code. Right now they figure that you and Toole were working together and they know that he's a crook.''

He saw the fear return to her face, so he knew his message was getting through. He had counted on her being more concerned for herself than she would be for Toole.

''The Japanese know that I'm with the U.S. government. They think I've been helping them track down American industrial spies. Now they've caught their spy, our friend Toole. And what I'm going to do is give them evidence to show that Toole was the only spy.''

''But we can't . . .'' she started to protest.

''We have to,'' he interrupted. ''They caught Toole dead to rights. If we try to save him, all we'll do is make them suspicious. We don't do him a favor by joining him in jail. But if we're to keep you out of jail, then we have to make the Japanese think that you're working with me. That you're part of the U.S. undercover team. That your role was to infiltrate the plot and find out if Toole was working alone or if he was working with Japanese insiders. So when I introduce you as my associate, all you have to do is tell them that as far as you were able to determine, Toole was working alone.''

"I won't do it!" she screamed. "It's the most dishonest thing I've ever heard of."

"Suit yourself," he snapped back. "But as I see it, you've got just two choices. You were either working for Toole or you were working for me. If you want to insist that you were working with him, I'll be happy to wrap up the case and let the Japanese take care of both of you. Hell, I've got nothing to lose. I got what I came here for... their goddamned supercomputer is out of action.

"But if you were working for me, then all we do is shake everyone's hand and walk out. And, kid, that's just the beginning. Because you'll have the supercomputer secrets and I'll have the contacts. We can put together one hell of a company when we get back to the States. Christ, we can even cut Toole in on the action. What are they going to do with him? Sentence him to two years and then give him a year off for good behavior? He'll be back in the country just about the time we'll be really getting things rolling. We'll be a team. Only then we'll be working for ourselves. We'll be way out ahead in the American supercomputer race."

"You want to take Fujii's code and use it for ourselves?" she asked. Cobb's bigger picture was just beginning to paint itself in front of her eyes.

"What would you like to do with it?" he asked sarcastically. "Turn it over to the Library of Congress? Or maybe bring it back to IAC, so that they can give you a bonus while they use it to make billions? Jesus, Karen, someone has to build on the information you've gathered. Someone has to get rich. Why shouldn't it be us? We're the ones who took the chances."

"Toole took the chances," she argued.

"And we'll make a place for him. For God's sake, will you just trust me! I'm not trying to screw Toole. But look at the facts. We can't help him now, and there's absolutely nothing to be gained for anyone by you going soft and joining him in prison. The smart thing to do is leave him here and go build ourselves a company. We'll have a place waiting for him when he gets out."

He could see that she still wasn't convinced.

"We can even help him get out. I've got friends and contacts in government. Once the furor dies down, it won't be hard to get our Japanese allies to release him. Believe me, I've thought this through from every angle. It's the only way. Trust me!"

She stared at him suspiciously. Trust him? That was out of the question. She wasn't sure whether he had always intended to take the supercomputer secrets for himself and had always planned to leave Toole behind in a Japanese prison. But she knew that most of the things he had told them when they were planning the operation were lies. And that opened the possibility that everything he was saying now was a lie.

"What do you want me to do?" she asked.

He smiled in satisfaction. "Just support my story." He bounded out of the chair and walked to the writing table. When he returned, he was carrying an envelope which he opened out onto the table between their glasses. "You're with the Justice Department," he told her. "Here are your credentials and a backgrounder on your assignment. Study it in case they ask any questions. What it basically says is that you infiltrated Signet and that Signet sent you here to work with Toole. The department directed you to accept the assignment so that you could find out who was cooperating with

Toole. Your opinion is that he was working alone. You're certain that Fujii wasn't working with him and you're not at all surprised to learn that Fujii was cooperating with the Japanese government. Say all the nice things about him that you want. God knows, he can use the help."

"And what does Toole say?" she asked.

He dismissed her concern with a wave of his hand. "Toole is a smart operator. He has nothing to gain by taking you with him. He certainly can't help his own cause. Hell, he carried enough plastic explosive into that place to level the whole building. Besides, he likes you. I don't think he'll want to see you get hurt."

She nodded that she understood. "There's just one more thing," she said as she reached over and picked up her champagne glass.

"What's that?" Cobb asked.

"This," she answered and with a flip of her wrist she threw the champagne into his face. "That's my toast to you, because you have to be the most miserable son of a bitch I've ever known. You're not good enough to share the same cell with J. P. Toole. And as for Fujii, they shouldn't even let you live on the same planet."

Cobb snatched a handkerchief from his jacket pocket and began dabbing at the spreading stains. But when he looked back up at Karen, he wasn't at all angry. As he answered, his face broke into a self-satisfied smile.

"Maybe you're right. I never did put much stock in character and goodness. What I trust is brains. And right now Fujii is looking for work as a janitor and Toole is being fitted for a striped suit, while I'm on my way back to the States to be a billionaire. So you figure out who has the brains."

"You're a bastard," she added.

"But I'm a smart bastard. That's why we will make such a great team. We're both smart. When I told you to trust me, I wasn't asking you to have faith in my good character. I was telling you to have faith in my intelligence. I'm smart enough to get what I want and if you play it my way, you'll get what you want. Never trust the good guys, lady, because they'll let you down every time. Trust a bastard. You can always count on a bastard to get what he wants. The trick is to make sure that the bastard wants the same things you do."

He walked to the ice bucket, took out another bottle and opened it. Then he refilled both glasses. As he handed Karen her glass, he said, "If you want to throw that one at me, too, go right ahead. The suit needs cleaning anyway. But if you're as smart as I think you are, you'll join me in a toast to our success. Because the bottom line is that you don't really have any choice."

He raised his glass to her and waited. Slowly, Karen brought her glass close to his. They touched glasses and then Karen watched him while he tossed his drink down. Then she brought her own glass to her lips.

"Partners?" he offered.

"To smart bastards," she agreed.

December 9th, 9:00 P.M., Tokyo

Toole thought he had all the answers. Unfortunately, it was too late to put them to use. His earlier instincts had been correct. He should have abandoned the plot and left the country. But he had stayed to protect Karen. Now, he realized, protecting her would cost him the next five to ten years of his life.

As he sat in his cell, really a locked bedroom on the top floor of the prison hospital, he had to admire how easily Cobb had taken him in. It had begun with their first meeting in Harrisburg, when Cobb had walked him outside the prison wall. He should have seen, right from the start, that Cobb wanted much more than just his expertise.

He had made the dumbest mistake imaginable in his profession. He had allowed himself to be flattered. "Pretty slick," Cobb had complimented him, referring to his Citibank caper, with lots of goodies added to show just how valuable his skills were to the government. He had accepted the implication that he was the only one qualified for the mission and had been tickled that the United States government would pay any price for his services. What services? All they had needed was some sleight of hand at a card table and an amateur's knowledge of computers. He provided no special skills. But what he did provide was a documented record as a thief and a reputation for running cons with computers. It should have been simple for him to figure out that what Cobb desperately needed was a credible felon. And once he had figured that out, his role in the scheme should have been apparent.

How had he missed it? The flattery, to be sure. Cobb had been smart enough to quote a price, not as payment but rather as testimony to the value of his skills. But there had also been the taste of freedom. He had been in jail and Cobb had staged their conversation outside the walls in a pastoral setting. There he hadn't promised Toole his freedom for cooperating. Instead, he had given him his freedom and then threatened to send him back for not cooperating. "Smart," Toole told himself, thinking of Cobb. "The bastard played me like a violin."

But how, Toole wondered, had Cobb been so sure that he would stay in line? Right from the beginning, on the flight to Boston, he had weighed his options. And two of the three options had involved his double-crossing the government agent. Cobb must have known that Toole had those possibilities. What made him confident that Toole would stay in the game until the last inning and would be waiting around to be the victim of his own reputation?

Could he have known that Toole would become involved with Karen? Was he smart enough to have guessed that once forced to work with a partner, Toole would never leave that partner behind? Had he selected an attractive, naïve woman as his computer expert specifically to keep Toole from running out? Or had that simply been a lucky break?

He climbed up out of the chair, finding it difficult to keep his balance. His ribs were heavily taped and his left arm was strapped to the side of his body to keep him from moving a badly dislocated shoulder. His head was still bandaged to protect the five stitches it had taken to close the wound in his scalp. He reached out and grabbed the bedpost for support, then lowered himself gently onto the bed.

Toole didn't even want to consider the other possibility. It seemed absurd. Yet he had been thoroughly taken in by Cobb in the beginning. He had to admit the possibility that he had been just as thoroughly duped by Karen in the end. Did she know the fate that Cobb planned for him when she lay in his arms? Was part of her assignment to keep J. P. Toole in line? Perhaps her love was the greatest con of all, played so skillfully that he still couldn't admit he had fallen for it. So entrapping that he was now ready to consign himself to a Japanese prison rather than risk betraying her.

It made sense. If Karen were part of Cobb's master scheme, then she would not have been putting herself at great risk by insisting on the meeting with Fujii. Cobb would have protected her just as he had protected himself. How ridiculous he must have looked begging Karen not to reveal herself to Fujii if Karen had known the whole scheme.

But he couldn't be certain. And because he was unsure, he had no way of fighting back. The Japanese had proof positive that he was the thief. First he had tried to steal the supercomputer programs. Then he had been caught in the act of destroying the supercomputer hardware, his pockets filled with records of the payments he had received and the airline tickets that he would use for his escape. His obvious guilt argued for everyone else's innocence. If he tried to involve Cobb, he would inevitably involve Karen. And the last thing the supercomputer plot needed was another innocent victim—if she was an innocent victim.

If only he could think clearly. There must be a logical explanation for the role she had played. There had to be positive answers that he could work with. But somewhere under the bandages, there was a drill bit still boring into the back of his skull. And his ribs were flashing like lightning with every breath that he drew. He could only get unfocused glimpses of the convoluted net in which he was entrapped. He couldn't think through the complete pattern of the twine.

He had two choices. He could fight back, charging Cobb with masterminding the scheme. He wasn't helpless. He had prepared some nasty surprise for Cobb on his trip back to the States. Maybe if he helped the Japanese catch a bigger fish—the whole United States government—he could bargain for a lighter sentence. Perhaps even for immunity! But, of course, the more he involved Cobb, the more he would involve Karen. There was no way that Karen could be innocent if Cobb were guilty. Or was there?

His other choice was simply to accept his obvious guilt. In fact, he could insist that he was operating alone; or operating with other Americans whom he would refuse to name. That would certainly aggravate his captors, and probably guarantee him a much stiffer sentence. But it would also assure Karen's freedom.

He could protect Karen only by playing his script exactly as Cobb had written it. Or he could play his own script. The problem was that he couldn't know which way to turn until he knew whether Karen was on his side or Cobb's. And that question tortured him more than his wounds.

He heard the key turning in the lock, and he tried to get out of the bed and into the chair. But his body responded much too slowly. His feet hadn't reached the floor when a uniformed guard opened the door. The guard stood back and allowed a young American in a dark business suit to enter. Toole pushed himself up from the bed, and held out his hand in greeting. "Mr. Wollensky," he started to say, but then he felt himself falling. The young American steadied him and led him to the chair.

"Let me call your doctor," Wollensky offered, but Toole shook off the suggestion.

"I'm fine if I stay in one place," he explained. "It's moving that gets me into trouble."

Wollensky nodded and spent a few seconds looking concerned. Then he got down to business. "I'm afraid moving isn't the biggest of your problems, Mr. Toole," he said. "We've been in contact with the Japanese and there doesn't seem to be very much that we can do for you."

"The American Embassy has struck out," Toole concluded.

"Well, not completely," the official answered. "We still intend to protect your interests in any way that we can. But I'm afraid that the Japanese are adamant. Usually, we can get them to release Americans who get involved with their laws into our custody. They're satisfied if we simply get them out of the country. But in your case, they intend to prosecute you under their laws. And I have to tell you that unless you cooperate with them, the penalty will be very severe. I think you should reconsider and let us get you a lawyer."

"What's a lawyer going to do for me?" Toole asked, implying that he already knew the answer.

Wollensky wasn't very enthusiastic. "Probably give you the same advice that we're giving you. Tell them who sent you here. Cooperate with them in their investigation. We can probably help you if you help them. But if you refuse to make a statement, we can't really work on your behalf. After all, the United States government takes a very dim view of industrial espionage."

Toole started to laugh, but the pain from his ribs cut him short.

"The U.S. government is opposed to stealing Japanese computer secrets?" he asked.

"Certainly," Wollensky answered. "We have patent and copyright agreements with these people."

Toole nodded his understanding. "Then I guess no one would believe that I was working for the United States government," Toole concluded.

Wollensky shook his head. "Please, Mr. Toole. This is no joking matter. Our government has been cooperating with the Japanese in their effort to expose you and arrest you. In fact, two American government officials will be presenting evidence against you at the preliminary hearing. And I can assure you that the Japanese will have very little sympathy for you if you insist on protecting the other people in your organization."

"Two?" Toole asked, suddenly becoming thoroughly interested.

"Yes," Wollensky said as he opened his briefcase and withdrew a folder of official papers. He flipped through the sheets. "Two people from the Justice Department. A John Cobb, who is the senior investigator on the case. And a specialist by the name of Karen Albert. I believe she infiltrated your operation on behalf of the government."

"I believe she did," Toole agreed. "And you say they have been cooperating with the Japanese government in its investigation? Do you know when this cooperation began?"

"Several months ago," Wollensky said. Toole's face went pale.

"Several months," Toole repeated.

"Yes. As I said, the United States government is fully committed to putting a stop to industrial espionage. So as you can imagine, they have a great deal of evidence against you.''

''I'll bet they do,'' Toole agreed.

''That's why I think you should have a lawyer and why I advise you to be completely cooperative. You have no reason to protect anyone. Why, the computer you were attempting to destroy doesn't even work.''

Toole looked stunned.

''So you see, there's nothing for you to gain by remaining obstinate. The secrets you're trying to protect are completely worthless.''

''It doesn't work?'' Toole asked carefully.

Wollensky reevaluated his statement. ''Well, of course, I can't be sure. I know nothing about computers. But I was told by the Japanese officials that the machine failed its test. Apparently they thought I knew, and were warning me that it made no difference to your case.''

''She did it,'' Toole said, a smile illuminating his face.

''She did what? Who?'' Wollensky asked.

''Nothing,'' Toole said, dismissing his own comment. Then he straightened his shoulders and tried to look forceful. ''Mr. Wollensky, please tell the Ambassador that I appreciate his interest, but I have no need of assistance. I'll handle my own defense.''

Wollensky opened his mouth in protest, but he stopped short of forming a word. He simply closed the briefcase as if he were shutting the lid on Toole's last hope.

''Can I help you back to your bed?'' he asked.

''No, thank you,'' Toole said. ''I think I'll stay up and begin working on my case.'' Wollensky knocked on the door, and the guard let him out.

She had done it. Somehow she had unscrambled the password and turned Fujii's superbrain into an idiot. She and Cobb had accomplished their mission and sunk Fujii's aircraft carrier. There would be no industrial Pearl Harbor. The steel hulls of American technology would stay afloat, at least for another few years. Probably until they rusted out and sank under their own weight.

And now, Karen and Cobb were making their escape—an escape they had probably been planning since the whole sick scheme had begun. What had Wollensky said? Karen had infiltrated his group. They had been working with the Japanese government for the past several months. All along they had been planning to leave him behind. His role in Cobb's grand plan had been to cover the retreat. And Karen had made certain that he played his role to the final curtain. He thought bitterly of their shared moments in her bed. She had done her job well.

December 10th, 9:30 A.M., Tokyo

They were all waiting when Toole was brought into the room. The government security official and the security officer from Fujii's company. A prosecutor from the Japanese Ministry of Justice. A police official from the barracks where Toole's arrest had been recorded, along with his interpreter. A Japanese attorney, assigned by the Justice Ministry over Toole's protest.

Wollensky from the American Embassy. Cobb, and seated beside him, Karen.

It wasn't a formal courtroom, but rather a conference room with a large central table surrounded by heavy chairs. Microphones were set at each place not for amplification, but simply to capture statements for the record. Toole had been told that this wasn't a trial, but rather a hearing in which the Japanese prosecutor would determine whether there was enough evidence to justify prosecution. In his case, as his appointed lawyer had explained in perfect English, there was little doubt about the evidence. The hearing would be strictly for the sake of adherence to procedure. "Don't bet on it," Toole had instructed his attorney.

His appearance had improved miraculously. The gauze wrap had been removed from his head, leaving just a small bandage in the center of the tonsure that had been shaved for his stitches. The strap that secured his arm was gone, replaced by a simple cloth sling. His white shirt with its tastefully patterned tie and the blue suit jacket hid the tape that circled his ribs. Toole ignored the pain that accompanied every motion and strode confidently into the room. He paused behind his chair and looked directly into each of the faces around the table, nodding to those he recognized. He lingered on Karen long enough to try a smile. Her eyes dropped. Finally he looked at Cobb and wasn't at all surprised to find two coldly confident eyes staring back at him. He had wondered how Cobb would react. How should a man respond when the ghost of someone he has ordered killed enters the room? His guess had been that Cobb would be unmoved.

Toole took his seat, slipped the arm out of the sling and rested it in front of him on the edge of the table. Immediately, the prosecutor leaned in toward his microphone and began speaking in stumbling English.

The hearing, he explained, was a preliminary review of the evidence to determine if a crime had been committed and if there were cause to begin criminal proceedings. Evidence would be heard and statements taken. As in United States law, he said for everyone's benefit, there was no presumption of guilt on the part of anyone. He raised his eyes and looked directly at Toole. "Nevertheless," he said, making it sound like three words, "statements made here can be cited in a trial." He advised all parties that they need not answer any questions or make any comments, but naturally he hoped for their fullest cooperation. "Cooperation," came out sounding like five words.

With his opening remarks delivered, he turned and nodded to the security officer from Fujii's firm. The man wrapped a hand around the bare of his microphone, cleared his throat, and in a low voice announced that he would read a statement prepared by Yamagata Fujii, an employee of his company, concerning an attempt by one J. P. Toole, an American citizen, to extort proprietary information from him. Toole's appointed lawyer interrupted politely to ask if the statement had been duly witnessed and notarized. While the security officer was explaining that it was, the prosecutor explained that such safeguards were not necessary for this type of hearing, which began a five-minute discussion in Japanese among the three men. Toole looked on unconcerned. When the discussion ended, the security officer began reading the statement, which told Toole that his lawyer had flunked his first test.

The statement recounted events that Toole had already figured out for himself. Fujii had been made aware of Toole's mission by John Cobb, a representative of the United States government. It had been decided, in the presence of government security officials, that Fujii would continue his contacts with Toole, and agree to supply Toole with information as it was requested. The intent was to follow the information—highly proprietary computer code—to the source of the conspiracy. As predicted, Toole had indeed attempted to extort the code from Fujii.

Next, a transcript of Toole's meeting with Fujii over the card table was read. Toole was stunned by the factual recitation of his own words. He had not realized that Fujii had worn a recorder.

Then, the security officer produced copies of the gambling checks that Toole had altered along with Fujii's doctored bank records. And then copies of the computer code that Fujii had turned over to Toole.

Finally, he reached under the table and hoisted a thick suitcase into full view. When he opened the lid, packets of cash spilled out onto the table. "One million American dollars," he told his startled audience. "This is the money that J. P. Toole delivered to Yamagata Fujii in payment for the information."

During the entire deposition, none of the Japanese had even glanced at Toole. Apparently it was impolite to stare at a man in his moment of shame.

The prosecutor asked how the bank records had been altered and received a blank expression in response. "We're not sure," the security officer answered. The bank, he explained, was still in the process of trying to trace the source of the false entries.

"So is Citibank," Toole thought, allowing himself a moment of self-adulation.

Next, the prosecutor turned to the police official, whose remarks were translated by an assistant from a chair in the second row. He recounted how the police had been summoned by the guard at Fujii's laboratory and had found Toole trapped beneath heavy equipment that he had apparently knocked over on top of himself. He described the plastic explosive that had been placed in the laboratory, and the wire connections that had been made to fire the bomb from an outside location.

Two points of his testimony were of interest to Toole. First was the explanation of how Toole had survived the crushing weight of the frame. As it fell, the police official said, the component blocks and cards had fallen forward. They had landed an instant before the frame and had broken the momentum of its fall.

"Lucky me," Toole told himself, running his fingers along the edge of the tape that bound him like a girdle.

The second surprise was the police officer's impression that there must have been one or more additional persons in the laboratory who had helped set the bomb. "The frame couldn't have been knocked over accidentally," he testified. It was much too heavy. "It was probably pushed from behind. And, of course, Toole could hardly have pushed it from behind, then run around it in time to be trapped by its fall." He speculated that probably Toole was pulling while one or more other persons were pushing, and that the structure had gotten out of their control and fallen on

Toole. No, he had no idea why they would have knocked over the frame. There was no need to destroy it in that manner since the explosion would have blown it to bits. And no, he couldn't explain how the frame had landed on Toole's back if he had been pulling on it and, presumably, facing it.

After a word of thanks to the police official, the prosecutor introduced John Cobb. Toole turned in his chair so that he would be looking directly at his accuser.

Cobb introduced himself as an agent for the National Security Agency of the United States, on temporary assignment to the U.S. Department of State. The title was impressive, drawing an admiring nod from the Japanese security officer and a wide-eyed gaze of amazement from Wollensky. Then he launched into his testimony, which he delivered with occasional glances at his notes.

"In February of this year, February the eighteenth I believe, the Japanese government informed the United States government that an American citizen, a Mr. Stanley Kaplan, had been apprehended in the act of stealing highly confidential commercial information. We were informed that the information clearly came under the terms of agreements between our two countries regarding mutual recognition of patents and copyrights. It was further the opinion of the Japanese government that Mr. Stanley Kaplan was not acting on his own behalf, but rather was an agent of an American corporation, Signet Corporation. Since United States policy recognizes the sanctity of patents and copyrights originating in friendly nations, the Department of State enlisted the aid of the Department of

Justice, and Justice, in turn, asked the help of my agency."

"Nothing new here," Toole thought. Cobb was telling the same story that he had put forward at their California meeting as his cover.

"We began a two-pronged investigation. I was assigned to work with Japanese officials and, as you know, I reported to you and presented my credentials. Miss Albert," and Cobb turned and smiled toward Karen, "was recruited from an American computer firm because of her technical expertise, and was infiltrated into Signet Corporations' California offices."

Toole stole a quick glance at Karen, who was involved in examining the cut of her fingernails. "So that's how they're playing it," he thought. "Karen was an American agent. She knew me because she was investigating me, not because she was part of my operation." But Cobb's statement posed a problem. Was this his effort to explain Karen's direct contacts with Fujii? Or was it true? Had Karen known all the details of Cobb's plan right from the beginning?

"Our investigations quickly identified J. P. Toole as Signet's operative in Japan. Toole was a convicted felon with extraordinary skills in computer technology. We could, of course, have arrested Mr. Toole at our leisure, but it was agreed with Japanese officials that our best course was to play along with his scheme in the hope that he would lead us to his superiors.

"Miss Albert, meanwhile, had been assigned by her superiors in Signet Corporation, who were ignorant of her true purpose in joining the company, to travel to Japan and assist Mr. Toole. She took it upon herself to form a relationship with Mr. Fujii in order to learn whether any Japanese employees of the corporation were part of the illegal industrial espionage scheme."

Cobb stopped his testimony while he consulted his notes. Toole again turned his attention to Karen. Who was she? What was her true role in Cobb's efforts to destroy the Japanese supercomputer? Was she counting on Toole's silence in order to escape? or had she been planning to use him as her scapegoat right from the very beginning? He needed to know her part in Cobb's plan before he could act. And she was the only one who could tell him.

"Our investigations," Cobb continued with a nod toward Karen, "have convinced us that J. P. Toole was Signet Corporation's only operative in your country. There were no Japanese nationals associated with his efforts."

The statement brought a smile of relief from the government security officer and an affirmative nod from the company's security executive.

"In the United States," Cobb concluded, "our people have closed Signet Corporation and are attempting to apprehend its officers. In Japan, we have concluded our investigations. We were about to recommend the arrest of Mr. Toole when we learned of his outrageous effort to destroy your computer system.

"Even though the technology involved proved defective," Cobb said sadly, "even though there is no such thing as a supercomputer, my government deeply regrets that American citizens were involved in efforts to steal your work, and then to destroy it. But we are pleased to have cooperated with Japanese officials in exposing and apprehending the culprits."

The Japanese were applauding before Cobb even finished his statement. He had said exactly what they wanted to hear. There was no supercomputer to upset the cherished relationship in which Americans spent all the research money to develop new technologies, and Japanese made all the profits building and selling the products which exploited the new technologies. The two nations were friends, not business enemies. And they would jointly prosecute anyone who tried to turn their relationship into economic conflict—by banishment, as with Fujii, or by imprisonment, as with Toole. Everyone had a place and everyone knew what that place was.

Cobb was smiling modestly, accepting the accolades of his audience. But Toole's eyes remained fixed on Karen. If she agreed with Cobb, then he had two choices. Let her escape with Cobb and become the victim that Cobb had always intended him to be, or take her and Cobb with him into the funeral pyre. But if she opposed Cobb, then there was a chance that he could save her along with himself.

As the applause died, the prosecutor nodded toward Karen. But her glance was still turned downward, and she missed the signal.

"Karen," Cobb said solicitously, "do you have anything further to add?"

She looked for a moment at Cobb and then turned her glance toward Toole. He tried to read her expression. There was despair in her eyes, but was it fear for the consequences of the truth she was about to tell or pity for Toole whom she was about to railroad into oblivion?

"Karen," Cobb repeated in a soft voice, "if you have nothing to add, I'm sure we'll all understand." He turned to the prosecutor. "As I said, Miss Albert is new to this kind of work. It's difficult for her to bring accusations against anyone." He reached over and, in a fatherly fashion, patted the back of her hand.

"Nice move," Toole thought. "Why should the Japanese want to press the issue? Why risk offending representatives of the American government? They had an agreed-upon villain. Everyone had done his job. And the technology was useless anyway! Once again, Cobb had told the prosecutor exactly what he wanted to hear. There was no need for further investigation.

Karen's voice startled him. She looked toward the Japanese officials and the sad despair was gone from her eyes. Instead, she looked angry.

"I do have a statement to make," she said.

Cobb's glib confidence seemed to drain from his face. "There's really no need . . ." he began to advise.

"As Mr. Cobb has stated, I am a computer specialist . . . a computer expert. And I am on special assignment to assist the United States government. But that's where the truth ends. After that, everything that Mr. Cobb said is a lie. In fact, Mr. Cobb is a lie. He's not just an embarrassment to the American people, he's a disgrace to mankind."

Cobb's jaw fell just as Toole's face spread into a smile. She hadn't been working with Cobb all along. And she wasn't about to join him now, even though her own safety depended on it. She was going to take them all down together in one final act of repentance, like Brunhild dragging Siegfried's horse into the fire. It was a noble gesture, but Toole wasn't ready for noble gestures. He had a better plan. And now was the time to put it into action.

December 10th, 9:40 A.M., Tokyo

The police were everywhere. It seemed to Kaplan that Smith had led him into a trap.

He had waited patiently in the taxi for two days, handing the driver an additional helping of Kado's savings every time the man seemed to be losing his patience. But even when he was paying a new assessment, his eyes never left the entrance to the hotel. Smith would be coming out; that was certain. And this time he wouldn't get away.

He had seen Kado rush from the building, waving his arms frantically as if he were trying to fly. A moment later, Smith had come through the doors, escorting a tall, stylishly dressed American woman. He had helped the woman into the taxi while the hotel doorman was bowing his profound respect.

Kaplan glanced to the end of the street. Kado's cousin was right in place, waiting in a parked taxi. Kado now turned his back on Kaplan and was doing his bird imitation toward his cousin. No matter which way Cobb headed, one of them would be waiting for him.

The taxi drifted away from the door and turned to the end of the hotel driveway. Kado bounded into the very next cab and was already moving in pursuit. Smith's taxi paused before entering the street, and then turned into the traffic and began moving toward Kaplan. He had screamed at his driver, gripping his shoulder with one hand while pointing at Smith's car with the other.

"Follow," he had commanded in Japanese, mimicking the sounds that Kado's cousin had helped him rehearse. His driver had moved out into the flow of cars, and fallen into position alongside Smith's taxi.

After a few intersections, they formed a line. Smith's cab pulled into the lead, with Kaplan's car directly behind, keeping bumper to bumper contact. Kado was leaning into the front seat of the taxi directly behind Kaplan's. The procession twisted its way through the city, and turned in front of the steps of the security offices. Kaplan watched the woman climb out and wait while the man he knew as Smith paid the fare. Then the man closed the car door behind him and walked with the woman up the steps.

Kaplan had already jumped from his taxi and had started up the steps when Kado grabbed him by the sleeve. With surprising strength, the little man swung him in a half-circle and was attempting to drag him back down to the street. "What's the matter with you?" Kaplan had shouted, tearing his arm free. "He's getting away." His response was a frantic stream of Japanese, accompanied by a pantomime that seemed to be a person directing traffic and blowing a whistle. After each characterization, Kado jabbed his finger toward the building.

"Yes, yes," Kaplan had yelled, "he went into the building." But as he turned to follow, Kado grabbed his sleeve again. He had torn his arm free, pushed Kado away, and darted toward the front door, taking the steps two at a time. Without looking back, he had dashed into the building.

Smith had vanished, probably into one of the elevators whose doors were opening and closing at the other side of the lobby. Kaplan rushed to the light board, picked up the column where the light was already ascending, and watched carefully until it stopped at a floor. Then he stepped into the next available car and pressed the button for the same floor.

When the door opened, he found himself staring into the faces of four Japanese policemen. Obviously he was about to be arrested and in a flash he considered his alternatives. Should he bolt through them and out into the corridor? Or should he push them back and close the elevator door in their faces? But before he could act, the officers stepped back, clearing a path for him. And as he walked uncertainly through their cordon, they smiled a greeting and tipped their heads in a gesture of respect. He watched over his shoulder while they boarded the elevator, then turned to find several more policemen standing in the hallway. As he looked around, he saw police everywhere, clustered around the water fountain, gathered in a lounge area, even in each of the offices that he could look into through the open doors. The damn place looked like a police station. And then he remembered Kado's pantomime and his friend's efforts to drag him away from the building. This must be the National Security building, where Kado had first picked up Smith's trail. That's what the diminutive Japanese had been trying to tell him. Smith had been leading him to certain arrest.

He saw two policemen walking toward him. He felt his heart stop, and for an instant thought of crashing through one of the doorways and into a room in order to escape. But then he noticed there was an American between the two officers, apparently a prisoner. The

American's arm was in a sling. The policemen and their prisoner stopped at a door directly across from him. When they pushed open the door, Kaplan saw Smith and his companion seated at a table.

He hesitated, leaning toward the room as if he were about to rush in, yet holding back to keep from throwing himself into the arms of the police officers who had just entered. It would take him only a second to thrash the truth out of Smith. But would the police give him a second?

He had to do something. He was surrounded by half the Tokyo police force. Undoubtedly they had been notified of his escape; his picture was probably hanging next to the Emperor's in every squad room in the city. It would be just a matter of time before he would feel the grasp of the law and hear the snap of the handcuffs around his wrists.

He was grabbed from behind. Kaplan wheeled murderously and saw the top of Kado's head. He looked down into pleading eyes, and this time he followed when his friend tugged at his shirt and led him down the corridor. As they passed the group of police officers gathered at the fountain, Kado offered a cheery greeting, which the men happily returned. Kaplan smiled and bowed his head and the officers returned the sign of respect.

Suddenly, Kado darted to one side, dragging Kaplan in tow. He pushed open the door to the men's room and swung Kaplan inside pushing him ahead until they reached the booths. Then he fired Kaplan into one of the stalls and slammed the door behind him.

Kaplan ran his massive hands up the sides of the walls. So this was where it had all led. All the months of physical training, the escape, the hiding, and then his brilliant scheme to catch Smith out in the open. It had all led to a three-foot cubicle that he was sharing with a toilet inside the headquarters of Japanese law enforcement. It had all been a waste. And the bitter frustration was that while Smith was only a few steps away, he might just as well have been on the other side of the ocean.

He was untouchable.

December 10th, 10:15 A.M., Tokyo

"Cobb is a liar," Karen repeated. "He didn't come here to protect your damn industrial secrets. He came here to steal them."

Cobb looked stunned. What in God's name was she doing? Didn't she understand that nothing she said could help Toole? All she could do was join Toole in the cell and probably take him along with the two of them. The prosecutor's eyes widened, then snapped quickly from Karen to Cobb and back to Karen. Wollensky, who had been rocking his chair backward, away from the table, bounced forward and nearly slid onto the floor. The two security officers began yelling at one another in Japanese and the police official, who had first leaned toward his assistant for a translation, clamped his hand over his own mouth as if he had just uttered an obscenity. Suddenly, everyone was talking at once, except the prosecutor, who was tapping his knuckles against the table in a plea for order, and Toole, who was smiling broadly at Karen. "You're okay, kid," he wanted to say, "but you haven't seen anything yet."

"Mr. Prosecutor," Cobb tried above the din, "it's obvious that the strain on Miss Albert has been excessive . . ." No one was listening to him, so he talked directly to Karen through clenched, smiling teeth. "What the fuck are you trying to do," he threatened. "I'll leave you here to rot. I swear to God I will."

Toole stood up from his chair, a motion that brought the two police guards springing to his side. He swung his good arm in a wide, overhead arc and brought the flat of his hand squarely on the table. The explosion snapped every head in his direction and brought instant silence to the room.

"My name is J. P. Toole," he announced. "I'm an agent of the United States National Security Agency and I'd like to bring these proceedings to a close as quickly as possible. I have a plane to catch."

Jaws slackened all around the room, followed by a hiss as the entire assembly seemed to gasp at once. "Holy shit," Wollensky said, breaking the silence. Toole looked at Cobb and found a face that looked as if it had been kicked in the groin. In Karen's eyes he saw the beginnings of laughter. He turned to the prosecutor, who was trying to dismiss what he had just heard by squeezing his eyes shut and then reopening them. "If I can have your attention, I think I can clear up this confusion right now."

"Mr. Prosecutor," Cobb said, rising out of his chair. But the prosecutor simply waved him back into his seat, never taking his eyes from Toole.

"You're a representative of the United States government?" the prosecutor demanded suspiciously.

"That's right," Toole answered. "National Security Agency, on loan to the Commerce Department."

The prosecutor's eyes narrowed. He pointed down the table toward Cobb. "Then, who is he?" he demanded.

"John Cobb is an officer of Signet Corporation, an American company that we have had under investigation at the request of our government. As Miss Albert has just stated, his purpose is to steal classified industrial information from your computer industry."

The company security officer shouted his interruption, starting with Toole, but finishing his statement in the direction of the prosecutor. "Impossible. Mr. Cobb has been working with us for the last six months to help apprehend the industrial spies." Now all the Japanese faces swung to Toole's end of the table, almost as if they were following the ball at a tennis match.

"Working with you?" Toole demanded, acting out the effort that was necessary to control his anger. "Or working you the way a pickpocket works a crowd? Wasn't he the one who advised you to print out your confidential software and turn it over to an extortionist? Is that how he was helping you apprehend industrial spies? By advising you to give the spies exactly what they wanted?"

He watched the puzzled looks on their faces and saw their eyes turn suspiciously toward Cobb. "Let me ask you something," he demanded. "Did any of you security experts ever check up on this man? Did you contact Mr. Wollensky here or anyone else from our embassy, and ask for Cobb's records? Did you contact Washington and authenticate his claims?"

The prosecutor turned balefully to the government and company security officers, who looked first at one another and then down at the table. "I'm afraid you didn't," Toole said, the anger in his voice replaced by compassion. "You let him just walk in off the street and claim to represent the United States government. Gentlemen, I can assure you, our government would never ask a friendly nation to turn over its valuable secrets to an extortionist.

"But don't be too hard on yourselves," Toole continued. "John Cobb is a master at his trade. In fact, before he joined Signet Corporation, he was serving three years in a federal prison for an espionage scheme in which he had raided the computer records of one of our leading banks."

"This is outrageous," Cobb interrupted. But Toole had the floor and he wasn't about to give it up.

"His mistake in this case was that he didn't even consider that Miss Albert might be a government infiltrator. So he made her a party to his scheme. Then he brought her here to support his lie. But, like myself, she is working for the government. She is well aware of who is trying to protect your classified information and who is trying to steal it."

"Holy shit," said Wollensky, this time more slowly.

The prosecutor was turning from Cobb to Toole and then from Toole to Cobb. He seemed to be trying to find the truth in their eyes. He settled on Toole. "But you were the one who approached Yamagata Fujii. He recorded your conversation."

Toole was nodding as the prosecutor spoke. "It had to be that way," he explained. "Consider for a moment our position. Your secret computer code had been delivered to an American company by an American citizen who had tuned into one of your telephone channels. You arrested the American, a low-level operative who obviously wasn't running the operation. What we needed to know was who had recruited him, who had planted the tap on the telephone line. It seemed likely that someone in Fujii's company or in his laboratory was part of the operation.

"So, we put your people under surveillance. I followed some of them myself. I'll be happy to turn over all the information we gathered on them. Their addresses. Their telephone calls. Their bank statements. We even learned their access codes to the computer. But you'll be very happy to hear that we found nothing. Found nothing because there was nothing to find." He looked at the company security officer. "Your people are extremely loyal, sir, and meticulously honest in their personal lives. You are to be commended."

"He was trying to compromise them," Cobb shouted. "He tried to steal their access codes."

"Why?" Toole demanded of Cobb. "Everyone in this room knows that Fujii had already turned the computer software over to me. Why would I need their access codes?"

He looked away from Cobb and continued addressing his Japanese audience, by now fascinated to the last man.

"I made contact with Fujii because there was the possibility that he was the one compromising his own code. The possibility!" he stressed in response to their aghast expressions. "After all, Yamagata Fujii is a world-renowned expert in a very valuable profession. Dozens of foreign companies have made him offers. If he were leaving to join a new company, wouldn't it make sense that he would try to take his work with him? Is it out of the question that he wouldn't have objected to pocketing a substantial profit in the process? If Fujii were conspiring and we tried to extort the same information from him, it seemed likely to us that he would contact the people to whom he was already supplying information. He would lead us to whoever was in charge of the operation. And, in a sense, that's exactly what he did. He led us directly to John Cobb."

"But you accepted the code that Fujii delivered," the government security official pointed out.

"Right," Toole agreed. "And then I turned it over to Signet Corporation who, as we already know, was involved in the plot. Signet, in turn, gave it to their new software expert for analysis. They didn't know, of course, that their new software expert was a government plant...Karen Albert." He bowed toward Karen and hoped her total confusion at the fabricated details he was narrating wasn't as obvious to the Japanese as it was to him. "And Signet, naturally, instructed Karen to deliver the code to their top operative in Japan." He turned back to Karen. "And to whom did you deliver the stolen code?"

"To John Cobb," she said, trying to make her words sound more like a statement than a question.

"Exactly," Toole concluded, realizing that in his monologue he was beginning to sound like Sherlock Holmes. "So our plan worked perfectly. Both Fujii and the code led us to the same person . . . John Cobb."

Cobb jumped to his feet. "I've had just about enough of this," he shouted. "I've been working with you people on a full disclosure basis for the last six months. I identified this man as your thief before any of you were aware of him. You know perfectly well whose side I have been working on. I would ask you to remember exactly where you apprehended J. P. Toole. As I recall, he was caught inside your top secret laboratory, wiring an explosive charge to your supercomputer. Now I ask you, does that sound like the policy of the United States government?''

Toole felt the eyes panning back toward him. ''An excellent point,'' he commented. ''If I may, I would like to turn to the statement of your own police for the explanation.'' He looked directly at the senior police official even though he knew that the man spoke no English. ''I believe in your statement you indicated that it would have been impossible for me to have pushed the frame over from behind and then run around it in time for it to have landed on top of me. I think it was your opinion that someone else must have pushed it over on top of me?'' He waited while the younger policeman translated, then watched the senior officer nod vigorously in agreement.

''That's exactly what happened,'' Toole continued. ''I was brought to the laboratory at gunpoint by two of John Cobb's assassins. They wired the charge, hit me over the head, and pushed the frame onto me. They expected that in the explosion all evidence of their crime would be destroyed. My body would be found among the ashes.

''Now, Cobb had already persuaded you that I was an industrial spy. So when you found my body, you would naturally assume that I had been killed by my own bomb. The case would have been quickly closed. It would have worked perfectly. . . if the bomb had exploded.''

''Absolutely fantastic,'' Cobb shouted, again leaping to his feet. ''That's the most incredible story I have ever heard.'' He wheeled on the two security officers. ''Gentlemen, how long am I expected to put up with this . . .''

"There's proof," Toole interrupted. "I can give you the location of a warehouse that contains an exact replica of the communications frame that was wired with the bomb. I think you'll find that the space was rented by Mr. Cobb. Or, if he has already disassembled the equipment, I think you'll find documentation to prove that he shipped components of the frame to the warehouse, and then back out again."

Toole paused dramatically. Then he continued, "I don't know exactly when he found out that I was actually a government agent. But from that instant on I was marked to die as the cover for his theft. Fortunately, he never learned that Miss Albert was working with the government or she most surely would have been with me, waiting for the bomb to go off."

The Japanese were looking at one another, with Cobb staring into their faces trying to see their thoughts. Karen was looking at Toole, suppressing a smile that was driving up the corners of her mouth. "Pure horseshit," she wanted to say in admiration. And Toole settled into his best choirboy expression. He had raised his chin, just as in his childhood on the basketball court. The Japanese had jumped to block the shot, leaving him an open lane to the basket.

"Gentlemen," Cobb said suddenly. His expression had gone from outrage to sweet reasonableness. "There's really a very simple way to settle this problem. What you have before you are two people claiming to be representatives of the United States government.

"In America, we keep meticulous records on people." He allowed a smile as he added, "Sometimes we think the records are too meticulous, bordering on invasion of privacy. But nevertheless, there are ample documents to prove conclusively who belongs to the American government, who works for Signet Corporation, and who is a convicted felon who has recently been relased from a federal prison. All these issues will be settled if you will simply ask Mr. Wollensky here...I'm sure no one doubts that he is a loyal American representing our Department of State...if you will ask Mr. Wollensky to use his good offices and check the records. I can sympathize with your confusion, but I think Mr. Toole's charade has gone on long enough."

The prosecutor turned to Wollensky.

"Sure," the young man said. "I'm dying to know who's who myself."

"We would be most grateful," said the prosecutor.

Cobb slid back into his chair and turned a toothy smile toward Toole. The smile narrowed maliciously when he pointed it toward Karen.

The prosecutor tapped his knuckles on the table indicating that he had reached a decision. "We will assemble here at noon tomorrow. Because there is no reason to assume anyone's guilt, you are all free to leave. But let me caution you..." His eyes moved meaningfully from Cobb, to Karen, to Toole, "against leaving the city. That would be very foolish. Noon tomorrow," he repeated forcefully.

"Noon tomorrow," Toole agreed with a comfortable smile.

Karen and Toole rose, nodded toward the prosecutor and left immediately. Cobb walked to the end of the table and began his apology to the government and company security officers. "This is appalling," he said with a despairing shake of his head. "I regret the embarrassment that this entire hearing must have caused you."

The Japanese faces showed no expression.

"He was lying," Cobb insisted. "Surely you don't believe that there was any truth in his charges. The man's a thief. A cheap con man."

"Noon tomorrow," the government official said. He bowed his respects.

Cobb felt as if he were about to be sick. He left the hearing room and searched the doors of the corridor until he saw the symbol for the men's rest room. He pushed open the door and ignored the familiar-looking diminutive Japanese who seemed to be playing with the water in one of the washbasins. Cobb walked to the first stall, pushed open the door and started to go in.

KAPLAN COULDN'T BELIEVE HIS EYES. God had just opened the lid of his python cage and thrown in a rat.

"Excuse me," Cobb said when he realized that the stall was already occupied. He started to back out, but then there was a flash of recognition. In the electric fire in the giant man's eyes he saw righteous anger and retribution. While he couldn't connect a name to the face, he understood instantly that this was the specter of past transgressions that had been chasing him through the paths of time. He knew that he was about to be slaughtered.

"Smith," the python hissed.

"Jesus," Cobb prayed. He remembered well who it was he had conned with that name—a fat dunce of an accountant he had thrown to the Japanese to trigger his plan. And this giant from another planet had to be his big brother—or perhaps his soul reincarnated into the body of an outraged ape. He ducked under the swiping hand, pivoted, and lunged back out of the stall.

Cobb reached the door. Had it swung out, he might have been able to plunge through and out into the safety of the corridor. But the door swung into the men's room, and while he was pulling on the metal handle, two hands crashed down on his shoulders and locked his torso in a vise. He felt himself being snatched into the air and he screamed against the door hoping that his voice would carry out into the hall. He felt his spine snap as he was hurled backward through the air. He saw the shapes of washbasins flying by, then hit the tile floor like a stone skipping over the surface of a pond. After he stopped bouncing, he continued to slide until his head crashed into the wall at the opposite end of the men's room.

He opened his eyes to see two enormous hands reaching down toward him. He was snatched from the floor by his armpits and found himself staring into the angry eyes, his feet churning furiously in space.

"You're going to tell them," Kaplan screamed, his voice as deafening as the whine of a turbine. "You're going to tell them everything."

Kaplan began shaking Cobb like a rag doll, making him appear to Kado to be the personification of the cement blocks. He hurled phrases into Cobb's face. "You're going to tell them how you conned me. You're going to tell them how you betrayed me. You're going to tell them how you left me to rot." He punctuated each phrase by snapping Cobb's body like a whip.

"Do you understand?" Kaplan kept demanding.

"Yes, yes, I'll tell them," Cobb promised after each order, but Kaplan wasn't satisfied with promises. He kept thrashing Cobb's body and firing out new orders.

Kado could see that Cobb was going to come apart. The furious shaking had to separate bones from ligaments and muscles from tendons. He sprung up on Kaplan's back to keep his friend from committing murder.

"You're going to take the blame," Kaplan yelled, oblivious to Kado's arms wrapped around his neck.

"I will," Cobb prayed.

Crack went his body as Kaplan shook him again.

When the two Japanese policemen rushed into the room to investigate the screams, they saw Kaplan spinning in circles as he throttled Cobb and tried to throw the rider from his back. They grabbed Kaplan's arms and then felt their own feet rising from the floor. Kaplan fired Cobb against the wall, then spun and tossed the two policemen back across the room. He picked Kado off his back with one hand and dropped him into one of the washbasins; where he landed with his butt in the basin and his legs dangling over the edge. Then he turned back to Cobb, who was in the process of sliding down the wall.

"I'll tell them everything," Cobb yelled, as Kaplan's hands reached out for him. This time the huge palms closed against the sides of his head. As he felt himself being lifted, he knew that his head was about to be torn from his body.

One of the policemen reached up behind Kaplan, swung his club in a compact arc and smashed it against Kaplan's skull. Kaplan set Cobb down carefully, turned on the policeman and snatched the club from his hand. He took the stick by its ends, broke it over his knee, and tossed the splintered ends on the floor. Then he turned back to Cobb, who was staring at the broken club, visualizing what the maddened gorilla could do to his arm.

"Please!" Cobb screamed. "I'll do whatever you say."

Kaplan again reached out for him, but at that instant a second club smashed against his shoulder. When he wheeled and grabbed for the club, he saw two more policemen bursting through the door.

He lifted the officer who had just struck him and threw him toward the newcomers, scattering them like bowling pins against the far wall. Then he felt Kado, who had climbed out of the sink, spring up onto his back. He spun violently, launching Kado into one of the booths. The first police officer grabbed him around the knees and tried to tackle him to the floor. While he was pulling his foot free, Cobb jumped up onto his back.

Kaplan lost his balance and tumbled to the floor, nearly crushing the officer who clung to his legs. Cobb was on top of him. He rolled over, his motion tossing Cobb under the row of basins. But before he could get up, another uniformed body came flying through the air and landed on his chest. Then two more policemen pounced on him.

He began peeling them off as if they were layers of sweaters. But suddenly he froze as something sharp dug into the soft flesh of his neck. Cobb had picked up the broken club and was pressing the splintered end against his throat.

"Hold the bastard," Cobb shouted to the officers. "Get some handcuffs on him." They didn't understand his command. But they were already pulling Kaplan's arms behind his back.

December 11th, 12:05 P.M., Tokyo

John Cobb wasn't surprised that Toole hadn't shown up for the hearing. When he strode confidently into the room, he smiled at all the Japanese officials who were waiting in their places, noted the empty chair that Wollensky had occupied on the previous day, and saw Karen sitting by herself at the end of the table. He took his place next to Karen.

"I think I can still get you out of this," he said softly, through a smile designed to make his whispered comments appear to the Japanese to be a simple word of greeting.

She didn't even look toward him.

"Toole is finished," he whispered. "Right now, he's probably trying to smuggle himself out of the country. He knows that as soon as Wollensky gets here with the records, this case is closed."

She didn't respond. Instead, she left her chair and walked out into the hallway to the water fountain. Cobb nodded apologetically toward the prosecutor, rose and followed her.

"Don't be stupid," he said when he was standing beside her, filling a paper cup with water. "I can get you off. I know what Wollensky is going to report on you. For Christ's sake, I wrote your damn records. I can explain your role. All you have to do is agree with me. Back up what I say."

"If you can get Toole out of this, I'll go along with you," she said.

He answered through clenched teeth. "Toole is finished. There's nothing we can do for him. It's you I'm talking about. You're either coming with me or you're staying here in prison. Which is it going to be?"

"I'm staying," she said without a moment's hesitation.

Cobb stared into her eyes and saw the determination. "Okay, then you're going to be just what your records say you are. An employee of Signet Corporation. See you in about ten years," he concluded as he walked past her and back into the hearing room.

The prosecutor was examining his watch. He turned and whispered to the police official, who stood up and walked toward the door. As he turned into the corridor, he collided with J. P. Toole.

"Mr. Toole," the prosecutor said, rising from his chair. "I was afraid that you had decided not to join us."

"Wouldn't have missed it for the world," Toole answered. "Actually, I have a great deal of trouble waving for taxis." He indicated his arm, which still rested in the sling.

As he walked to his place, he smiled at Karen, who almost laughed with pleasure to see him again. Then he looked directly at Cobb. "I thought you'd be crawling into the hold of a freighter," he said.

Cobb sneered. "I think you're in for a surprise, Toole," he answered.

"I love surprises," Toole said as he settled into his chair.

They all turned toward the doorway at the sound of footsteps running in the corridor. Wollensky's form flashed past the opening, followed by the screech of leather heels on the tile floor. He reappeared, his jacket open and his necktie thrown back over his shoulder.

"I'm sorry," he said as he ran around the table to his seat. "It's the time difference. These reports just came in a few minutes ago."

As soon as Wollensky was seated, the prosecutor tapped his knuckles on the table. Then he turned in his chair to face the representative from the American Embassy.

Wollensky opened his briefcase on the table and took out a stack of teletype sheets. He closed the case and slipped it under his chair. Then he lifted the pages and began to read.

"Karen Albert. An employee of IAC Corporation, Advanced Systems Research Divison. On leave from her company beginning April thirtieth of this year. Temporary assignment as consultant to United States Department of Justice in a matter of industrial espionage involving corporate and individual citizens of the United States. Specifics available only to persons with *Secret* clearance..." Wollensky looked up from the document. "There's biographical information... education, family, that sort of thing. Should I read it?"

Cobb looked startled. It wasn't the record that he had prepared for Karen. The report made no reference to Signet, or to the payments that Signet had made to her account. Something was wrong. He looked at Wollensky, who was droning on through the details of her biography. "What the hell is the matter with the embassy," he thought. "Don't they know how to do a record check?" He had left the information in the most obvious places. How the hell could they have missed the Signet connection he had planted?

"John Cobb," Wollensky said, turning to a new page. "A principal shareholder in Signet Corporation, an American corporation involved in the development of advanced computer systems..."

"What?" Cobb shouted, exploding to his feet.

The prosecutor motioned for him to be seated.

"That's a lie," Cobb said. He started up along the edge of the table toward Wollensky. "Let me see that," he demanded.

"Be seated," the prosecutor ordered.

"But that's bullshit," Cobb shouted.

"Take your seat," the prosecutor commanded, "or I'll have the police officers take you to your seat." His voice left no doubt that he meant exactly what he said. Cobb retreated to his place, never taking his eyes off the paper that Wollensky was holding.

Wollensky continued. "Convicted of fraud in January of last year, specifically of using interstate telephone lines to illegally alter to his own benefit the records of banks in New York, New Jersey, and Pennsylvania. Sentenced to three years' imprisonment. Released after serving one year of his sentence on March first of this year."

"That's him," Cobb screamed, jumping up and jabbing his finger toward Toole. "You dumb son of a bitch, you've got the names mixed up. That's Toole's record."

The prosecutor nodded to the police officers, who left their post at the door and started around the table toward Cobb. Cobb dropped back into his seat and listened while Wollensky added background information that was clearly his own. He looked over at Toole, who was examining the bruises on the back of his hand. And then he understood what was happening.

"You changed my records," he said in a tone that was barely audible.

"Wait until you hear mine," Toole said without looking up.

"There's an additional report on Mr. Cobb," Wollensky offered when he had finished Cobb's personal data. "I asked for a search of files of government employees. It's quite thorough. There is no one named John Cobb, no one with Mr. Cobb's Social Security number who is presently on the payroll of the United States government."

Cobb didn't have to listen to the report on Toole. He now knew exactly why Toole had gone back to the United States. With his toy computer and his dimestore modem, he had broken into all the relevant data banks and rewritten all the records. It wouldn't have surprised him if Toole's record showed him to have been America's first astronaut.

"J. P. Toole," Wollensky intoned, turning to a new page, "is a federal employee, listed as a case supervisor for the National Security Agency. He took this position in January of 1984. Toole joined the federal government as an attorney with the Department of Justice in September 1980..." He continued through an illustrious career, which began with Toole serving as a captain in the United States Navy legal branch. Then he started into biographical data, beginning with his graduation, magna cum laude, from Harvard Law School.

Karen was biting her lower lip, shaking with fear that she might burst out laughing. Toole had told her about the entrapping records that Cobb had prepared for the two of them. And he had hinted that he had used his time in the States to prepare for the worst. But she had never suspected what that preparation might be. Now, all she hoped was that he hadn't credited himself with the Heisman Trophy.

Cobb rose wearily after Wollensky closed his file. "Mr. Prosecutor, I really must protest. Every one of those records is a forgery, engineered by Mr. Toole, who is quite adept at forging computer records. I must ask that Mr. Wollensky talk directly with some knowledgeable person in the government. And because he is affiliated with our Department of State, I would suggest that he talk directly with the Secretary. The Secretary of State knows me well."

The prosecutor acknowledged the comment but his expression made no promises. He looked down and examined the notes he had spread before him. "Mr. Cobb," he asked, "have you ever used a..." He grasped for a word, but couldn't locate it. He whispered a question in Japanese to the police official, who in turn whispered in Japanese to his interpreter. It was the interpreter who finished the question.

"A pseudonym. The prosecutor asks if you have ever used a name other than your own."

"Of course not," Cobb snapped, his indignation clearly boiling beneath the surface.

"You have never given your name as Smith?" the prosecutor persisted.

Cobb dropped limply back into his chair. He knew instantly where the questions were leading. "Well, yes. Of course. In the line of my official duties I have had to...withhold my true identity. In that capacity, I may have used Smith. It's quite possible."

"And did your official duties as a representative of the United States government ever include tapping telephone lines here in Tokyo and copying the computer code that was being transmitted over those lines?"

"Certainly not," Cobb answered.

The prosecutor pointed toward the door and one of the policemen followed the signal out into the corridor. All eyes turned to the opening, which was suddenly filled by the massive form of Stanley Kaplan. His hands were cuffed behind his back and he was attended by two additional policemen who watched him cautiously.

"Mr. Kaplan," the prosecutor asked, "do you recognize any one of the persons in this room?" The question was unnecessary. Kaplan's eyes were already boring into Cobb and the muscles in his neck were as tight as cables.

"That son of a bitch," Kaplan answered, pointing at Cobb with a snap of his head. "Him. Smith."

"This person," the prosecutor continued, pointing a finger directly at Cobb, "told you that his name was Smith?"

"Yeah!" Kaplan responded. He was beginning to breath heavily, his chest rumbling like the ground a moment before the eruption of a volcano.

"Did he ask you to undertake any mission on his behalf?"

Kaplan talked without moving his lips. "He's the one who had me copy telephone transmissions and send him the tapes. He's the one who set me up in that pottery factory. And when I got caught, he left me to rot." The weight of his words caused him to lean toward Cobb, and by the time he finished his statement it took both policemen, pulling on his cuffed hands, to keep him from leaping over the table.

"Where did he have you send the tapes?" the prosecutor said.

"To Signet Corporation," Kaplan said, "in California."

The prosecutor nodded. Then he turned to Cobb, who was leaning back in his chair trying to keep as much distance as possible between himself and Kaplan.

"Was it in your capacity as an agent of the United States government that you gave this man Smith as your name?"

"No, but you don't have the complete picture..." Cobb tried.

"Was it in your capacity as an agent of the United States government that you hired this man to steal Japanese industrial secrets?"

Cobb was shaking his head trying to formulate some sort of coherent answer.

"Who were you representing when you directed him to send those secrets to Signet Corporation?" the prosecutor pressed on.

"One moment," interrupted the attorney who had been appointed to represent Toole. "It seems obvious that Mr. Cobb here should be represented by counsel. Shouldn't I have a few moments with him before he answers any further questions?"

The prosecutor looked disdainfully at the young lawyer and then at Cobb. "Mr. Cobb, would you like to consult with an attorney of your choice?"

"What the hell do I need a lawyer for?" Cobb yelled. "I'm a representative of the American government. I demand that my embassy contact the Secretary of State."

"Yes," the prosecutor agreed. "Mr. Wollensky, will you contact your superiors for a direct comment on Mr. Cobb's status?"

Wollensky assured him that he would.

"In the meantime, I think we have sufficient reason to detain Mr. Cobb. I direct that he be placed in police custody until we hear from Mr. Wollensky.

"Mr. Toole and Miss Albert. I sincerely regret the difficulties we have caused you." Toole was already waving his hand to indicate that the difficulties were of no concern. "Further, I think the Japanese people owe you a great debt for your efforts." Toole allowed himself to turn pink with embarrassment. "It will be my pleasure," the prosecutor continued, "to write directly to your superiors and commend your fine work."

"No need," said Toole, rising. "The United States is always pleased to be of service to a friendly nation. But there is one favor you might do me."

"Of course," said the prosecutor.

"This man Kaplan. He seems insignificant now that we have apprehended the top man in the conspiracy. I believe he was tricked into his actions and I believe that he has already paid a severe penalty for his mistake. I wonder if you would release him into my custody if I guarantee to have him out of your country by nightfall?"

The prosecutor consulted with the government security officer and then with the police official. "Will the embassy request his release?" he asked Wollensky. Wollensky nodded.

"In your custody," the prosecutor said. "But the police will accompany him to the airport."

"Thank you," Toole said, starting around the table and shaking hands with the Japanese. When he reached Wollensky, the embassy official whispered, "I really thought you were the spy. I never would have pegged you for a secret agent."

"If you did, it wouldn't have been a secret," Toole responded with a smile. "And now, gentlemen, if I may have my property, I'll be on my way"

"Property?" the prosecutor asked.

"The million dollars," Toole said. "With our balance of payments, we can't just leave it here."

"Of course," the security officer laughed. He translated Toole's comment for the police official, who howled with delight.

"But we should count it and get a receipt," the government security official said, as he placed the case on the table and snapped it open.

"Did you take any out?" Toole laughed.

"Certainly not," the security officer laughed back.

"Then it's all there," Toole said as he took a piece of paper and scribbled out a receipt.

Cobb awakened from his shock in time to see the Japanese close the case and hand it to Toole. He jumped to his feet. "You're not going to let that crook walk out of here with a million dollars?" he demanded. "That's United States government property."

"That's why they're entrusting it to a government official," Toole answered. He held out his hand to John Cobb. "As one American to another, I want to wish you the best of luck."

"You know I'm going to get you, don't you, Toole?" Cobb demanded.

Toole glanced at the two policemen who were standing on both sides of Cobb. "Not any time soon, I don't think."

Karen had gathered her things. "Good-bye, Cobb," she said pleasantly. "I'll see you in about ten years."

Toole slipped his arm out of the sling and offered it to Karen. In his good hand, he carried the million dol-lars. They left together.

December 11th, 8:00 A.M., Washington, D.C.

The Secretary of State unfolded his copy of the *Washington Post* as if he were unwrapping a bomb and peeked cautiously at the headline.

"Pentagon Admits $3 billion Overrun on Supermissile," it said.

"Thank God," he prayed in relief. Now the Secretary of Defense would be getting his share of publicity.

The *Post*'s headlines over the last week had been a litany of diplomatic disasters. The Russians had walked out of talks designed to establish the seating protocol for disarmament talks. They hadn't left a forwarding address. The top general of a Latin American junta, who had just paid a state visit to the White House, had been overthrown by a People's Democratic Committee for Freedom, who immediately sent a representative on a state visit to Cuba. A militant Senator from Kansas had promised to supply Taiwan with cruise missiles, ruffling the feathers of the People's Republic of China. The French, who had already left NATO and the EEC, were now toying with the idea of leaving Europe. The Israelis had taken the position that they wouldn't negotiate with anyone who wasn't Jewish. And the New York City police had towed away the King of Norway's automobile while he was speaking at the United Nations.

Moments after he read each headline, before he could crack the top of his morning egg, the President had been on the telephone. Today, it would be the Secretary of Defense who drank his coffee cold.

He opened the paper next to his plate, lifted the silver lid from the dish in front of him, and selected a slice of buttered toast. Then he poured his coffee, tipped in a heaping spoon of sugar, and stirred absently while he began leafing through the pages. "Serves the little bastard right," he thought of the Secretary of Defense while he scanned the lead story. The man had seized the run of diplomatic errors to nuzzle up closer to the President and suggested that perhaps military intelligence might look into the operation of the normal diplomatic channels that seemed to have been delivering a great deal of misinformation. "Maybe I should suggest that State lend him a couple of bookkeepers," the Secretary mused.

It was on page six that he caught an INS piece datelined Tokyo. "Japan Charges American in Computer Theft," the headline read. The copy began: "An American, John Cobb, has been detained by Japanese security officers..." He felt the toast stick in his throat.

He remembered Cobb. It was back in April when the man had come to his house with some harebrained scheme about getting the Japanese to destroy their own computers. He had thrown him out, hadn't he? He remembered some of the details of their meeting. Supercilious little wimp. More concerned about the vintage of the wine than he was about plotting against a friendly nation. Hope he likes the vintages they serve in prison.

Wait a minute. He hadn't thrown him out. He was going to, but then Cobb had threatened to appeal to the President. That's right. The guy was a friend of the President.

He reached for his telephone and dialed the White House switchboard. The operator put him through to the President's secretary. After a few minutes he heard the President's voice.

"Good morning, Mr. President," he said.

"Fucking Pentagon," the President answered.

"I saw the story," the Secretary said. "Three billion dollars and only a week after we cut ten million from the school lunch program. I guess the *Post* will have a field day."

The President growled. "It would be worth three billion if they could fire the damn thing into the *Post*'s newsroom. But I understand it couldn't hit the Atlantic Ocean. Christ, they've nicknamed the damn thing the 'boomerang.' They're afraid to test-fire it for fear it will come back and get them."

"Three billion," the Secretary repeated.

"Well, at least it douses the fires under you. Nothing like a good Pentagon scandal to get State off the front page," the President chided. "I hope you called me with some good news."

"No disasters," the Secretary assured him. "But maybe a small problem. Do you remember a guy named John Cobb? He was on some kind of NSA assignment, I think, using Commerce as a cover. It had to do with a computer that the Japanese were about to introduce.''

''Yes,'' the President said, his voice suddenly calm. ''What about him?''

''The Japanese have arrested him,'' the Secretary of State said.

''Jesus Christ,'' the President answered.

The tone of the President's voice assured the Secretary that Cobb wasn't as small a matter as he had hoped. ''It seems likely that we'll be hearing from the Japanese. They always ask our cooperation on these matters. Background information for starters and probably some investigative help within our own country. And, of course, we comply. Should this guy get any special treatment from us?''

''What guy?'' the President asked.

''John Cobb,'' said the Secretary.

''I've never heard of him,'' the President said. ''And for God's sake, make sure that no one in government has ever heard of him either. If he was stealing computer secrets, he can't be working for us. We don't do that sort of thing.''

''I understand,'' the Secretary answered. ''I'll see that it's taken care of. I was just concerned that he might be a friend of yours.''

''A friend? I don't associate with people who steal,'' the President barked. ''I never heard of him. You never heard of him. Nobody who wants to stay in this administration ever heard of him. If the Japanese ask, tell them we have no knowledge of John Cobb and absolutely no interest in John Cobb. Tell them to put him in jail. And while you're talking to them, ask them if they have any room for our Secretary of Defense.'' He clicked off the line.

The Secretary of State reached for his egg, set it in his egg cup, and began cracking the top. It looked as if it was going to be a good day. God knows, he deserved one.

December 11th, 4:00 P.M., Tokyo

Karen gasped when she saw the knife on the small table in front of Fujii's altar. It confirmed her worst fears. He was a proud man who had little patience with failure. When failure visited his own life, he wouldn't hesitate to inflict the penalty upon himself.

She had rushed straight from the hearing room to Fujii's house, rung the bell and then knocked on the door when the bell brought no response. There had been no sign of movement inside. Finally she had tried the door, which had pushed open easily. She called his name into the silence and became alarmed when there was no answer. Inside, she had walked through his library with its collection of Japanese epics and replicas of victorious ships and airplanes. Then she had remembered the room where Fujii had destroyed the memory of the *Akagi*'s defeat and she had thought of how he might destroy the memory of his own defeat. She had run through the garden to the room and slid open the door.

The Buddha Who Is to Come waited in the tokonoma, but the coals in the brazier before it were cold and dusty. A small table was placed in the center of the room, directly in front of the shrine. The fifteen-inch blade, drawn from its scabbard, waited on the table.

"Three times I knelt with it in my hands," Fujii's voice said behind her. She wheeled abruptly. He was standing in the doorway, wearing Western clothes; dark slacks with a white sweater pulled over his open-necked shirt. His face was sallow, with dark blotches at the corners of his eyes. She could see immediately that he hadn't slept since his disastrous demonstration.

"I didn't answer because I didn't think I wanted to see you," Fujii said. "But when you came into the house, I thought that at least I ought to congratulate you. You did an exceptional job with my computer."

"I'm sorry," Karen said. She looked down at the gleaming blade. "I wouldn't blame you if you used that thing on me."

"No," Fujii answered. "That one can be used only on oneself. It's part of a set. There's a much larger sword for enemies."

"I deserve it more than you do," Karen said. She glanced again at the knife. "You . . . won't . . ."

Fujii forced a smile. "No," he answered. He walked to the table and lifted the weapon by the handle. He touched the point with his fingertip. "When I held this against my belly, I wasn't afraid. I just felt stupid. I remembered that the Captain of *Akagi* had tied himself to the ship's anchor so that he would go with it to the bottom of the Pacific. But his crew thought that losing the ship was bad enough. They didn't want to lose a valuable naval officer as well. So they cut him free and took him off *Akagi*. I decided I still had a great deal of work to do. I guess I don't believe in useless gestures. And pushing this into my stomach would have been a useless gesture." He slid the blade back into the scabbard.

Karen followed him as he walked back through the garden and into the main room. "May I get you something to drink?" he offered. "I have some scotch." She shook her head. He continued into the kitchen and poured a drink for himself, then brought it back to the low table where he gestured toward one of the cushions. She sat uneasily.

"I had to talk to you," she began. "I wanted you to know that I never meant to do this to you."

"Please, don't . . ." he tried.

"I have to say this," Karen persisted, "although I have no right to ask you to listen. But it wasn't...you. I thought I was fighting against a machine."

"You were," he told her calmly. "And you beat it very badly. You were a complete success."

"It was a challenge," Karen continued. "When they told me about the computer, that it had to be derailed, I took it as a challenge. Almost a game. And then when I got here, I started working with the computer... talking to it for hours and hours each day. At first I was almost walking around it, looking at it in awe. It was so far ahead of the best machines that I'd ever worked with."

He acknowledged the compliment with a tip of his glass.

"Then I began to understand it. I started to see the weaknesses. But it was just a machine, so it didn't seem so bad to outsmart it. Then we met. I began to realize that the machine was really you. It was daring because you were daring. It was brilliant because you were brilliant. And I guess I knew that when I took the Akagi computer down, I'd be taking you down as well.

But by then, things were too far along. I was in over my head. I should have stopped but I didn't know how."

"You shouldn't apologize for your victories," Fujii cautioned.

"That's not what I'm trying to do," Karen corrected. "What I want you to know is that I never would have gotten into this if I had known you. I wouldn't have come here to hurt you. I never would have agreed to destroy the computer if I had understood how much of you was in the computer."

She watched for his reaction, but there was none. "Does anything I'm saying make sense?"

Fujii nodded.

"I guess I'm hoping that you won't always hate me," she concluded.

Fujii set his glass on the table and looked directly at her. "You didn't destroy the Akagi computer," he told her. "I did."

She looked shocked.

"If I had done it their way," he continued, "you couldn't have destroyed it. But I insisted on doing it my way. My superiors wanted me to proceed slowly... cautiously. But I insisted on a large, public demonstration. They wanted me to work with a larger team and share the information so there would be many people fully versed in the new technology. I wanted to keep it to myself. They wanted numerous copies of each part of the code. But I didn't want anyone else to demonstrate any part of my work. So I kept the only copies...the ones you destroyed. If I had played by the rules, you wouldn't have been able to hurt us. Too many people would have understood the work. There would have been too many copies of the code. So, you see, it was my own arrogance that sunk Akagi. I'm the one that I have to forgive. The problem is that I'm not yet ready to do that."

Karen couldn't allow him to blame himself. "But if you had worked their way, would you have been so far ahead?" she asked. "No team could have duplicated what you created in your own head."

"Perhaps," Fujii agreed. "But it would have been safer to work in the more traditional way. What I didn't understand is how well you knew me. You had to know exactly how I worked. You had to be certain that I would keep the only copies for myself. Otherwise your plan could never have succeeded. I was the inventor of the Akagi program. But I was also its greatest weakness. And you saw that weakness. Was that your insight?"

"No," Karen said. "Toole saw it. He read everything you had written and talked with people who had worked with you."

"Toole," Fujii repeated. "I took him for a fool. He's not what he appears to be."

"That's his profession," Karen agreed. But then she asked the question that had brought her to Fujii's home. "What will you do, now?"

He smiled. "For a while, I'll do just what I've been doing. I'll feel very sorry for myself. It's a pleasant way to get over one's mistakes. But then I'll get back to work. It will take a few months to reconstruct the code. Perhaps several more months to persuade my offended leaders to let me get on with my work. I still hope to beat you, even though your company will be starting where I left off."

"I'm not going back to my company," Karen said. "And I'm not going to compete with you. I'm just going to take everything I know and try to build a supercomputer. The best machine I can conceive."

"For the Americans," Fujii said, stating what he thought was obvious.

"No," Karen said. "For anyone who is interested in a new kind of computer. Remember when I visited here before? I asked why we had to be on different sides since we were both trying to do the same thing. You said that that was just the way it was. Well, I don't agree. I don't believe that you and I have to be competing against one another. I believe that if we worked together we could come up with something far better than the Akagi computer."

"I work alone," Fujii reminded Karen. "That's what gets me into trouble."

"Can't we work together?" she asked.

He looked at her for a long time without speaking. "You know I was going to send you to prison?" he asked.

She nodded that she knew.

"After I . . . the night you bathed with me . . ."

"We were both trying to hurt each other," Karen admitted. "But that's in the past."

His amazement was obvious. "You're serious about working together," he said.

"We could get the backing," Karen explained. "We both have reputations . . . and experience. Only it would be on our terms. We would build the best damn computer anyone has ever seen. And we'd sell the technology to anyone who wanted to buy it. Japanese, Americans . . . it would benefit everyone."

"Exciting," Fujii admitted, "but naïve. That's not the way the world works."

"It's the way I want to work," she insisted. "I'd rather be working with you than against you. Why don't you come with me?"

He was startled by the invitation. She was obviously serious and he was pleased with the idea. But he shook his head. "Not now," he answered. "I'm not ready to get back to work yet."

"But you'll think about it," Karen prompted.

"It's not a very conventional idea," he warned her.

Karen answered. "That's why it should appeal to you. You're not a very conventional person."

"I'll think about it," Fujii promised.

She got up, offered her hand, which he accepted, and started to leave. Fujii followed her to the door. "I'm glad you came," he said. "I must admit that I was beginning to hate you. At least during the moments when I wasn't hating myself."

"Think about it," Karen repeated. "Instead of digging a trench and throwing bombs back and forth at each other, we could be helping each other. We'd get a lot more accomplished. I'll let you know where I am as soon as I get settled."

"I promise," Fujii answered. He watched her walk away from the house. Then he called after her. "You're right about one thing. We could build a very elegant machine. Very elegant indeed."

December 11th, 8:00 P.M., Over the Pacific

Toole rested his feet on the million dollars and poured his whiskey over the ice cubes. He leaned back into the soft, first-class seat, raised his glass toward Karen, and proposed a toast.

"To John Cobb, for bringing us together."

Their glasses clinked. "Even the devil has his good days," she answered.

"And to you," he said with a second lifting of his glass, "for making it happen. As beautiful a piece of work as I've seen. If there were a hall of fame for con artists, I'd propose you for membership."

"It was an accident," she answered modestly. "To tell the truth, I'm still not sure I understand exactly what we were doing. Just who the hell were we working for? John Cobb? The government?"

"A little of both." He laughed.

"And who in God's name was Kaplan? Did you know that he was going to walk into the room and drive the final nail into Cobb's coffin?"

Toole shook his head. "Kaplan was a pleasant surprise. It was really touch and go until he named Cobb as the person who had hired him. Fitting, though. The first person Cobb tried to screw was Kaplan and Kaplan ends up being the last person in the brief but illustrious career of John Cobb, the con man."

"Cobb set up Kaplan?" Karen asked.

He nodded. "It was quite a scheme. Each of the players was carefully selected for a very specific role. The problem was that like all actors, we began padding our parts."

She looked puzzled, so Toole went back to the very beginning.

"Derailing the Japanese supercomputer presented some rather unusual problems. You couldn't steal it, because the Japanese would certainly recognize their own technology when it showed up in an American computer. And there was no point in trying to destroy it. The supercomputer was really an idea and how do you destroy an idea? The only thing our geniuses could do was discredit it. But to do that, you had to understand it. Cobb and his secret government types had to get inside the Japanese supercomputer program. And that was the problem. How do you get the Japanese to invite Americans into their most secret technological development? The answer was to create a problem that would cause the Japanese to ask for American assistance. Kaplan was the problem."

Toole raised his hand to the stewardess and pointed to their glasses. She rushed off to bring them two refills.

"Kaplan had the exact qualities that Cobb needed. He wanted to be a spy and he wasn't experienced enough to keep from getting caught. So Cobb hired Kaplan and set him up in Tokyo to copy software transmissions from telephone lines. Then he invented Signet Corporation as Kaplan's employer. It was just a matter of time before Kaplan got caught, which gave the Japanese a clear-cut case of an American involved in industrial espionage. Naturally, they complained to the United States government and our government responded by sending a top official to Japan who would help a friendly country put an end to this outrage.''

"John Cobb."

Toole nodded. "Which brings us to part two of his master plan. Cobb needed a plot that he could help the Japanese investigate. As part of the investigation, he would get the Japanese to turn over their top secret code so that the code would lead them to the higher-ups in the bogus scheme. So he went out and got himself a suitable schemer. Yours truly.

"I had all the necessary qualifications. A prison record. A background in computer fraud. It would be child's play to get the Japanese to believe that I was the bad guy. So while they were watching me, they wouldn't be watching Cobb. Right from the beginning, he planned to turn me over to them as proof of the sincerity and effectiveness of his mission. Like Kaplan, I was an expendable part of his plan. The fact that I was able to figure out that Fujii's arrogance was the weakness in the Japanese supercomputer program was a bonus."

The stewardess returned with fresh drinks and took away the empty glasses. Toole passed Karen's drink to her and gestured another toast.

"So you were expendable," Karen said, picking up Toole's story.

"Right. And so were you," he answered. She seemed shocked.

"I had the right credentials for stealing the code," Toole continued. "But as I told you a long time ago, no one would believe that I could analyze it and sabotage it. So to complete his cover story, Cobb needed a bona fide computer expert that he could capture and turn over to the Japanese. If everything had gone according to plan, you would have destroyed the code. The Japanese would have used the mined code in their supercomputer and decided that the supercomputer was useless. Then Cobb would have concluded his investigation by handing the two of us over to the Japanese. The result: the Japanese supercomputer would have been derailed and the Americans would have looked like heroes for helping the Japanese capture American spies."

"Quite a plan," she agreed.

"Genius," Toole concluded, "except no one followed the script that Cobb had written. Instead of rotting in jail, Kaplan became incensed, broke out of prison, and set out to find the man he knew as Smith. Instead of buying the ease with which Fujii was compromised, I got suspicious. I started to investigate the real role that I was playing."

"And that finished Cobb's plan," Karen offered.

"Not quite," Toole continued. "You were an even bigger surprise. He expected you to tend to your computers. When you came out of the closet and began meeting with Fujii, Cobb had some very significant problems."

"Why?" she asked. "He wanted to turn me in as a spy anyway. When I met with Fujii, all I did was add to the evidence against myself."

"True," Toole conceded. "But by then Cobb had changed his role as well. All of a sudden he was in possession of the most advanced computer program in the world. And he was working with someone who understood it and could probably perfect it."

"Me?" she asked.

"Bingo," Toole agreed. "It suddenly dawned on him that if he could get you to work with him, he could be the owner of the first company to introduce a truly advanced computer system. He saw lots of big bucks with his name on the account. Why should he just go back to Washington, receive a handshake from the President at a private meeting, and then start counting the years until he could retire on his government pension? Screw the government! If he could get you to team up with him, he could really strike pay dirt. But then you introduced yourself to Fujii as my associate, which meant you had to be a spy. The last thing he wanted was you in a Japanese prison, so he had to figure out a way to get you out of a trap that he himself had set for you."

She nodded her understanding. It all seemed to make sense.

Toole continued. "I figured out his scheme when I went back to the United States and saw what he had done with our records. When he turned us in, the Japanese would naturally want background on each of us. Cobb had fixed it so that our records and involvement would confirm the fact that we were crooks. I changed the records to make him look like the crook. At the time, I didn't know how I would ever get to use the records I invented, but I knew we would be in better shape after I changed them."

"How did you ever manage to get into official records?" she asked.

He smiled. "How many computer hackers do you think there are in the United States?" Then he answered his own question. "A couple of hundred thousand. Sometimes they're so proud of their successes that they post the telephone numbers and access codes on computer bulletin boards for anyone with a personal computer to see. The more sophisticated hack-

ers sell their information to illegal services. Do you
know that I can buy my way into just about any department store charge account record for about a
hundred bucks? Fifty on weekends."

She laughed. "With your help, I could become one
of America's ten best-dressed women."

"It all came together at the hearing," Toole said.
"The computer records I had planted. Kaplan's appearance. Once I knew which way you were going to
play it, the rest was easy."

"Me? How else could I have played it?"

Toole smiled. "You had me worried," he confessed. "If you had sided with Cobb and agreed that I
was the one stealing the supercomputer secrets, the
hearing would have ended right then and there."

"I couldn't have done that," Karen insisted indignantly.

"You could if you had decided to work with Cobb.
After all, you didn't know what I was planning to do.
It looked as if Cobb was going free and I was going to
jail. The smart move on your part would have been to
stick with him. But once you called him a liar then it
was obvious that you were on my side. That gave me
the freedom to go on the offensive."

"Freedom," Karen pursued cautiously. "I don't
understand. You mean that if I had sided with Cobb
you wouldn't have fought back? You wouldn't have
demanded that they get our records from the United
States?"

He didn't answer.

"Let me get this straight," she persisted. "If I had
agreed with Cobb, then you couldn't have attacked
Cobb without attacking me. So you would have just sat
there with your mouth shut and gone to prison."

He ignored the statement and tried to signal the stewardess for another drink. But Karen grabbed his arm and turned him toward her. "Why was saving me more important than saving yourself? You're supposed to be a con man, not a humanitarian."

"Right," he answered. "And you were an amateur. You didn't know what you were getting into. It just didn't seem right that you should end up in prison because the rest of us were trying to screw each other."

Karen let go of Toole's arm and slid back into her seat. "Nothing makes sense," she mumbled half to herself. "The straight shooter from the United States government turns out to be a crook. The bastard we're trying to con turns out to be the only honest person in the whole affair. Now the convicted felon ends up being a humanitarian. Nothing figures!"

"Don't be too surprised," Toole said. "Didn't the amateur end up pulling off the scheme after the professional had failed?"

He waved away the dinner the stewardess tried to set before him, leaned back and closed his eyes. As they flew to the east, the darkness came quickly, and the drinks only added to the toll of fatigue. He should have fallen asleep quickly, but his mind was churning. There were decisions to be made and the time for making them was slipping away along with the daylight.

"Are you asleep?" she asked in a whisper.

"I can't sleep on these damn things," he responded without opening his eyes.

"I visited Fujii," she said. He didn't seem particularly surprised.

"Funny," he answered. He sat up in his seat and blinked his eyes open. "I was thinking of doing the same thing. But I guess I knew he wouldn't be thrilled with my company."

Karen told him about their meeting; about her own plans for continuing her work on the supercomputer and her hope that Fujii might agree to work with her.

"You and Fujii," he said pointedly.

"No," Karen answered. "Not that way. But I think we'd get a lot done if we worked together. Professionally, I think it would be great for both of us."

"You'll make a dynamite team," Toole said. "Sign me up for half a million of your start-up capital." He reached down and took the briefcase from under the seat and slid it under the seat in front of Karen. "My half-million plus your half-million. You've already got a million to get started."

She looked shocked. "We can't keep that money," she said.

He laughed. "Who do you think is going to take it back? The government? No one is going to claim the money that was used to steal Japanese computer secrets. As far as Washington is concerned, this money doesn't exist. It's just like John Cobb. No one in Washington is going to admit that he exists either. So I guess you and I are stuck with it. And I've just invested my half in you and Fujii. I'm betting that the two of you can pull off a miracle."

He settled back into his seat, closing his eyes as if to block out all further discussion of the topic. But Karen's voice broke through once more.

"I didn't sleep with him . . ." she started.

"Karen, you don't owe anyone any explanation," he interrupted. "Christ, he's probably the only person in the world who can understand half the things you say."

"The night at his house," she continued. "I knew what he wanted and he thought he knew what I wanted. I was going to make the trade. Anything to bring down that computer."

Toole opened his eyes and turned in his seat toward her. "Please don't embarrass yourself," he said, his own uneasiness at the topic completely obvious. "Look, I'll admit I was mad as hell. I thought...I hoped you and I...so when you came home with your clothes half on, I was...pissed. But I knew why you did it and when I heard that Akagi had crashed, I knew you had gotten what you needed. Hell, I've done the same thing dozens of times."

"I didn't go to bed with him," she repeated, now annoyed at the ease with which he assumed that their own affair had held no meaning for her. "I let him con me into his tub and I knew what was supposed to come next. But I kept chattering away like an idiot, hoping to keep him talking. He put his hand on my knee and all I did was talk faster. God, but he must have been enjoying himself. And then his hand was sliding up the inside of my leg. But I couldn't. No matter what it was that he might tell me, there was no way I was going to..."

A smile was spreading across Toole's face, with laughter already showing in his eyes.

"Don't you laugh," Karen warned him. "I've already been laughed at. I came out of that tub like the killer whale at the aquarium. I don't remember climbing out. I just flew out. Next thing, I was running through his garden, stark naked and soaking wet with my clothes in a ball in my hand. And he was laughing so loud I hoped he would fall off his seat and drown himself..."

Despite her warning, Toole was laughing, with tears beginning to run down over his apple-red cheeks. Karen turned away in embarrassment and stared out the window.

"I'm sorry," Toole was finally able to say. "But, Christ, it must have been funny. You trying to get your pantyhose on over wet legs in the middle of the garden."

"I didn't put them on," she said coldly. "I stuffed them into my pocket. And if you had cared enough to notice, you son of a bitch, you would have seen that my bra was on inside out."

He burst out laughing. Her head snapped toward him with fiery anger in her eyes. But then her lips began to quiver, and in an instant, she was laughing louder than he was.

When she regained her composure, she finished making her point. "So, anyway, I couldn't go through with it. And I didn't."

He nodded, but he didn't ask the question that she was hoping for.

"Don't you want to know why I couldn't go through with it?" Karen prompted.

He shrugged. "Listen, I'm glad you didn't. But you don't have to explain anything to me. As far as I'm concerned..."

"Yes, I do," she said, her anger beginning to return. "Because you are concerned...unless you think that sleeping with someone has no meaning to me...that I just tiptoe from one bed to another."

"Karen," he tried to interrupt, afraid to hear what he hoped she might be about to say.

"I jumped out of that tub because I thought of you. I could have done it to myself to get his goddamned password. But I couldn't have done it to you. You would have gone to prison for me and I would have lost the Akagi rather than bed down with anyone else... except you."

Toole looked at her for a long time. Then he smiled. "I thought of a hundred different ways of asking you if we could... stay together for a while. But none of them made any sense." Then he corrected himself. "They made sense for me. But they didn't make much ·sense for you. I mean, with what you know, you can go anywhere. Do anything you want. The last thing you need is to get tied up with a felon. You're a genius. What did you tell me?—maybe a dozen people in the world can do what you do. The bottom line on me is that I'm a crook. It doesn't seem like much of a bargain for you. I don't see how it could ever work."

"Trust me," Karen said.

"That's not the problem," Toole answered. "The question is whether you can trust me? I've never made a commitment in my whole life. Or whether we can trust whatever is happening between us. Does it make sense for a computer genius and a jailbird to fall in love?"

A mischievous smile broadened her mouth. "You've never listened to Masakado," Karen told him.

"Masa... who?" Toole wondered.

"A Japanese shogun who lives in the middle of downtown Tokyo," Karen said. "He tells the Japanese not to question things just because they don't make sense. If something works, leave it alone, even if you can't explain why it happens to work."

His eyes narrowed.

"I think we work beautifully," Karen said.

Toole reached out and took her hand. "You think Masakado would approve of my being in love with you, even if I have no right to be?"

"I think he'd be delighted," she answered.

December 11th, 10:00 P.M., New York

"I guess you two are stuck with me," Kaplan said.

Toole and Karen were watching the luggage piling up on the carousel in New York's Kennedy airport when they heard the voice behind them. They turned together, their eyes first focusing on a forest of hair that filled an open neckline, then moving up to the dark round face. Kaplan's white teeth flashed. "I'm released into your custody," he reminded Toole. "So where are we headed?"

"Mr. Kaplan..." Toole started to say.

"Stanley," the giant answered. He held out a hand in greeting and Toole risked a handshake. It proved to be amazingly gentle.

"Stanley," Toole tried again, "I'm glad you caught us. I never did get a chance to thank you properly. Your testimony was invaluable in convicting our friend John Cobb."

"It certainly was," Karen added.

"Cobb?" Kaplan questioned.

"Smith," Toole corrected. "Smith's real name is John Cobb. He's a veteran industrial spy and he was trying to steal some very important industrial secrets."

Kaplan nodded. "So was I. I was working for him. His point man. Then, when the whole thing collapsed, he left me to take the rap. The guy is a pig!"

"I understand that you nearly disassembled him," Karen said by way of small talk.

Kaplan nodded. "All I wanted him to do was tell the truth. I didn't mind being caught. I'm a professional, and the risks go with the territory. But I didn't like being forgotten. I got him the information he wanted and then he didn't even try to get me out. He could have helped me by just telling the truth."

"The problem," Toole advised, "is that John Cobb...Smith to you..is incapable of telling the truth."

Karen reached for a large suitcase that was approaching on the carousel. Kaplan leaned past her and snatched it up as if he were plucking a grape from a vine.

"Were you ever in any other profession, Stanley?" Toole asked as Kaplan set the case down behind them. "Moving pianos? Or buildings?"

Stanley laughed. "I wasn't always this strong. In fact, I was a few pounds overweight. But I did a lot of working out while I was in prison. No, I joined the company right out of college..."

"Central Intelligence," Toole interrupted, obviously impressed.

Stanley nodded. "They recruited me in my senior year. I was studying to be an accountant, but the CIA seemed more exciting. I should have stayed with accounting."

Toole reached toward his trunk, but Kaplan again intervened. In his hands the trunk seemed no heavier than a Ping-Pong ball.

"What will you do now?" Karen asked.

He shrugged his shoulders. "Whatever Mr. Toole says, I guess. He's government and I'm in his custody. So I'm going to play it straight. I've had enough of prison."

Toole cleared his throat. "Stanley," he began uncertainly, "there are one or two things I should clear up. First, I'm leaving government service. I'm turning my attention to the private sector. Karen and I have decided to try our hand at launching a computer company. Secondly, I don't think you should take the notion of custody quite so literally. The Japanese simply had no reason to hold you any longer. Putting you in my custody was a convenient way of disposing of your case. It had nothing to do with adoption."

"Then I'm free," Kaplan seemed to discover. He didn't seem overjoyed by the idea.

"As a bird," Toole said. "The Japanese government has no claim on you and neither does the U.S. government."

Kaplan nodded. "Then I guess I should say thank you. If you hadn't spoken up for me, I'd be sharing a cell with . . . Cobb."

"I don't think so," Toole answered. "The Japanese are much too humane a people to leave Cobb in a cell with you. But let's say we're even. You did me a favor and I was happy to return it."

Kaplan piled the luggage together and asked Toole and Karen where they were going to take it. Before they could call a porter, he had all the trunks and suitcases under his arms.

"What about your baggage?" Karen asked.

"I left in a hurry," he explained.

Toole and Karen walked out to the cab stand, carrying the briefcase that bulged with its million-dollar contents. Kaplan was right at their heels, a mountain of luggage traveling on the legs of a dancer. Toole pulled up short.

"Let's take a limousine," he suggested to Karen. He raised the briefcase. "We can afford it. And then maybe a suite of rooms at the Plaza. We could put together a few vacation days before we get down to work."

She laughed. It was the happiest laugh he had ever seen her enjoy.

They marched off in a new direction with Kaplan still holding up the rear. He dropped the luggage into the trunk of the car, ignoring the chauffeur who was trying to help. Then he beat the chauffeur to the door and pulled it open for Karen.

"Good-bye, Stanley," she said as she shook his hand.

"Good luck," Toole added, bending through the door and sliding into the seat next to Karen. Kaplan slammed the door behind them.

He stood at the curb while the chauffeur started the engine and waved forlornly as the car began gliding away. But the two figures in the back seat seemed already absorbed in one another. They weren't even looking at him.

Suddenly the brakes screeched, the back end of the car rising abruptly. As it settled back down, the door opened and Toole's head popped up above the window frame.

"Did you say you were an accountant?" Toole called above the traffic noises.

"Right," Kaplan yelled back.

Toole disappeared for a moment, but quickly popped back up out of the car. "Karen has just reminded me that our new company is going to need an accountant. We were wondering if you might be interested in the position?''

Kaplan's face exploded in a grin.

"If you'd like a lift into town, we could talk about it on the way," Toole shouted.

Kaplan started running toward the car. "I'd like to be the comptroller," he began yelling before he was halfway there. "I've always thought I'd make a great comptroller."

Toole looked back in at Karen and shook his head.

"Some spy!"

The *Choice* for Bestsellers
also offers a handsome and
sturdy book rack for your
prized novels at $9.95 each.
Write to:

The Choice for Bestsellers
120 Brighton Road
P.O. Box 5092
Clifton, NJ 07015-5092
Attn: Customer Service Group